BY JOHN BOYNE

NOVELS

The Thief of Time
The Congress of Rough Riders
Crippen
Next of Kin
Mutiny on the Bounty
The House of Special Purpose
The Absolutist
This House Is Haunted
A History of Loneliness
The Heart's Invisible Furies
A Ladder to the Sky
A Traveler at the Gates of Wisdom

NOVELS FOR YOUNG READERS

The Boy in the Striped Pajamas
Noah Barleywater Runs Away
The Terrible Thing That Happened to Barnaby Brocket
Stay Where You Are and Then Leave
The Boy at the Top of the Mountain
My Brother's Name Is Jessica

STORIES

Beneath the Earth

A TRAVELER AT
THE GATES OF WISDOM

A
TRAVELER
AT THE
GATES OF
WISDOM

A NOVEL

JOHN BOYNE

BOND
STREET
BOOKS

DOUBLEDAY
CANADA

Bond Street Books and colophon are registered trademarks of
Penguin Random House Canada Limited

Library and Archives Canada Cataloguing in Publication

Title: A traveler at the gates of wisdom / John Boyne.
Names: Boyne, John, 1971- author.
Identifiers: Canadiana (print) 20200240447 | Canadiana (ebook)
20200240501 | ISBN 9780385695855 (hardcover) |
ISBN 9780385695862 (EPUB)
Classification: LCC PR6102.O96 T73 2020 | DDC 823/.92—dc23

Jacket design: Christopher Brand

Printed and bound in the USA

Published in Canada by Bond Street Books,
a division of Penguin Random House Canada Limited

www.penguinrandomhouse.ca

10 9 8 7 6 5 4 3 2 1

BOND
STREET
BOOKS
Penguin
Random House
Canada

FOR MY BROTHER, PAUL

AUTHOR'S NOTE

Country names in the chapter titles refer to their current designations in 2020.

All other geographical names—cities, towns, villages—are as they were at the time of the story, or at their earliest known historical designations.

CONTENTS

PART 5 · THE THREE JEWELS

PART 6 · MILLENNIUM

PART 7 · PLUM BLOSSOM MELODIES

PART 8 · THE REFUGE OF THE WORLD

PART 9 · THE SHADOW OF MY SHADOW

PART 10 · A DEVIL'S PROMISE

PART 11 · GOOD AND BAD ANGELS

PART 12 · THE SUN, THE MOON AND THE STARS

EPILOGUE

PART 1

A TRAVELER
IN THE
DARKNESS

PALESTINE

A.D. 1

O N THE NIGHT THAT I WAS BORN, my father, Marinus, left
our home while my mother was in labor and, over the eight
hours that followed, slaughtered a dozen infant boys, the
sons of our neighbors and friends, each one under the age of two
years.

He owned four swords, including a pair of gladii and an ornamental sica that had been handed down through three generations
of our family, but he chose the smallest weapon in his arsenal, a
triangular dagger with a wooden handle and silver blade known as
a parazonium, to end each of the babies' lives. A ruby jewel of considerable value lay at the center of the quillion, its liquid blush ready
to reflect the blood that spilled from the bodies of the children.

A man of duty, he did not hesitate as he marched from door to
door, searching each house for hidden nurslings before plunging
his knife into the heart of every boy he found, and while mothers
screamed in horror and rained curses down upon his head, fathers
stood silently in corners, mute and impotent, knowing that if they
dared to speak, the blade would surely find its way across their
throats before their sentence came to an end. Older siblings trembled in fear as they watched Marinus go about his dark business,
soiling themselves, frightened that they, too, were about to face the
judgment of the gods for some unspecified crime, but no, once the
babe had been dispatched from this world for the next, my father
barely glanced in their direction before making his way to the next
house, and the next, and the next after that, for there were more
babies to discover and more lives to bring to a premature end.

After each murder, he wiped the blade clean on his tunic, the
fabric growing increasingly discolored as the sun began to peep

over the horizon in the east, a fiery witness to unspeakable crimes, and soon the gray disappeared beneath an incarnadine coat.

Of course, Marinus was not the only man engaged in sanguineous misadventures that night. More than thirty other soldiers had been deployed by King Herod to the towns that surrounded Bethlehem, from Ramat Rachel in the north to Rafida in the south, and from Har Gilo in the west to Juhazm in the east, until more than three hundred infant boys were put to death for the crime of being a potential King of the Jews.

When my father returned home in the early morning, his spirit dyed with a barbaric tint that could never be erased, I was suckling at my mother's breast and he placed a trembling hand upon my skull, resting it there for a moment as he gave me his blessing and begged forgiveness from the immortals atop Mount Olympus. When he took it away, a trace of blood was left in its wake, a deadly deposit, and I've always wondered whether some residue of his crimes remained indelibly upon my soul, a tattoo invisible to all but the eyes of the gods, a reminder of the massacre of the innocents that was taking place as I filled my lungs with air for the first time.

. . .

There is, of course, an unhappy irony to the fact that he dispatched a dozen babies from this world, for he would be responsible for bringing the same number into it over the course of his life, although few would survive past their infant years.

He also saw off four wives, although none, I hasten to add, at his own hand, and while my mother, Floriana, was the last woman to marry him, she would not be the last to share either his bed or his home.

Marinus's first marriage took place when he was only twelve years old, a forced contract with his cousin Iunia, the ritual taking place in a stone temple in the town of Za'tara, where they were both born. The marriage was not a success. His father and uncle, greedy men with cruel dispositions, spent their lives slipping between periods of hostility and camaraderie and their children paid the price for their inconstancy. The couple being so young, it was said that all four parents stood on either side of the wedding bed on the night of the ceremony, issuing crude instructions to their naked, frightened offspring on how to achieve consummation, and when Iunia fainted in distress and Marinus burst into tears, they were soundly beaten and informed that they would not be permitted to leave the marriage chamber until the act had been completed to everyone's satisfaction.

Iunia died less than a year later, giving birth to a son, my brother Junius, her fragile young body so ill prepared for motherhood that it was torn apart by the trauma of childbirth. Although saddened, my father must have grown accustomed to the pleasures of matrimony, for he took a second wife almost immediately, a servant girl named Livia, who gave him a half-dozen more children, most of whom survived only a few months at most, before she was caught in a rainstorm, succumbed to a fever and died of it within a week. And then there was a third wife, Capella, who tumbled into a well while under the influence of wine and was discovered months later, her body already in an advanced state of decomposition. And a fourth, Reza, who was found hanging from a rope, a victim of her own malaise.

Marinus had been fond of his wives and was, by all accounts, a more considerate husband than many in Bethlehem, never raising a hand to any of them in anger, but he had never truly loved them. That emotion was reserved until shortly after his twenty-second birthday, when he laid eyes on my mother for the first time. And although he would not remain faithful to her, monogamy being an unnatural concept to him, I believe that he felt a deeper emotion toward his fifth wife than he had toward any of her predecessors.

· · ·

My father loved women, all women, and was as indiscriminate with his favors as a dog in heat. He said that tall women excited him, but short women were good for his soul. Thin women made him joyful, but fat women made him giddy. He himself was a magnificent beast of a man, tall and broad, with virile good looks, powerful chest muscles and a set of golden curls that fell to his neck, capturing the sunlight and adding a reflective glint to the deep sapphire eyes that drew his conquests in, hypnotizing them and fooling them into believing that there was poetry hidden behind his beauty. His only blemish was a horizontal scar across his left cheek, the result of a childhood argument with another boy. But this imperfection only enhanced his splendor, for without it, women said, he would have been so exquisite that he could scarcely have been called a man at all.

Skilled in the ways of seduction, he rarely faced opposition to his desires, taking whoever he wanted, whenever he wanted, regardless of class, age or marital status. Indeed, Marinus was as likely to be found in a virgin's bed as her grandmother's, and on the rare occasions when his advances were rebuffed he assumed the woman suffered from a disorder of the mind and took her anyway, for he recognized no one's rights but his own and those of his peers within the Roman legion. He was a brute, certainly, but people adored his company, and I, like them, was desperate for him to love me, to show some added favor toward me as his son. This was a battle that I would never win.

When Marinus and Floriana first met, my mother was promised to another man and only a week from her wedding. She was not in love, of course, but a woman who felt any emotion other than gratitude toward the man who had chosen her would have been regarded as an eccentric. The marriage had been brokered by her father, Naevius of Bethlehem, who accompanied her to the marketplace that morning to negotiate with one of the street vendors over the price of his raisins. While the men haggled, Floriana slipped away, making her way toward one of the textile stalls, where she ran her hand along some dhakai cloth that the trader claimed had been imported from the kingdom of Vanga at great expense.

"Very beautiful," he assured her, placing his hands together, as if in prayer, to convince her of his honesty. "In that distant place, women make their dresses from these fabrics and their husbands fill their bellies with many babies."

It was while Floriana was inspecting the man's wares that my father emerged from the doorway of a nearby house and caught sight of her for the first time. He'd spent the morning in bed with the wife of a local tax collector, ravaging her three times in quick succession as payback for the percentage of his wages that he was forced to return to the imperial purse, but his erotic spirits were ignited once again when he saw the great beauty standing on the other side of the street. He observed the sensual manner in which her fingers stroked the material, her tongue running across her upper lip in pleasure as she caressed the cloth, and felt a longing inside him different to the basic desire for sex that stalked his every waking moment. Here was a new emotion, igniting in the pit of his stomach before coursing through his veins and stimulating every nerve ending. Sensing his gaze, my mother turned and glanced in his direction, flushing immediately, for she had never looked upon so handsome a man before. For her, too, something that had lain dormant inside began to stir. She was only sixteen years old, after all, and the man to whom she was betrothed was almost three times her age and so corpulent that he was known to all as the Great Elephant of Bayt Sahur. They had met only once, when he came to inspect her at her father's home, as one would scrutinize a brood mare, and I imagine that she was anticipating the wedding night, if she even knew what it involved, with a mixture of dread and resignation. Now, it took an act of will on her part to turn away from Marinus and, unsettled by such alien and disquieting emotions, she made her way from the stall in search of a quiet place to catch her breath.

Before she could go too far, however, he had crossed the street and was standing before her.

"You would walk away from me?" he asked, smiling, barely cognizant of the musk of perspiration and sex that emanated from his body. He visited the bathhouse only once every few weeks, when the stink from his pores became too much even for his own nostrils, but somehow his aroma often proved an intoxicating perfume.

"Do I know you?" she asked.

"Not yet," he replied, breaking into a wide smile that allowed the dimple on his right cheek to reveal itself and the scar on his left to whiten. "But that's easily remedied." He took a step back before bending at the waist to offer a polite bow. "Marinus Caius Obellius. A member of the Roman garrison stationed here in Judea. And you are?"

"The daughter of Naevius of Bethlehem," she said, casting a quick look to the other side of the market, where her father was still lost in negotiations.

"The merchant?" asked my father.

"Yes."

"But you have a name of your own, too, I suppose?"

"Floriana."

"I'm surprised that such a man would allow his daughter to walk the streets alone."

"I'm not alone," she said, daring to play with him a little. "I'm with you."

"But I'm a very dangerous man," he replied, leaning forward and lowering his voice. "I have a reputation."

My mother blushed. Already, he had gone too far for her. "In fact, he's just over there," she said, nodding in her father's direction. "Perhaps you should continue on your way. He may not take kindly to you addressing me."

Marinus shrugged his shoulders. He'd never cared for such niceties before and had no intention of starting now. Permission, after all, was for common men, not for Roman legionnaires who looked as if they might name Jupiter and Venus as their progenitors. "You come to the marketplace with your father," he asked speculatively, "instead of your husband?"

"I have no husband."

"My heart rejoices."

"But I will. A week from today."

"My heart grieves."

He looked away, considering the probable chain of events that lay over the days ahead, and as he considered various options for ridding her of her betrothed, my grandfather marched over to protest against the young man's insolence at addressing his daughter in a public place. Floriana drew her veil across her face and took a step backward as Naevius stood before them, insisting that he would summon the Roman Guards if this stranger dared to behave in such a disrespectful fashion ever again.

"But I am of their number," said my father, smiling in a friendly manner, for he was free of his duties on that particular day and dressed in the informal style of any Judean citizen, although he had barely pulled his clothes together from his encounter with the tax collector's wife. "Marinus Caius Obellius," he added, offering another bow, hoping that his manner would suggest that he was a man of good character and not some opportunistic predator wandering the market in search of virgins to seduce.

Naevius hesitated a little now, for he had spent his life in fear of authority but could not stand for the insult either, particularly when the traders on the street were watching.

"My daughter is a married woman," he said forcefully, and Marinus shook his head.

"No," he said. "Her wedding day has yet to come."

Naevius turned to glare at Floriana, who blushed furiously and looked down at the ground.

"A matter of seven days, that's all," protested Naevius. "And then—"

"Seven days is a long time," replied my father. "We might all be dead in seven days. Or seven minutes. Surely I might be allowed to offer my own proposal before it is too late?" He softened his tone and reached out to touch the older man on the arm in a gesture of humility. "I mean you no disrespect, sir," he said. "But when a man encounters such a great beauty as your daughter, a girl with the lineage of a proud house behind her, it is only natural that he should seek to make her his wife. Don't you agree?"

"I do," said Naevius, puffing up his chest at the platitudes. "But it's impossible, of course."

"Why?" asked Marinus.

"Because of the Great Elephant of Bayt Sahur," replied my grandfather, leaning forward and opening his eyes so wide my father could see the veins that ran across the sclera like aimless tributaries.

"And what has he to do with anything?"

"He is to be my husband," said my mother and, at her interruption, Naevius raised his hand to strike her for her insolence, but my father reached out and caught that same hand in midair, urging peace.

"You would give your daughter to the Great Elephant of Bayt Sahur?" he asked, infusing his tone with as much deferential outrage as he could summon. "A man who is so fat he can scarcely fit through his own doorway? A man known to break the backs of the unfortunate donkeys tasked with carrying him? Why, he would crush every bone in her body on their wedding night, if he could even find his cock within that vile mass of quivering blubber. The Great Elephant of Bayt Sahur? No, sir, the Great Whale! The Great Whale!"

"He's a man with a healthy appetite, it is true," conceded my grandfather. "But he's also wealthy, you can't deny that. One of the wealthiest merchants in this region. And he's been widowed for almost a month, so it's natural that he would seek a new woman."

"Did he not kill his last two wives?" asked Marinus.

"Yes, but they were unfaithful to him," replied Naevius with a shrug. "So, he was within his rights."

"He fed the first to a lion then stripped the skin from the second over the course of a week."

"I have heard it said," admitted Naevius. "He is ingenious in his cruelty."

"Then your daughter wanders into dangerous territory," said Marinus, shaking his head. "I wonder that a man of your dignity and reputation could permit such a match when a better opportunity stands before her?"

TURKEY

A.D. 41

THAT BETTER OPPORTUNITY which my mother would come to enjoy included a small house, built from a combination of mud bricks dried by the sun and rough-hewn stones that acted as quoins, giving us a slightly more elevated status than most of our neighbors. Wooden beams packed with clay kept us dry from above, while the earthen floor beneath our feet was covered intermittently with paving stones. We slept in different corners, without privacy, but a fire burned from morning till night in a central stove that served the dual purpose of keeping us warm and cooking our food.

My father, Marek, was not a man much given to humor, which makes it all the more surprising that one of my earliest memories is of him marching through the door with tears of laughter pouring down his face. I had started walking a few months earlier but was still uncertain on my feet and I stumbled across the room to greet him, eager to be enveloped in his mirth.

"You're in good humor," said my mother, Folami, looking around as he sat down and swept me onto his knee while she continued with her bread-making. My father's wages as a Roman legionnaire in Cappadocia could scarcely support a family of six, as we were then, but my mother was well regarded in the province for her baking skills and women appeared at our door every morning, proffering copper coins to purchase her loaves and pastries. She spent most of her days with her hands immersed in flour, dough, yeast, poppy, flax and sunflower seeds, giving her a distinctive scent that has always offered me a feeling of safety and comfort whenever I've stumbled across it.

"New orders came through today," said Marek, using the heel of his hand to wipe his face dry. He kissed me on the top of my head and I reached out to trace the scar that ran down his left cheek. It was only a couple of inches long, but its narrow gully, a perfect fit for my tiny fingers, fascinated me. "Issued by Quintus Veranius himself. It seems that a ship arrived in the port of Bartin yesterday, direct from Rome, carrying the most curious cargo."

"Oh yes?" replied Folami. The wives of the soldiers had their own collectives, of course, where they gossiped and exchanged the pieces of intelligence that their husbands had let slip across the table or between the sheets, but for the most part Cappadocia was a quiet place, far removed from the daily intrigues of our Imperial over-lords.

It had not always been so. Centuries before my birth, Alexander the Great had tried to conquer the region but been rebuffed by a people who loved their King, and it was only when the civil war began that the state lost its independence through its equivocation over who to support, Pompey, Caesar or Antony. It took the Emperor Tiberius to bring us to heel, turning a once-proud city into a Roman province. The citizenry accepted its defeat with good grace, life becoming peaceful afterward, the Roman Guards assimilating well and little enmity existing between the conquered and the conquerors.

"More than one hundred stone heads," continued my father. "They're being transported south, even as we speak, to be attached to statues."

Folami paused in the mixing of her dough and turned to look at him, raising an eyebrow. "I don't understand," she said. "They've sent heads but no torsos?"

"The torsos are already here," he replied. "They've been here for decades. At the temples, at the courthouse, along the roads. Every statue in Cappadocia is to be decapitated and the new heads are to replace the old. The same thing is taking place all across the Empire."

"And let me guess," said my mother. "They depict—"

"The Emperor Caligula, of course. Jupiter on his throne will become Caligula. Neptune with his trident will become Caligula.

Even the female deities—Juno, Minerva, Vesta, Ceres—they are all to become Caligula. O fortunate eyes that will be able to gaze upon his features wherever they turn!"

My mother shook her head. "So, you are to turn yourself into a stonemason and defile the images of the gods?" she asked.

"You know me," he replied, setting me back down on the floor and walking over to embrace her. "Whatever Rome demands."

I watched, feeling comforted by the affection that existed between them, a warmth that was disturbed only by the arrival of my older brother, Jouni, who came in and observed their mutual affection in distaste. Jouni was about ten years old at the time, the son of my father's second wife, and I was frightened of him, for he rarely acknowledged me, other than to commit some random act of violence, and when he spoke to our father, it was without fear, an attitude that Marek respected. His behavior stood in stark contrast to my sister, Azra, the daughter of his third, who treated me like an animate doll and could sometimes be suffocating in her jealous affections.

"So, every statue is to look like Bootikins," said my father, deferring to his first-born's sensibilities and returning to his seat by the fire. "And I've been placed in charge of the project. An honorable task, don't you agree?"

"The Emperor is as vainglorious as he is ridiculous," said Folami. "I've heard that he enjoys congress with his sister, wants to make a consul of his favorite horse and believes himself to be a god. Don't be surprised, Marek, if the next news that reaches us is of his death. The knives will take him down if he continues to behave in such an excruciating fashion."

"Wife," said my father quietly, a note of caution creeping into his tone, for humor was one thing but remarks such as these could be overheard by ambitious neighbors and reported back to the governor. My brother looked at her with disgust on his face. He was a true servant of the Empire, turning around and disappearing outside again without a word. I can recall the expression on his face as he left. Revulsion. Hatred. Anger. But then he had never got along with his stepmother and perhaps it was inevitable that their troubled relationship would one day reach an unhappy end.

· · ·

Of course, the statues were not the first heads to be separated from their shoulders by my father. When he met my mother two years earlier, she had been only seven days from an arranged marriage to one of the wealthiest merchants in central Anatolia, a man so corpulent that he was known to all as the Great Bear of Kayseri. Having been enchanted by her beauty, and then daring to speak to her in the marketplace, Marek learned of her upcoming nuptials and made his way to the groom's home the following morning with an offering of gold, which he hoped would liberate Folami from the engagement.

The Great Bear agreed to receive the young legionnaire but was unmoved by my father's request. "My wife has been dead for almost a month and my bed has remained cold since then," he told him, half amused and half insulted by the paltry amount of coin that Marek was offering in exchange for the girl. "A house needs a woman in it. And my children need a mother. Fusun is young, her hips are broad, and she can bear me many more. A man must procreate! If I were to—"

"Folami," said my father, correcting him.

"What?"

"Her name is Folami," repeated my father. "With respect, sir, if you do not even know the girl's name, you cannot be in love with her."

The Great Bear threw his head back and burst out laughing before reaching for a tray of candies that sat on the velvet cushion next to him. "Why are we speaking of love?" he asked, stuffing his mouth with a fistful of sweets before letting his tongue slowly lick the sugared residue from his fingertips. "I thought we were discussing marriage. Two very different things, my friend."

"But there are so many more girls in Cappadocia," argued Marek. "Some even more beautiful than Folami. A man of your stature could have his pick of them."

"If you believed that, then you would not be here talking to me. You would be pursuing them yourself."

"Still, if you don't care about her one way or the other—"

"What makes you say such a thing?" asked the Great Bear, frowning.

"You've said yourself that love and marriage are two very different things."

"Yes, but you want this girl. Therefore, she has become an item of value, to you at least. And I don't walk away from items of value when they have already been promised to me. Regardless of your entreaties and your womanly talk of love, I've made an arrangement with the girl's father and have no intention of turning my back on that. A man's good name is all that he has and mine would be diminished if I canceled a brokered agreement. As for this pathetic offering"—and here he threw the pouch of gold back at my father, where it landed with an insolent jingle at his feet—"I wouldn't sell you a dog for that, let alone a young beauty of child-bearing years. Have you looked around, Marek of Cappadocia? You must see how wealthy I am?"

My father, a proud man, was stung by the humiliation but not ready to give up on Folami quite yet. If he could not win her through commerce, then he would claim her by force. His favorite kilij hung in a scabbard by his side, a saber that had been handed down through three generations of our family, and as he reached for it, the ruby jewel at the quillion catching the light, the Great Bear simply clicked his fingers in an uninterested fashion and four guards approached from each corner of the room, unsheathing their scimitars and pointing them toward Marek's throat.

"You were thinking of killing me?" asked the Great Bear, shaking his head more in pity than in anger. "Better men than you have tried, my friend. Better men will again. And perhaps, someday, one will succeed. But not you. And not today."

"If you will not give the girl up," said Marek, "then at least fight me for her. We can use any weapon you choose. Or none at all. We could fight as men do, with our fists."

"Don't be ridiculous," replied the merchant. "Why would I enter into combat with you when I would most certainly lose? You're young and strong. I am neither of those things."

"Then choose a champion, and either he will fall, or I will."

The Great Bear considered this and stroked his many chins. Finally, he nodded. "I suppose it will be an entertainment, if nothing else," he conceded. "At present, the days are so warm that I cannot bear to leave the villa and I am in need of amusement. I accept your challenge, Marek of Cappadocia. But I choose four champions, not one. The four men who face you right now. If you defeat them all, you may take the girl. Do you accept my offer?"

My father looked around. The men in question were healthy specimens, undoubtedly useful with their swords, but he was skillful, too, and had a prize worth fighting for, while they did not.

"I accept," he said, spinning around and, in a moment, using his kilij to lift the head from the first of his opponents, the man's skull tumbling to the floor and rolling toward the Great Bear, who stopped it with the tip of his slipper, laughing in delight at how swiftly my father had acted, and clapping his sticky hands together as the three remaining guards gathered their wits. It was noted afterward by one of the servants that this had all happened so quickly that the head continued to live for a few seconds, its eyes darting back and forth in surprise at being trapped beneath the Great Bear's foot, before blinking twice and remaining open in death. Marek was fast on his feet; for a large man, he had the nimble tread of a dancer, and in anticipation of this clash, he had sharpened the blade of his kilij to a fine edge the night before and it took the head from another guard easily before he turned his attentions to the two that remained. One, the younger of the pair, looked terrified and his sword-arm trembled noticeably as my father lunged at him. He stumbled backward with a defeated cry as the saber pierced his heart and Marek turned now to the final guard, who fought valiantly but was no match for his opponent and soon found himself pinned against the wall, the blade of my father's sword pressed against his neck.

"I have taken three of them," said Marek, turning to the Great

Bear, who had grown pale now, perhaps nervous that his own body might be lighter by the weight of a head in a few moments. He had removed his foot from his slipper and was massaging his toes through the hair of the first soldier's skull. "Will you let me spare this boy's life and take the girl, as promised?"

"I am a man of my word," said the Great Bear, dragging himself to his feet, no easy task for a man of his girth. "The girl is yours when you have defeated all my champions. That is the deal that we made and you must honor it, as I will."

My father did not waste a second, and before the boy could find a voice to cry out for mercy, his shoulders, too, had been relieved of their load.

Without returning home to change his bloodied garments, Marek made his way to my grandfather's house and claimed his bride.

Several weeks after my father had decapitated every statue in Cappadocia and replaced the heads with carvings of the Emperor, two events of note took place.

The first was that Folami was proven right, and Caligula was assassinated, and the second was that I went missing.

Although I was too young to understand the importance of what they were discussing, I sat alongside my siblings while Marek recounted the gossip that was spreading across the Empire from Hispania to Judea and from Germania to Carthage.

"He was attending a performance of some squalid play in the palace," he told us. "And, in his usual charming way, he was mocking the actors and being scornful of the senators in attendance, each of whom was keeping one eye on the stage and one eye on their Emperor in case he laughed, so that they might laugh, too. During an interval between the acts, he announced that, depending on whether meat or fish was served for lunch, he would have half of them tossed into the Colosseum later in the day as a treat for the lions. *All of you on my left,* he said, *you die if it's fish. And all of you on my right, you die if it's meat.* Then, as he made his way toward his private dining room to discover what might lie beneath the cloches, he was approached by Cassius Chaerea, a member of the Praetorian

Guard, who stabbed him in the shoulder. When he fell to the ground, Chaerea held him down and slowly carved his way through the Emperor's neck with a rusty knife."

"So it's not just the statues that have lost their heads," remarked my mother with a shrug.

• • •

A few days later, Folami brought some loaves to the marketplace, leaving me under the supervision of my brother, but Jouni, bored by the prospect of spending an afternoon indoors with an infant, and pleased by any opportunity to disobey his stepmother, went out to meet some friends, and when Folami returned a few hours later, I was nowhere to be found.

My father arrived home soon afterward and together they went from house to house in search of me, but with no success. My mother was inconsolable and when Jouni returned home that night, unaware that I had gone missing, he was thrashed soundly by Marek, a rare punishment, for my father had a weakness for his children and was rarely violent toward any of us.

As my father was a member of the Roman Guards, there was a suspicion that I had been taken by a Cappadocian resident who had either suffered hardship at the hands of the protectorate or was seeking revenge for the conquest of his region. Known criminals were dragged from their beds and tortured in the streets in a quest for answers, but if any of them knew who had taken me, or why, or where I was being held, they did not say.

The events of that week remain a mystery to me. I have no memory of the circumstances that brought me home again either, but family legend has it that, seven days later, Marek and Folami were woken in the middle of the night by a loud rapping on the door. When they opened it, they discovered me sitting in the dust outside, crying bitterly. Despite the number of questions my parents asked, I could tell them nothing, and whether this was because I had been threatened by my abductor or was simply too traumatized to speak, I do not know.

The next evening, I was examined by a local physician, who found no signs of brutality anywhere upon my body. It seemed that

during my absence I had been fed and well cared for. The only sub-
sequent curiosity was that as we made our way home we passed a
blind woman on the street and I did everything in my power to go
to her, but having misplaced me once, my mother was loath to let
go of me again. Despite my insistent weeping that I belonged with
this stranger, I was taken back to the comfort of my family home
while the blind woman, whose name was Teseria, continued on her
way alone, uttering not a word but pointing toward the sky, where
the stars had started to glimmer in the darkness.

ROMANIA

A.D. 105

ON ANOTHER DARK NIGHT a few years later, my mother, Florina, gave birth to twin babies. Their screams of bewilderment as they entered the world echoed her own tortured cries of pain. For a child of my age, it was a brutal symphony and I felt sure that she would die. I sat trembling, my hands pressed against my ears, dreading what the future might hold for the motherless boy I was sure to become before the sun rose.

It was her fifth pregnancy, but none of the children, other than I, had survived. Florina, who was much given to motherhood, was determined that these babies—a boy named Constantin and a girl called Natalia—would survive and to this end she began training my older brother, Juliu, to help with her small dairy business so she could devote more of her time to their care without causing our household income to suffer. At first, Juliu refused, believing this to be women's work, but my father was equally committed to the survival of his offspring and ordered him to do exactly as he was told. Marius's natural authority meant that none of us would have ever dared to disobey him, but my brother saw this as yet another reason to resent his stepmother. No matter what she did or how much kindness she showed him, he could not make his peace with her.

We lived in the coastal town of Kallatis, on the banks of the Black Sea, across which Jason and the Argonauts had once sailed in their quest for the Golden Fleece. When he was not being dispatched by the King to fight the Roman armies who were threatening to invade our land, my father was a fisherman, operating a small boat with weathered sails that had been passed down from his grandfather to his father and now to him. Juliu preferred being on the sea with Marius, a more masculine pursuit than the one in which Florina was trying to engage him, and I didn't blame him. On the rare occasions when my father brought me out on the boat, I found myself equally thrilled by the action of the waves and the shoals of fish that we caught over the course of a day. Most of the sons of the town fished with their fathers, bringing back sturgeon, eel, shad and even the occasional angel shark to sell in the marketplace, and it was assumed that these boys would, in the fullness of time, assume their fathers' businesses when they were no longer young enough to take to the water. But while I enjoyed being at sea, I knew that this would not be the life for me. I wanted much more from the world than that.

For as long as I could remember, I had been an intensely creative child, preferring to be left alone to play in the sand dunes or on the beach, where I would gather stones and pebbles, arranging them in shapes that were pleasing to the eye, pulling flowers from rushes and using them to create designs that would survive only until Juliu returned, always preferring to scorn my naïve efforts at art by scattering my hard work to the winds with a single kick. Even at home, I would spend hours drawing rough sketches in the dust of the floor with my hands, my mind already filled with images of strange worlds and people that I longed to know. I had a curious sense that these ideas would one day manifest themselves in the real world and that my destiny was not to remain isolated in our small town but to spend my days among tribes and cultures alien to my own.

"An artist, not a warrior," my mother remarked once, looking down at the images I had crafted in the ground. One showed a boat sailing down a river, the sailors carrying saws in their hands. Another a man and woman standing by a well while a beast faced them down. A third displayed the bars of a prison cell. My father examined them, shook his head and spat in the fire in disgust.

"I'll see that beaten out of him," he grunted, but even then, even at such a young age, I knew that I would never allow that to happen.

What fascinated me the most, however, were the stars. It thrilled me to lie outside when the sun had set, staring up at the constellations in the night sky, drawing imaginary lines between each shining instant and wondering who, if anyone, might live within those bright patterns. In my dreams, I floated among them, a traveler in the darkness, looking down at the world from an orbit that I was still too young to comprehend. And when I suggested to my parents that I would like to live among the stars someday, they simply laughed at my foolishness.

From the day of their birth, I took an interest in the twins, who stared up at me from their blankets with expressions of curiosity upon their faces. Perhaps because Juliu showed no affection toward me I determined to be a good brother and it didn't take long for me to become their protector. My sister Andreea resented this, and so jealous was she of my affection for the babies that she took great delight in tormenting them. Naturally, it pleased my mother to see her son so devoted to his siblings' well-being and, while my father found my attentiveness to be unusual in a boy, he offered no protest. As the months passed and they put on weight, it became clear that the infants would survive the hazards of the first year and they soon became thriving, noisy members of our household.

Florina, however, was not so lucky and in the wake of the twins' birth she grew ill, taking to her bed. The sounds of her crying out in agony terrified me, reminding me of the night that she had given birth. I adored my mother and felt certain that she was close to death once again. My father, too, was fearful, summoning an apothecary who prepared foul-smelling potions concocted from various roots and nettles for her to drink and ordering that she remain prostrate until her body had had time to heal from the trauma of so many confinements. When he returned for a second visit a few days later, I overheard a conversation between them as they discussed how her fever had broken at last, but the pain was still so concentrated that her face was as gray as the walls of our small dwelling.

"Be warned, Marius," he said. "If she were to become heavy with child again, both she and the baby would die. There is no doubt of that. Do not lie with her unless you are content to risk her loss."

My father sat by the fire, a frown settling upon his face as he considered this. "She cannot be a wife to me anymore?" he asked, deeply upset, for he bore the unusual quality of loving Florina and a more uxorious man could not be found anywhere in our village.

"She can," said the doctor. "Just not in the marriage bed. She is still capable of cooking, cleaning, mending clothes, the natural wifely duties, but you must restrain yourself if you want her to live. Her womb suffered too great an insult during the birth of these last two babies and will not stand any further affront. It will rupture, the poisons will enter the bloodstream and she will die a most agonizing death."

"Then I shall touch her no more," declared my father, standing up and nodding decisively, as if forging a sacred covenant between himself and his creator. "I can live with having no more children, but I cannot live without Florina."

"You can have as many more children as you want," said the doctor, correcting him. "Just not with your wife. There are others, of course. You must not deny yourself that which is natural to a man. Remember, the towns that surround us are filled with nubile young women, particularly since we've lost so many men fighting the Romans."

And at this, I observed a spark of interest ignite my father's face, a light blush that made the scar on his left cheek inflame a little. Perhaps he would never have betrayed my mother under normal circumstances, but given permission by a man of medicine? Well, that changed matters considerably.

• • •

Although he was at his happiest on his fishing boat, Marius was fiercely loyal to the King and had fought against the Roman dogs intermittently over the years, whenever the Emperor Trajan sent his legions into Dacia. Many of his childhood companions had laid down their lives during those wars and my father nursed such a grudge against the imperial powers that when our great King Decebalus broke the peace treaty, leading Trajan to dispatch even more troops into the region in retaliation with a plan to vanquish us for generations to come, he entrusted his fishing boat with Juliu and set off once again with the Dacian army for Sarmisegetusa.

By now, my mother had recovered her health and returned to making soft cheese and nut butter to sell to our neighbors, but she wore her melancholy around her like a cloak. From time to time, I discovered her weeping silently on her bed, her hands pressed against her empty belly. It was not that she was still in pain but the fact she could no longer bear children that upset her so greatly. And perhaps she feared losing the affections of her beloved husband, an idea which he would have dismissed as impossible but which would, in time, prove painfully accurate.

Around this time, another fisherman, Caturix, befriended my brother. He was older than Juliu, almost twenty, and a youngest son, which meant that he had no hope of inheriting his father's boat. He made his living around the shores of Kallatis, helping those who were either too ill or too incapacitated to put in a full day's work. In my father's absence, he labored alongside Juliu, going out on the boat with him every morning and carrying the catch to the market at the end of each day. Occasionally, my brother would invite him back to our house to eat. Florina had no objection to feeding him—he was helping our family in a time of need, after all, albeit for a basic pay—but as young as I was, I could tell that Juliu's new friend had more than food on his mind.

Caturix was handsome, but in an entirely different way to my father. Where Marius wore his blond curls with narcissistic pride, Caturix tied his dark, straight hair into a knot at the back of his head. While my father was a broad, muscular man, Caturix was of slighter build but tall and strong with sinewy muscles that relaxed into noticeable blue veins along his upper arms. Like my father's, his hands were the hands of a fisherman, scored with the markings of ropes and blades, the knuckles red with bruises and pockmarked from fishing hooks that had embedded themselves in his skin over the years. I found myself rather in awe of this engaging young man, and even though he barely registered my presence in the household, I envied Juliu the time he spent with him on the water, for here, I thought, was an older brother to whom I could give my allegiance.

Had I known what it was to flirt with someone, I would have recognized that Caturix was flirting with my mother in a subtle fashion, complimenting her on her food, her dress, how neatly she maintained our home and, starved of attention since my father had gone away, it was obvious that she was flattered by the courtesy he displayed toward her. After a while, he began to bring small gifts with him when he visited. A colorful stone that had been washed in by the tide, perhaps. A velvet cushion he had purchased in the market. A dried flower. Now my admiration began to turn to annoyance and I started to resent his intrusion, for I knew that my father would not approve of these regular visits.

Juliu, on the other hand, seemed to encourage the friendship, seeking any opportunity to throw Florina and his new friend together.

"An extra portion for Caturix tonight, my father's wife!" he shouted one evening, banging his fists on the table as we sat down to lean rations. It was Juliu's custom to employ this formal term whenever he addressed Florina, trying to keep their relationship as distant as possible. "His heart is heavy."

"Why so?" asked Florina, placing some extra rice on his plate and passing it across with a piece of salted fish. I watched as Caturix glanced in her direction, a half-smile playing across his lips. When he caught her eyes, she blushed slightly.

"The girl he loves does not love him in return," continued Juliu with a melodramatic sigh, and Caturix threw him a reproachful look.

"I can't believe it," said Florina. "What girl could say no to Caturix? She should be pleased to find such a good husband."

"It's not marriage that he's after," said my brother, sniggering. "His ambitions are a lot earthier than that."

"Juliu!" said my mother, frowning deeply, for she did not care for vulgarity.

"I only speak the truth," replied my brother.

"And have you spoken to the girl in question, Caturix?" asked Florina. "Have you expressed to her the stirrings of your heart?"

"I have not dared."

"Why not?"

He shrugged his shoulders. "I could not bear for her to refuse me. I would as soon slice off my ears than hear words of rejection."

"But you do not know what she might say until you ask," Florina replied. "Perhaps she has feelings for you, too?"

"There are complications."

"What sort of complications?"

"She has a husband already."

"Ah," said Florina, shaking her head. "Then you must look elsewhere. After all, any woman who would betray her husband would not be worthy of you. Forget her, Caturix, that's my advice to you."

"Forget the most beautiful, the most tender, the most interesting woman I have ever met?" he replied. "You might as well ask me to forget my own name."

Florina looked around the table and smiled. I suppose she enjoyed the idea of a little gossip. "Will you not tell us who the girl is?" she asked, leaning forward, and Caturix shook his head.

"I cannot," he said.

"Her husband, then? Is he old? If he is, then perhaps nature will free her sooner than you think."

"He's not old," replied Caturix. "But he is away, playing at war, so perhaps the gods will take my part and strike him down."

"You shouldn't say such a thing!"

"If it offends you, then I take it back. But he has been gone these three months now and his family have heard nothing from him. He fights the Roman dogs and might be locked in a cage being transported back to the Colosseum to tarry with the lions, for all we know. Or he could already be dead. Anything is possible."

Florina stared at him and then, to my surprise, her amused expression turned to a frown and then to anger, and she stood up, gathering the empty plates from the table noisily. I did not then understand what he had said to upset her so greatly but, a moment later, she declared that it was time for him to go home and that it would probably be a good idea if he dined separately from us from now on. Caturix simply nodded and left, his head hanging low, but when my brother pushed his chair back to follow him, Florina grabbed him by the arm and held him tightly, her fingers digging deeply into his skin.

"Is this your doing?" she asked. "Are you trying to cause mischief?"

"I don't know what you mean," he replied innocently. "You don't think he meant . . . ?" He threw back his head and burst out laughing. "My father's wife, have you looked in a mirror lately? Your face is gray, your hair is lank and your eyes have grown tired. Not to mention the fact that you're as barren as an untilled field. You can't imagine that a man like Caturix would—"

"You've been a troublemaker from the start, Juliu," she snapped. "I know this is your doing. If there's any more of this scheming, then Marius will hear of it."

He pulled his arm free from her and his laughter turned to scorn. "You don't get to tell me what to do in my father's house," he insisted. "While he is gone, I am master here and you and your brats live under my protection. You would do well to remember that."

Three nights later, I was lying on my mat next to Florina's bed, the twins breathing heavily in the cot next to me, when I heard the door open and a shaft of light slunk deceitfully into the room. My mother was asleep but, alerted by the intrusion, she opened her eyes, sat up and looked toward the door to see who it was that disturbed us at such a late hour.

To my astonishment, it was Caturix! Here he was, when darkness had fallen, walking in a disrobed state toward my mother's bed, his feet as quiet upon the floor as the padded paws of a cat, his engorged member guiding him toward his prey.

"What are you doing here?" hissed Florina, pulling at the rough hemp sheet she used to keep her warm about her body. "You can't be—"

"Juliu said that I might visit you. He passed on your message."

"What message?" she asked.

"That I should come and lie with you tonight. I promise, no one will ever know."

In a flash, she jumped from the bed and ran from the room, followed quickly by a naked Caturix. A vociferous argument broke out in the room beyond and the next morning, when I awoke, my mother was alone in her bed and Juliu was nowhere to be found.

IRAN

A.D. 152

WHEN MY FATHER, Marwan, returned from waging war against the Romans in Armenia, the atmosphere in our home changed considerably. Having taken part in countless battles and witnessed the violent deaths of many of his friends, his senses had grown overwrought, his temper was more easily provoked and he was less patient with his children. Too much noise would drive him into a fury; at his worst moments he was Ishtar, covering the Earth with storms and turning all the rivers to blood.

Part of his ill humor could be put down to the mysterious disappearance of my brother Johan, of whom there had been no news since he vanished two years earlier. Some said that he had been spotted outside a temple in Ctesiphon, carrying a monkey on his shoulder and a tiger cub on a lead while begging money from strangers. Others claimed that he had traveled as far as Mithradatkirt, where he'd married a direct descendant of Arsaces himself and was living a life of extravagant splendor. Still others suggested that he had never left our village at all but had been murdered by his stepmother, his body thrown into an empty well or buried beneath the foundations of one of the new dwellings that were being constructed in the village next to our own. Marwan quizzed Fabiana frequently about the events leading up to the boy's departure, but she remained vague in her answers.

"He always hated me, you know that," she protested. "And yes, we argued while you were gone, but I didn't throw him out and nor would I ever have caused him harm. We went to sleep one night, all of us, and the following morning, when I awoke, he was gone. That is all I know."

Marwan accepted this for now, but a new remoteness developed between my parents and when he returned to the shore to rebuild the boat-repair business that had fallen into decline since Johan's departure, his attitude suggested that he felt it to be a less worthwhile trade without an heir by his side. Occasionally, I would accompany him, but I was still too young to be of any practical use and he would grow angry with me as the day wore on, eventually returning home in bad humor.

It upset me to recall how loving my parents had been before the war and, despite my mother's best attempts to return their relationship to an affectionate place, her efforts were in vain. At night, when they retired for bed, I could hear him groaning in frustration before rising, dressing and disappearing into the night without explanation. At such times, I would slip from my cot into the bed next to Fabiana, whose weeping upset me greatly, and do my best to comfort her. She would hold me tightly and kiss me on the forehead but remained inconsolable and when I asked where my father went so late at night, all she would say was that he searched for the pleasures she herself was no longer able to afford him. Although I was too young to understand the meaning of her words, I swore that I would never turn away from her or abandon her for another, a promise that made me weep, too, and soon the pillow was damp from our mutual distress.

"But you will, my beloved son," she said with a sigh. "Boys always do."

During this time, our friends and neighbors lived, as we did, in a state of perpetual readiness for more conflict, for the amnesty between our ruler, Vologases, and the Emperor Antoninus Pius was a fragile thing at best. Our beloved Parthian Empire, may the gods look over her with mercy, existed in a state of constant tension with its Roman counterpart. And while I loved my father, I longed for the day when he would be called upon to don his battle armor once again, for the war between the empires had as its counterpoint a certain peace at home. At the back of my mind, however, I began to wonder whether aggression was the natural state for our species and if I, too, would one day be forced to raise a sword against an unknown enemy.

I must now speak more of my older sister, Abeer, who from the start combined a brilliant mind with a jealous nature. By the age of one she could draw with great skill. By five, she was a talented horse rider and by nine her swordplay was the envy of many. She was witty, too, and tough, and brave, displaying all those characteristics that my father longed for in a son but which he considered wasted on a daughter. Like me, she spent much of her time seeking his approval, but he was less interested in his female progeny; the children who concerned him most were the absent Johan and myself. The male twin, Constans, suffered from a feeble mind and was sent away as a child to be a servant in a rich man's house before drifting out of our lives forever. The rest were bred as future wives and mothers, nothing more.

For the most part, Johan had tolerated Abeer, but his affections were muted when, as a child, she bested him in a tournament of warriors. Carrying only a wicker shield and a short spear, she managed to overturn him in front of our entire village, leaving him begging for mercy as the tip of her blade kissed his throat. It was a moment that I savored, for I rarely saw Johan reduced to the role of supplicant, and his face turned scarlet when he suffered the insult in front of his hooting friends.

By the time Abeer turned eleven she was already a noted beauty and, when it became obvious that she would blossom into an exquisite woman, one of the elders made inquiries with Marwan about securing her as a bride for his son. My father refused the request, determined that no one would take his daughter to a marriage bed before her sixteenth birthday. He did not seek a great alliance or any financial advantage, after all, and I think he hoped that she would marry a man who would prove tender toward her, as he had been toward my mother when they first met.

Most of the boys in our village were half in love with Abeer. The braver ones collected posies of dried flowers and left them by our door, watching from behind trees as she gathered them in her arms and inhaled their perfumes. They were deeply jealous of her friendship with Hakan, a crippled boy who lived alone with his mother, Nera, nearby. Hakan, who was the same age as my sister, had stumbled into the path of a frightened horse when he was only three years old and had been lucky to survive the accident. His legs had been badly broken, however, and the incompetent doctor who attended to him did nothing to fuse the bones back into their proper places so, as the years passed, the lower half of his body became misshapen and he could walk only with the aid of sticks, which he fashioned himself from the wood of the silver birch trees that grew on the outskirts of our village, carving two crows into the handgrips. He was relentlessly bullied, but Abeer took him under her protection from a young age and such was her reputation as an indefatigable pugilist that few would have dared to mock him when she was by his side.

For my part, I found Hakan to be a frightening creature with his contorted legs, which reminded me of clusters of ginger, bent as they were in unpredictable directions and with strange protrusions lurking beneath the skin. When he sat near me, I dreaded his flesh coming into contact with my own and would shuffle along the seat to stay as far from him as possible. I wasn't proud of myself for this—I knew it wasn't his fault that he had suffered such a ghastly injury—but nevertheless, I could not bring myself to treat him with the affection or kindness my sister did and wished that he would stay away.

And so I was naturally dismayed when my father returned home from the riverbank one evening with this same boy in tow, declaring that Hakan would be our guest until further notice.

"I found him on the street crying," he explained, tousling the boy's hair, which was dark and unkempt and in need of cutting. "Nera has gone to visit her dying mother and, heartless creature, has left him to fend for himself. I couldn't allow it. So I invited him to stay with us until she returns."

Fabiana turned around in surprise from her cooking and, although she was fond of Hakan and had a generous nature, it was obvious that she was surprised by her husband's sudden rush of altruism.

"But where will he sleep, Husband?" she asked.

"With the boy," he replied, nodding in my direction.

"And how long will his mother be away?" she continued, but

Marwan simply shrugged his shoulders and sat down, waiting for a plate of food to be put before him. The conversation had come to an end.

I spent the evening dreading the night that lay ahead. The notion of Hakan's body and mine pressed together in my tiny bed in a state of undress horrified me, and when the time came and he hobbled into the bedroom where I was already lying naked beneath the thin sheet, I began to weep, running into the kitchen to ask my parents whether I might sleep in their bed instead, a request that was summarily refused. My father looked at me with such disgust that I cried even more, for I hated to shame myself in front of him.

Marwan, having fought in so many battles and witnessed so much butchery over the years, was barely conscious of Hakan's deformity and saw my tantrum as nothing more than the selfishness of a child too spoiled to share a bed with another, while Fabiana understood why I was protesting and scolded me for my callousness. Still, I lay awake much of the night and, whenever he turned, some part of those twisted limbs would make contact with my own and I would withdraw from him even further.

As the weeks passed and Nera had still not reappeared, I asked whether Hakan might not share Abeer's bed instead—after all, I reasoned, he was her friend and not mine—and my father struck me in anger. I did not realize that asking two eleven-year-olds to sleep together would be to land them in disgrace as well as a marriage contract.

Abeer forgave my unkindness, for she could never stay angry with me for long, but when I asked her why she liked Hakan so much, particularly when he was an outcast with the other children, she replied by saying that I had answered my own question.

"His isolation is what makes him interesting," she told me, sewing a set of yellow ribbons into the hem of her skirt, for among all her other talents, Abeer was an excellent seamstress. "Hakan saves all his best stories for me. All his ambitions. All his secrets."

I liked the idea of secrets and asked her to share them with me, too, but she smiled and shook her head.

"Will you marry him one day?" I asked, fearful that he might become a permanent member of our family, but she remained silent as she returned to her sewing. She must have missed a stitch, though, for she winced and drew a finger to her mouth. When she pulled it away, a drop of blood fell on the material of the freshly decorated dress, leaving a perfect red spot at the center of one of the ribbons.

"Here," she said, holding the bleeding finger out toward me. "Kiss it better."

I took the finger into my mouth, tasting the saltiness of the blood, and sucked on it. When the bleeding stopped, I watched, transfixed, as she pricked the top of a second finger, producing the same result, and told me to kiss this one better, too.

"You'll do anything I ask, little brother, won't you?" she said thoughtfully as I held this finger in my mouth. "I like that."

A month later, Nera returned at last. It was evening time and our family, along with Hakan, was seated around the fire, eating lamb stew flavored with saffron. Winter had come, the nights had turned cold, and my mother was repeating some gossip she'd overheard in the marketplace that morning when we heard footsteps approaching from outside. We turned around as one, for it was unusual to have visitors at that time of night.

The door opened and Nera entered, looking exhausted and hungry. Hakan jumped up and hobbled toward her, crying out her name in delight. She was holding a bundle that, at first, I took to be food, a symbol of her gratitude to my family for taking care of her son. But no, a confused mewling from the parcel revealed that she was carrying a baby, an infant, and she parted the two sides of the blanket to reveal a tiny head and scarlet lips that suckled at her finger, just as I had suckled at Abeer's.

"Well?" asked my father, staring at her.

"A girl," she said.

He nodded and sighed, closing his eyes for a moment before returning to his place at the fire. "Wife," he said, addressing Fabiana but not daring to look at her. "Nera and my daughter will live here with us from now on. There will be no arguments, no discord. This is how I want things to be and this is how they will be."

The silence that followed this speech seemed to last for an eternity. I looked at my mother, whose face fell in a mixture of distress and shame, her entire body slumping in a manner that suggested she had not only been defeated but knew she had no way of fighting back. A kind woman, she turned to Nera, speaking the words of welcome that were as natural to her as breathing.

"You must be hungry after your walk," she said. "Let me offer you a plate of food."

ITALY

A.D. 169

AS OUR NEW and unconventional family life formed over the following months, my discomfort around the boy I began to think of as my cousin diminished and we formed an unexpected friendship. However, it would not be long before I was forced into the company of another playmate, one far less friendly and far more dangerous than any I had yet known.

The Emperor's son, Commodus, and I met for the first time at the interminable funeral procession for Hadrian's heir, Lucius Verus. He was seated on the right hand of his father, Marcus Aurelius, while I, as the son of one of the senior members of the Praetorian Guard, held a position of honor to the rear of the main dais. He happened to glance in my direction during one of the eulogies and, when he caught my eye and offered an extravagant yawn, I burst out laughing and had to cover my mouth with my hand to hide my disgrace. A moment later, he whispered something into the Emperor's ear and was given leave to vacate his chair. As he walked proudly past my row, his head held high as befitted a child of his elevated status, he indicated that I should follow him, and soon we were making our way back toward the palace together.

"If I had to sit there for another minute," he declared, waving a regal hand in the air, "I might have drawn the dagger from my father's side and cut my own head off. I promise you that when I am Emperor, events like those will be kept as brief as possible. And there will be more sacrifices to the gods. I enjoy a good sacrifice, don't you? Otherwise, everything becomes so boring. I love the sound of screaming, it's like music to me."

I wouldn't have dared to disagree, but in truth I had been sorry to leave the pageantry, having looked forward to the moment when my father, Maarav, would lead the cortège carrying the body of the late warrior emperor, which was being venerated that afternoon. Lucius Verus had been the one to finally defeat the reviled Parthian Empire and their wicked King, Vologases, broadening the expanse of the Roman Empire so significantly that the Senate had deified him only days after his death. Maarav had played his own part in these victories and I was filled with pride for his achievements.

"Yes, Highness," I replied, already in thrall to Commodus, who looked like a young god in his elaborately stitched toga picta with stripes of Tyrian purple running along the arms to signify his exalted rank. "I would have gouged my eyes out with my thumbs if I'd been forced to stay another moment."

He turned to look at me in some surprise before bursting into laughter. "You're the son of Maarav, yes? Of the Praetorian Guard? I've noticed you around the palace grounds. You're noisy. Too noisy, at times. You must learn to remain quiet. Otherwise, someone might decide to cut out your tongue."

I apologized for my indiscipline and swore to mend my puerile ways, although the accusation was harsh, given I was surely among the least boisterous children in Rome. I began to tell him more about my father and the campaigns in which he had fought, but he quickly grew disinterested. Maarav may have been an important member of the Palace Cavalry but, to the prince, he was just another worthless plebeian, a mortal lingering in the company of the divine.

He took me to his rooms, which were elaborately decorated, and I examined the tapestries on the walls, the work of the most extraordinary craftsmanship. Each one depicted a great Roman victory, from the Battle of Silva Arsia almost seven hundred years earlier, marking the birth of the Republic under Lucius Junius Brutus, to Julius Caesar's great triumph over the Gauls at Alesia. I reached out to touch the fabric and was moved by the astonishing blend of strength and fragility represented in each stitch. My admiration for such things was exactly what made my father despise me so; he saw it as unmanly and symptomatic of a weak or even feminine disposition, but I did not care. Even then I valued beauty above all other things.

But the tapestries were not the only luxurious items on display. The drapes that hung around the boy's bed were crafted from velvet, the sheets from satin, while the rugs that lay upon the stone floor, brought back from the Dacian Wars, were the very ones King Decebalus himself had once walked upon. The only thing to upset the perfect tranquillity of the room was a pair of dogs with yellow ribbons tied around their necks that had been asleep by the fireplace upon our arrival and whimpered in fear when we entered, rushing to hide beneath the trio of klinai that stood by the window. Commodus ignored them, but I observed how they remained on their guard throughout my visit, the younger, no more than a puppy, trembling violently. I wondered what occurred in these rooms every day to make the poor animals so frightened.

"Do you play tali?" he asked, lifting a pouch of sheep's knucklebones from a table and emptying them onto the floor. The game was a popular one among Roman children; we would toss the small bones in the air then try to catch them on the front of our hands, a more difficult proposition than it might sound.

"Of course," I said, and he indicated the cushion opposite him. When I sat down he threw the bones up quite high, catching all but two. He was a skilled player.

"My father, the Emperor, speaks highly of yours," he declared after a lengthy silence during which we concentrated on the game. "Were it not for his good opinion, I wouldn't have invited you here today. Naturally, I cannot allow just anyone into my bedchamber. You don't smell as bad as some of the other children, I'm pleased to say. Although you're uglier than most."

"Thank you, Highness," I said.

"My father says that your father has two wives," he continued when my turn came and I managed to catch only one, a defeat in which he took extravagant pleasure. "Can this be true?"

"Not quite," I said. "Maarav is married to my mother, Fabia. But there is another woman, Noemi, with whom he has a daughter. And Noemi herself has a son."

"The cripple?" he asked.

"Yes," I said, feeling defensive for Hagan, for I had grown to recognize him as a boy of uncommon sympathy and understanding and I valued his presence in a mostly female home. The note of contempt in Commodus's tone offended me, but I would not have dared to challenge him.

"And your mother does not object to such an unusual arrangement?"

"She would never go against my father's wishes," I said.

"Of course not. That would oppose the natural order of things. But I daresay she is grieved by it?"

I remained silent. In the two years since Maarav had introduced us to his mistress, the women of the house had formed a strong matriarchal alliance, and they had become more sisters than rivals.

"From now on," he told me then with a decisive nod, "you are to come to the palace every day. You may sit outside my rooms and, if I wish to play with you, then I will. If I don't, then you will be completely ignored and make no noise. Is that understood?"

"Yes, Highness," I said, bowing my head, and, our pact made, we played a few more games of knucklebones until I defeated him at last. I leaped up with a delighted cry and he immediately grew incensed, pushing me over and kicking me so hard in the ribs that I felt the breath leave my body. More violence followed and, when he began to kick me in the face, he sent two of my teeth flying across the floor. Even as I lay there, with blood pouring down my chin, I blamed myself for displeasing him and swore not to do so again. Commodus, I realized, was not one to be gracious in defeat.

• • •

Over the weeks that followed, I obeyed the young Caesar's instructions to the word, stationing myself outside his rooms during the day, in anticipation of his pleasure. Sometimes he would summon me inside to play dice or tabula and, although I made sure never to achieve a victory over him again, he would usually find some reason to lash out at me before sending me on my way. More often than not, however, I would be left sitting outside without food or water and, if he passed in the corridor, he would ignore me, as if I were no more important than a tile on the wall.

After eight consecutive days when I did not lay eyes on him, however, but watched as members of the household entered and left his bedchamber with expressions of concern on their faces, I began to wonder whether something untoward had taken place within. My anxiety only increased when I discovered my father waiting for me at home on the ninth morning, saying that he would accompany me to the palace that day. Fabia was weeping and held me to her with such intensity it was as if she believed she would never see me again. When Maarav and I left, she buried herself in Noemi's shoulder, crying inconsolably.

As we walked the short distance from the barracks, where the families of the Praetorian Guard lived, my father took my hand in his and surprised me by saying that I was a good son.

"Perhaps I have been slow to show you the love that a boy should expect from his father," he added quietly. "But my affections were so strong for your brother Joao that when he disappeared I grew anxious of allowing those feelings to develop for another."

I said nothing of the fact that he had shown a want of emotion toward me since long before Joao's departure.

"But I am proud of you this day," he added. "Very proud."

"Thank you, Father," I said, looking ahead toward the great stone doors, where a tall, bearded man stood in wait. I was convinced now that, having outlived my usefulness, Commodus had decided to add me to the lions' lunch menu. When the man stepped forward to receive us, Maarav knelt down, taking me in his arms and embracing me with almost as much fervor as my mother had earlier.

"We must each do what we can for the glory of Rome," he said. "And you, my son, are making the greatest sacrifice of all. You will bring great honor to our family name."

He stood up, turned and walked away. I felt sick inside. Whatever was going to happen would happen and there was no point in resisting.

The tall man, left in charge of me, rested a hand on my shoulder before introducing himself as Galen, a physician from Pergamon who had the honor to act as personal doctor to the imperial heir.

"Am I to be eaten?" I asked, and he frowned, looking as if he had not quite understood my question. "By the lions," I added, and he shook his head, laughing a little, as he led me down the familiar corridor.

"No," he said. "At least not today."

"Does His Highness wish to play, then?" I asked, and Galen sighed.

"You are aware of the plague?" he asked me, and I nodded, for over recent months the people of Rome had spoken of little else. The sickness had arrived in the city with troops returning from Western Asia, killing hundreds of people in only a few weeks. Typically, victims would come down with a fever before suffering the filthy scourge of diarrhea, at which point they would be confined to their beds in a delirium. Next, they would lose the ability to speak, a terrible rash forming at the back of their throats that made swallowing a most painful experience. Soon, the skin would erupt in a multitude of abscesses, engorged with pus, that covered the face and body. Then there would be nothing to be done; the patient would either recover or die. It did not discriminate between social ranks.

"Of course," I replied. "But I'm healthy and have shown no signs of illness. My parents say that I've never been sick a day in my life."

"I don't care about you," he said dismissively as we approached Commodus's door. "But those who are struck down must be kept in strict quarantine, in order to avoid any further spread of the disease. I'm sorry to say that the Emperor's son has developed symptoms and is very ill."

I hesitated, stopping in the corridor, and he turned around.

"The boy is lonely," he continued. "He needs companionship. Someone who will sleep next to him, deliver his food and take care of his needs. Your reputation is high, and I believe that you have been a playmate of the prince in the past?"

"Yes," I said, feeling frightened at the prospect of being cast inside the infected room. "But I don't think he likes me very much. He beats me frequently and calls me names. I can't be the right person for such a task. I'm not even of noble birth and—"

But Galen cared nothing for my protestations, opening the door before pushing me inside and quickly pulling it closed again.

I looked around and took a deep breath, hoping not to let any of the infected air into my lungs, but of course I could not manage this for more than a few seconds. The room stank of vomit and excrement, there was uneaten fruit rotting on one of the tables, and when I looked toward the bed I saw Commodus lying there, one hand thrown across his face, the other beckoning me forward. I took small steps, hoping that he would tell me to stop before I put myself in any further danger, but instead he urged me closer and closer.

"You are good to come," he whispered, his voice a dry croak, almost unrecognizable from the confident, belligerent boy I had come to know and fear. "I grow lonely here, and both my father and mother are too frightened to visit. Even my sister Lucilla, who swore that she loved me above all others, has not set foot inside this room. Perhaps she hopes that she will usurp my position and become empress if I die. The gods would never allow such a perverse outcome, would they? I am divine. My place is on the mountaintop with Jupiter, Mars and Apollo."

As I moved nearer still, I saw how altered his face had become since our last encounter. His skin had turned blotchy and pockmarked, the signs of the plague all too visible. He reached out a hand and I had no choice but to take it. Commodus would surely perish, and I would succumb to the disease next.

"Can I get you some water, Highness?" I asked, but he shook his head. He patted the other side of the enormous bed and asked me to lie next to him, for comfort's sake, and I removed my sandals and did as requested.

"I would have been a great emperor," he croaked, and I nodded, for I was young enough to believe that the old ways were the bad ways and that when my generation came to power a revolution would begin. In my mind, despite his many cruelties toward me, Commodus represented change.

"Don't give up hope," I told him. "Remember, half die and half survive."

"The gods long to have me among their number," he said list-lessly. "They crave my wisdom, so summon me to Olympus. I feel it, more so every day. It's understandable, of course. I was always too good for this world."

Outside the door, when Galen had pressed my task upon me, I had been frightened, but here, in the sick room, on the very preci-pice of infection, I found that I was ready for whatever might come next. I reached over and placed a kiss upon Commodus's forehead, my lips grazing against a grotesque carbuncle, and, while the stench that emanated from his body was repulsive, I held him beside me in the hope that he would feel some comfort, and soon, in this false tableau of devotion, we both fell asleep.

• • •

For several weeks we carried on like this. A knock would come from outside and our meals would arrive, a banquet for the young prince, who could barely eat, and a few miserly scraps for me. I was hungry, of course, but would not have dared to touch his food. Occasion-ally, Galen would speak to me through the door and ask how fared the patient before leaving potions which I administered to Com-modus, feeling less revolted now by the bursting blisters that marked his countenance.

And then, one day, to my surprise, he began to show signs of improvement. His deliriums ceased, as did the rasp in his throat. His appetite returned, he ate all the food that was brought to him and, when I bathed him in a mixture of hot water, goat's milk and coconut oil, the infected skin slipped from his body, leaving behind only red scars as souvenirs. Almost a month after my sequestration had begun, the doors were flung open and Commodus returned to the court, healthy and revived, and without, I might add, a single word of thanks. And I, too, returned home to my family, where I was welcomed with tears of joy from Fabia and Noemi and obvious pride by Maarav.

Throughout the entire experience, I was fortunate not to suc-cumb to the plague myself. Indeed, I never displayed a single symp-tom of the disease and told myself in private moments that perhaps I was stronger than anyone believed, stronger even than the Emperor's son himself. And although a man can never know what the gods have in store for him, my immunity to the epidemic suggested to me once again that I was destined for a long life, one filled with incident, and this pleased me, for there was much that I wanted to achieve before laying down my burden.

PART 2

THE GREAT

HUMILIATION

SWITZERLAND

A.D. 214

My FATHER, Marvel, liked to recount the story of how an ancestor of his, a man named Lonus, made a valiant attempt at murdering Julius Caesar, long before the conspirators drew their daggers on the floor of the Senate. Our people, the Helvetii, were only days from defeat at the Battle of Bibracte and, finding the idea of capitulation to such savage trespassers repugnant to his nature, Lonus rode directly into the Roman army camp, his swinging sword ripping the heads from three unsuspecting legionnaires before charging in the direction of the tent where Caesar was consulting with his generals. Had it not been for the quick thinking of Crassus, who hurled a spear between the shoulder blades of the would-be assassin, the fortunes of the Roman Empire might have turned out very differently. I didn't like to point out that the narrative in which he took so much pride had not only ended in failure but also in the death of his forebear, who, having survived the spear, had his fingers and toes removed with a blunt knife before being skinned alive and roasted slowly over a spit.

He told the story once again on the night that the young men of our village set up camp on the Alpine mountain land that we called home, where he and the other elders planned on training us to fight the Romans. There were perhaps one hundred gathered there— every male over the age of fourteen—a small army in comparison to the cohorts that would soon arrive from Italy, and to my surprise I found myself among their number, despite the fact that I was only ten years old. It was the first time that my father had permitted me to accompany him into the world of men, and my mother, Fabiola, protested strongly, claiming that I was still too young to be involved in warfare.

"Julian would not have been too young, Wife," he replied, nodding toward me dismissively. "If my firstborn had not vanished, then it would be him accompanying me to the mountains and not this one."

"And what of me, Father?" asked my sister Alba, who, despite being a girl, was far more suited to combat than I.

"You're worth more than the boy, that's for sure," he told her. "But no, Daughter, you must stay at home. The mountain is no place for women."

"I would kill ten Romans for every one that he would," she insisted, raising her voice.

"I don't doubt it," he said. "But I cannot allow it. Even the idea is a sacrilege."

"What about me?" asked Hagune, and, although Marvel regarded him admiringly, he shook his head.

"A boy with twisted legs would be even less use than a girl," he said, resting his hand upon the boy's head. "But your bravery earns my respect. As does yours, Alba."

"So the one person who doesn't want to go is the one who goes," she replied, rolling her eyes and placing a hand against a tile on the wall, as if to steady herself. "To be a healthy boy is all that matters in this life, isn't that right, Father?"

• • •

At our mountainside camp, Marvel trained the young men in techniques of hand-to-hand combat, aiming to build our confidence as we prepared to defend ourselves against the expected onslaught of the Empire's finest soldiers.

We were each given a sword, a shield and a dagger, but little else, making us lighter on our feet than our Roman counterparts, who typically carried several days' worth of rations and digging equipment in their backpacks. We fought at various intervals, one man against two, three, four or five, each one building up muscle and stamina and never daring to appear sluggish, for my father could be a brutal taskmaster and was happy to take out his anger on anyone who was not performing at the level he demanded.

In the evenings, however, he transferred his attention from our bodies to our minds, recounting the legends of our Helvetii ancestors and listing the crimes that the Romans had committed across their plundered world since Mars had first placed twin boys in the womb of the Vestal Virgin.

I was the youngest there and, while I was pleased to be given an opportunity to earn my father's respect, the violence and brutality that played out before me every day was upsetting. Of course, the men were considerate toward me on account of my youth, but the image of a warrior's sword swinging toward me as I raised my shield to stop myself from being slaughtered was a terrifying one. The fact that my opponents laughed when I fell over and held their swords high, as if to slice me in two, only added to my fear.

With all of this activity going on, and with so many hot-blooded young men trapped on an isolated hilltop with stirred emotions and no women to keep their passions at bay, perhaps it was inevitable that an accident would eventually take place. Late on a cold, damp afternoon, only a few days before the Romans finally appeared, my father pitted me against a boy, Loravix, six years older than me, who was considered something of a coward. I think Marvel sought to humiliate him, or me, or both of us, by gathering the entire army to watch us and mock our chaotic and uncoordinated moves. The men formed a circle and my father roared whenever we swung too soon or our footwork became careless. Loravix directed his sword toward me and I raised my shield to defend myself, aiming my own at his ankles, but he leaped in the air as he had been trained, swinging deftly and narrowly avoiding lifting my head from my shoulders. My father shouted from the sidelines that we were expected only to fight, not to kill each other, and I swung again, expecting to make contact with his shield, but Loravix chose this moment to turn in Marvel's direction and, as he did so, he dropped his right arm. My own was moving too fast to stop and, to my horror, my sword sliced cleanly through his wrist, relieving him of a hand, and in a moment, blood poured from the stump. Horrified by what I had done, I grew dizzy and, as Loravix started to scream, I turned my head to vomit on the ground. Others came quickly and bound the wound, but there was nothing that could be done and the boy was sent back to the village. I was inconsolable, but my father surprised me by behaving in a solicitous fashion, maintaining that if it hadn't happened in training, then it would have happened on the field of battle anyway, and it would have been Loravix's head rolling down the mountain, not his hand.

Later that night, however, he discovered me at some distance from the camp, urinating against a tree, and spun me around, slapping me hard across my face with his glove. I was taken unawares, uncertain what crime I had committed now, and as I stumbled, he hit me again, and once more until I was lying prostrate on the ground. My crime, of course, had not been maiming another boy but vomiting in front of the other men. Marvel hated any display of weakness, particularly one that reflected badly on him.

"I'll make a man of you yet," he said, looking at me with contempt as I rolled on the grass, trying not to weep through the pain. "When this is over, when we have chased the Romans away, it will be time for you to stop spending so much of your days around women and learn how to be a man. Like me."

• • •

We fought valiantly but, faced with an entire cohort of Roman legionnaires, our small army found itself outnumbered five to one and it took only a few hours for the Empire to bring us to heel. Just over sixty of our men were brutally slain and the remainder were brought back down the mountain in chains. The ankles of each man were shackled together and it was a grim sight to observe the defeated villagers lined up, humiliation carved into their faces and an expectation of death in their eyes.

As the battle raged, I had hidden as instructed in a tree, watching in horror as men I'd spent weeks with were slaughtered before my eyes. When the remaining rebels were captured, a group that included my father, I was surprised to see them being led back toward the village rather than killed on the spot.

Watched over by a smaller group of soldiers, they awaited the arrival of the centurion Priscus, who had been charged with supervising the stone wall fortifications that surrounded Rhaetia. He had not taken part in the battle, probably thinking that our ragtag group of rebels was unworthy of his attention, and failed even to appear that night, when the chained men could be observed collapsed on the ground in their manacles, half-asleep and starving, stinking of piss, shit and vomit. The dead bodies had been recovered the previous day before being piled atop a pyre and the women had been given permission to burn their lost husbands and sons. The stench of roasted flesh in the air lent a sickening perfume to our defeat and the night was filled with the calamitous sound of weeping and mourning.

I followed at a safe distance and managed to return to my father's house under cover of night without discovery. Fabiola and Naura were comforting their children, who were traumatized by the horrific sights and smells, so it was Alba who first saw me slink through the door, and she cried out in delight as I stumbled inside. In a moment, they were all upon me to offer kisses and hugs, my mother, the woman I had come to think of as my aunt, the twins and my crippled cousin. I answered their questions as best I could about what had taken place and, while they were terrified at what might happen when the centurion finally arrived, they were at least relieved that my life had been spared.

The entire village was summoned outdoors the next morning when Priscus rode in on a white horse fitted with a fine turquoise-colored saddle, flanked by four young contubernales carrying the flag of the Roman Republic, a golden eagle, its wings outstretched across a garland of laurels, with the letters SPQR—*Senatus Populusque Romanus;* the Senate and People of Rome—printed beneath it. Priscus was an enormous man, unnervingly tall and broad, with a startling yellow beard. I looked at the filthy men shackled on the ground; how could they compare in splendor with their muddy skin and rough, worn clothing? Priscus must have felt the disparity, too, for he did not even offer us the respect of dismounting his horse, humiliating his captives by remaining aloft as he addressed the surviving men, women and children of Rhaetia.

"Helvetia is conquered," he shouted, "and these tedious local skirmishes waste all our time! Many of your neighbors died yesterday, more still will die today. A message must be sent to others who would defy the rule of the Emperor Caracalla."

He looked around at the row of men before him, who had been dragged to their feet now and stood in a long, single file. At his signal, four of the legionnaires moved behind the first group of men, each one drawing his sword and raising it vertically in the air, so it was pressed against the base of a prisoner's neck. The women screamed, begging for mercy, but Priscus held his hand out, demanding silence. When all that could be heard was muffled weeping, he turned to the first soldier and rotated his hand so the thumb pointed upward. The soldier sheathed his sword and stepped down the line, so he was now standing behind the fifth man, at which point he withdrew the sword once again and held it as he had before.

There was a great cry of relief that our first neighbor had been spared but then Priscus held his hand out again, this time turning it so the thumb pointed toward the ground, and as he did so the second soldier's sword descended through the spine of a man who had once carried me on his back as a child and who cried out for only a moment before collapsing to the ground, dead. The crowd screamed, the soldier moved along the line and Priscus granted mercy to the third man in line, then execution to the fourth, fifth and sixth, mercy to the seventh, death to the eighth. It seemed that half were being reprieved and half killed, although the order was random and there was no way to tell whether the next man would live or die.

I glanced toward my father, who was standing close to the end of the line, and saw no fear on his face, although the scar on his left cheek seemed more inflamed than usual. I held my breath, watching the murderous hand of the centurion, certain that he was going to bring my father's life to an end, but no, he saved him, and while he may not have wished to show any emotion, I thought I could see a trace of relief on Marvel's face.

By the end, only sixteen men were left alive, and Priscus addressed us for the final time.

"Every man that remains, every woman, and every child, you

have forfeited the right to live as free people. You are now bound in servitude and will be taken to Rome, where you will be purchased by new masters and work for them according to their whims. And if you want to blame anyone for your change of circumstances, then look only to yourselves."

SOMALIA

A.D. 260

THE NIGHT BEFORE the slave auction took place, my father, mother and aunt sat down to discuss how many new purchases we would make at the fair. It had been almost two years since Bal Priscumi, the slave trader from Mombasa, had last come to the Seat of the Shah with fresh attainments and many of the great households, including our own, were in need of replenishment. My mother, Furaha, was in charge of domestic arrangements but had already discussed her needs with Nala.

We owned eight slaves already and Makena had a strict rule that we should neither give them names nor permit them to use the ones they had employed before coming to Sarapion, as names were for people and slaves were not people, but chattel, subject to the whims and desires of their owners. One to Five had lived in a hut toward the rear of our property since before my birth, Six had arrived when I was a child, while both Seven and Eight had been acquired the last time that Bal Priscumi had come to town. It was a source of great distress to Furaha, however, that we owned so few; she believed that a family like ours, with wealth and position, should keep twice that number, but my father preferred to keep his slave numbers low, saying that being greeted by such miserable, ungrateful faces every morning got his days off to a bad start.

"Why are they so unhappy anyway?" he asked. "They should feel honored that we purchased them in the first place."

"Who knows?" replied Furaha with a shrug. "You cannot expect me to understand the minds of slaves. The point is, Husband, that we need nine more. It shames me to see how empty our slave hut is compared to—" And here she named neighbor after neighbor after neighbor who were better endowed with slaves than we were. This was always an effective way of winning an argument with Makena, for he could not bear to be viewed as inferior in status to anyone.

"Nine more to house, nine more to feed, nine more to look at," he groaned, placing his head in his hands in frustration. "While you two sit around all day doing nothing?" He looked from Furaha to Nala, who bowed her head and remained silent. Typically, she did not involve herself in matrimonial disputes, allowing my mother to make the case for both of them.

"Us? Do nothing?" cried Furaha, throwing her arms in the air. "All we do is work, Nala and I, from morning till night, because the slaves you've bought in the past are so useless. Lazy good-for-nothings from Nubia and Punt who act as if they should have the freedom to live their own lives instead of according to their mistresses' wishes. You won't even consider buying strong, young slaves because heaven forbid that we diminish our coffers! We have more money than anyone for miles around, but will you spend any of it?"

"We have it because I won't spend it!"

"Then what use is it? Will you still cling to it in your shroud?"

"All right!" cried Makena, growing weary of her shouting. "But why nine? Why so many?"

"Two for cooking and three for household work," said Nala without hesitation.

"And two more for the garden," added Furaha. "The garden is a disgrace, Husband, as you can see, because Three and Five are getting too old to manage the land."

"That only makes seven," replied my father, counting them off on his fingers.

"And two more to help with the children," said Furaha.

"The children are your responsibility!"

"Two more to help with the children," she insisted.

"And where are they to sleep, these wonderful, strong young slaves? We would own . . ." He thought about it for some time and I could see his lips move as he calculated the number. "Seventeen slaves in total. So, tell me, Wife, where are they to sleep?"

"In the slave hut, of course," she said. "The others can make room. We will put Two and Four out onto the street for their laziness, and Three and Five can join them, as they are too ancient to be of any use anymore. So, in truth, our numbers will only rise from eight to thirteen."

"Good Brother," said Nala quietly, using the peaceful tone that she always employed at such moments and the name she sometimes assigned to her lover. "Beloved Sister Furaha is correct to say that your name is held in less esteem since you own so few slaves. These new additions will only enhance your position in the town. We do not speak to cause you weariness or upset, only out of love and concern."

My father considered this and, knowing that he could never win when these two combined forces against him, gave in and nodded his head.

Nala, I realized, was more skillful at convincing him on these matters than my mother, who was growing into a more aggressive presence in our home. Of course, she knew that Makena had taken several new lovers in the village, much younger than either she or Nala, and lived in fear that one of them would give him a baby and the pair would also be brought to live among us.

"You win, as you always do," said my father. "But if you want these slaves, then you must choose them yourselves. I have better things to do with my time. Nala, you go. You have more sense than my wife." He stood up to leave but then, thinking better of it, turned back. "And take the boy with you," he added, nodding in my direction. "He can keep hold of the money."

• • •

The marketplace was busy but our status in the town ensured that most people stepped aside to allow Nala and me through. Many attended solely out of interest, lacking the resources to make any purchases but keen to observe the drama of the afternoon.

Traders from the town had set up tables to take advantage of the increased business that the slave fair would bring. There were food stalls selling teff pancakes, sambusas and quraac, jewelers holding precious gems in their hands, and a display of ornamental objects, including a golden eagle, a silver statue of Minerva and a collection of glass fruit that captured the sun, sending prisms of color onto my palms when I held them aloft.

The sale was due to take place in the colonnade at the center of Sarapion and pillars had been erected on the dais where the slaves could be tied up and examined without fear of their trying to escape. Nala and I took our place at the front, alongside other wealthy men from our town, and they looked so surprised to see a woman given such responsibility that I took my father's pouch of money from my pocket and tossed it from hand to hand so they could see I was no longer a child but had at last earned Makena's trust. The purse was filled with gold fragments and arrowheads, and I felt a surfeit of pride to be the guardian of such treasures.

At the end of the row I noticed the tavern owner, Vinium, whose daughter was my father's latest mistress. I had spied on them recently, following Makena through the town to a hut in a forest where she waited for him. When he appeared, she smiled and removed her dress without a word and I almost cried out in pain to see how beautiful she was. My father took her, quickly and without any pretense at tenderness, and I felt a mixture of contempt and confusion at his actions. After he left, I climbed down from the tree where I was hiding, and as I turned to make my way home, the girl, Sanaa, emerged from the hut and discovered me. As our eyes met, I felt sick with humiliation, but to my surprise she simply smiled lasciviously at me, asking whether I wanted to indulge in the same games as my father.

"You're young," she said, loosening the strap of her dress from her left shoulder and letting it slip down just enough that I could see her breast, the enticing heft of it and the darkened nipple which both excited and terrified me. "But every boy must learn to pleasure a woman at some point."

I wanted to touch her but was embarrassed by the unexpected engorgement beneath my tunic and, uncertain how to conduct myself in this moment of potential initiation into the ways of adults, I ran away as fast as I could, hearing her mocking laughter echo through the forest. Returning to the village, I fell to my knees and prayed she would not betray me to Makena, who would surely have beaten me, had he discovered that I had been spying upon them.

"I wonder how they feel," I said quietly now, shifting uncomfortably in the chair.

"How who feel?" asked Nala, turning to me.

"The slaves. Being bought and sold like this. Is it an insult to their dignity?"

She shrugged her shoulders, as if I had asked her to explain a simple fact of nature, like why the sky was blue or why we needed sleep. "It hardly matters, Beloved Nephew," she said. "They have no dignity. They're only slaves, nothing more. Their feelings are not important. I don't know if they even have any."

"Seven has feelings," I said, because only a few days earlier I had discovered it crying in the corner of one of our fields when it should have been busy herding cattle. When I asked why it was weeping, it replied that it missed its home. Naturally, I pointed out that Sarapion was its home now, but it simply shook its head, looking at me with something approaching hatred on its face. For as long as I could remember, I had barely noticed those who toiled at our pleasure, any more than I noticed the grass or the well or the rugs on our floors, but Seven's reaction had confused me and made me question why some were masters and some were slaves.

"Seven is headstrong," replied Nala. "It needs to stay with the animals where it belongs. Eight can be emotional, too. When it gave birth last year and Makena sold the baby, it wouldn't work for days afterward. Your mother and I had some sympathy but, eventually, even we grew tired of humoring it. Still, whenever Eight passes me by, it gives me a look as if it dares to have an opinion about me."

I remembered that event from the previous summer. No one knew who had put the baby inside Eight but my father had insisted on selling it as soon as it was weaned. He got a good price for it, too, I remember, but Eight had screamed for hours afterward and it could only be silenced when a gag was put in its mouth. Now it never spoke at all, but I was surprised to learn that it continued to show such disrespect toward my aunt. Like a wild horse, I thought, it had been broken.

There was a rustle of noise in the colonnade now as Bal Priscumi appeared, older and fatter than I remembered him from his last visit but his yellow beard as impressive as ever, followed by a group of men, women and children, each with their heads cast down and wearing distraught expressions upon their faces, which were far blacker than mine or any of the residents of Sarapion. The whites of their eyes were studded with blood-red veins, which frightened me. They were almost naked, too, the men and boys wearing nothing but loincloths around their waists, the women and girls draped in rags that barely covered their private parts. I stared at the young girls, who wrapped their arms before their breasts, and felt desire for them, just as I had felt for Sanaa. This longing had been a con- stant concern of mine in recent months. Where once I had felt no interest in girls, believing them to be useful only for housework and child-rearing, I had recently found myself staring at them in the street and, when one glanced back at me, feeling an inexplicable anxiety, along with a desire to touch myself, for I had lately discov- ered that my body could provide previously undiscovered pleasures if manipulated carefully.

In a deep voice that carried across the marketplace, Bal Priscumi announced the number of slaves on sale—sixteen men and just over twenty women and children—and I wondered whether we would be able to buy the required nine if others were equally interested. Nala walked over to inspect the men, ordering them to show her the soles of their feet, to run on the spot, to flex their arms and display their muscles. She ran her hands over their skin in a way that suggested she was already their mistress. She lifted the loincloths of some and examined those parts that made them men and, when she reached out to weigh these same parts in her hand, the slaves wore expressions of humiliation on their faces. Next, she turned to the women, examining their hands for signs of hard work and their teeth and gums for symptoms of disease, as one might study a stal- lion or a brood-mare before deciding whether or not to make an offer. The children were not of much interest to her but she moved around them anyway.

When she was finished, we consulted over the pouch of money

before approaching Bal Priscumi to begin our negotiations. She wanted five men, Nala said, indicating which ones, and four women.

"What about a child?" I asked, looking toward the younger group, who were clearly frightened to be the subject of such intense scrutiny.

"We have enough children," said Nala, shaking her head.

"Just one, though," I said. "A female. One who will have years of work ahead of it. Perhaps that would be a real bargain, Aunt?"

Nala considered this for a few moments before nodding. "Perhaps," she agreed. "But just one. Choose whichever one you like the most."

I walked past each child slowly, looking them up and down, and when I stood before the prettiest of the girls, I reached out to lift the base of its dress, just as Nala had done with the men's loincloths. The moment my fingers touched it, however, the boy standing next to the girl reached out for one of the branding irons that sat in the hot coals ready to mark each item as the property of a new owner. Had I not leaped back in time, I might have found myself scarred for life. Instead, the tip of the iron merely glanced across the skin of my neck. I cried out in pain, for it burned badly, and I could not have been more surprised by the impulsive actions of this slave if one of the cows in our fields had begun to relate the gossip of the herd to me.

The boy began shouting in a language that I did not understand, but I sensed, by the uncanny resemblance between them, that they were brother and sister and, for some reason, it had taken offense at my touching its sibling. I would have liked to strike it back but the slave trader was already beating it with a stick so I returned to the girl.

"This one," I said to Nala, and I turned back to it, smiling to show that I meant it no harm, but its face hardened and it looked at me with nothing but hatred in its eyes. I lifted its dress then and was pleased by what I saw.

Still, it seemed that my mother, Furaha, had been right. Some slaves were given to incitement and curious bursts of emotion and we had to be careful which ones we purchased. I wondered for a moment whether it might be better to buy none at all, and to wait until another day, when more obedient slaves might be brought to the marketplace, but Nala had already struck the deal with Bal Priscumi and now it was time for me to make the payment.

That done, we shackled our belongings together at the ankles and led them home.

SOUTH KOREA

A.D. 311

TWO YEARS LATER, in the house to which we had been taken against our will, I took a life for the first time.

From the moment of the Great Humiliation, I felt a sickness gnawing at the pit of my stomach, one that twisted around my guts and pressed into the core of my being. The pain was there when I woke in the morning, it grew worse throughout the afternoon and by nightfall it was almost unbearable. Not for the last time in my life, I realized that I longed for vengeance and for this to be taken in blood.

It was difficult not to blame Honored Father for subjecting our family to this degradation. He had lived his entire life in the town of Binjeon, on the banks of the Gongneungcheon River, where he repaired boats for the fishermen who sold their daily catch in the marketplace. It was honest work; it afforded us a small house, clothes for our backs and shoes for our feet. We never went hungry. But Honored Father was greedy, resenting having to pay taxes to the sacred landowners, and so, with the support of men he had known since childhood, he rebelled against the tariffs that had been part of life in Binjeon since Dangun first descended from the heavens to create the glorious land of Joseon. The uprising was always destined for failure and the insurgents were punished by having their freedom and the freedom of their families revoked. We were placed into the custody of a slave trader, who brought us to Incheon, where we were purchased by the great trader of spices Cheong Yeon-Seok, who in turn took us to his home in Wiryeseong to live out the rest of our lives as chattel, assigning us numbers in place of our given names.

How I despised Honored Father for his pride! He who had always looked down at me for not wanting to spend my life chopping wood to repair hulls or cutting cloth for sails! He who belittled me by speaking of Older Brother as the lost hero of our family, despite his having deserted us years before and disappearing into who knew what life of debauchery or crime! He who ridiculed me for not rolling around the streets like an animal, fighting with the other boys, drawing blood and having blood drawn, for preferring a life of contemplation and artistry!

Ha, to that!

I recount now the story of that ignoble afternoon when Honored Father returned home to discover Gentle Mother teaching me the venerable art of sewing. She was making a new dress for Older Sister from a spool of fabric imported directly from Goguryeo and was putting the finishing touches to her craftwork by using thread the color of dragon-fire to run along the hem. Watching her, I imagined a different design, marking it out in the sand at my feet with a twig, a pattern that reflected the flow of the great Han River. To weave this into the dress, I suggested, would be a most beautiful thing. Gentle Mother took delight in this idea and I asked whether I might be permitted to undertake the task myself. She agreed, and I had been working on the garment for perhaps two hours, lost in the sheer ecstasy of creativity, when Honored Father returned and kicked me from my stool, throwing the dress into the fire, where it fizzled into nothingness even before Gentle Mother's cries had come to an end. Honored Father beat me while I was on the floor, saying that it shamed him to witness his son engaged in the work of women.

"Ha!" I cried through my tears, enraging him further by insisting that the creation of beauty was worth every beating that he might inflict upon me, that I would simply find another dress, another needle, another set of threads to create my own designs. He threw his hands in the air then, beseeching the heavens to explain why they had inflicted such a son upon him, but I cared not for his insults, crying "Ha!" again and "Ha!" a third time, which led Honored Father to kick me in the face, silencing me so that I could "Ha!" no more.

I hated myself for weeping, but his brutality injured not just my body but my mind, too. Still, whenever I felt maltreated, I could console myself by knowing that one day I would leave Binjeon forever, just as Older Brother had done, and make my own way in a world where, if I wanted, I could sew night and day! All that was taken away from me, however, when Honored Father decided that he was too good to pay his taxes!

. . .

From the moment that I first encountered him, I despised Cheong Jung-Hee, the son of my master. A year older than me, he had been present when I was bought, poking at me and my siblings as if we were pieces of fruit that needed to be squeezed to discover whether we were ripe enough for his taste and pulling our clothes asunder to examine our bodies. That much-loathed villain rode his own horse back to Wiryeseong while the rest of us were thrown into a cart, and the sight of his fat body bouncing up and down on the back of his unfortunate beast made me red with anger. When we stopped to allow the horses to rest, his servants offered him chicken stew flavored with gochugaru to eat, washed down with flasks of miyeok guk, and he made a point of gobbling it down in front of us, mocking our hunger. What he didn't finish, he simply threw away, laughing when he saw how we longed to lick his leftovers from the street. Gentle Mother and Respected Aunt wept, such were the pangs of hunger in their stomachs, and he called them vile names, for which he received no reproach, for Honored Father simply sat toward the back, staring out across the fields and, I prayed, regretting the bad decisions that had led us toward the Great Humiliation.

It took several days, but finally we arrived at a large estate where Cheong Soo-Min, our master's wife, explained in a bored voice what our roles would be now that we were no longer free. Honored Father was taken to work in the fields while Gentle Mother and Respected Aunt were given the degrading tasks of cleaning floors on their hands and knees. Older Sister was taken inside the house to work in the kitchen and I was told that I would be a factotum, expected to appear at any summons, day or night, and to do whatever was required of me. A small hut stood toward the rear of the house with six cots, and that was where Older Sister and I, along with four other children who worked on the estate, were expected to sleep. An image of three candles, the middle one extinguished, was carved into the door and, in hot weather, the roof was pulled open and I could stare up at the sky, which fascinated me.

"Someday I shall live among the stars," I remarked to the boy on my right-hand side one night, and he laughed and mocked me, so I punched his face and never did he mock me again! Ha!

Each cot was separated from the one next to it by a thin curtain and, while it was small comfort, I was glad that Older Sister and I were adjacent to each other so we could whisper words of encouragement before we found the solace of the dream world.

The fat pig, Cheong Jung-Hee, spent almost as much time in the kitchen as those who worked there because he could not go from one hour to the next without stuffing his face full of food. He was so overweight that his body was always slick with perspiration, and just to look at him made my stomach turn in revulsion. He had more chins than I have fingers! Ha! Sometimes he would throw things on the floor for no other reason than to tell me to pick them up. He loathed me as much as I loathed him but I took pleasure in the knowledge that it infuriated him to see me so lean and handsome when he was a disgusting monster who made girls want to rip the eyes from their faces in abhorrence, lest they ever witness his vile visage again. When he caught me kissing one of the kitchen girls, he grew scarlet with rage and, pulling my shirt off, instructed two other slaves to tie me to a post so that he could beat me with sticks. Afterward, when I fell to the ground, bleeding and faint, he took out his tiny ding-dong and pissed on me, a stream of stinking yellow effluent that made me want to tear the skin from my body and wander the world as a skeleton of blood and bones!

He reserved most of his attention, however, for Older Sister, coming into the kitchen night and day to tell her to make him some kimchi jigae or a few steamed mandu dumplings. As she cooked, he would step closer to her, pressing his corpulent body against hers, and on more than one occasion she ran from the kitchen in tears as he insulted her with his desire. Then he would grow angry again and throw the half-cooked food on the floor, leaving me to clean up

the mess that he had left behind. I longed to see Honored Father
to tell him what was happening and form a plan for our escape, but
we had been kept apart since our arrival.

I knew that if Cheong Jung-Hee continued to behave as he did,
it would be left to me to defend Older Sister's honor.

· · ·

The moment of reckoning came late one night when Cheong Jung-
Hee's behavior finally became too transgressive. The days leading
up to this had been very busy as my master, Cheong Yeon-Seok,
had invited the elders from the town for a ceremonial dinner and
the entire household had been working endlessly in preparation for
it. My tasks had included sweeping the driveway, peeling vegetables
and roasting oats for the visitors' horses. More humiliation, that I
should be forced to prepare better food for the animals than I was
given to eat myself! Ha!

In the evening, I was outside, emptying the vegetable peelings
into a trough for the pigs and having to endure the torment of listening to that brute, Cheong Jung-Hee, who was seated with a
friend of his, Ghim Do-Yeon, a boy with no honor. It was well
known that he had mistreated a local girl of low birth, committing
the marriage act with her and putting a baby inside her belly against
her wishes and then refusing to take her as his wife. Ignoble boy!
She had been driven into exile by her family, who blamed her for
allowing Ghim Do-Yeon to steal her virtue, even though it was
common knowledge that he had forced himself upon her. Nevertheless, Cheong Jung-Hee idolized him, following him around like
the disease-ridden dog that he was!

"Look how skinny he is," said Ghim Do-Yeon, pointing in my
direction, and it was true that you could count my ribs through my
skin. "And he stinks, too! I can smell him from over here!"

"He's the stupidest of all the slaves," said Cheong Jung-Hee.
"And so ugly to look at. Never have I seen a boy with such a miserable expression on his face. He turns the milk sour."

I looked at him, my hands clenching into fists. I might have attacked him then, only this was when Older Sister emerged from the
kitchen carrying a bucket of slops, and when she came toward me

silently, the boys stopped their mocking, looking her up and down with the demon lust in their eyes.

"And who is this pretty thing?" asked Ghim Do-Yeon. "I haven't seen her here before."

"That one's even stupider than her brother," replied Cheong Jung-Hee. "But yes, she's nice to look at. Hey, come here and sit on my knee, kitchen girl!" he called to her, and Older Sister stared at him for a moment, her facing growing red, and she shook her head, turning back for the house. "I said come here!" he shouted then, leaving her with no choice but to obey. When she got close to him, Ghim Do-Yeon grabbed her and pulled her onto his knee. She let out a scream and, at that same moment, Cheong Jung-Hee reached for her dress and pulled it apart at the chest, her breasts spilling out. The insult was too great, and I dropped the pail, ready to run over and rip his head from his shoulders, but his mother chose this same moment to appear and he released Older Sister, who ran crying back toward the kitchen.

Later that night, when we were settled into our cots, Older Sister was still upset by the humiliation that had been visited upon her and I held her for a long time, swearing that I would remove us from this wretched place as soon as I could. I returned to my own bed and was close to sleep when I heard the door to the hut open and the sound of bare feet padding across the floor. At first, I wondered whether I was already dreaming, for there was no reason for anyone to be there at that time of night, but then I saw the great hulking shadow of Cheong Jung-Hee on the other side of the curtain, the one that separated my cot from Older Sister's, and a moment later heard the sound of muffled cries as he held his hand over her mouth.

My anger built into a great whirling tornado inside my body and I jumped from the bed and pulled the curtain aside, only to find that filthy animal on Older Sister's bed, pulling at her clothes with one hand while trying to push her legs apart with his knee. He stopped for a moment when he saw me, then climbed off her, pushing me back onto my own bed with a curse before dragging the curtain across, and I saw the shadow once again attempt to mount

her. I ran into the kitchen and looked around, hoping to find something that I could use to stop him, and when I saw the silver statue
of Minerva that stood on the windowsill, I lifted it from the shelf
and ran back to Older Sister's cot, jumped on the bed behind
Cheong Jung-Hee and bashed it down against the back of his head!
He groaned and fell to the floor and I hit him again, and again, feeling more powerful with every thrust of my arm.

A horrible gurgling sound could be heard from his body as he
died, and then a great explosion of blood burst from his mouth,
covering his lips and chin. A moment later, his body jerked in spasm,
his head fell to one side, and when I dared to lean down and look
him in the eyes, I knew that I had killed him.

I do not regret my actions! He was an animal and he deserved to
die! Ha!

PART 3

A
MASTER
CRAFTSMAN

ERITREA

A.D. 340

HER NAME WAS LERATO, which, in my language, means "beautiful woman," but she was not quite a woman yet, any more than I was a man. Halin and I first noticed her on a cold spring morning soon after the drought that had plagued our land for two years finally came to an end, when the great trader of spices, Chuseok, transported her to Adulis. Having purchased her a few days earlier, he made a point of parading the girl, along with a dozen new slaves, through the marketplace at the busiest time of the morning. Chuseok had not always been treated with great respect, for he was uncommonly short and round, like an obscene orb of blood and blubber, and throughout his life he had suffered at the hands of mocking tormentors, who referred to him as the Great Ostrich of Asmara, but the spice market was a lucrative trade and he was determined to see his status recognized in his hometown.

Lerato wore her hair cropped tightly to her head and her eyes were unnaturally large. Her cheeks were gaunt, perhaps from hunger, and the bones beneath her neck were prominent. Even from a distance, the clarity of her blue pupils was dazzling. She was so striking that neither I nor my cousin could keep our eyes from her. I pressed Halin to speak to her, for, despite his infirmity, he was much better at talking to girls than I, with a talent for making them laugh over silly jokes. I remained shy and self-conscious and was almost alone among the boys of my village yet to commit the act that defines the border between childhood and adulthood. But when Lerato walked by, three steps behind her master, Halin could not summon the courage to speak, and nor could I, but still, she seemed aware of my gaze, for when she turned to look in my direction our eyes met and I felt a stirring inside unlike any I had known before.

So distracted was I by her beauty that I could barely concentrate on my work for the rest of the day. Old enough, at last, to be liberated from the demands of my father, I had become a craftsman of the wooden steles that served as eternal monuments to the dead in the graveyard at the edge of our town. Only the wealthy could afford to honor their loved ones in this way, of course; the rest buried their people without markings, but as humility was in short supply among my neighbors, even those with little money aimed to raise their prestige by availing of my services whenever a family member passed to the other side. As my skills grew, so did my reputation, and families had started to compete with each other to commission the most ornate memorial.

I had been crafting steles for almost two years by now, using the wood from local oak trees to fashion structures that could rise to twice the height of a man, if required, and a third of that size in width. Typically, I kept the edges straight, forming a pleasing curve across the top, but my great skill lay in fashioning the designs on the front that would act as testaments to lost souls. Before starting, I would spend some time with the bereaved family and images would form in my mind, as if summoned by a rare ghost, and once they took shape, I would begin my work.

On the day that I first spoke to Lerato, she arrived in my workplace accompanied by her mistress, Sumin, who had recently lost one of her eleven sons in mysterious circumstances. Sumin, it must be said, was not grieving her loss with any great fervor. The boy had been an effeminate sort, much given to loud behavior and unrefined conversation. Once, a few years earlier, when we were still boys, he had come upon me in the bathing pool with his ting-ting hard and asked me to stroke it, and I did as he wished but later felt shame for my actions and hoped that Manu would not find out, as he would have surely whipped me for my vulgar behavior.

The boy had been discovered in his bed a few mornings earlier with his head bashed in by a statue of the Roman goddess Minerva, and it was assumed that his father, Chuseok, had murdered him, but he claimed that no, a servant boy had committed the brutal act before escaping into the night. Still, even though their son had shamed them in life, the family would not allow him to disgrace them even further in death, so Sumin had come to my workshop to commission a stele that might properly reflect her family's position.

"I see your reputation is well earned," she said, looking around at some of the work I had on display. "They say you are quite the craftsman. Who trained you in your art?"

I bowed deeply to acknowledge the compliment. "No one, Mistress Sumin," I replied. "These skills have been with me since childhood but, naturally, I have labored to improve them. I feel at my most content when working with wood and chisel."

She ran her fingers along a stele that was due to be collected later in the day for the grave of a young girl who had been mauled to death by a lion. In the design I had depicted her ascending to the heavens while all the animals of the world bowed in supplication toward her, begging forgiveness for what a single errant member of their kingdom had done.

"I want it to be taller than these," she said, walking around the workshop and examining the blocks of wood that would be stripped of their bark before I began to carve them. "Let us say fifteen feet tall."

"Fifteen?" I asked in surprise. "That is taller than any I have made before."

"Good. That's what I want."

"You don't think it might look a little—"

"A little what?"

I wanted to use the word *ostentatious* but could not bring myself to say it, for fear of insulting her.

"You cannot do it, Craftsman?"

"I can," I said, bowing my head in supplication. "Indeed, it will be an interesting challenge."

"And I want a mask carved into the front that shows my son at his most fierce."

"And the skirts he enjoyed wearing?" I asked innocently. "Would you like these to be included, too?"

She slapped me hard across the face, knocking me over, and I fell to the ground, my hand pressed against my cheek, trying to understand why my comment had offended her so deeply. After all, it was a simple fact that the boy had worn skirts and, sometimes, I had seen him crush beetles and the claws of lobsters into a wet paste so that he could create a rouge for his lips and cheeks. If I had observed all of this, then surely she had, too. I placed my left hand on a small table that held some of my brushes and into which I had carved the image of a hawk carrying twigs for the creation of a nest, and stood up.

"You will depict my son engaged in his favorite pursuits," she said as I rose. "Hunting, fishing, running. Throwing spears and javelins. Wrestling. Climbing mountains."

"Of course, Mistress Sumin," I said, ignoring the fact that I had never once seen the boy participating in any of these activities. Chastened, I turned to glance in Lerato's direction. She was standing before a stele I had completed only that morning and which was intended for the wife of a local sheep farmer. It was rather plain in its way but had a certain elegance in its beveled trim. At the center, I had carved the woman's face in profile, surrounding her with images of needlework, as the woman had been known as an excellent seamstress. At the top, I had included an image of three candles, the middle one extinguished, for she had been the mother of three sons, one of whom had died after falling into a well.

True, it was not the most original or inventive of my works, but it pleased me to see Lerato admiring it. When she reached out to run her hand along the furrows, I felt a stirring at the pit of my stomach and found myself unable to turn away from those long, thin fingers, envying the wood the intimacy of her touch.

"What's the matter with you?" asked Sumin, hitting me on the shoulder now, but this time I did not fall over. "Your face has gone quite red. Do you have a fever?"

"No," I said, shaking myself back to life. "My apologies, Mistress Sumin, my mind was elsewhere." I looked around and walked to the other side of the room, where an enormous block of wood stood ready for use. It seemed to be around the size she wanted and I had intended to split it in half and use it for two steles. When I suggested using it, she nodded and asked how long it would take and the price. Both replies were met with her satisfaction, a date was set for the monument's completion, and soon she was on her way.

As they left, Lerato turned to me and smiled. Her teeth were dazzlingly white against her black skin. "Did you carve that?" she asked, pointing toward the stele that she had been examining earlier.

"Yes," I said, my voice catching slightly in my throat. "I carved all of them."

"You lean a little too heavily on the base of your chisel," she said. "Try holding it up more and trusting your thumb and forefinger to do the work for you. You might find you have more success that way."

I said nothing, feeling astonished and outraged that a slave girl would dare to tell me my business. Afterward, I looked at the stele in question and realized that she was right. This was something I could work on.

. . .

A few days later, and struggling with my design for the boy's memorial, I began to worry that I might be forced to abandon the entire thing and start over, which was most unusual for me. Typically, once I began a project, I became completely immersed in it to the exclusion of all other matters. But the truth was, I was so distracted that I simply could not concentrate on my work.

I had fallen in love.

There were many girls who I had liked before but none who had affected me quite so deeply and, no matter how hard I tried to concentrate on the task in hand, my mind would turn to this girl, to this captured slave, and I would abandon my workshop and wander the streets in the hope that we might meet unexpectedly at the marketplace or the fish traders' stalls by the sea. Before I conceded defeat on Sumin's request, however, I recalled Lerato's advice and held my chisel higher as I worked and, to my surprise, the images started to form before me, false images, yes, but the images that the dead boy's mother had insisted upon. Soon, much sooner than I could have expected, it was ready, and I felt proud of my achievement, certain that my beloved had inspired me at a crucial moment.

I longed for her to return to my workshop so that I could show her what I had created in her honor.

. . .

My father, Manu, had always wanted me to become a warrior like him and play my part in the interminable wars that raged around the Aksumite kingdom, but it seemed that he had finally abandoned hope that I would ever live up to his expectations. His greatest wish, I think, was that I would be brutally killed on the field of battle so that he could carry me home in triumph to my mother, around his shoulders like a slaughtered lamb. He called me lazy, a coward, a half-man, but I was none of these things; I was simply more interested in the act of creation than destruction. Manu was embarrassed by my inclinations, but I could not be other than I was and, awake or asleep, images stole into my mind and I sought ways to reproduce them, in chalk or stone or wood or metal. I was happy to draw pictures in the sand with my toes if that was all that I had to work with. People I had never known, places I had never visited, all of which seemed entirely real to me. And when they appeared, I knew that I had no choice but to reproduce them before they disappeared like sugar in water.

Naturally, this led Manu to bemoan constantly the disappearance of his first son. While I often wondered what had become of my older brother, I also found myself occasionally cursing his name. He had treated me poorly when we were children, but he remained my brother and my mind turned to him more often than I might have expected. Now that we were both adults, I wondered whether we might be able to honor that bond, were he to return.

A few months before I met Lerato, I chanced upon a hidden cave on the banks of the Dahlak river and found myself crawling through its narrow entrance, where I discovered a long, flat wall, stretching perhaps one hundred feet from one side to the other. Its virgin innocence affected me greatly and, in the silence of the fissure, I felt as if it were whispering to me, breathing unheard words that had been waiting many centuries for me to arrive. I placed my hand flat against the stone and a shock ran through my body. Unexpected images formed in my mind and I knew that if I wanted to pull them from my imagination into the real world, then here was the place to do so. I sat on the ground and stared at the granite blankness for a long time, my arms occasionally stretching out and drawing designs in the air or conducting the birds in the sky. That night, when I returned home, I gathered up all my chalks, as many different colors and textures as I could find, and set them aside to take with me the next morning.

I woke early, the cave calling out my name. When I arrived and stepped inside, I found it a cool and welcoming place. I felt embraced by its isolated longing and wasted no time, simply taking the first piece of chalk that came to hand and standing at the very center of the stone, where I drew a great vertical line, then another in parallel to it. I sketched a series of statues, beginning with the plinths before moving to the bodies, and when I reached the heads, I felt a curious urge to create confusion, as if the heads and torsos came from different works and had been pressed together by undisciplined hands. And even though the finished effect appeared strange and disordered to my eyes, it also felt right.

At the far left of the wall I drew a marketplace, chalking small stick figures to represent the people of an unknown village as they went about their business. From nowhere, an elephant appeared, and then a great bear. I drew without thinking, my hands allowing the images to pour through my fingers, as if they had been waiting for this moment to be released into the world.

When I arrived that morning, I knew I wouldn't leave until my task was completed and had brought provisions with me to last a week, sleeping in the cave at night, and waking early each morning, my body bristling with energy. Every day, I moved across my stone canvas, connecting images and stories together, lost in the creation of a world that was as unfamiliar to me as it was exciting. Later, I would learn that I had spent twelve days in the cave and might have stayed even longer had I not finally been interrupted by voices from outside. I turned toward the entrance in fright as the shadows appeared and soon revealed themselves to be a group of men, led by my father, Manu.

"He's here!" he cried, holding up a hand to stop the other men from entering. "I've found him." He was carrying a torch of fire and only when he crawled through the entrance and held it to my face, almost scorching my skin, did I realize that I had been working in near-darkness since my arrival. I did not understand how I could have seen my drawings but, somehow, they had been entirely clear to me. As surprised as I was to see Manu there, I was also frightened by the furious expression on his face. He grabbed me by the shoulders. "Your mother is in torment. We thought you had left us, like your brother did. Or that you were dead."

"No, Father," I said, dropping to my knees in humility. "I was drawing, that's all."

He held the torch out toward the wall and walked around the cave slowly, examining my work. More images appeared in the new light, some that I could not even remember creating. A boy lying sick in his bed while another tended to him. A mountaintop where a group of men were gathered. A marketplace where a group of slaves were lined up next to each other, shackled together by chains. I stared as he did, feeling both curiously distant from my work and inexorably connected to it. I was both witness and participant.

"You did all of this? This is how you have spent this time?" he asked me in a low voice, and I nodded, uncertain how he would respond to this.

"Yes, Father," I said, placing my hand against the stone, as I had done when I first discovered the cave. Giving in to neither pride nor violence, Manu simply shook his head and looked at me with an expression on his face that I could not decipher. Saying nothing, he turned around and left the cave.

Once he was gone, I turned back to the wall, wanting to examine my work in more detail, but the spell had been broken. He had taken his torch with him and I was now plunged back into darkness, a darkness that had not mattered to me before but that now made all my efforts invisible to my eyes. I reached my hand out once again and had to believe that the art I had created still existed beneath the gloom, and that someone, someday, would discover it again.

CYPRUS

A.D. 365

ARISSA DID INDEED RETURN to my workshop as I had hoped and, some months later, we were married in a ceremony of great joy on the banks of Chrysochou Bay. The most revered elder from our village laid his hands upon our heads as we knelt before him, chanting the prayers and oaths that committed our lives to each other. My mother, Flania, sprinkled us with the petals of bozea plants while my aunt, Nula, offered the fruit of the eastern strawberry trees to those who had gathered to celebrate with us. I received the tattoo of the married man, a small black mark upon my right wrist. There were many tears of happiness, including, to my father's embarrassment, my own.

I barely slept the night before, so exultant was I to join my spirit with one whose intelligence, grace and beauty overwhelmed me. To be in Larissa's company was to feel at peace with the world; until we met, I had never felt such a deep sense of harmony. Her very presence brought me to be at one with the ground beneath my feet and the sky above my head. On the morning of the ceremony, I looked up and observed the flight of a hawk carrying twigs for the creation of a nest and smiled, believing this to be a portent for our future.

My mother was a fine artisan of jewelry and had taught me many of the skills that had served as the foundation to what I hoped would be my life's work and, unknown to Larissa, I had spent weeks crafting a necklace of iron to present her with on the morning of our wedding. My reputation as a skilled metalworker had grown in recent years, to the point where wealthy women sought me out to create bespoke jewelry for their ears, necks and wrists. Some flirted with me, for like my father I had grown handsome, with a head of golden curls. One, in fact, had been so determined in her efforts to seduce me that by the time she finally abandoned hope I had crafted a dozen or more pieces for her, enriching me considerably. But I had remained an innocent in physical matters until my first romantic encounter with Larissa and it pleased me to know that we had reserved the pleasures of the flesh for each other.

For many months we had been spending time together, walking the hills around Akamas, eating at the marketplace, and swimming in the bay, after which we would make our way in lustful excitement toward a cave we had discovered at the foot of the mountains where we made love and explored the astonishing terrain of each other's bodies. It was a quiet place, where only the sounds of the waves lapping against the shore provided a serenade for our desire, and when we were spent, Larissa liked to examine the carvings on the wall, running her hands along these strange images from the past, wondering who had created them and why.

Larissa did not have a family of her own—her parents had both died when she was a girl—but was employed as a cook in the villa of a wealthy trader of spices. She was, perhaps, more ambitious than I for our future together, seeing something in my work that she felt could prove successful outside the island. I was not rich, nor did I expect to grow rich, but my status had risen and my neighbors respected my artistry. Even my father, who had always hoped that I would join him as a builder of boats for the fishermen on the banks of Morphou Bay, had made his peace with my decision and had turned his attentions to a young man from our village, who some said was his illegitimate son and who showed much more interest in following in his steps than I.

"Everything you create is so beautiful," Larissa told me, examining different pieces of jewelry in my workshop—necklaces, pretty hooks to hang from the ears, gold-studded bars that could be placed through the eyebrow—"and they should be seen more widely. You could trade, not just here in the villages around Akamas, but further east, too, on the far side of the island. We could hire someone to bring your wares there or go together to establish your reputation. Perhaps in time, we could even speak to the captains of the trading ships that sail to the lands across the sea."

I admired her ambition and, although I had no great wish to set myself up as some materialistic merchant, I found myself won over by her enthusiasm. In truth, my needs were simple. I wanted a wife, some children, and to be allowed to practice my art without interference. If my business grew bigger, I might need to take on apprentices, and would the work be truly mine if I did so?

On the morning of our wedding, I presented her with the piece that I had been working on, placing it carefully around her neck. It was one of the most beautiful necklaces that I had yet designed. Five rectangular panels chained together, and I had employed a texture hammer to craft images of Artemis and Aphrodite on the left pairing, Hera and Selene on the right, and in the center I had chiseled the face of Ishtar, the Queen of Heaven, a goddess worshipped by the people of Mesopotamia some thousand years before. Inlaid at the top of each panel was a single pearl I had collected from the sea, diving to capture hundreds of oysters until I found the perfect mollusk, and at its heart that most unusual of jewels, the blue pearl with a pink overtone that seemed rich in history. Larissa wept when she saw what I had created for her and I cried, too, for we loved each other deeply, and I thanked the gods for the knowledge that, by nightfall, we would belong to each other forever.

· · ·

Ours was not the first marriage my family was to celebrate that year, for the betrothal had just been announced of my older sister, Abira, to the head of our army, Atlium. It seemed like a poor match to me, since Atlium was more than ten years older than she and already had four children with his first wife, who had jumped from the rocks to her death a few days after discovering that she was bearing a fifth.

Abira didn't care much for the idea either, knowing that she was being taken on as little more than a nursemaid to a group of motherless infants, but my father insisted and, of course, it was not her place to question the wisdom of men. Flania had pointed out that, approaching twenty years of age, this might be Abira's last opportunity to find a husband.

"Who says I even want one?" said my sister, rolling her eyes in annoyance. She was an ill-tempered creature at the best of times but talk of marriage had only increased her irritability.

"What kind of girl does not want a husband?" cried my mother in reply, throwing her hands in the air, as if she could not believe the ingratitude of her stepdaughter. "I've never heard of such a thing."

On the day that Abira's engagement was announced, I discovered her sitting on her bed, weeping at the prospect of the life that lay ahead for her, and tried to console her by pointing out that, as Atlium was already thirty, he would surely die soon and then she would be free to return to her old life.

"But the children," she said, her face a mask of distress. "The moment he travels to the next world, they will become my responsibility. You think I want to be stuck with four mouths to feed?"

"Then what do you want?" I asked, confused, for like my mother I could not conceive of a girl who did not long for a man to marry, a home to keep and children to care for. And although I sometimes found Abira's deep attachment to me unsettling, I cared for her and hated to see her so unhappy.

She shook her head now and looked me in the eye, and it was as if she were trying to see deep into my soul.

"If I told you," she said quietly, "you might be shocked."

"I'm not easily shocked."

"Then perhaps I should tell you my idea."

"I want to hear it."

"Even if it's something that the gods might not approve of?"

"We don't know the minds of the gods, Sister," I pointed out, taking her hands in my own. "Just tell me. It might not be as scandalous as you think."

She hesitated for a long time before speaking.

"Do you remember that afternoon in the mountains?" she asked eventually.

I stood up, releasing her hands as if they were flames. We had agreed never to discuss the matter again and I, for the most part, had locked the memory away in a part of my mind that I did not care to revisit. The incident in question had taken place a couple of years earlier. I had been walking through the forest, searching for peculiar and interesting stones that I could use for my jewelry, when I heard the sound of muffled screams in the distance. I followed their echo and, to my horror, discovered my sister being pressed up against a tree by a fat pig of a boy, Heevin, who was attempting to perform the marriage act with her against her will. I stood there, transfixed at first, not quite understanding what was taking place, for I was still young at the time and uncertain of the way of these things, but then she turned her head in agony and saw me standing there, watching. The expression on her face was one of such pain that I knew I had to act.

I looked around, searching the ground for something I might use as a weapon, and settled on a heavy rock that I could just about carry between my hands. I ran back and, before Heevin could turn around to stop me, smashed it down upon the back of his head. He stumbled, reaching a hand slowly around to his neck, before turning to stare at me with despair and confusion in his eyes, and then falling to the ground, dead.

Both Abira and I had stared down at him in shock before she turned away, pulling her clothes back together. When I asked her what had happened, she told me that she had been out searching for fresh mushrooms when she heard the sound of footsteps behind her. She knew the boy—we all knew him—for he had been discourteous to her on many occasions in the past, calling her vile names and telling her the things that he would do to her if she were his wife. When she saw him following her, she knew immediately that he meant her harm. She ordered him away but he refused and, before she knew it, he was pushing her up against the tree, ripping at her clothes and trying to put his toolie inside her. Which was when I appeared.

We ran from that place, Abira and I, and when Heevin's body was discovered a few days later, no one knew who had attacked him, or why. Some said it was a forest spirit, others that a bird had taken on human form when he tried to steal from its nest, attacking him for his larceny. But Abira and I knew the truth and revealed it to no one.

"I never think of that," I told her now. "And I don't wish to discuss it. As far as I'm concerned, it never happened."

"But it did," she said. "You saved me then, Brother, and you could save me again. It would be an act of love on your part, not of cruelty."

I stared at her, feeling that sense of disorder that she often occasioned in me, for Abira was a strange creature, one whom I had never fully understood. What was she asking of me now? To kill the man she was to marry?

Later that day, as I saw Atlium engaged in conversation with my father, planning the wedding feast, I feared what she might do to him in the future. Or what she might ask me to do on her behalf.

• • •

After our marriage ceremony, Larissa and I walked hand in hand along the road that led to the tip of the peninsula. We had not yet told any of our friends or my family that I had put a baby inside her and as we stood there, my hand pressed against her belly, I felt more happiness than I knew was possible.

"When this one is born," I said, "and when you are well again, we will create another life, and another after that, and another after that. We will teach each child the order of the plants, the birds and the animals, and they will look after us when we grow old."

"Will you be strict with him?" she asked me, for she was certain from the manner in which the fingers on her right hand tingled in the mornings that our first child would be a boy.

"Strict, but never cruel," I said. "He will learn that there is more to the world than war and, if we have luck on our side, he will never have to fight in one."

Larissa shook her head. "There are always wars," she sighed. "When one finishes, another begins. Such is the destiny of boys. They all die young."

"I didn't," I said.

She smiled and we kissed, looking out across the sea toward the island of Crete, which lay far in the distance. It was a place of which I had heard many stories, and I hoped to visit it one day. An unexpected sound burst through the air and, when I looked up, it surprised me to see how all the birds in the sky were flying in the same direction, toward the east of our village.

"They're scared," I said, confused by their uniform pattern. "Something has frightened them."

"Tomorrow, we must tell your mother and father our news," said Larissa, less interested in the unusual behavior of the flock than I. "They will want to know that they are to be grandparents."

"Yes, tomorrow," I agreed, as the sound of the birds squawking overhead became even louder and more disconcerting.

"Husband," said Larissa, looking out into the sea. She gripped my arm suddenly, her tension growing. "What is that?"

It was a fine day and I stared out, uncertain what I was looking at. Where usually the sky met the sea at the place of the horizon, now both seemed to have been replaced by a great white wall, rising higher by the moment. My mind could not make sense of it. I knew this view like I knew my own reflection and, through storms and tempests, I had never witnessed anything to compare with this before. It was as if the Earth were rising up and closing over onto itself. We watched in horror as the wall of water drew ever closer and Larissa let out a scream when we realized that the sea had drawn itself up into a single great tide and was charging toward us, preparing to swallow us within its frosted surf.

"Run," I said, grabbing her by the hand, and we raced back along the path in the direction from which we had come, but every time I looked around, the waves had grown taller and taller, until they almost reached the sky. It was the end of the world; I was certain of it.

"Wait!" cried Larissa, slowing down and pressing a hand against her stomach as I tried to drag her along. "The baby."

I turned to urge her to follow me, but before the words could leave my mouth the waters had fallen upon us, our hands separated and we were washed away.

GUATEMALA

A.D. 420

SLEPT BADLY, my dreams poisoned by memories of the great
shaking of the ground, and when I rose, the people of my village
had not yet emerged from the darkness of the night. I felt a weakness in my stomach and forced myself to eat some of the plantains
and queso blanco that my kindhearted aunt, Nála, had left out for
me the night before. The flavors were rich and my body awoke
quickly as they roused my senses; in my grief I had been depriving
myself of sustenance, but the piquancy of the food forced me back
into a life that I wanted only to abandon. When my plate was empty,
I longed for more, so I plucked some ripe avocados from the trees
as I made my daily pilgrimage to the other side of Yax Mutal.

The journey to the North Acropolis took me past the workshop
where I had spent the last few years crafting sandals for both men
and women to wear. It was a lucrative trade, one that I enjoyed, and
I had grown highly skilled in my work. From a young age, I'd found
myself fashioning footwear for my mother and sister and, although
my father had beaten me for it, it was my passion, a revelation that
further diminished me in his eyes.

"Sandals," he would remark, spitting the word out as if it were a
sour taste on his tongue. "That a son of mine should waste his time
on something so trivial."

"You would prefer to cut the soles of your feet against the sharp
stones that lie along our pathways?" I asked him, for as I grew older
and more confident I began to take some pleasure in goading him.
"If bloody feet are what you prefer, Father, then you may give me
back the pair that you wear this very day."

The task itself was both complex and beguiling. I paid a hunter
to bring me the hides of animals, which I would cure over a number
of days, de-liming them first in a paddle before tanning and dyeing

them and placing a cork sole beneath the skin. My great flair, however, was in turning the sandals from the functional to the beautiful; in order to achieve this transformation, I hired village boys to collect as many colored stones and bits of glass from the beaches as they could, which I would then bead into the stitching. Men preferred their sandals to be plain but women loved my decorative touches and competed with each other for the finest pieces. My order book was always full and, once, when I discovered a blue pearl with a pink overtone and laced it into the toe of the right shoe, I was paid so much money for my work that I could have easily abandoned my trade for several months and suffered no diminishment of my livelihood.

My workshop had been closed, however, since the great shaking, a phenomenon that the gods had sent to claim the life of my wife, Latra, and our unborn child, along with those of many more of my neighbors. My days since had been filled with sorrow, my nights with weeping, and when friends came to offer solace, I sent them away, frustrated by their attempts to comfort me. More than once, I had spoken roughly with these good people and, although I despised myself for such fits of distemper, I could find no warmth inside my soul.

Latra and I had only been married a few hours when the noises began to sound from beneath us and, at first, we had laughed, for it seemed as if the Earth were grumbling from hunger. But then cracks began to appear in the streets, great fissures that ripped at the earth beneath our feet. I watched in horror as some of our older neighbors, those who were not fleet of foot, fell screaming into the crevices that opened up and led to the core of the world. None of us knew what was happening but we ran toward the safety of our homes, even as the temples and stone houses tumbled around us. We had almost reached our hut when Latra cried out that she needed to stop, that the baby was hurting from within, and foolishly I agreed that we should pause. She sat down to catch her breath while I ran to the well to fetch cold water to soothe her forehead, but when I returned, she was lying on the ground, an enormous stone from that same building having fallen upon her.

Her eyes were open, blood was running down her forehead, but all life had been extinguished. I was certain that the end of the world was upon us. It was not, of course, for by nightfall the land had fallen still once again and it was left to those of us who remained to gather the bodies of our dead and carry them, in dumbfounded grief, to the burial grounds.

For weeks now, I had walked every day to the Acropolis, where Latra had been laid to rest, and sat by her grave, talking quietly to her in the vain hope that her spirit would hear my words and respond, perhaps through whispers on the wind or the symbolic appearance of a glorious quetzal that might sit upon my shoulder and sing in a language that none but I might understand.

Others came throughout the day, too, visiting the resting places of their loved ones, but most ignored this part of the graveyard, where the common people lay, and made their way instead to the central area, where the great towers and ornamental sarcophagi stood, beneath which lay the bones of the great family of ajaws who had ruled our land in the past. These dilettantes would make a huge show of laying flowers and keening histrionically over the graves so that the guardsmen could see both their devotion to Storm Sky, who ruled over us now, and their eternal fidelity to the memory of Spearthrower Owl, the greatest ajaw of them all, under whose eternal benevolence the world continued to thrive. I despised their posturing, for what did they know of true grief? Their displays were the stuff of theatre and, had I the energy, I would have marched over to decry their stupidity, but, of course, I did nothing, said nothing, saving myself for hushed conversations with my beloved, silent Latra instead.

As I sat by her burial place, I thought of Orpheus. Like me, he was an artist, one whose heart was filled with music, and like me, he had lost the woman he loved on their wedding day, Eurydice, when she was bitten by a snake and died. Afterward, Orpheus could play only mournful music and the gods, in a moment of tenderness, allowed him to plead his case for her return to the world of the living. Won over by his suffering, they granted his wish but with one stipulation: that he must walk ahead of Eurydice, not looking on her face until they were back on mortal terrain. He could not resist, however, turning back too soon, and the moment he laid eyes on his beloved, she disappeared forever.

The gods would not allow me any such entreatment. Latra was lost to me, and so I had decided that today would be my last visit to the graveyard, for I no longer wished to engage with a memory of my wife but to see her in the flesh once again, to hold her hand, to press her body against my own, and so I had come to tell her that she and our child would not be lonely in the other-world for long, as I would join them soon. I had resolved to entrust my body and spirit to Ixtab, the Goddess of Suicide, who I believed would welcome my sacrifice and accompany me on my journey to the heavens, where my beloved would be waiting for me.

As I left, I noticed a boy walking along the path whose face was familiar to me and called him over. He was the one who crafted the steles for the burial places of the wealthy, fine wooden sculptures, sometimes as much as fifteen feet in height. Not everyone could afford such luxuries, of course, but what need had I of money when I was preparing to leave this world for the next? Some months earlier, I had admired a stele that he had carved for the murdered son of a wealthy merchant and been impressed by his skill at crafting images of hunting, fishing, running, throwing spears and javelins, wrestling and climbing mountains, even though the dead boy had shown no aptitude for any of these things. I spoke to the craftsman now, telling him stories of Latra and asking him to fashion something in her honor, a memorial to her, to me and to our unborn child. He would find the money under a red stone in the corner of my workshop the following morning, I told him, more than enough for his troubles. He agreed to the commission and I felt satisfied as I went on my way that while our lives would soon be forgotten, a monument would be built to our existence and it would be a beautiful thing that might last through the ages.

As I passed that same workshop on the way home, however, I was surprised to see my father, Manrav, standing outside, pulling at the doors which I had tied together earlier with a length of sisal rope. When he turned and saw me approaching, he looked me up and down with a mixture of contempt and pity on his face. He was getting older, I could see that; his hair, once golden and luxuriant, had thinned and grayed, and the scar on his left cheek lay pale against his coarsened skin. Although it was not in his nature to be compassionate, he had shown some degree of consideration toward me since Latra's death.

"Your doors are locked," he told me, shaking his head in irritation. "And only this morning, while I have stood here, two women and a man have come by looking for new sandals. Then they complain to me that you are not here to receive them."

"I'm not making sandals anymore," I said. "My business is at an end."

"So, all this time when you said that that was what you were born to do," he replied, "and that you would prefer to spend your days stitching hides together for the feet of strangers rather than fighting as men do, all of that was a lie?"

I had no answer to this and felt no desire to argue with him.

"Your tears must end," he said quietly, reaching out a hand in an uncharacteristic display of tenderness and laying it on my shoulder for a moment before thinking better of it and pulling away. "Death comes to us all, my second-born son. But the living must walk the Earth until they are summoned home. You know this."

"That summons comes too soon for some," I said.

"You grieve. It is natural. But there are other women. Many other women. You do not have to be alone. Look at Attilian, our great warrior leader. He has already forgotten his previous wives as he prepares to marry your sister. You should follow his example."

I looked at him in disbelief. We were different men, my father and I, and I did not share his appetite for variety. I had loved only one woman, had lain with only one woman, and would never look on her face again while I drew breath. But I would join her soon, I was determined on it.

"Leave me alone," I said, brushing past him, and he spun me around, slapping me sharply across the face, and I stumbled, falling to the ground in a daze. I felt an anger burn inside me as I looked

up at him and would have leaped to my feet and struck him in return, had he not been my father.

Instead, I simply stood up and turned my back on him, continuing on my way, wondering how he would feel when the news of my
death reached him and he recalled that our last interaction had been
a moment of violence.

· · ·

On making the decision to end one's life, concerns about the past,
all worries about the future, begin to dissipate and, in their place, a
sense of calm descends over the mind and body. If we could remember those moments in the womb, long before the waves broke
and we were thrust outward, against our will, into the horrors of
the universe, then we would recognize the inexorable connection
between the two.

Alone in my hut, I took a bundle of rope and cut four feet with
a sharp knife, making an *S* shape from what I held before drawing
the standing line beneath the two ends and looping them around
six times to ensure that the noose would be tight. I did not want to
struggle when I fell, nor did I want to feel any pain, and I prayed
that my neck would break quickly.

As I was making the final adjustments to the knot, however, I
looked up and noticed a figure standing in the doorway. It was the
blind woman, Tiresia, whom I had known for many years and whom
I had long believed had cared for me during my mysterious absence
from my home when I was an infant. She was the oldest person for
many villages around us and was venerated by all, not least because
her dead husband, Aapo, had been a revered ajaw, one of our most
beloved, before the other-world had summoned him home, too.

Despite her lack of sight, Tiresia had taught me my hieroglyphs
when I was a boy, and I had delighted in drawing the tiny pictures
and letters that made written communication between our people
possible. I had learned the depictions for hundreds of words and
could deploy them with ease, but Tiresia knew thousands more and
it had always fascinated me how she could draw with such ease
while not being able to witness the results of her efforts.

"Son of Manrav," she said, stepping inside, and I laid the noose down on the floor beside me, startled by her unexpected appearance. "You are not at your work today? Your order book is empty?"

"My days of stitching sandals are behind me, Wife of Aapo," I told her. "May his name be remembered forever in glory."

She gave a small, mocking laugh. "The women will be very disappointed to hear this," she replied, taking a seat on a wooden bench that ran down the side of my hut. "You must know how much they value your work, those vain creatures. They use your skill to betray their husbands."

I shrugged. Vanity, I knew, was a growing curse among our people and my work contributed to this.

"Your wife is lost to you in this world," she continued, "and so you believe that you have no reason to live. I am right?" I stared across at her but uttered not a word. "I came here today for I dreamed that you had prayed to Ixtab to pluck you from this world and fly you to the heavens."

"And if I did?" I asked, impressed by her gifts of prophecy but determined that I would not allow her to dissuade me from my course of action. Among our people, after all, suicide by hanging was seen as a sign of great honor, not of shame.

"Latra was a good woman," she said, her tone softening. "She brought me food from the marketplace when I was ill and rubbed soft ointments into my hands and feet. She did not deserve to be taken when the great shaking occurred. But others were taken, too, of course. Many others. And their loved ones have learned to live with their losses."

I nodded, aware that I was not alone in my grief, but this was of no consolation to me.

"Fix another rope for me, then, son of Manrav," she said with a sigh, glancing around my workshop, and I turned to her in surprise.

"I don't understand."

"My grandson died in the great shaking, too. You did not know this?"

I shook my head.

"So, fix another rope," she repeated. "I will ascend to the heavens with you. My life has been long. Perhaps it is time to see what glories await me in the next one."

I shook my head. "That, I cannot do," I told her. "I will not help you in this matter, Tiresia, Wife of Aapo."

"And why not?"

"You are old," I said. "Your time is nearly done. The gods will call you home soon enough. You don't need to go this way. It will be painful."

"For a few moments, perhaps," she replied. "But after that, there will be peace. And that is what we all seek, isn't it? Peace?"

I lifted the rope again, drawing it back and forth between my hands. "I ask only for silence," I told her, the words catching in my throat as I fought back tears. "Nothing more. My head is filled with Latra from wake to slumber. I think only of the times that we spent together and the memories that we will never now create. I have been robbed by the gods."

"And why would they do such a thing, son of Manrav?"

"I don't know."

"You do. Ask yourself why."

I looked away. "I don't," I insisted.

"A life for a life," she said.

I felt a chill run through me. What did she know of the crimes that lay on my conscience, even if it was a justifiable response? No one, other than my sister, had ever been privy to it. Not even my wife.

She reached across now and took my hand in hers. Her skin was cold, her flesh a thin layer around bony fingers. "You must not give in," she said, her voice strong and determined. "There are many lives ahead of you yet, son of Manrav. I see them all. One day, you will live among the stars."

"The only place that I will live is in the other-world," I replied, standing now and raising her to her feet, walking her to the door, desperate to be rid of her. "You were good to come, but now you must leave me to my choices. As I must leave you to yours."

She sighed and placed the flat of her hand against my cheek. I felt an urge to close my eyes and sleep there, but a moment later she was gone, continuing along the road, her head bowed. I turned and glanced around the workshop, looking up toward the roof, which was strong enough to hold the weight of a falling body. I saw a spot, reached for a nail and hook and ascended a chair to hammer them into the woodwork.

When I was certain that it was secure, I set a stool upon the floor and stepped upon it, placing my head within the noose. Closing my eyes, I breathed in slowly and whispered my wife's name.

HUNGARY

A.D. 453

REACHED UP toward the hook to take down the dress, placing it carefully over the wooden mannequin in the center of my workshop. It was difficult not to take some pride in what was surely my finest creation to date. I had used a blend of four exquisite materials—silk, satin, damask and lampas—and stitched the fabric together using golden threads interwoven with silver to lend a sparkling effect. The hem played host to a series of gemstones, each of which was particularly suited to reflecting candlelight, and the dye that I'd employed—a dramatic shade of blood red, contrasted with the virgin white of the sleeves—was ambitious and stunning to behold. I stood back and took in the effect I had created, feeling that most human of traits, vanity. Without question, I was the finest dressmaker that the Huns had ever known.

Finally, I was snapped out of my narcissism by the sound of the door opening and I turned to see my sister Abrila stepping inside. Protocol dictated that I bow low in recognition of her new and exalted status, but she rolled her eyes when I did so, placing a hand beneath my chin to raise me back up to my proper height.

"Don't ever do that again, Brother," she said. "It's embarrassing for me."

"And if one of your husband-to-be's soldiers witnessed me not paying the homage to which a future queen is entitled," I told her, "he would score a cross down my belly and drag my intestines onto the ground. Which would be embarrassing for me."

"Still," she said, smiling a little at the image, for she had a certain bloodthirst to her nature, "I can't bear how everyone's attitudes have changed toward me since that pig demanded my hand. It's not as though I even asked for this marriage."

This was not a conversation I wanted to have. My sister had

hinted to me before how I might help her escape this detested match and, anxious about what she might have in mind, I had worked hard to avoid discussing it ever since.

"But I must say, you've surpassed yourself," she said, reaching out to stroke the material of the dress that she would wear later that evening. "I don't think I've ever seen anything quite so beautiful in my life. If I actually loved my betrothed, I'd be delighted."

"You're unhappy, I can see that," I said, sitting down on the floor opposite her. "Not at all how a bride should feel on her wedding day. But perhaps it won't be so bad. After all, Attila is the greatest warrior the world has known since Alexander. As his wife, your name will enter into legend, too."

"You think such things matter to me?" she asked, standing up again and moving around the workshop, picking up a length of sturdy sisal rope that I used to lock the doors at night and pulling it firmly between her hands, as if she were trying to choke someone. Then, discarding it on the floor next to a pair of sharp silver scissors, she lifted different dresses from their hooks and held them against her body before returning them to their places. Some had been commissioned by the wives of Attila's generals and were due to be collected later in the afternoon. Others were for the speculative buyers who drifted in and out whenever my workshop was open. Since the announcement of the marriage, I had been incredibly busy, for the women were as competitive in their fashions as the men were in their fighting, and I was looking forward to more restful days ahead when Attila and Abrila were finally joined as one.

"There are many who would find that a great privilege," I suggested.

"I prefer to live in this world," she countered. "Not the next."

I glanced toward the door. She had closed it upon entering and we were alone, so I dared to speak freely.

"If you're really that unhappy, Abrila," I said, aware how naïve my words would sound to her, "then perhaps you could tell Attila that you've changed your mind?"

"Changed my mind?" she repeated, laughing bitterly. "You say that as if I had some choice in this matter to begin with. He selected me before he went on his last campaign, writing to our father to tell him to have me ready for tonight. You know that. I had no say in any of it. Let us not pretend otherwise."

"Women rarely have a say in the man they marry," I pointed out. "That is not the way of the world."

"Latiro did," she replied, and when she saw the stricken expression on my face, she reached out and took my hand in hers, holding it tightly. "I'm sorry, Brother," she said. "That was unkind of me."

Although the initial pain of my wife's loss had begun to lessen, I often thought of the evening that I had tied a noose around my neck, intending to end my own life, only to pull back at the last moment, either too afraid to go through with it or too hopeful that there might yet be something worth living for. Since then, I had learned to live with my sorrow although, some days, the scar tissue felt rawer than others. "I know you don't love Attila as I loved Latiro, but—"

"Love him?" she asked. "How could I love him? He's old, he's fat, his teeth are yellow, his breath smells like dung and his head's too big for his body. Also, they say that his man-parts are malformed and riddled with disease."

I laughed. I had heard these rumors myself, but then it was well known that our glorious leader ravaged every woman he could find, regardless of rank, and that when he was on a campaign, as he usually was, he thought nothing of spending his lust with other soldiers or even animals. I did not envy what lay in store for my sister in her marriage bed later that night.

"I should have accepted Hakin's offer," she said with a sigh. A year or two earlier, Hakin, the boy we called our cousin, had dared to ask our father for her hand in marriage, but he had refused. Abrila, however, had been touched by the proposal. She liked Hakin, as most girls did, for he was handsome despite his infirmity and had a way about him that charmed all. Had our father been in the grave, as Latiro's was when I asked her to be my wife, she might well have accepted him and been spared this unfortunate fate.

"Well, it's too late for that now," I said. "Anyway, your husband will likely be waging war hundreds of miles from here in a few days' time. What else does he ever do? He only reappears here for a week or so every year. You won't have to suffer his attentions for too long."

"Even one night is more than I can stand," she said, standing up and lifting a jar of red dye from a shelf, removing the cork plug from the top and sniffing the contents.

"I thought it would have a much stronger scent," she remarked, returning it to its place with a curious expression on her face.

"No," I said, shaking my head. "It doesn't smell of much at all. But be careful with it, though. It remains toxic in that form."

"So, if a person were to mistakenly ingest any of it . . . ?"

"They would surely die."

We didn't speak for a long time but continued to look at each other.

"You're not thinking of—" I asked, standing up and placing my hands upon her shoulders. "Abrila," I said. "You know that when Latiro was killed I, too, came close to ending my life. But I thought better of it. You mustn't allow your mind to follow the same path."

"Oh, my poor, sweet, innocent brother," she said with a smile. "It's not my life that I'm thinking of ending."

• • •

The wedding party lasted for many hours and Attila did not so much as glance in Abrila's direction throughout the entire event. This was not his first marriage and he drank so copiously that I wondered whether he would even be able to perform his matrimonial duties when he and my sister finally retired to the bridal chamber. Throughout the evening, instead of paying court to his new wife, he talked exclusively to his friends, the soldiers who had returned with him from the most recent campaigns in Italy. Occasionally, drunken fights broke out between these men, leaving some severely beaten and being dragged senseless from the hall, much to the amusement of the host and his guests.

I observed my father sitting a few seats along from the general, chewing his way through an entire cooked chicken, the juices flowing down his chin and onto his tunic. Every so often he would laugh at some exchange with his neighbor before banging his fists down on the table enthusiastically. At one point, he caught my eye—I was seated toward the back of the hall—and looked away quickly. It shamed him that a son of his had made the bride's dress.

"I thought it was very beautiful," said my mother, who had helped dress Abrila earlier. "Not so much a dress as a work of art."

"Thank you, Mother," I replied. "I've learned most of my techniques from you."

"Some," she said, placing a hand atop mine, and I frowned to see how translucent her skin was becoming as the years passed, the pale blue veins visible beneath. "But I was never much more than a gifted amateur. You, my son, are an artist."

When Abrila entered the room wearing that same gown, a hush fell among the party and even Attila deigned to look her way, stroking his beard before whispering something into the ear of the man seated next to him, something so apparently hilarious and undoubtedly vulgar that the man spat a mouthful of wine across the table. I looked away in disgust. I had never belonged among these rough men; they were a breed apart to me. They lived for fighting, for drawing blood, for killing, while all I cared about was beauty. My Hun brethren delighted in carrying the heads of their enemies back with them from their campaigns, the skulls rotting in open cases, while my greatest pleasure came from the sensation of a fine brocade between my fingers.

An hour passed, and another, and another, and I was looking forward to being allowed to escape the festivities for my bed when Abrila approached my table and touched me on the arm, indicating that I should follow her. We left the hall together and ascended the staircase, making our way along the viewing gallery toward a smaller flight that looked down over a galley area. The further we progressed, the louder came the sound of grunting mixed with the sound of crying. My sister pointed toward our right, where, in the candlelight, I watched as Attila engaged in the marriage act with a girl who could not have been more than twelve years old. The girl was weeping as he took her, thrusting himself in and out as he stole his violent pleasure, and throughout his exertions he gnawed on a leg of lamb that had been almost cleared of its meat. Eventually, he threw himself forward with a triumphant cry before pulling out and pushing her onto the floor and then tossing the spent meat bone on top of her. She lay there, curled in a corner, as he marched away, barely taking a moment even to tie his tunic to cover his indecency.

"And that girl," said my sister quietly, nodding toward the child who lay on the floor, tears rolling down her face, blood tainting the hem of her gown. "You know who she is, don't you?"

I shook my head.

"The youngest daughter of Kreka."

I swallowed in disgust and felt the food that I had consumed at the banquet churning in my stomach in revolt. Kreka had been an earlier wife of Attila, dead these ten years now. The child with whom he had been fornicating was his own daughter.

"So, Brother," she said. "Are we going to let him do that to me? Or, worse, to the children that he might give me? Or do we take action?"

• • •

The dyes that I used in my dressmaking were composed from various ingredients, depending on the color required, but almost all required nightshade, sapphire, keese wing, the leaves of the silent princess plant, Octorok eyeball, swift violet, thistle and hightail lizard. In addition, for the red I had used for Abrila's dress, I employed spicy pepper, the tail of the red lizalfos and four Hylian shrooms. Despite the abundance of component parts, the resultant mixture was as inoffensive to the nose as it was damaging to the body.

I was overwhelmed with fear as Abrila and I entered Attila's bedchamber, for to be discovered there would have led to me being put to death in the most creative fashion, but I summoned the courage to follow, carrying a vial of the poisonous liquid in the pocket of my tunic. The room itself was enormous, the bed large enough to fit four or five people, and rumor had it that he took advantage of its size frequently when he was in the palace.

On a table in a corner sat a flagon of wine and two cups.

"There," said Abrila, nodding toward the jug. "Pour it in."

I took the vial from my pocket and walked slowly toward the

table, glancing back time and again toward the door in case one of the Hun soldiers entered, but there was no one standing guard outside, as all the men were still enjoying the revelry taking place in the great hall. Uncorking the small glass bottle, I held it aloft, but something prevented me from following her instructions.

"I can't," I said, turning to my sister.

"You can. Just do it. We don't have much time."

I tried, I truly did. But this was not like the time I had discovered her being raped by that pig of a boy. My actions that day had been spontaneous and he had deserved to have his skull caved in. This, on the other hand, was an act of premeditated murder. I shook my head and stepped away.

"Give it to me, then," hissed Abrila when she saw my hesitation, grabbing the vial off me and emptying it quickly and without any sign of remorse into the jug, lifting the vessel to swirl it around so the dye would be evenly dispersed in the liquid. "Good," she said then, smiling in satisfaction as she walked toward the door. "Come on, Brother, I am saved."

She returned to the wedding party then, while I stepped outside into the night air, questioning how culpable I was for this deed. True, I had not poured the toxic mixture in myself, but I had provided it and allowed the act to happen before my eyes. I could hardly claim innocence and the gods saw all.

The next morning, the palace came alive to a great cry of consternation. Abrila had run screaming from her marriage bed after waking to find her new husband dead beside her, having choked on his own blood. As the men took the body for burial and wept that they had lost the greatest Hun who ever lived, the women surrounded his bride to offer comfort in her loss. When she caught my eye, however, I saw the hint of a smile upon her face and she nodded, as if to acknowledge my complicity in her actions. Her cold-heartedness unsettled me and later that day, when I returned to my workshop, I found that, for once, the urge to create was lost to me.

AFGHANISTAN

A.D. 507

WHENEVER MY SPIRITS were low, I made my way into the barren wasteland of the Bamiyan Valley, where I felt a certain intimacy with the sandstone mountains surrounding the basin of our town. As a boy, when I first grew interested in masonry, I spent most of my time there, selecting blocks of stone that had fallen from their moorings and using my hammer and chisel to create replicas of animals, people or whatever strange fantasies appeared in my mind.

Often, my ideas emerged directly from my dreams—a boy in shackles; another climbing a rope into the sky; a boat overturning on a stormy sea—and I would wake with the images pulsating so vividly through my mind that re-creating them in stone seemed almost as necessary to me as breathing.

My workshop was thriving now, my order book filled with commissions for religious icons, usually statues of the Buddha, which could be placed in a doorway to ward off evil spirits. Soon after the dramatic events of my sister's marriage, my cousin, Hakang, began to look after the financial side of my business so I could concentrate exclusively on my craft, a fine arrangement since he was skilled with numbers while I was not.

Perhaps it was a combination of both our talents, however, that led to my reputation growing further afield and to an unexpected summons to the palace of Vārāha Rilna, where I was offered an opportunity that was as intimidating as it was exciting.

A messenger arrived unexpectedly one morning with instructions that I was to ride with him to the city, where the Sultan wished to meet with me. What could a man as great as he want with one as simple as I, I wondered? But of course I had no choice but to obey and when I arrived in the city after several hours' riding, I was brought to a bath-chamber where four young women waited to wash me, a most embarrassing ritual but one which was deemed necessary, as the messenger said that I smelled like a donkey who had been rolling in its own filth for a week and that to present myself before His Majesty in such a disgusting manner would be the gravest of insults.

The women removed my clothes and led me toward a deep bath. Steam rose from the surface of the water, infused with the most intoxicating perfumes, and it was a relief to submerge myself beneath its dark surface. I had not received the touch of a woman since my wife had been killed and I found myself torn between desire and embarrassment as the women removed their clothes, too, stepping into the bath with rough sponges to rid my skin of the dirt and dust of the road. My lust betrayed itself easily but they seemed immune to my discomfort and, when I was eventually clean and dry again, they dismissed me as if I had been of no importance, just another priapic visitor, albeit one who had not tried to molest them.

Dressed in fresh clothes, I was led into the receiving chamber, my body scented with exotic oils and my hair pressed slick against my head, and fell immediately to my knees to kiss the floor, holding this position until I was given permission to rise. When that moment came, I found myself too intimidated to look directly at the Sultan himself, keeping my focus somewhere around his chest area, while trying to ignore a pair of monks standing at his right hand, one of whom was smirking at my obvious uneasiness.

"Your reputation has reached our ears," said the Sultan, who was short and squat with an extraordinary pile of yellow hair that sat in a pyramid formation on the top of his head, culminating in a peak that looked as if it might be sharp to the touch. He lifted a bunch of grapes from a bowl and examined them for a moment before tossing them to a young boy seated at his feet on a turquoise pillow. The child snipped a few off with a pair of sharp silver scissors, tasted a handful, did not die instantly, and threw them back to his master, who ate a few noisily, masticating them between his teeth. "They say that you are the finest stoneworker in the region and have crafted many beautiful Buddhas for your neighbors."

I thanked him for his kind words and agreed that yes, I believed I had some skill in this area.

"Your father works with stone, too?" he asked me. "You have followed in his footsteps?"

I shook my head. "My mother, Your Majesty."

"Your mother?" he repeated, sitting forward in surprise.

"Naturally, not as an occupation," I said, correcting myself. "But she has always been skilled with stone and chisel and she taught me proficiency as a child."

"Most peculiar."

"In another world, she might have been a fine mason," I added.

"Thankfully, we do not live in such a place," he grunted, waving this observation away. "Let us speak no more of women. I was asking about your father. What sort of man is he?"

"He's a soldier, Your Majesty," I replied. "Or, rather, he was a soldier."

"He's dead?"

"No, but having spent a lifetime fighting, his body begins to betray him. He has taken to his bed, where my mother and aunt wait upon him and are martyrs to his every whim."

"He is a difficult patient?"

"A very difficult patient, Your Majesty."

The Sultan nodded and considered this for a moment. "Still, he must be proud of you," he remarked, and I decided not to admit that my father had, in fact, little regard for my work, simply bowing my head in agreement, at which point he introduced me to the older of the two monks who stood by the throne, a man named Sanavasi, who walked forward now in tiny, pitter-patter steps that reminded me of a small duckling. He pressed his hands together, closed his eyes and bowed before me and I mirrored the greeting.

"It pleases us to commission a statue of Siddhārtha Gautama Buddha to be built into the rockface of the mountains in the Bami-yan Valley," said Sanavasi in a voice that was so high I wondered whether those parts that made him a man had been removed at a young age. "It pleases us to invite you to take charge of this project. It is to be a birthday gift for the Sultan's wife and in honor of his fourteen children."

I looked at him in surprise. It was true that all of my work to date had been constructed from stone taken from the valley, but it had always been my practice to transport large blocks to my workshop, where I would create my idols. I had never even conceived of carving images into the rockface itself. Still, there was no reason why such a thing could not be done and I found the idea intriguing.

"Am I to think that the statue would be visible to those who pass by the mountain?" I asked.

"Yes."

"A statue somewhat larger than a man, then. Somewhere for travelers to rest and pray?"

"Not quite," he replied, in a perfect soprano. "It pleases us to imagine a statue so enormous that it could be seen from a great distance. In doing so, it would show our devotion to the Buddha, may his name be remembered forever in glory, and become a source of great inspiration to our people."

I considered it. "How big are you thinking?" I asked.

"Imagine one hundred and twenty men standing atop each other," said the Sultan, rising from his throne now, thrusting his hand beneath his robes and scratching his manhood. When he was done, he reclaimed his throne and held the same hand out for one of his dogs, who came and licked it hungrily.

I stared at him, uncertain that I understood him correctly. I had never heard of such a structure before. The tallest statue I had carved to date had been only twice my own height, and even that had taken some considerable effort. To make a statue sixty times those dimensions would be an astonishing feat.

"I hope you are not going to say that it is impossible," said the Sultan, narrowing his eyes.

"No, Your Majesty," I replied, even though I thought that it might be the case. "However, for such an edifice, I could not possibly work alone. I would need many men to work under my command, obedient to my orders, while I designed and supervised its construction."

"How many men?" asked the Sultan.

"At least forty," I said, plucking a number from thin air, uncertain whether he would laugh at my request or not.

"It pleases us to afford you this number," said Sanavasi, so quickly that I assumed he'd already thought this far ahead and would have offered me more, had I asked for them. "The statue you create will survive through the ages and the name of our great Sultan will be spoken of with reverence by children many centuries from now. We thank you."

At this point, the Sultan dismissed me and Sanavasi led me into a smaller room nearby, where we discussed the logistics of the project, the time it would take to complete and my payment. It was a sizeable amount, but more important than this was the honor that they were granting me. When I left the palace a few days later, I was determined to create the greatest statue that the world had ever seen.

. . .

The first months on the project were the most difficult. It took time for the scaffolding to be erected and for the sanding down of the surface to be completed, a process that made the stone flake, which in turn led to many of the workers coughing up blood as they dug deeper into the rock. I spoke to Sanavasi about this, who declared that anyone who died during the creation of the Buddha would surely be taken directly to heaven on the wings of an angel in gratitude for their sacrifice, a response that did not seem a great reward to the men when I passed it on to them. Alerted to the disquiet, Sanavasi sent soldiers to patrol the site, ensuring that the men worked even harder.

As the statue began to take form, I directed operations from a group of huts that had been erected at the foot of the mountain. Hakang continued to assist me and, as well as keeping a careful account of the daily costs, he ensured that my sketches and plans for each different part were carefully numbered and filed. But as I was the only designer, I struggled to keep up with the pace of the work and worried that it would not be finished on time. As the Sultan had remarked on my last morning at Vārāha Rilna that any delay would be met by the forfeiture of my head, I had good reason to want everything completed by the agreed date.

To an outsider, therefore, it might have seemed like a stroke of great fortune when a young man named Peren arrived one morning in search of work, but the truth was that his appearance, innocuous as it originally was, would prove the catalyst for the chain of events that would dominate the next decade of my life and lead to more betrayal, bloodshed and grief than I could ever have possibly imagined. If I could return to that day, I would have stood by the entrance to my hut and, at the moment of his first appearance, slapped his horse to turn it around before sending him directly back to the town that had spawned him.

He was an exceptionally handsome young man with thick dark hair and bright blue eyes, and had grown up further east, toward Kamboja. Word had spread from village to village of the Sultan's commission, and he had been drawn toward it by a passion for working with stone. When we first met, however, he shocked me by declaring that he did not actually believe in Siddhārtha Gautama Buddha—he credited no supernatural entity or deity for our existence—and saw our work as having only an artistic value, not a spiritual one. I had never encountered anyone who would dare to utter such blasphemous remarks and, while my initial instinct was to invite one of the soldiers in to draw his pulwar and decapitate him on the spot, Hakang, who had been seated in the corner of the workshop, watching the young man intently as he spoke, was more gracious and asked him to wait outside while he discussed the matter with me in greater detail.

"Men are different in that part of the country, Cousin," he told me, laying a hand on my arm, for I had grown light-headed with rage. "They do not all believe as we do."

"But would it not be a sacrilege to permit an infidel to work on the statue?" I asked. "What if someone discovered his heresy and word got back to Sanavasi or, worse, to the Sultan himself? We would all lose our heads."

Hakang glanced out through the open door to the valley, where Peren was seated on the ground, his head thrown back in the sunshine and his eyes closed. Who did he think provided those glorious rays, I wondered, if not the divine Buddha? A moment later, the boy removed his tunic to reveal an impressively muscular frame, carved as fluently through his skin as the stone we worked on. While I turned away in contempt for both his atheism and narcissism, Hakang seemed captivated and continued to stare at Peren with an expression on his face that I had never seen before. A moment later, he lifted his crutches and carried himself to the hut's entrance, where he called out to our visitor, inviting him back inside.

"Show us what you can do," he said, picking up a tooth chisel, a rondel and a carving hammer and nodding in the direction of a block of stone some three feet in height and two feet in width. "If you can discover something beautiful within the stone, then my cousin might think you worthy of a position here."

I shook my head, unconvinced, but allowed Hakang his indulgence, and when Peren lifted the stone and the tools and carried them outside to a shady area, my cousin turned back to me with an enormous smile on his face. I worried that he was exerting himself too much, for his face had grown quite flushed and he appeared to be lost in some sort of silent reverie.

Hours later, when the sun began to set behind the mountains, Peren returned to the hut, presenting us with a sculpture of the four-armed Vishnu, a crown upon his head, an orb in his hand, and an intricate throne for him to sit upon. I examined it carefully, inspecting the depth of the cutting and the integrity of the stone, before being forced to admit that he was a man who had some skill, although it certainly needed refinement. Nevertheless, I remained concerned by his unorthodox views and expressed as much to Hakang.

"We promised him a job, Cousin," he replied, and his enthusiasm for the young man began to irritate me. I had never known him to care so much about any of the other workers before. What made this new arrival so special?

"*You* promised," I corrected him. "Not me."

"He will be a worthy addition, I'm sure of it. You always complain that you don't have the time to design the entire statue alone, and when a gift from the Buddha falls into your lap like this, you turn away. Look, you're already exhausted and it's only been a few months. How will you feel by the end of it? Assuming you still have breath in your body."

I examined Peren's work again, running my hands across the surfaces. It was good, yes, but it was not extraordinary. There were others onsite who were equally talented but who had not been offered any exalted position. Still, I had to admit that the young man had a skill that might surely grow in time, and that would only be to my advantage.

In the end, I gave in to Hakang's enthusiasm. "If you like him so much, then tell him to be here early tomorrow morning and I'm sure I'll find something for him to do."

His face lit up. I could scarcely recall when I had last seen him so happy and it pleased me to give him such cheer, for his life was often a lonely one. Now that we were men, it seemed that he regretted the fact of his twisted limbs much more than he had when we were children, for he made no attempts to seek a wife; perhaps, I imagined, out of fear that eligible young women or their fathers would laugh at him. But still, despite his infirmity, he moved so quickly toward the door to give Peren the good news that I feared he might trip over his crutches and humiliate himself entirely.

• • •

Almost a year after the project had begun, the statue was finally close to completion. As promised, the Buddha stood one hundred and twenty men in height, carved into the rock and looking out across the valley wearing a timeless expression that combined benevolence and sagacity.

And yet, just as the joy of finishing was coming my way, tragedy struck. None of my family had come to visit the site during construction, so I was surprised to observe my sister Abir riding toward us at great speed one afternoon. When she reached the workshop, she jumped off her horse and came running over to Hakang and me with tears in her eyes and, after she spoke, I turned toward the enormous Buddha, wondering why he would betray me in such a cold-hearted fashion after I had devoted so much time and care to his construction. I longed for an answer and had to remind myself that this, of course, was not Siddhārtha Gautama Buddha himself, but just a replica, carved from a mountain. Stone, not deity.

Perhaps, I thought, Peren had been right all along. Perhaps there was no benevolent God looking over us. Perhaps we were alone in the universe, with no past lives to atone for and no future lives to anticipate.

YEMEN

A.D. 552

WHEN MY SISTER APPEARED with the news, I was already preparing to make the journey from Aden to Sana'a to present the Great Malik with the miniature figurines he had commissioned for the Honored Malikah's birthday. The sixteen tiny statues were carved from butter wood and represented the Malik himself, his wife and their fourteen children. Each one was no bigger than the first phalanx of my thumb but the detail in the faces and bodies was, I thought, exceptional.

Years earlier, when I had first started to craft my tiny sculptures, people had laughed at me. *They're so small,* they said, *why would anyone want such pathetic things?* But once they observed the precision that went into carving every tiny face and body, they reconsidered their mockery and my order book had begun to fill.

When Albia announced through tears that we needed to return home without delay, I glanced at my cousin, who had been out of humor all morning, ignoring the companionable jokes that usually defined our time together. Perhaps we both assumed that my father was beginning his journey from this world for the next, since Maurel had been ill of late, but when we arrived at our dwelling, a much more unexpected and sorrowful shock lay in store for us.

For as long as I could remember, I had called Núria my aunt, but strictly speaking we were not related in any sense. However, we had always liked and respected each other, particularly since I'd embraced Hamu as a cousin, enjoying the kind of relationship with him that I had always longed to have with my long-since-disappeared brother.

In those early years, Maurel had divided his affections equally between my mother and aunt, visiting the beds of each one on al-

ternate nights, but as they grew older, he abandoned them almost
entirely for younger women.

But Núria's health had deteriorated in recent months, too, and
I'd discovered her on more than one occasion in the marketplace,
seated on a bench while breathing heavily and pressing one hand
against her chest. When I placed my own hand upon hers, it felt as
if her heart were trying to break through the skin, and the panic in
her eyes reflected the fear in my own. An apothecary visited her in
our home but declared that women must suffer through their infir-
mities, for Allah had made it clear that their primary purpose was to
bear children and to fulfill the tasks that men demanded of them.
Only once did she take to her room for a day and, even then, we
had to distract Maurel from noticing her absence in the kitchen.

• • •

When death finally came for her, Núria had already spent most of
her morning washing clothes, preparing food and feeding the livestock. Earlier she had cooked some fatoot with beef's liver for Hamu
and me before we set off for my workshop, and as she wrapped the
mutabbaks that we regularly took with us for our lunch, I sensed an
awkwardness in the air. Hamu and his mother had always loved each
other dearly. That morning, however, things had felt very different.

When Hamu had sat down on the turquoise pillow that he favored, Núria had turned away from him and he'd stared at the floor,
an expression of utter abjectness on his face. It was obvious that my
aunt had been crying and when she placed our breakfast before us,
he'd reached for her hand, but she'd pulled away, saying, "Not now,
Hamu; later," before returning to her chores. Before we left the
house, and while I was placing my sandals upon my feet, I overheard him speaking to his mother in a low voice, begging her forgiveness, and when I stepped inside, I found her seated at the table,
her head in her hands, as if a great tragedy had been visited upon
her. I looked from one to the other, but neither spoke, Hamu's face
growing red with a mixture of fury and embarrassment as he
brushed past me on his crutches.

I reached down to kiss the top of her head, the familiar and comforting scent of the apple perfume she used in her hair filling my

senses, but as I walked away, she took my hand, pulling me back to her.

"Did you know?" she asked, looking at me with a degree of disappointment in her eyes. "Are you a part of this?"

"Did I know what?" I asked her, and she searched my eyes for an answer but, finding only ignorance there, released me, and I went on my way, confused by her question. It was the last time that we would see each other.

Of course, their lives had been difficult from the start. Hamu had not been born with twisted limbs; they had been the result of an accident when he was three years old. It was unfortunate in so many ways, not least of which was the fact that the girls of our town looked at him with great desire in their eyes, for there was not a boy in our village who possessed such astonishing physical beauty, and he would have been a much-sought-after husband had he not been cursed with this deformity.

Núria, however, had always been a wonderful mother to him, and my mother, Farela, had grown fond of him, too, encouraging the friendship between the two of us, although once, in a moment of candor, she had confided in me that she did not trust him entirely.

"Be careful of him, my son," she told me, watching as he carved a pair of eagles into the handles of his new crutches. "You think he loves you as you love him, but I fear there is another side to him."

"And what side might that be?" I'd asked her in surprise.

"Envy," she replied. "Hamu hates your freedom, the skill you have with your hands, the fact that you have not been damaged physically. If he can ever find a way to hurt you, he will."

At the time, I had laughed it off, thinking it a ridiculous idea.

There were times when I wondered whether it was Hamu's good looks that made everyone adore him. I was certain that had I been as pretty, my father would have shunned me entirely or sent me to an orphanage and yet even he had an affection for this good-natured boy, treating him much as a benevolent uncle might, an affection that I never resented. In my innocence, I believed it was impossible not to love Hamu.

It was my mother who discovered Núria's body, soon after lunch, when she returned to the house and found her old friend lying in the dust behind the coop where the chickens hatched their eggs, her hand clutched to her chest and a terrible grimace affixed to her face. She ran to my father's room in tears and he came outside to pick his lover's body up, before carrying her inside the house and laying her upon the table.

"Her heart," he said quietly to my mother, taking his wife's hand and kissing it, allowing a rare moment of tenderness to pass between them. "It must have given out on her at last."

When Hamu and I arrived home, we discovered my mother washing the body in preparation for the burial, which according to our custom had to be before the sun set. I wept copiously and unashamedly but, to my surprise, Hamu shed no tears, simply staring at his mother with an indecipherable expression on his face. He was trembling noticeably, though, and when I reached out to take his hand in friendship, he shook me off and rushed from the house, his crutches banging noisily upon the stone floor.

Within hours, prayers were being said over Núria's body, which had been wrapped in a shroud. Together, my father and I, along with two of our neighbors, carried her to the burial ground, where she was laid in a grave and covered in earth while her soul ascended for the final judgment of Allah.

When we turned to go back home, I was surprised to find that Hamu was no longer there.

. . .

I found it difficult to sleep that night, memories of my aunt running through my mind. Conscious of the long ride that lay ahead of me the following day, I rose early and decided that a walk might soothe my emotions. Strolling toward the shore where the fishermen had lined up their boats in a neat stripe along the beach, I glanced in the direction of the repair shop on the peninsula that represented the last port before the great and mysterious continent of Africa.

It was quiet, save for the sound of the occasional bird in the air or animal scurrying through the undergrowth. Beneath my breath I hummed a love song that my late wife had often sung to me after we made love in the caves nearby, a place I rarely visited anymore.

In fact, I had gone only once since her death; running my hand along the images carved into the stone I had been overwhelmed by the sensation, feeling a shock against my skin that was so powerful I pledged never to return.

I had walked for some time and was thinking of turning back for home when I heard the sound of weeping and followed it carefully. A figure revealed itself slowly and to my surprise I discovered Hamu seated in the undergrowth, staring out to sea, tears rolling down his face. He startled when he saw me.

"Cousin," he said softly as I sat down next to him. I said nothing for a time, but when it seemed that his silence would prove interminable, I decided to speak.

"I miss her already," I said, picking up a handful of sand and allowing it to sieve through my fingers onto my toes. "But she lived a good and honest life. She would not want you to be unhappy, Hamu. Death comes to us all, my friend."

"You don't understand," he said.

"I understand how it feels to lose someone you love," I reminded him. "I understand what it is to mourn."

He hesitated for a moment, acknowledging the truth of that remark. "Still," he said at last, shaking his head. "This is different. After all, you were not responsible for your wife's death."

"No," I admitted. "But then, you were not responsible for Núria's either."

"I was."

"How?"

"She saw me," he whispered. "Last night. She saw me. That's why she didn't want to talk to me this morning."

I turned to look at him and frowned. "Saw you?" I asked. "Saw you doing what?"

"You can't guess?" he asked.

"Cousin, I don't know what you're talking about."

"Parona and I," he said, looking down and pressing a hand against his eyes as if to block out the world.

I turned back to the sea, considering this. The only Parona I knew was the boy who had recently come to help me in my workshop, sweeping floors and sharpening my tools. A remarkably hand-some and muscular youth, certainly, and one whom Hamu had taken under his wing, for they spent much time together, laughing and sharing private jokes.

And then, of course, I understood.

"You mean . . . ?" I began, unwilling to put the profanation into words, and he looked back at me, wiping his tears with the back of his hand, before nodding.

"She saw us together," he said. "That is why she would not talk to me this morning. That is why her heart gave out on her. It is all my fault."

I could scarcely find the words to express my surprise. I had never imagined that my cousin had such a deviant taint to his nature, al-though I knew that such men existed, of course. There had been a boy in our village a few years earlier, for example, who had been of such a mind, and he had been murdered in his sleep on account of his perversion. And while the perpetrators had never been caught, it was believed by all that his parents had committed the act.

"You must not indulge in such sinful thoughts," I warned him eventually. "Allah has said—"

"I don't care what Allah has said," he snapped, and I drew in my breath at the heresy.

"Hamu!"

"It's so easy for you, isn't it?" he said, turning to me now with venom in his eyes. "Normal in every way. Legs that work. One wife already buried and another in your future, no doubt—"

"Hamu," I repeated, growing angry now. "You are grieving, so I will make allowances for any indiscretion on your part, but have a care with your tone."

"Everything, your entire life, has come easy to you," he contin-ued, ignoring my warning. "But what about me? What is there left for me?"

I looked toward the water while Hamu calmed himself, saying nothing now. Somehow, I found myself reaching out and taking his hand in mine. He was, after all, my cousin and I loved him as deeply as he loved me. Nothing, I was sure, could ever change that.

PART 4

A
FACE CARVED
IN STONE

SRI LANKA

A.D. 588

THE ROAD FROM NEGOMBO to Anuradhapura was notoriously treacherous, taking me through mountainous terrain and those parts of the country where bandits and killers were known to dwell. Considering the value of the goods that I was carrying, I felt anxious about making the journey alone and had considered asking my cousin to accompany me, but, as he remained lost in his grief, I guessed that he would prefer to remain at home.

I was riding to the capital for an audience with King Aggabodhi, who had commissioned me to create a set of bronze replicas of the royal family as a birthday gift for his Queen. Earlier in the year, when he dispatched his emissary to Negombo, our entire village had taken pride in my receiving such an honored assignment. Casting my own bronze from a mixture of copper, zinc, lead and bismuth, I worked day and night for months on the pieces—there were sixteen in all—before wrapping them in a fabric covering and placing them in my satchel for the journey ahead. I looked forward to visiting the royal palace and seeing the expression on the King's face when I presented him with my work, the finest pieces that I had yet created.

I expected that it would take me three days in total to reach the capital and, on my first night, I stopped in Padeniya, to eat, rest and allow my horse time to recover. The inn was situated in a long rectangular building, constructed entirely from stone, and three of the walls were divided by a dozen or more partitions where travelers could sleep on heavy blankets thrown on the floor. The landlord confirmed that there were a few still available that night and I left my bags in one, hoping that the man sleeping in the cell next to my own would not prove himself a thief. I glanced in his direction as I passed; his back was turned to me so I could not see his face, but something about the manner in which he lay there, with one leg wrapped behind the other, made me feel that I knew him from somewhere. The memory did not immediately reveal itself to me, however, so I continued on toward the center of the hostelry, where a large gathering place could be found, replete with tables and servant girls offering food and drink. At the rear of the structure was a place for livestock and the coop where the chickens hatched their eggs, along with a bathhouse. Entering the steaming chamber, I nodded to the three or four other men already relaxing in the water and, divesting myself of my clothing, stepped in to join them while a group of young women poured perfumes and balms about our shoulders, massaging their unguents into our hair. The heat of the bath relaxed me and I allowed myself a deep sigh as I stretched out and closed my eyes, the pores on my face opening to let the dirt of the roads seep from my skin.

The girls were all pretty, but there was one in particular who caught my eye, for she seemed shyer than the rest, remaining mostly silent while her sisters joined in the bawdy jokes of my bathmates. I was accustomed to the obscene conversation of men in places like this—even in Negombo, which prided itself on being a more cultured part of the country, the men treated the women of the bathhouses like whores. Still, despite my desire to block out my surroundings, I remained conscious of the girl I admired, who was standing in a corner of the room, mixing a fresh treatment in a stone bowl from spices and oils. She seemed a little too sophisticated and elegant to be forced to endure the badinage of libidinous men and I shrank back against the side of the enormous tub when she came over, hoping to make it clear that I was traveling alone and not a member of their party. As another of the girls began to bathe the fattest of the men, he grabbed her hand and pushed it down into the water between his legs, making the rest all laugh uproariously when she tried to pull away. It was a disgusting sight to behold but there was nothing that I could do, for there were four of them and only one of me and they were already looking in my direction as if they resented my silence.

"You look angry, friend," said one of the men. "You don't like a girl to touch you?"

"I like it well enough," I replied. "When she has chosen to do so."

He laughed and shook his head, rolling his eyes contemptuously. "Don't act the innocent," he said. "You're old enough to know how these places make their money."

I chose not to engage in this dialogue and he soon grew bored of taunting me, rising from the bath, his tumescence an insult to my eyes, before taking one of the girls into a side room from where we were treated to the sounds of his exertions. So disgusted was I by his behavior that I considered leaving, but at this same moment, the girl I liked came over with her bowl of perfumed lather and began to knead it into my skin, producing a deeply comforting sensation. Beneath her breath, she sang a lullaby about a many-colored butterfly that could scarcely be heard above the sounds of laughter from the men, but it was soothing, and when I closed my eyes, I imagined myself a child again, in a time of peace.

When my bath was over, she invited me for a massage, leading me to an empty stall, where I lay down upon towels that had been warmed by hot rocks. As she worked her fingers into the knots of my back, I felt more at ease than I had in a long time. It had been an eternity since a woman had touched me with such feeling and as I let out an involuntary sigh I found, to my embarrassment, that I, too, was growing aroused.

Noticing this, she reached her hand down between my legs as she had undoubtedly been trained to do, but I took her softly by the wrist and shook my head.

"You don't want this?" she asked, confused, appearing worried that she might have displeased me in some way.

"Not today," I said, covering myself up. "But thank you."

She glanced around anxiously. From the other side of the bathhouse door I could hear the noise of the inn as it seeped through the walls, and she told me that the landlord, her father, would beat her if he suspected that she had not satisfied me.

"Your father would do this?" I asked in surprise.

"Of course," she said. "He has beaten me since I was a girl. This is what men do, no?"

"Not all men, no," I said. "And you have satisfied me. Truly, you have. I don't want anything more, I promise. If I am asked, I will only sing your praises."

She nodded but was clearly baffled by my refusal. I suspected that no man had ever refused her ministrations before and, for a moment, I wondered whether it would be kinder simply to allow her to do what was expected of her. Instead, I dried myself with a rough towel and donned my clothes once again before making my way toward the door, looking forward to the food that awaited me.

Glancing back once more, however, I noticed the innkeeper's daughter watching me, and our eyes held each other's for an unusually long time. And then—slowly, as if she were unaccustomed to such things—she smiled.

. . .

I slept late the next morning. When my eyes finally opened, I pressed them closed again in the vain hope that I might find my way back to the warm, welcoming land that I had just departed, but it was not to be. I rose and dressed and returned to the center of the hostelry, where the innkeeper, a big brute of a man, had laid out food for breakfast. As most of the other travelers had already woken and departed, however, there was little left for me.

"Eat," he told me, pointing toward the scraps that remained on the table. "It's that or nothing."

I looked at the scraps that remained in disappointment but soon forgot my hunger when the girl who had massaged me the previous night reappeared. I blushed a little, remembering that she had featured quite prominently in my lurid dreams, and when she glanced in my direction, she seemed confused by the blossoming redness of my cheeks, before placing some potato curry and a little dahl before me.

"Where did you get that?" asked her father, grabbing her roughly by the shoulder, and she lowered her eyes when she replied.

"It would have gone to waste otherwise," she said. "I heated it up in a pan for our guest."

He seemed unimpressed but walked away, disappearing into another room, and when I summoned the courage to ask the girl her name, she told me that it was Kasi. I smiled and told her that in my village, this was a word that meant "radiant."

"I do not feel radiant," she replied with a shrug.

"Sometimes our greatest luster comes from within."

"You are leaving this morning?" she asked, ignoring my pathetic attempts at flattery, and I nodded.

"I am."

"For where?"

"I travel onward to Anuradhapura," I told her.

"They say that there are great palaces there," she replied, glancing toward the door as if she could scarcely even imagine a world that existed beyond her own narrow universe. "And the most powerful men in the land live there in splendor. The ladies bathe in goat's milk and the men cut each other's heads off if they dare insult a woman."

"It is true, I think."

"But it is a long way from Padeniya. You will not make it there today."

"No, I plan on breaking the journey overnight again," I told her. "In a place like this, I expect. And then, all being well, I will arrive in the capital tomorrow."

"Be warned that there are robbers along these roads. Many who would slit your throat for the sandals on your feet. You are a merchant? You are carrying goods to trade?"

"No," I told her. "I am a simple craftsman, that's all. I work with bronze. Let me show you."

I returned to the small cubicle in which I had slept, passing the man who had seemed familiar to me the night before. He was awake now, too, but stood with his back to me as he packed his belongings in his satchel and, although I once again felt the strange twist of recognition, I did not want to leave Kasi alone for too long and so retrieved my saddlebag, removing one of the packages before bringing it outside and handing it to her. I had chosen a small replica of a child, the entire piece less than half the size of my palm in height, and her eyes opened wide in admiration as she examined it. I couldn't stop myself from staring at her; her pupils were of a blue tourmaline such as I had never seen before.

"It's beautiful," she said, holding the figurine in the air, where the light streaming through the window caught hold of it, sending a spark of gold dancing against the gray stone wall of the hut. "You made this?"

"I did," I said. "It represents Uttia, the youngest of King Agga-bodhi's children. It's the Queen's birthday in a few days' time and I was commissioned to fashion bronze icons of each member of the royal family as a gift."

"But how do you create something so intricate?" she asked, and I explained my process in simple terms.

"It can be dangerous, though," I told her. "Should any of the roasted clay fall on your skin, the pain can be excruciating. Look at what I have endured over the years."

I held out my hands, displaying the small burns and scars that I had acquired since my childhood experimentations with bronze had begun.

"This one," I said, pointing to a small black welt on the third finger of my right hand, "was one that I received while making this very replica. It still stings, especially in heat."

She examined it for a moment before standing up and disappear-ing into a side room. I stared after her, uncertain whether I had said something to offend her, but when she returned, she was holding a small bowl filled with a white paste, infused with the scent of laven-der and the aloe vera plant, before taking my hands in her own and massaging the cream into my skin. The sensation was both soothing and stimulating, the touch of her skin against my own deeply affect-ing.

"Tell me your name, traveler," she said, and when I whispered it to her, she repeated it back to me, her voice carrying like music in the air. I took my right hand back and placed it behind her head, pulling her forward slowly, but just as our lips were about to meet, a sound came from behind and I saw two of the men from the pre-vious night's bath stepping into the room. Noticing my sculpture on the table, one reached across and lifted it, weighing it in his hands. I watched in fear, nervous of saying anything in case I antagonized him and he dashed it on the stone floor. When he tossed it to his friend, my heart somersaulted and I cried out. Fortunately, the other man had sure hands.

"This must be worth some money," said the second man. "Where did you buy it?"

"I didn't buy it, I made it," I said, and they looked at each other for a moment before grinning and throwing it back to me. I wrapped it in its packaging again, thankful that no harm had come to it, and returned to my food as the men left some coins on the table and departed.

"Pigs," said Kasi after the door closed behind them. "They come from the Kelani river, passing through here once a month, and treat all the girls like filth."

"Have they hurt you?" I asked.

"Of course," she said, and from her expression, I knew that she understood me very well. "Many times. But who can stop them?"

I felt a great rage burn within. The idea of those animals performing the marriage act with this girl against her will offended me to my core. Images of slaughter came into my mind but I brushed them away, for I had already been responsible for two deaths in my lifetime and I did not wish to add a third to that number.

Finally, the food eaten and the time passing, I had no choice but to gather my things. As I prepared to depart, Kasi met me at the door.

"You will come back again?" she asked me, and I nodded.

"On my way home," I told her. "I'll be in Anuradhapura for several days, I think, but I will sleep here again on my journey back to Negombo."

She leaned forward and this time, uninterrupted, we kissed.

When I went outside to collect my horse from the stable, I felt a burst of exhilaration within my chest. Riding north, it seemed as if I were being swept along by the Buddha himself.

GREENLAND

A.D. 623

M Y SECOND DAY of traveling proved so arduous I began to
wonder whether my father had been right when he predicted that I would surely perish before finding Angerdlánguak, the leader of the Eskimo people of the North, who, it was
said, had six thousand men at his command. I doubted the world
could even contain such a vast number of souls.

"You've never traveled more than a few miles from home,"
M'arak had remarked the night before I departed, not long after
we'd buried my aunt and he had failed to persuade me to remain at
home until the weather turned. "You can't even cast a fishing hole
without falling in. And you expect to travel hundreds of miles without incident?"

"I've only fallen in once," I told him irritably. "And that was
when I was a boy and Jôrut pushed me."

He shook his head. "You'll find yourself in the Unknown World
before the day is done."

In truth, I had been anxious about the journey, but I believed
that I had both the will and the stamina to survive whatever hard-
ships might come my way. After all, Angerdlánguak's own man,
Børge, had traveled from the northwestern tip of the world to our
village without incident and he was old and fat while I was young
and healthy. Although it was true that Børge had brought eight
men to assist him on his journey, along with one hundred dogs,
while I was traveling alone and had only six canine companions to
drive my sledge.

Following the directions that Børge had given me, I steered a
straight northern path without veering too close to the western
fjords.

Journey north for three days, he had told me. *Soon you will hear us, soon you will sense us, soon you will find us.*

The conditions were not vastly different to home, the snow was neither deeper beneath my feet nor heavier as it fell from the sky, and I felt in the best possible position to survive the trek. I simply had to ensure that my course was true and my resolve remained strong. I wore the skins of two caribou, one with a layer of fur pressed against my skin and the other with a layer facing out. My hands were encased in fish-skin gloves and, over the previous week, my cousin Haansi had killed four seals and fashioned a new set of mukluks for my feet that rose as far as my knees. My handsome young assistant, Parkk, had sung a lullaby about a many-colored salmon when Haansi presented the mukluks to me and the two had collapsed in laughter, although I'd failed to see the joke.

The dogs did their best to keep up a good pace but, late in the afternoon, my eyelids began to twitch involuntarily from snow blindness and I feared that the drift would prove so deep the sledge would struggle to make sufficient progress. From time to time, I checked the pouch of amulets stored in my satchel to ensure their safety, for if I were to drop them, they would be lost forever and my entire journey would have been for nothing. Of course, I wore a charm around my own neck, too, a simple talisman made from wolf skin and feathers that I'd fashioned in the days leading up to my departure. Whenever my spirits drooped, I pressed my hand against it, allowing its energy to infiltrate my bones and encourage me to keep going.

Fortunately, I had slept surprisingly well the night before, and as hour followed hour, I consoled myself by thinking of the girl I had met, K'asalok, and how much I looked forward to seeing her again on my journey home. It had been a long time since I'd felt such stirrings for a woman and I wondered whether she might be persuaded to share my life and give me children, an idea that had been on my mind for some time now, for at twenty years of age, I was beginning to grow old and as yet had no sons to carry on my name.

. . .

When a cluster of igloos finally came into view in the distance, I drove the dogs on even faster. There were, perhaps, twenty or thirty large-sized dwellings spread out across the ice so I estimated that at least four hundred people must live in the community, and as I pulled the pack to a halt, a group of men gathered around a fishing hole paused in their conversation and one set his rod down to walk toward me. I greeted him respectfully, asking whether I might find accommodation for the night among his people.

"Your name, stranger?" he asked, and when I told him, he frowned, struggling to pronounce the syllables.

"Still, as long as you can pay, I don't care what they call you," he said, adding that his own name was Eipe. "But you'll find it a dark night for us here. We say goodbye to our oldest friend this very night. He travels toward the Unknown World in a few hours, so our spirits are low."

I assured him that I had come with enough money for my lodgings and offered my sympathies for the great sadness that had descended upon his people. A group of children emerged from one of the ice-chambers and took my dogs to be housed and fed while I followed Eipe into the largest of the igloos, where a meal of steamed walrus and musk oxen was served to me. I fell upon it like a wolf and my spirits lifted. An elderly man sat in the center of the room on a raised chair and I watched as dozens of men, women and children approached him, knelt down and invited him to place his hands upon their heads while he closed his eyes and muttered an incantation over them. I had never witnessed such a practice before and wondered whether he was a holy man of some description. His skin was weather-beaten, marked with so many grooves and crevices that only the presence of a pair of bright blue eyes betrayed his humanity. Something about his bearing suggested to me that he had endured much pain in his long life.

"Some, it is true," replied Eipe when I made this observation to him, and I watched as he observed the scene with a mixture of affection and sorrow in his eyes. "The man's name is Gudmundur. He was once a teacher here, so is known and revered by all. He taught most of my friends and me how to hunt, fish, throw spears, climb mountains of ice. Also, he is my father."

I looked up from my meal in surprise. "He is the focus of much attention," I remarked. "Has he achieved some great milestone?"

"It is he who is traveling to the Unknown World," replied Eipe with a regretful smile. "We are saying goodbye to him and receiving his blessing before his journey takes him to the land from which no man may return."

This was not a practice that was common in the southern parts of the country, but I had heard that the further north one went, the more prevalent it was. I found the custom to be strange, even a little barbaric, but it was not for me to express an opinion on their ways.

"He is ill," continued Eipe. "His memory is gone. His body can no longer support his desire. He cannot look after himself or contribute to the community. And so, we must say farewell. And you, stranger," he asked, looking directly at me now, although I noticed how his eyes regularly returned to the line making its way past his father. "What brings you here?"

"I travel toward the far north," I told him. "The great chieftain, Angerdlánguak, awaits my presence."

He raised an eyebrow, clearly impressed. "You are an intimate of his?" he asked.

"No," I replied. "I am simply a maker of amulets and was commissioned to create some as a gift for his wife." I reached into my satchel, which I kept close at hand at all times, and took one out. There were sixteen in total and the one I chose was the most elaborate by far, intended for the Overlord himself. Fashioned from the feathers of longspur, brant and steller's eider, I had used pieces of glass to capture the light, and threads of scarlet and gold to symbolize his glory. At its heart, I had placed an image of an owl, to symbolize wisdom, and a spearthrower above the bird's head to represent courage.

"You are quite the craftsman," said Eipe, handling the amulet with the care of one who understood the importance of beautiful things. "I imagine a charm like this must be of considerable value."

I smiled but chose not to reveal just how much Angerdlánguak had agreed to pay me. I had only just met this man, after all, and was fearful that my treasures might be stolen while I slept, if not by him, then by someone overhearing our conversation.

"Do you get many travelers through here?" I asked, changing the subject, and he shook his head.

"Not many," he replied. "Although another man did arrive earlier today. Also from the south. He will be sleeping in the same igloo as you tonight. Ah." He looked over to where his father was rising slowly to his feet and nodding in his son's direction. "It is time," he said. "Will you join us?"

As an outsider to their community, I was uncertain whether I should take part in the ritual or not, but Eipe insisted and so, to avoid causing insult, I agreed to accompany him.

We left in a group, Eipe and Gudmundur leading the procession, the rest of the villagers following in a close group behind, singing a mournful song as we made our way toward the water. It was a march of forty minutes or more and, after the long journey that I had endured throughout the day, I began to regret not taking to my bed immediately after my meal, for I was greatly tired. Eventually, however, I heard the sound of waves lapping the shore and knew that we had arrived.

When we stopped, Eipe chanted a prayer for his father while the rest of us bowed our heads, and then he and Gudmundur, along with a woman and some children who I took to be Eipe's family, embraced Gudmundur without tears. He walked with purpose toward the bank, where two men stood waiting for him. A large iceberg had been carved out of the landscape and they guarded it carefully, lest it float away, until Gudmundur stepped upon it. When he did, they released their grip and he sat down, his legs crossed beneath him, his face a mask of peace and contentment such as I had never witnessed before.

The men stepped away from the bank now and the gentle waves took both the iceberg and its cargo out to sea. As Gudmundur floated away, songs filled the air and he drifted toward the Unknown World. When the fog descended and he could no longer be seen, we turned as one back toward the village.

• • •

When I retired to my igloo that night, I chose to remain awake until my fellow traveler appeared. Soon, he stepped inside, his face covered in a mask of wolf skin to ward off the cold. He was a big man, tall and strong, and he paused as he looked down at me. Although I could see only his eyes and mouth, it seemed to me that he broke into a wide smile.

"Were you not told that you would have a companion for the night?" I asked, doing my best to sound friendly, for it was well known that wanderers in these parts could turn aggressive at the slightest provocation. It was the cold and the hunger that made each of us wretched and I did not want to have survived the treacherous conditions of my journey only to be murdered in my bed.

"I was," he grunted. "Although I didn't expect it to be you."

I frowned as he walked over to the other side of the room, where the skins of a dozen or more animals had been laid for him to sleep within.

"Do we know each other, friend?" I asked, and he nodded but didn't turn around.

"I saw you this morning," he said. "At the village in Parquoia. You were eating breakfast while trying to charm that girl."

Of course, it was the man who had been asleep when I arrived at the previous night's igloo and who had somehow seemed familiar to me. He'd marched past me before leaving and I hadn't wanted to look at him in case he took a larcenous interest in my amulets.

"And where are you traveling to?" I asked as he lifted four or five of the animal hides and slipped in between them, the mask still covering his face.

"The same place as you," he said. "To see Angerdlánguak."

"How do you know that's where I'm going?"

"You told the girl. You were bragging to her, were you not? To secure her affections?"

I opened my mouth to disabuse him of this notion but could not find the words. After all, he was right.

"What brings you to the Overlord?" I asked.

"He gave me a job to do and I did it. I return now to claim my reward."

"Might I ask how you make your living?"

"I kill people."

I swallowed nervously and could see from the manner in which his mouth twisted upward that he welcomed the fact that I found his remark unsettling.

"A man insulted one of Angerdlánguak's daughters before making off in the night," he explained. "So I was sent after him to achieve satisfaction. Do you see that bag over there?" He glanced in the direction of a black bag, made from the skin of a walrus. "It contains the man's head and his cock. The latter thrust inside the former. I'll show them to you if you like."

I slunk deeper into my own hide, hoping that we would both go to sleep and this conversation might come to an end. "Thank you, but no," I said.

"It's an amusing sight," he replied with a shrug. "And what about you, what takes you to Angerdlánguak's home?"

"Something far less dramatic," I said. "I'm a craftsman. A maker of amulets. I was asked to design a set for the Overlord and his family."

He laughed. "Women's work," he said, and although I took offense, I was not going to challenge him lest my own head ended up in the bag, too. "Still, I suppose you were always good with your hands, weren't you? From the day you were born, you preferred making things to fighting. It's one of the reasons that you and M'arak were never close."

I stared at him. What he had said was true, but how could he know such a thing? And how was he familiar with my father's name?

"Have we met before, friend?" I asked, sitting up now. "You seem to know a lot about me."

"You don't recognize me, Brother?" he replied, reaching up and pulling the wolf-mask from his face. "Still, it has been a long time. And we've both changed."

I gasped in astonishment, for I could scarcely believe who I was looking at.

It was my missing brother.

It was Jôrut.

PERU

A.D. 665

HAD OFTEN SPECULATED about when, or if, Jalen would reenter my life, but when I had imagined a potential reunion, I had pictured him riding into our village, clothed in the robes of the wealthy, a beautiful wife and a flurry of red-headed children by his side. I had never expected to encounter him again in the unassuming setting of a brick hostelry in the city of Pachacamac.

"I still cannot believe it's you," I said when we left our beds and stepped outside to take the night air. The evening was cold and neither of us could conceive of sleep after such a great surprise. "It's been so many years since we last saw each other."

"Too long for brothers to be separated," he said. "I wondered whether you might have forgotten me by now."

"I could never do that," I replied, shaking my head. "Every day I've wondered where you were, whether you were still alive, whether you were happy—"

"Happy?" he said, frowning, as if he had never even considered such an extraordinary notion. "Are there happy people in the world? Do you know many? I should like to meet them if there are. Still, it's only chance that brings us together again now." We sat down in the dust, our backs pressed against the stone wall of the inn. "And if I'm honest, I haven't thought about our family in years. I haven't dared."

"We thought of you. We all did."

"Really?" he asked, looking doubtful. "I doubt your mother regretted my departure."

"You're wrong," I insisted. "But she never understood why you disliked her so much or why you treated her with such disrespect. She never betrayed you to our father, you know."

He turned to look at me with an expression of surprise on his face.

"I assumed that she would have told him what I did the moment he returned."

"From that day to this, she has never uttered a word on the subject, I swear it. As far as Mavra is concerned, you simply ran away. He's never known the reason why."

He looked down at the ground and nodded, his expression proving to me that he regretted his actions.

"It was a silly, childish prank," he said finally, his voice cracking for a moment as if he might weep, but he coughed then to mask his shame. "Born out of jealousy. I meant no harm by my actions. I was just a stupid boy, that's all. Fabi was a good woman, I realize that now, and I was selfish and spoiled. Is she still alive? Is our father?"

"They both are," I said. "And our oldest sister and several other children that our father has begotten over the years."

"How many?" he asked.

I thought about it, counting off names in my head. "Seven," I said cautiously. "Maybe eight? I'm not sure. There's probably a few I don't even know about."

"Some more by your mother?"

"Yes. And you may recall that fidelity was never Mavra's greatest attribute. The children have been borne by various women of the village. Well, girls of the village, I should say. They're more to our father's taste."

"And he's allowed to behave in this way?"

"He's an elder. If a girl's father or brothers protest, he simply challenges them to a fight and, so far, he's never found himself in the dust on account of his actions."

Jalen paused for a long time, considering this. "He was a difficult man, as I recall," he said. "Unlikely to stay loyal to any woman for long. I take after him in this regard."

"You've been unfaithful to your wife?"

"I never married," he said. "Like our father, I prefer variety. And you, Brother?"

I recounted for him the story of my wedding day and how Laritel had been taken from me within hours of our union by a tornado that had blown across our village. I suffered a double loss that day, I added, for she had been pregnant with our child at the time.

"And you haven't married again?" he asked, offering no sympathy, which I found refreshing.

"No," I said. I considered telling him about the girl whom I had encountered the previous night and who had already taken a firm hold of my heart, but as I had no guarantee that either she or he would play any further role in my life, I decided against it for now.

"A man needs a woman," he said determinedly, slapping his left hand on the ground between us. "Without one, how can he be called a man?"

"I have a cousin, Hakal," I told him, "who prefers men to women."

"Many do," he replied. "We've all tried that, haven't we? If there are no women around and one is surrounded by compliant boys, then they're better than nothing. But the pillar and the stones have never really been to my taste. I prefer the welcoming valley. And this Hakal, he is happy with the man he loves?"

"I think so," I said. "The boy works for me and is popular among the laborers, although I'm not sure how great his skills are."

He nodded and turned away and I wondered whether he had missed out on family life, having run away from us all at such a young age.

"And your life, Jalen?" I said. "Tell me what you have done with it."

He stood up now, so quickly that I jumped, and walked along the path, kicking his sandals in the dust. I gained the impression that he was rarely asked to tell his story and was uncertain where he should begin.

"After I left our village," he told me, "I didn't go far at first. In fact, I hid nearby for several days, wondering whether I should return and beg your mother for forgiveness. Finally, I realized that I could not bear to humiliate myself before her and walked north for a few weeks instead, to towns and villages that I had never heard of, places where even the language was unfamiliar to me. In one such place, Valina, I found work training the sons of proud houses to fight, for in that part of the country there are interminable skirmishes. I proved my worth so well that a wealthy spice trader named Conquiga sent for me and invited me to be his champion."

"His champion?" I asked, looking up at my brother, who was picking up pebbles and tossing them into the distance, where they landed soundlessly in the dust. "Meaning what exactly?"

"Conquiga is master of a land that spans to the horizon," he told me. "Thousands of men, women and children fall under his patronage. He works hard for the prosperity and education of all. Some years ago, he created a rather unusual system of justice for lawbreakers. The sole judge, he hears these cases and, if he decides that a man is guilty of the crime with which he has been charged, then the law-breaker is given a choice of punishment. He can either forfeit a limb immediately or agree to fight me in public. Should he choose the former, then I take my sword and immediately slice an arm or leg from his body. Should he choose the latter, we engage in single combat and all the man has to do is draw a single drop of blood from me and he will be set free. The moment I draw blood from him, however, he stands convicted and loses his head, regardless of the seriousness of his crime. Theft, murder, an insult against a neighbor, it doesn't matter. The choice is his."

"And you agreed to such a random law?" I asked.

"Of course," he replied with a shrug. "It paid well, and look at me, Brother, I am not easily defeated."

It was true. Like our father, Jalen was a mountain of a man, his body a carefully carved terrain of muscle, sinew and vein. Recalling the beatings that he'd inflicted on me when we were only children and his strength was far less developed, I dreaded to think of the damage he might be able to wreak now.

"And you still hold this occupation?" I asked.

"No," he said. "My fortunes changed when a trio of bandits came to the town. They stole from merchants, raped the women and burned buildings to the ground. It took dozens of men to capture them. After their trial, Conquiga offered them the same justice that he offered everyone else but, in their case, he said that all three should take me on together. It was not a fair fight, but I think he wanted to test me. Naturally, they agreed, but not one could draw blood so I defeated them easily. By the end of the afternoon they were lined up on a dais side by side, where I took a sword to each of their heads. I resented Conquiga, however, for this. It was obvious that he'd grown weary of my victories, so I resigned my position. But my reputation had spread and since then I've been known as the greatest fighter in the country, at the employ of wealthy men. Whoever can pay the most, I am his to command."

"And the bag in our room?" I asked, for he had told me earlier that the moccasin satchel he carried contained a dozen left hands, all of which he was bringing north with him.

"Thieves," he said. "Petty thieves. Small larcenies, nothing important. But my employer wanted to make an example of them. He was not going to cut their heads off like Conquiga. A hand from each would suffice."

"And this work?" I asked. "It gives you pleasure?"

He seemed surprised by the question, as he had when I'd asked whether he was happy. "It doesn't displease me," he said. "It's work as much as any other work. And I enjoy watching the faces of men as they're led to their deaths. Some quake like cowards, some are brave like men should be, some try to offer words of wisdom to which no one pays any attention."

"A strange curiosity," I said, shivering a little. "And how many men have you killed?"

"Who can tell?" he replied with a shrug. "A hundred? Two hundred? A thousand? I don't keep count. And you, Brother? We live in dangerous times. Are you telling me that you have never dispatched a man from this world for the next?"

I turned away, not wanting him to see the expression on my face. Unlike him, I had the deaths of only two people on my conscience—a boy and a man—but I did not take pride in either. If anything, their memories haunted me. "No," I said.

"I can always tell when a man is lying to me," he said after a moment. "Do you know how?"

"No," I replied.

"His lips move."

He let out a great roar at this and I laughed along, somewhat nervously. When he sat down next to me on the dust again, he slapped his hand down on my knee so hard that I had to stop myself from crying out; any harder and he would have surely snapped the bone.

"Will you come home with me, Jalen?" I asked, when he had settled down again. "When both our tasks are done, I mean. Will you come home and see our father before he dies?"

He breathed in heavily. "I'm not sure," he said. "Would he welcome me?"

"I know he would."

"He might have forgotten me by now. It has been many years."

"I can assure you that that would never happen. The great sorrow of his life is that he lost you. He still speaks of you often and blames whoever is in his sight for your disappearance. In fact, in recent times, he has been speaking of you more and more, thinking that you are at home, that you are in the next room, that you have taken a walk by the shore, but I fear that his mind is playing games with him. Sometimes, he thinks that we are all still children again. He can't seem to keep his thoughts straight."

"I will think about it, Brother," he said. "But for now, I think it's time for sleep, don't you? We both have long rides ahead of us in the morning."

As we climbed into our beds, he put on a pair of fish-skin gloves to keep warm and I remembered how, when we were children, this was the time I dreaded the most, for he would wait until I was almost unconscious before crawling quietly toward me and jumping upon me, pounding me about the face or body with his fists, refusing to leave me alone until he had either made me cry or my father had come in to separate us. It was foolish of me to feel a grudge over such things after so many years—these were the antics of children, after all—but nevertheless, I felt a distinct sense of anxiety as I drifted off, knowing that he was only a few feet away from me and that his enormous body could be upon me in a moment, should he choose to attack.

Still, the next morning, I felt disappointed to discover that my brother had left without even saying goodbye. When I inquired of our host, I was told that Jalen had risen at dawn, leaving a few coins in payment, before saddling his horse and riding off.

"Did he leave any message for me?" I asked.

The innkeeper shook his head. "Not a word," he said.

Had it not been for the fact that he had encountered him, too, I might have almost imagined that I had dreamed the entire reunion. Now there was nothing left for me to do but saddle my horse, collect my belongings and ride north, where a king awaited me.

BULGARIA

A.D. 710

A WEEK LATER, having delighted the Khanbikeh and her fourteen children with the carved images that the Khan had commissioned, I returned from Varna with more than just a satchel of gold coins about my person; I also brought a wife.

Katia and I had met only twice before I offered to commit my life to her, but from our first conversation a bond of affection and trust had existed between us and I knew that we could make each other happy. She was honest with me about her life up to now, brutal in her narration, and while some suitors might have found her history intolerable, I reserved my contempt for a man who would allow his daughter to be treated in such a despicable fashion.

I passed her town on my journey home and we left together, under cover of night, Katia fretting over what might happen when her father discovered her absence the following morning. She had tried to run away once before, she told me, and her back still bore the scars of the whipping he'd inflicted on her. *Leave me again*, he'd said then, *and I will hunt you down and strip the skin from your bones.*

We rode slowly back toward Madara, the better to get to know each other, and on the second day I recounted the story of how I had first become interested in carving images into stone. I had still been a boy at the time, tormented by the most vivid dreams of cities and people I had never visited or known, and felt a great urge to capture those visions before sunlight allowed the apparitions of night to dissolve into nothingness. I carved into the walls of our stone hut, and the huts of our neighbors, and each image, when completed, made me feel as if I had summoned up a memory from some undiscovered country that lay deep within my soul. I described some of these carvings to Katia and she seemed moved by my passion. She was not an artist herself, she told me, adding that her talents as a seamstress were also nonexistent so I should not presume my new wife would be able to mend my clothes with any great skill. None of that mattered, I told her, for she could embrace motherhood and spend her energies building a home for the family we would create together. I expected her to be joyful at this suggestion and was mildly disconcerted when she said that she hoped for more from life than this.

"Of course I would like children someday," she added, sensing my disquiet. "But other things are important to me, too."

"Such as?" I asked.

"I'm not sure yet," she replied. "I've never been given the opportunity to dream before, but might not my dreams be as vivid as yours? After all, cooking, cleaning and child-rearing are tasks that a man and woman can share."

I turned around on the horse to glance at her, wondering whether she was teasing me with such a perverse idea, and when I saw how well she contained her laughter, it made me smile. I liked the idea of a wife with a good sense of humor.

"These are strange jokes," I said. "If I am not careful, you will be calling me wife, and I calling you husband!"

"We don't need to go quite that far," she said, her tone remaining serious. "But you must realize that I've spent every day of my life doing whatever men demanded of me. And my father, may his name be forever cursed, convinced me that I was put on this Earth for no other reason than to serve at their pleasure. Thanks to you, I'm free of all that now. But that doesn't mean I want to exchange one form of servitude for another."

"I didn't buy you, Katia," I told her quickly so she would not misunderstand my intentions. "And I only want you to be happy. But when you say 'free'—free to do what exactly?"

"Something," she said, laughing now at last. "Anything. Whatever can give my days some meaning. Don't worry," she added, wrapping her arms around me, for she could tell that I was growing anxious by her unexpected reach for independence. "I will be a good wife to you, I promise. Just don't expect a delicious gyuvech stew or a tasty pogacha every evening when you return home.

They're completely beyond my abilities. But you will have no cause for complaint. You liberated me, Husband, and I'll make sure you never regret that."

I remained silent. I was surprised by how deeply she thought about the world, but it pleased me, too, for I had always been drawn to strong-willed women. My sister Albena had once shown such fire in her belly but had allowed those flames to be extinguished since marrying for the second time, giving birth to four babies in four years and tying herself to a man who was unworthy of her. She had become a nag, regularly complaining about the mundanity of her days. Still, at least she hadn't asked me to murder her new husband, which was progress of a sort.

"We will be happy, I promise," said Katia, her tone growing seductive now, and when she whispered my name into my ear, I grew aroused and pulled the horse to a stop so that we could rest awhile in the fields.

• • •

When we arrived at my village, my family were immediately welcoming of my new love, with the exception of Albena, who was distrustful and hostile. I wasn't surprised to find her there—she preferred to be in our father's home than her own, where her corpulent husband, Xanthe, spent most of his time eating, planning his next meal or enjoying the memory of his last one. Xanthe had once been a soldier, like Marin, and it was our father who had imposed the match on his eldest daughter soon after her first husband's suspicious death. There had been much misgiving about Albena's role in his unexpected departure from this world and our father had convinced her of the wisdom of taking a much older man for a husband in order to restore respectability. Xanthe was so enormous that he was known as the Great Hippopotamus of Madara and we all assumed that he would not last more than a few months and then she would be free again. And yet, as year followed year, he continued to breathe and to eat and was obviously capable of undertaking his marital duties, as children kept appearing, much to my sister's distress.

Although I had only been gone from Madara for a few weeks, my

mother embraced me like a long-lost son and even my father struggled to his feet, surprising me by how happy he was to have me
home again. I was shocked, however, by his appearance, for he had
aged considerably in my absence, growing gaunt, his illness strip-
ping the fat from his face. I felt an urge to turn away out of respect
for the strong and fearsome man he had once been. To see him reduced to a shadow of that intimidating warrior was upsetting, but I
knew that he would despise any excessive emotion on my part and
so I said nothing, simply bowing my head so he could lay his hands
on me in a prayer of thanks for my safe return.

"You journeyed back without difficulty?" he asked me.

"A trio of bandits tried to rob us as we rode along," I told him,
hoping that he might be impressed by such daring, "but I outrode
them."

"I knew you'd come back one day," he said, his eyes filling with
tears. "They said you were gone forever but I knew better. You've
come home to say goodbye."

"He thinks you're Javis," said Albena, standing up and rolling her
eyes as she directed him back toward his seat by the fireplace. "You
may as well just pretend that you are, Brother, it won't make any
difference. This morning, he was convinced that I was Old Paravi,
who churns the butter in the village, and she's twice as old as me
with a face full of warts. And yesterday, he mistook Floza for a
goat."

"He did not mistake me for a goat," said my mother, turning
around and sounding annoyed by the accusation. Even now, after
all these years of betrayal, she still defended her husband against all
complainants. "He mistook the goat for me. There's a difference."

"There was a goat and there was you," replied Albena, rolling her
eyes. "And he didn't know which was which. It's not as if—"

"I'm not Javis, Father," I said, stepping past her and kneeling
down before him. "He was your first-born son. I am your second."

"No," he said, looking irritated by my response. "You're too
strong to be that worthless creature. He ran away from home many
years ago, may his name be forever cursed. No, you're Javis. I'd
know you anywhere."

My mother looked at me with an expression that suggested it might be kinder to leave him with his delusion.

"I've brought a surprise with me," I announced, standing up again and looking behind me, ready to introduce my new wife to them, but—I hadn't noticed until now—she had remained outside, hesitant to come in until invited. "Katia," I called, looking out onto the street and beckoning her forward. "Come in! You have a new family to meet."

She stepped inside shyly, her head bowed, and the room fell silent in surprise. Even Albena's babies stopped their caterwauling for a few moments as they stared at this glorious apparition.

"While I was away," I said, turning back to them, "I had the great fortune to fall in love. Katia and I were married along the road from Varna."

My parents and sister looked at me in surprise, saying nothing at first, but then an expression of joy spread across my mother's face and she stepped forward to embrace her new daughter, smothering her with kisses. Katia, moved by such an unexpected display of emotion, wept, and even Marin looked pleased that I had brought such a wonderful treasure home.

"If I was a younger man," he said, signaling her to come closer to him and patting his lap, an invitation that she declined, "it would not be my son's bed you would be climbing into tonight."

"Father!" I cried, but Katia turned to me and gave a small smile, letting me know that she did not feel insulted. I had explained to her on our journey how my father's mind had become disordered in recent times and that she should not be surprised if he made unsuitable remarks. In truth, she was accustomed to much worse slurs.

"You're a great beauty," said Floza, smiling at her and holding her face in her hands. "My son is lucky to have found you."

"We're both lucky," she replied. "He's been very kind to me. You brought up a man of great honor."

"You can't have known each other very long," said Albena, stepping forward now and looking her new sister up and down as if she were a dress that she was considering purchasing. "Are you with child? Is that why he married you so quickly?"

"No," said Katia, shaking her head. "Not yet." She threw me a sly look, for while she may not have been pregnant when we left Varna, it was entirely possible that she was now.

"Such a thing to ask!" said my mother, slapping Albena gently across the arm.

"It just seems strange to me that he would wed with such speed, that's all, considering how long he's been in mourning for a girl he was married to for only a few hours. I thought that was the great love affair for the ages?"

"We're happy, Albena," I told her. "I will always cherish the memory of my first wife but now it is time to set my sorrows aside and enjoy love once again. It's what she would have wanted for me, just as I would have wanted it for her, had—"

"Where was it that you met?" Albena asked, interrupting me and addressing her question to Katia.

"A half-day's ride south of Varna," she replied.

"And what did you do there? For a living, I mean? Who are your people?"

Katia hesitated. We had agreed how she would answer such questions, but still, this would be the first time she would be forced to lie and I sensed that this, along with cooking, cleaning and housework, might be another skill that she lacked. "I worked in the marketplace," she said. "Selling needles."

"Your hands are very soft for one who sold needles," said Albena, reaching forward and grabbing them so sharply that Katia let out a cry of surprise. "Not a single scar. Most seamstresses have hands that look like cracked clay."

"She always wore gloves," I said, stepping between the two and throwing Albena a look of annoyance. She had always been possessive toward me, but I wanted no trouble from her now.

"Gloves," replied Albena with a smile. "How clever of her."

. . .

A month later, settled back into life in Madara, I found myself out by the town walls, examining the stone. So pleased was Khan Terval by the images that I had fashioned in his palace that he had commissioned me to create more here, in my hometown, and I was planning something magnificent, an image that had appeared in my dreams repeatedly of a horseman spearing a lion while a dog ran behind, giving chase. I hoped to create my most intricate work yet and the Khan had promised to fill my coffers once again if I could complete it within six months, in time for the anniversary of his ascension to the throne.

A sound distracted me from my thoughts and I spun around, surprised to see my father standing behind me, for he almost never left our home anymore.

"You startled me," I said, walking over to him. "How long have you been there?"

"Not long," he said. "I've been watching you, but you do nothing. You just stare at the walls as if you're expecting them to speak to you."

"That's exactly what I'm doing," I replied. "If I stand here long enough, the stone will tell me what it wants from me."

"But why do you do it?" he asked. "What is it all for?"

"For eternity, I suppose," I told him with a shrug. "If I create something beautiful, then when people pass by our town in the future and witness what I left behind, they may feel as if they are being watched over by a ghost from the past. Don't we all hope for some form of immortality? We might not be able to breathe forever but there are other ways to stay alive."

Marin sat down heavily on a stone and sighed, wiping the perspiration from his face with the back of his hand. "I longed for a son different to you," he said quietly, and there was no anger in his voice now, no recrimination, just sorrow. I sat opposite him and looked him directly in the eyes as he spoke. "I wanted you to become a great warrior. For you to bear our family name with honor. Instead, you take chisels and carve pictures into walls, like a child. When you were a boy, you were different. You were tough then, always getting into fights and always winning. But something happened to you. What was it, my son? I don't recognize you anymore."

"No, Father," I said, reaching out to touch him on the arm, where his once-solid muscle had now deteriorated into loose skin. "You're confused. That wasn't me. That was Javis."

"Javis," he said, and something shifted inside his mind again as he looked up at me. "Will he ever come home, do you think?"

"You will see each other again one day in the future," I said, taking his hand now. "Perhaps not in this life, but certainly in the next."

"You believe in such fantasies?" he asked before turning away. There was something of the young Marin in him then. I could see the phantom of his youth in that strange smile. "I fought four men to win your mother's hand," he said after a long pause. "Did you know that?"

"Yes," I said, for this was a story he had told many times.

"I took the heads off two guards quickly, then plunged my sword through the heart of the third. I wanted to spare the fourth boy, he was young and frightened and had asked for none of this trouble, but I was given no choice. And so, he lost his head too. But the reward was a good one, for your mother was mine by nightfall."

"Back in Ohrid," I said, for this was the town where my mother and he had met.

"No," he said, looking down at the sand. "Not in Ohrid. In Cappadocia."

"Cappadocia is in the Ottoman Empire, Father," I told him. "You have never traveled as far as that."

He smiled at me, stroking my face with his hand, and shook his head, as if I were the one in the wrong.

"It was Cappadocia," he insisted. "I have traveled further than you know. As have you, my son. My journeys might be at an end now, but so many lie in wait for you. Do your memories never surprise you? Do you not dream of the past and the future and recognize both with equal clarity?" He leaned forward and grasped me by the wrist, a hint of his once-intimidating strength returning in that moment as he gripped me tightly. "Your shadow falls both behind you and before you while you stand between the two pretenders, a mask across your eyes."

I felt a shiver run down my spine, something otherworldly that unsettled me deeply. His confusion was too upsetting for me so I stood up and walked back toward the walls with my tools, hacking a loose piece of rock from the surface. Holding it in my hands, I used my chisel and hammer to carve a rough portrait of Marin's face into the stone and, when I was finished, I blew the dust away and held it up to the light. Not my finest work, but a passable portrait.

"See, Father?" I said, walking back to him. He was slumped over now, as if he had fallen asleep. "Isn't this better than fighting? This stone will last forever. It will still be here long after we have both become one with the dust."

I held it out to him, saying his name over and over, even as the tears fell down my cheeks. Finally, I let the stone drop to the ground and gathered my tools before placing his body on the back of my horse and leading it slowly back toward our village, where we would soon begin the burial rites.

MEXICO

A.D. 752

THE FUNERAL TOOK PLACE before the sun went down and, afterward, as my mother's spirit traveled onward toward the unknown place, I felt a deep sense of melancholy to know that I would never see her or my father, who had predeceased her by only a few months, again. Their bodies lay in the same earth now, their quarrels hushed at last, their bones intermingling as they began the business of transforming themselves in communion with the soil and the worms into new forms of life. As my mother's shroud disappeared beneath a blanket of loam and mud, my sister Adria drew attention to herself with an outpouring of the most dramatic keening, falling to her knees while tearing at her clothes and hair, determined that all who surrounded her should be in no doubt regarding the depth of her grief. Her husband was not there to console her. The man had grown so thin in recent months that it was frightening to see his bones press against his skin. It was as if his skeleton were trying to break through its translucent casing. And so it fell to my wife, Kalisha, to drag her to her feet and offer words of comfort. I considered this contemptible behavior on Adria's part since she had so often been a source of conflict between our parents and had in fact been responsible for the argument that caused my mother to lose her temper and collapse in a faint, hitting her head so hard against the stone floor that she took to her bed, dazed and incoherent, before leaving us in the night, a lonely end to a life that had been filled with kindness and love. The fight had been over a piece of marketplace gossip that suggested Adria was behaving indiscreetly with a handsome boy barely on the cusp of manhood, the grandson of one of my late father's friends. Adria did not deny the accusation. In fact, she seemed to take a certain pride in her seduction of the lad.

Although I retained a natural loyalty toward my sister, I had long since grown disenchanted by her behavior, not least because she had taken against my wife from the moment I first brought her to Teotihuacan, treating her like a person who could not be trusted and going out of her way to be unpleasant. At first, her spitefulness had been subtle—referring to her by my first wife's name, for example, or leaving the table one place short when she cooked for the family—but in time it became obvious that these little acts of tyranny were designed to hurt. There was a possessiveness to Adria that had always unsettled me and we shared such dark secrets that I had begun to feel that it might be healthier if there were more distance between us.

"Why does she hate me so?" Kalisha asked one evening as we walked along the Avenue of the Dead, making our way toward the Pyramid of the Sun. The structure itself was centuries old and I liked to imagine my forefathers dragging stones toward it under the gaze of the Cerro Gordo, confident that their descendants would enjoy the fruits of their labors until the end of time. The designs across the rockface depicted panthers, snakes, elephants, as well as beasts that were unfamiliar to me, and whenever I pressed my hand against the stone, I felt that I was drawing in the essence of generations past.

Once, as I climbed to the summit, I had stood alone to stare across the landscape of the city and a combination of blistering heat and an empty stomach must have played tricks on me, for I experienced a series of curious visions. The pictures that flickered across my mind seemed so real that the sun rose and set twice more before my daze began to clear. During that time, I felt the spirit of Spearthrower Owl descend upon me and since then, whenever I had felt in need of inspiration, I had come here, hoping that I would receive another revelation but, to my disappointment, the phenomenon had never been repeated since. "What did I ever do to insult her?"

"It's not you," I said, lifting our hands together and kissing her fingers tenderly. A small boy walking past giggled at our display of affection, and when I stamped my foot against the cracked clay beneath me to startle him, he ran off with a scream. "She's had a bad strain to her character since childhood. There are things that she's done—"

"Such as?"

I hesitated. I did not like keeping secrets from my wife but had decided against revealing some of the more iniquitous moments of my life.

"She has a temper," I replied. "And she hates to be challenged. In your case, I think it's because she's always felt envious of any woman who I love more than her."

"Was she equally rude to Laria?" she asked.

"No," I said, shaking my head. "Although, since she lived for only a few hours after our wedding, Adria didn't have much opportunity to come between us. But it's best not to think about these things. She can't hurt you in any way, my beloved. No one can. Not while I have breath in my body."

Kalisha appeared unconvinced. A gentle woman, she hated conflict, and it hurt her to be on the receiving end of any animosity, particularly when she had worked so hard to win the affections of my family. Of course, Adria's great triumph over my wife was that she was now the mother of six children while Kalisha and I had yet to bring a baby into the world. There had been moments of hope, when her belly had started to grow big, but on each of those occasions, she had woken in the night with blood spilling down her legs, the child lost to us before it even had a chance to witness its first dawn.

"Brother, you must be pleased with your choice of bride," Adria remarked on her most recent visit to our home, and I'd turned to her warily, certain that some clever insult was about to come my way.

"I am," I agreed, doing my best to make my voice heard above the clamor of my nephews and nieces, who were like farmyard animals in their want of manners. "Is there a reason you suggest this now?"

"Because life must be a lot more peaceful when you're not surrounded by shrieking children," she replied, waving a hand toward her boisterous flock. "A barren field has a certain serenity to it, after all."

Kalisha looked across in shock at the crude nature of these remarks before stepping outside, lost in her own thoughts. Although initially reluctant to become a mother, she now longed for it and her monthly disappointment had become a source of great distress to her.

"Was that really necessary?" I asked, rising now to follow my wife. "Why must you be so cruel?"

Adria merely shrugged her shoulders. "Honestly?" she asked. "It helps to pass the time, Brother. I have to find my pleasures where I can."

· · ·

As I was, at heart, a peaceful man with no passion for warfare, perhaps it was a little incongruous that I had been crafting swords since I was a boy. There was such satisfaction to be found in selecting a choice piece of steel, heating it to the right temperature in the scalding heart of a forge and then using my hammers to create a fine, smooth blade. The design of the grip was particularly important to me, as was finding an appropriate jewel for the pommel, and I signed each of my creations with the symbol of the pyramid on the chappe, an autograph to mark the sword as one of my own. My skills as a craftsman were well known and, while I was content to make a weapon for anyone who could afford my price, I was at my happiest when asked to create an elaborate sword for some wealthy soldier who wanted his instrument of death to be admired by his victims even as he used it to remove their heads.

It was while I was working on one such piece for a local ajaw, a beautiful foil with a star-shaped emerald as its centerpiece, that my cousin Hagi entered my workshop on his sticks, followed by the boy, Perro. Any sword that bore my pyramid needed to be of the highest merit and, unfortunately, Perro had not proved himself to be worthy of the task and so, a few days earlier, I had been forced to tell him that I could use him no more. He'd taken the news badly, although not quite as badly as Hagi, who had been avoiding me ever since. I felt a certain sense of dread, therefore, when I saw them arrive together.

Putting down my tools, I stepped away from the forge and greeted them politely.

"You're busy, Cousin?" asked Hagi, looking around at the collection of blades, hilts and scabbards that were scattered on tables in various stages of preparedness.

"As ever," I replied.

"Too much for one man, I suppose?"

I smiled. It hadn't taken long for him to get to the point. "Hagi," I said. "I know you're upset that I wasn't able to continue Perro's employment, but—"

"I'm just worried for you, that's all," he said, sitting down and propping his crutches up against the wall. "To have so many commissions and be forced to spend such long hours here. Your wife must miss you, surely?"

"My wife is content," I said, a note of caution in my tone. I understood his desire to recover his friend's job, but I didn't appreciate his invoking Kalisha's name. Still, recognizing that I'd caused some difficulties for Perro, I stepped over to the steel box I had built into the wall, and for which I and I alone had the key. Opening it, I withdrew some coins and handed them to him. "I know it's not much," I said. "But this should keep you going until you find something else. You're a skilled worker, my friend, and in time perhaps you will—"

"If he's so skilled, then why are you sending him away?" asked Hagi, raising his voice now.

"Because he's not good enough," I said. "Not for me. It's that simple."

"I know I can improve," said Perro, speaking now for the first time. "If you would have patience with me, I'm sure that in time I—"

"I'm sorry," I said, shaking my head. "I don't have time to be anyone's teacher. My work keeps me busy enough as it is without adding mentorship to my duties."

"Cousin," said Hagi, standing up and hobbling toward me, taking my hand in his. "Perro tells me that if he cannot return to work here, then he will be left with no choice but to return to Tapachula."

"Well, so be it," I said, uncertain why he thought this would have any particular effect on me. After all, I barely knew the boy, I was not responsible for his welfare, and if he was to return to his own family in the south of the country, then I would likely have forgotten him before they'd even finished welcoming him home.

"But his village is three weeks' ride from here," continued Hagi, raising his voice now in frustration. "If he goes, he will never return."

I stared at him, feeling a growing sense of irritation. Turning to Perro, I asked him whether he might leave Hagi and me alone for a few minutes and he nodded before stepping outside. When he was gone, I closed the door and turned back to my cousin.

"What is this all about?" I asked. "I know you're fond of the boy, but—"

"I'm more than fond of him," he said. "We care deeply for each other."

"You don't mean that you're still engaged in intimacies with him?"

"I love him, Cousin," said Hagi. "He must stay here. I cannot go with him. Tapachula is not the place for a cripple like me. His family would never accept me."

I considered it for a moment but knew that I could not change my mind. "I'm sorry," I replied. "I don't want to hurt you, you must know that, but you're behaving like a fool."

"A fool?" he repeated, looking outraged.

"Yes, a fool. Find a wife, Hagi. I know you think that no woman would want you with your twisted—"

"It has nothing to do with that," he insisted. "I don't want a wife; can't you understand that? I want Perro! Only Perro!"

"And I want to return to my work," I sighed, running a hand across my eyes in exhaustion. "So, if there's nothing else?"

"I've never asked you for anything before, Cousin," he said, stepping so close to me now that the look of determination on his face frightened me a little. "I've been your friend and ally since the day my mother, may her name be remembered forever in glory, brought me to your house as a child. But I'm asking you for this. Let Perro work for you. Please. Train him. Allow him to stay in the village. I'm begging you, Cousin. Do this for me and I will never ask for anything again. Not as long as I live."

I turned away, wondering whether there was a way that I could give him what he wanted. The look of desperation on Hagi's face was almost enough to convince me to reconsider, but, in the end, I knew that I had to put the consistency of my craftsmanship before any personal loyalties and so, with regret, I shook my head.

"I'm sorry," I told him. "There is very little that I wouldn't do for you if I could. But you ask too much, my friend. On this matter, I cannot help you."

He closed his eyes and breathed heavily through his nose, remaining that way, as if trapped in stone, for almost a minute. When he opened them again, he looked at me with an expression I had never seen before, one of contempt mixed with a desire to inflict pain. Such coldness unsettled me, and I hoped that he might say something to forgive my refusal, but instead, he simply gathered his sticks and walked slowly out of the workshop.

EGYPT

A.D. 767

LOOKING BACK, I wonder whether perhaps I behaved selfishly in placing my standing as an artist over a friendship that had endured since childhood. But having spent my entire life on the banks of the Canal of the Pharaohs, painting images on the hulls of the ships that transported their goods along the towns and cities between the Nile and the Red Sea, I did not want to see my position usurped by any of my competitors. It was the same consideration I put into choosing my commissions, preferring the more complicated and extravagant ideas, and it pleased me to know that the routes of the silk trade were populated by dozens of boats enlivened by my art.

And so, when the great Caliph Al-Mansur, may his name be remembered forever in glory, announced that he was closing the passageway as punishment to the rebellious states in the south, I grew worried that my business would no longer be viable. My wife, Khepri, an optimist by nature, did her best to reassure me that we would survive on what we had saved until the notoriously fickle Caliph reversed his decision, but I could tell that she was worried, too, particularly now that our family of two had become three, our son, Eshaq, being almost a year old by then.

This came as a further strain on a life that was already suffering under the weight of uninvited troubles. My beloved cousin, Hager, with whom I had scarcely exchanged a cross word in two decades, had become estranged from me. Even when I became a father, he failed to offer his congratulations or to bring a gift for the child, despite knowing how long Khepri and I had waited to be so blessed. And, as if one family discord was not enough, my sister Abra's regular complaints and insults, not to mention her insistent belief that I could somehow resolve them for her, had become so overwhelming that I dreaded seeing her walking toward me, her face always red with fury and perceived slights.

"We could move further north," I suggested one evening when Khepri and I were discussing our savings, which were beginning to diminish as my contracts dried up. "Toward Alexandria, perhaps?"

She looked across at me in surprise. "I thought you didn't want to leave your hometown?" she said.

"I don't," I replied. "But if I cannot work, then we cannot eat. And I left it once before, remember? When I met you. So I'm not frightened of what the world might hold for me."

"And your family?" she asked. "I find it hard to imagine you living without them."

I shrugged my shoulders. After all, my parents were both dead, Hager and I weren't speaking, and Abra was an endless source of distress. Perhaps it would do me good to start afresh elsewhere.

"The only people I need are you and Eshaq," I told her. "What do you say? There's nothing to stop us leaving if we want to."

She considered it for a moment before nodding her head. "It could be a great adventure," she said, her face lighting up as she smiled. "Why not?"

. . .

Of course, when I told Abra of our plans to leave Ismaïlia, she grew enraged.

"It's her fault, isn't it?" she said, spitting out the words like pomegranate seeds. "She's making you do this! This has been her plan all along."

"I assume you're talking about Khepri?" I asked, weary of her jealousy.

"Who else would I mean? She has you just where she wants you, Brother. She won't be happy until she's taken you away from everyone and everything that you've ever known."

"The canal is closed, Abra," I cried, throwing my hands in the air in frustration. "Tell me, how do I make my living painting hulls when there are no hulls to paint? Explain that to me and I will reconsider!"

She shook her head violently, for, of course, there was no solution to this conundrum. Sitting down at her table, she put her head in her hands and began to weep. From the next room, I could hear her husband singing songs to himself. The tallest man in Ismaïlia, one whose height almost defied possibility, he was as skilled a singer as I was a fighter.

"You can't leave me alone with him," she said, lowering her voice now. "Please, Brother, I cannot bear to be around him, and at night, when he touches me . . ." She shivered, wrapping her arms around herself. I had no interest in knowing the details of their connubial activities, nor did I want to picture how a man so uncommonly tall achieved congress with a woman so exceptionally short.

"Sister," I said, turning away and putting my hands to my ears. "Please. No more, I beg of you."

"I could always come with you," she suggested, and I turned back to her with a frown.

"Come with me where?"

"To Alexandria."

"And what about your husband?"

"Oh, who cares? He can stay here. It's not as if I have any feelings for him, other than disdain. He was supposed to die long ago, remember? I would never have married him if I'd known that he was still going to be alive all these years later."

"And your children? You would abandon them, too?"

"They're monsters, every one," she said, dismissing them with a wave of her hand. "All they do is drag me down every moment of the day. The problem is, they're always *there*. I never have a moment to myself. No, let the children remain with Xart, he seems fond of them anyway. The oldest can look after the next in line, then she can look after the next, and so on."

"The younger ones have barely started walking!"

She considered this. "I suppose they'll just have to look after themselves," she said with a shrug. "It will toughen them up. They'll probably end up thanking me for it one day."

I shook my head. The depths of her cruelty astonished me at times. "No," I said. "Absolutely not. It cannot happen."

"But why not?" she asked, kneeling on the floor and taking my hands in hers. "Haven't we always taken care of each other in the past? You protected me once before, Brother, if you recall? Twice, in fact."

I closed my eyes and pulled away.

"I need you to save me again," she continued, her voice growing quieter now. "Once more and I will never ask anything of you for the rest of our days. Just take me to Alexandria. When I'm there, I'll leave you in peace, I promise. I'm still an attractive woman, or so people tell me. Perhaps I could find a new husband and—"

"No," I insisted, raising a hand in the air.

"But why not?"

"Because it is not my place to separate a husband from his wife. Let alone leave a group of children without a mother."

"Well, what if Xart was to meet an accident?" she asked, growing animated now. "Would you take me with you then? And if I brought one or two of the children with us, would that soothe your conscience? Which ones are your favorites? Pick a couple and they can come. Any except the baby. He never stops mewling."

"Stop it!" I shouted, jumping to my feet. "Whatever schemes are running through your mind, you can forget them, as I won't be involved. Khepri, Eshaq and I will be leaving in a week's time, just the three of us, and you will stay here, so make your peace with it. I won't discuss it any further."

Again, her expression changed, this time from entreatment to disgust. "Eshaq!" she said, rolling her eyes and looking at me as if I was a fool. "You don't even know that the boy is yours! I've heard stories, Brother. I know that you like to act as if Khepri is a saint among women, but she has a past. And a scandalous one at that."

"What are you talking about?" I asked, growing angry now. "Where have you heard such things?"

"Oh, gossip spreads as easily as disease, you know that. From what I've heard, your angelic wife was once quite popular with the men of Wadi Rum. All those lonely travelers, looking for a willing body to help them discharge their passions. She offered a good service to them, too, didn't she? I don't blame you for bringing her back to Ismaïlia with you. She must know tricks that honest women don't."

My hands clenched into fists. It took all my willpower not to strike her down.

"Perhaps she's continued her ways here?" she mused. "Have you never considered that? Does she like variety, Brother? After all, Eshaq doesn't really look like you and—"

"For you, of all the women in this town, to call my wife a whore," I said, marching quickly toward the door before I lost control of my emotions. "When the dogs in the street know how many boys you've seduced."

"Someone needs to introduce them to the delights of the flesh," she said without an ounce of repentance in her tone. "Their enthusiasm is always stimulating. And unlike Khepri, I don't charge them for their pleasures. What I give, I give for free."

I couldn't find words to express my disgust but, as angry as I was with Abra, I also felt a certain anxiety. She had never been one to accept defeat gracefully. Until my wife, son and I had the palaces of Alexandria in our sights, I knew that I would not feel safe.

· · ·

A week later, on my last day in Ismaïlia, I made my way down to my workshop to collect the last of my brushes and paints but also to say farewell to the friends I had made in the boatyard over the years. Many of them had worked alongside my father and, as I had grown up in their company, they were like surrogate uncles to me.

A friend who worked as a carpenter on the shore, Sef, arrived to complete the purchase of some tools that I was leaving behind, and we sat outdoors, drinking jugs of his home-brewed heket, and reminiscing as we looked over the banks of the canal, wondering whether it might ever host ships again. As we talked, I observed a man walking along the path and slowing down a little when he noticed us, although not drawing to a halt. He was strongly muscled, with a shaved head and a familiar expression, and he wore a pair of intimidating daggers on either hip, a star-shaped emerald rooted into the hilt of one. When he caught my eye, he smiled in a peculiar way, betraying no hint of warmth.

"Who was that?" asked Sef when he'd passed. I shook my head, trying to place the stranger. I knew him from somewhere but could not, at that moment, recall exactly where our paths had crossed. In Alexandria, I wondered? Was he a servant of the Caliph?

"I'm not sure," I said, unsettled by his strange countenance. "Did you recognize him?"

"No, but it looked as if he knew you," he replied, and then we let the matter go, watching as the sun began to descend. When the time came to say farewell I embraced my old friend, wishing him great luck in life, before stepping back into the workshop for one final look around. A box in the corner caught my eye and I took it in my hands, kneeling down to examine its contents. Illuminated designs for hulls that no one had wanted as yet, images that were too elaborate or colorful for current tastes but that might be of use in my future endeavors. One in particular attracted me. A design based on the constellations of the stars. When I was a boy, I had often thought of such things and was surprised now to find that this fascination had found its way into images that I had no memory of drawing.

I packed them into a dark brown leather satchel with my initials carved into the pelt, hoping that, once we were living in Alexandria, I might persuade the Caliph to allow me to experiment even more. I would talk to Khepri about it once we left, I decided. I would show her my designs and seek her advice. Surely she would feel proud at how far we had both come from the disreputable inn where we had first met in Wadi Rum.

Wadi Rum.

As the name of that terrible place came into my mind, a burst of recognition tore through my body with a powerful shock. The papers I was holding fell from my hand, scattering around my feet, and I leaped up, growing dizzy, so much so that I was forced to reach a hand out to steady myself against the wall.

The man. The big, burly, daggered man who had smiled at me

outside. I remembered now where I had seen him before. Our paths had crossed only once, a few years earlier, when I had traveled north to the Caliph's palace, staying in this man's inn to break the tedium of my journey, and he had denied me breakfast because I'd woken late. And then, upon my return, I had stolen his daughter from that poisonous house, bringing her to what I hoped would prove a better life. Had he been looking for her ever since?

Leave me again, he had told her once, *and I will hunt you down and strip the skin from your bones.*

And, sure enough, she had left him.

I raced through the streets. As I passed Abra's home, I saw her standing outside, emptying a bucket of dirty water into the street, and she watched me as I ran past her. It was the only moment when I slowed my pace, and I saw her face break into a smile as enigmatic as my wife's father's.

"Still planning on leaving, Brother?" she shouted, but my heart was pounding so fast in my chest that I could not even conceive of replying. I ran on, putting her from my mind, my lungs starting to burn with the effort, and finally, when my home came into sight, I narrowed my eyes, praying that I would see my wife and son standing outside, carrying our belongings to be loaded onto the buggy for our journey.

But no; to my dismay, the street was empty.

I stopped outside our door, my hands on my hips, bent over and breathing heavily, frightened to go inside for fear of what I might find there. A voice sounded from behind me, whispering my name, and I turned to see Tesera, the blind woman whom I had known since I was a child.

"You must go inside, son of Mavira," she said, standing next to me and placing her hand upon my shoulder.

"I can't," I said.

"You must see what he did."

"What did he do? Tell me. Don't make me look."

"Your wife is lost to you," she whispered. "Your son, too. Gone to the world from which no man may return." She reached into a pouch and removed two small glass vials filled with a transparent liquid, offering one to me. "You can drink this if you want," she said. "And you will join them before the sun rises in the morning. But if you do, then I will drink the other. My life has been long. Perhaps it is time to begin the next one."

I stared at her. The door lay open before me and I knew that the moment I stepped inside, the life I had once known would come to an end and I would be faced with a new reality, one that would be filled once again with pain and grief. This would be the last moment of hope that I would feel for many years.

"You must not give in," she said, burying my head in her shoulder. "There are many lives ahead of you yet, son of Mavira, and I see them all. One day, I promise it, you will live among the stars."

. . .

I chose to use the two daggers that the innkeeper had left behind. The first lay next to the corpse of my wife, from which the skin had been stripped, as promised, before being piled in a pyramid of horror next to her mutilated body, while the other was pressed into the abdomen of my son, Eshaq.

I sat with the bodies until the sun set. Perhaps I thought about burying them; perhaps I didn't. This is a time that I cannot recall. I had already lost one wife and child and barely survived the trauma. At least with them, it had been an act of nature, one for which no mortal man had been responsible. But this, what had taken place in my home, was a premeditated massacre. All I could see was my sister Abra standing outside her own house with that inscrutable smile on her face.

Of course, I decided, Abra was responsible for these slaughters.

She had tracked down Khepri's father and revealed our whereabouts. This was how far she would go to keep hold of me. What had happened to her, I wondered? What had made her so possessive that she would cause the death of my wife and son in order to satisfy her own desires when she surely knew our own relationship would come to an end at that same moment?

Regaining my senses, I placed the daggers in my pockets, their blades still wet with blood, and made my way through the town. Some of my neighbors stared at me in surprise, wondering why I was still there, but I ignored their questions and continued along the road, never more determined than I was at that moment. I was in no hurry and felt a strange sense of contentment, knowing what I had to do next and how easy and satisfying it would be.

When I reached Abra's house, I walked inside calmly and discovered her sitting in a chair, repairing one of her husband's tunics. I stepped toward her without a word, placing my right hand around her throat and lifting her against the wall. It had only taken a moment and I was gratified to see the expression of surprise and terror in her eyes.

"Because I wouldn't bring you with me?" I whispered. "For that, you would see them die?"

She gagged, trying to speak, her eyes bulging in their sockets, but I squeezed her tighter about the throat.

"Now you will experience what she experienced," I said, loosening my grip. "If you have anything to say, now is the time to say it. Because your life is about to end."

I took one of the daggers from the pocket of my tunic and pressed its sharp tip against her right eye. I thought it would be a just punishment to slowly, very slowly, press upon the hilt until it passed through her skull and emerged on the other side.

"It wasn't me," she said, choking. "I swear it wasn't me. I didn't write to him."

"Of course it was you," I said, spitting my words against her face. "*Gossip spreads as easily as disease,* that's what you told me, remember? You knew about her. You found him. He came. And he killed her. He killed Eshaq, too. Was that part of your plan? To have the blood of an innocent child on your hands, along with that of my wife?"

"It wasn't me!" she insisted as my grip tightened against her throat.

"You were the only one who knew!" I roared, my emotions coming through at last. "Who else could have told him, if not you?"

"I confided in someone," she cried, tears rolling down her face. "If I am guilty of anything, Brother, it is of betraying your wife's secret. But nothing more!"

I took a step back, loosening my grip now, and there was something in her expression that gave me pause.

"Who?" I asked in confusion. "Who did you tell? Who would hate me enough to find Khepri's father and bring him here to commit such monstrous acts?"

She coughed repeatedly, horrible choking sounds that suggested just how close I had brought her to death. And at that same moment, as she tried to draw breath, another voice echoed in my mind.

The voice of my mother.

Be careful of him, my son. You think he loves you as you love him, but I fear there is another side to him . . . If he can ever find a way to hurt you, he will.

"Hager," I whispered, looking at my sister with disbelief in my eyes.

"He was here," she said. "He blames you, Brother, for the boy he lost. He hates you. He's always hated you, since we were children, only you were too blind to see it."

I stared at her. It was inconceivable that the man I thought of as a cousin would go to such terrible lengths for vengeance.

"He never imagined that she would be killed," she continued, reading my mind. "Or that Eshaq would die, too. He thought only that her father would take her away, back to Wadi Rum. Back to his whorehouse. He wanted you to lose your love, as he had lost his. He didn't know what the man was capable of. If you'd seen him, if you'd seen how upset he was—"

"You saw him?" I asked.

"He came here," she said. "Not long before you. He was distraught."

"Where is he now?"

"Gone," she said, shaking her head. "He knew what you would do when you discovered their bodies. You'll never find him, Brother. He took a horse and fled. He didn't say where. The world is his to travel."

I nodded, then took a step forward again, our bodies separated only by the rising and falling of our stomachs. I looked my sister in the eye, certain that she had told me all she knew and that she had spoken the truth. She might not have been the one responsible for the death of my loved ones, but she had given my cousin enough information for him to take that duty for himself.

Khepri's father had taken good care of his knives. The first slid easily through Abra's clothes before entering her heart, while the second made quick work of her skull. I saw her eyes open wide in surprise for a moment, then horror, then agony, before turning black and lifeless.

So I had three deaths on my conscience now. But now, at last, my life had a purpose. No matter how long it took to find him, I would track my cousin down and make him suffer for what he had done.

PART 5

THE
THREE
JEWELS

IRELAND

AD. 800

HOPED ONLY FOR PEACE when I arrived at the monastery. At first, I felt a degree of caution about approaching the tower, uncertain whether or not I, a man of no particular religious scruple, would be turned away from a place of holy men. But after several hours of sitting in a field with my back pressed against a willow tree, doing all I could to present an innocent facade so that any of the monks observing me from their embrasures would feel reassured that I presented no threat to their way of life, a door opened at the base of the stronghold and an elderly man clothed in brown robes stepped outside. He looked at me for a long time before glancing left and right warily to see whether I was alone and then summoned me forward with an expression that suggested uncomplicated acceptance.

He spoke not a word as he led me through the stone ramparts and up a winding staircase, where, at the top, he knocked on a wooden door and waited for a voice from inside to call out that we might enter. When we did, I found myself in a cold, sparsely furnished stone room, where I took a seat opposite a tightly tonsured abbot, Brother Finbar, and tapped a finger to my lips to indicate that I was a mute. This was one of the few lies that I told during my time there, and it was a deceit that I did not maintain for long, but I had no desire for conversation and did not want to explain to these men the circumstances that had brought me there.

I had chosen Kells because word had spread throughout Ireland of a Great Book that was being illustrated there by a group of monks. The illumination of manuscripts had been my calling since I was a boy. Brother Finbar asked me some questions about my life and why I had come to him and I managed, through paper, quill and ink, to convince him that I had spent some years in an abbey in the barbarian country across the water but had been repulsed by their godless ways and love of ornament and felt that here I might rediscover the life of simple servitude that had first drawn me to the Lord. Also, I added, I had a very particular set of skills that might prove useful to him.

I had carried some of my designs with me in a dark brown leather satchel with my initials carved into the pelt, illustrations that I'd taken from my workshop in Wexford on the morning that I left, having buried my second wife and son in the local cemetery and hidden the body of my sister in a mountain grave that I dug overnight. There had been some questions raised about Ailbhe's sudden disappearance but, in a stroke of good luck, one of the more handsome youths of the parish vanished that same day, running away from a violent father, and it was generally assumed that she had joined him, for she had a predilection for boys of his age.

The abbot looked through my pages now, examining the intricacy of my work, and I could tell by the expression on his face that he was impressed.

"Your designs are very fine," he told me. "How long have you devoted yourself to your craft?"

I held both hands in the air, the fingers separated from each other.

"Ten years," he said. "And you worked on sacred books for the heathens across the way?"

I nodded.

"They'd have been sorry to see you go, I imagine," he said. "There's monks here who've been working on the Great Book for years, they're twice your age and don't have half your skill. Tell me this, though: you're showing me nothing but papyrus here. Have you worked on calf vellum before? Because that's what we're using."

I nodded again.

"And iron gall ink? It soaks into the page as quickly as anything I've ever seen. You've no room for mistakes, or days of work can be squandered in a heartbeat."

I nodded for a third time, then shrugged my shoulders as if to suggest that I had practically invented calf vellum, when, in truth, I had never even heard of such a thing. Glancing toward the cross on the wall behind him, I noticed a wooden statue of Jesus staring back at me with pity in his eyes, and I wondered whether He could look into the depths of my soul and see both the mendacity and the rage that coexisted within.

"You're fierce thin, all the same," continued Brother Finbar, looking me up and down with a frown. "Have you eaten? Are you starving, is that it? Did they not feed you on the boat across, no?"

I shook my head but waved a hand in the air to say that I was fine, despite the fact that I was ravenous, for it had taken me five days to walk the distance from Wexford to Meath and I'd had precious little to eat along the way. But the sun was waning, and I guessed that, soon, the monks would gather together for their evening meal, when I would surely be invited to join them. I could wait until then for sustenance.

"We'll welcome you so," said the abbot, handing me back my drawings and taking me downstairs to introduce me to the men whose company I would be sharing, forty of them, old and young, all of whom sat at long wooden tables waiting for their stew and watching me carefully to decide whether or not I might represent some threat to their positions. This might be a holy place, I would soon learn, but there was a hierarchy to it that would not be challenged.

The monks were informed that I was an Englishman, but I was no Englishman, and regretted not having told Brother Finbar that I was Scots or French or some other nationality, as there was not a man in the country who would stand up to let an Englishman sit down. Still, they were men of God, even if I was not, and I hoped that they would treat me fairly.

"The poor man has no voice," the abbot continued as the pots of food arrived. "So, don't be trying to get into any conversations with him, as you've more chance of drawing blood from a stone. Am I right, Brother?" he asked, turning to me, and I smiled beatifically. "Grand so," he said, indicating an empty seat next to an elderly man who I would come to know as Brother Ultan. "Sit down there now, like a good man, and eat your stew while it's hot."

I did as instructed and the food might have been hot, cold or somewhere in between for all the difference it made to me. It was food and it was good and while my spirits had all but abandoned me over the previous week, it gave me a sudden and much-needed sensation of well-being.

. . .

The work itself was more rewarding than I could possibly have hoped for and, to my surprise, I found that daily life in the monastery suited me as I grew to appreciate its unvarying repetition. I woke shortly before five o'clock in the morning, when I joined the monks as we made our way toward the chapel for Lauds, and then, after breakfast, we separated into different groups. There were two cellarers who organized the meals throughout the day, three sacrists who maintained the books in the library and took care of the vestments, a half-dozen or more who toiled in the gardens, growing vegetables and looking after the livestock, while the rest of us were the artists who spent our hours working on the Great Book. We'd stop at noon for the Little Hours of the Divine Office, partake of a small lunch and then return to our work in the afternoon before vespers and dinner. It was painstaking work, hard on the eyes, but the hours passed like seconds.

I had been charged with working on a page of the Gospel according to Saint Matthew and, before I began, I spent a few days studying the work that the monks had already completed in order to bring my illustrations into line with theirs. It was thrilling to observe their artistry. I'd never seen anything so intricate and recognized that, in these men, I had at last encountered not only my artistic equals but my superiors. Losing myself in their skillfulness allowed me to quieten my grief and I was grateful for such relief. There was no conversation as we worked; instead, each monk bent over his page with pens and inks, trying to capture as much of the light as he could before evening fell. A page could take as much as a month to complete and was set aside only after it had been approved by Brother Finbar, who employed a large magnifying glass with a carving of a snake on the surround to check every image and word. Naturally, we used the Vulgate as our source, the Latin Bible that Saint Jerome had composed for Pope Damasus four hundred years earlier, and our task was to transcribe it exactly.

Mistakes could be costly, as was proven when Brother Daragh made an error that spoiled weeks of effort. He'd been transcribing the Sermon on the Mount from Chapter Five and slipped from "Blessed are the peacemakers" to "Blessed are you when people insult you" without adding "Blessed are those who are persecuted because of righteousness" in between the two. The page was close to completion and if it hadn't been for another of the monks happening to glance at it and noticing the oversight, it might have made it all the way to Brother Finbar's desk. Poor Brother Daragh saw all his work on the page ruined and he tore it into shreds, scattering the scraps on the floor as tears dripped down his face. I wanted to offer solace, but as none of the other monks even glanced in his direction, let alone tried to console him, I did nothing, lest I betray the fact that I was not truly one of them. The poor man barely recovered from the trauma, however, and died a few days later. Although, in fairness, that was because a rabid dog bit him when he was out for a walk and he came down with an infection, so the two events were not, in fact, connected. Although there were some who suggested the fatal injury had come about as divine retribution from a vengeful God.

I was careful that no similar errors should appear in my work, poring over every word, drawing, line and color to ensure that my lettering and illustrations were as close to perfection as I could achieve. I created an image of six peacocks wrapped together, a symbol of eternal life, and the ink fell on the page as if it had been torn from its natural bed centuries before and was only delighted to be reunited at last. At night, when I fell into my bed, my hands a rainbow of color, I felt fortunate to have discovered the monastery and might have even begun to believe in a God to whom I pretended to pray, had it not been for the fact that he'd already robbed me of two wives, a son and an unborn baby, when I had done nothing but try to live an honest life. No, there was no god for me, save

Nemesis, the old Greek deity whose purpose in the eternal sphere was to exact vengeance upon wrongdoers and miscreants.

· · ·

Occasionally in the evenings I would take a turn about the gardens, my eyes needing to relax after a day of squinting over a set of intricate illuminations, and it was on one of those nights, as the sun began to descend, that I encountered Brother Ultan, who I had sat beside at dinner on my first night at the abbey. Brother Ultan was the oldest member of our community and looked every day of his eighty years. A bag of skin, sinew and bones, he had a face full of white whiskers and a mouth full of yellow teeth. Age had not diminished his faith, however, for he was one of the most devoted of the monastery's congregation. I witnessed him weeping regularly at church and when I saw him emerge from the confessional on a daily basis, I wondered what sins could possibly stain the soul of a man who had spent so much of his life cloistered within these bulwarks. He slept in the cell next to mine and our beds would have been pressed together, were it not for the stone wall that separated us.

On this particular evening, however, he waved in my direction and I nodded back, intending to walk on, but he beckoned me toward him, and, for politeness's sake, I obeyed. Strolling over, I took my place on the bench next to him and, for a time, we remained silent as we sat side by side enjoying the beauty of the land that surrounded us. When he finally spoke, however, his question could not have surprised me more.

"Tell me this and tell me no more," he said quietly. "Who is Kathleen and who is Éanna?"

I turned to look at him, astonished to hear those names spoken aloud, for I had neither heard nor uttered them since taking my leave of Wexford some months earlier. I thought about standing up and walking away but Brother Ultan was studying me with a faint smile on his face and I saw that he meant no malice by his question. "You can answer in words rather than signs," he added after a few moments. "I know that you're no mute, even if you've fooled everyone else into thinking otherwise."

"How did you know?" I asked, and it had been so long since I had spoken aloud that the words cracked as they came from my lips, my voice sounding like a foreign instrument even to my own ears.

"Sure don't I hear you through the wall?" he asked. "Every few nights, when you have one of your nightmares, I hear you calling out their names. Kathleen and Éanna. So I've grown intrigued, you might say, although of course this is none of my business and if you don't want to tell me, then I won't press you for an answer."

I looked down at the grass beneath my feet. It was true that my sleep was often disturbed and there were nights when I woke in a cold sweat, but never had I imagined that I had cried out and been overheard.

"Kathleen was my wife," I said, deciding that it would do me good to have a confidant. "And Éanna, my son."

"They're dead, I suppose?"

"They are," I said.

"Will you tell me how?"

"Murdered," I told him. "Kathleen ran away with me against her father's wishes, so he hunted her down and killed her, along with the lad. It took him a long time to find her, but I should have known that he wouldn't stop until he did. I'd put him from my mind long since. I thought we were safe. I was a fool."

"And that's why you're here, is it?" he asked. "Because I know you've not taken holy orders, no matter how easily you've tricked Brother Finbar. When you first arrived, it was obvious that you hadn't the first clue when to stand, when to sit or when to kneel when you were at the Mass. Did you not attend as a boy, no?"

"It wasn't part of my life," I said.

"Are you not a believer?"

"If I ever was, I'm not any more."

"Then why did you come here? Why not somewhere else?"

I thought about it for a long time before answering.

"I came for the silence," I told him. "And for the peace. Right now, I know that it is best if I am at a remove from the world. I've committed acts that would surely send me to hell, if I believed in the existence of such a place. I need a period on my own before I undertake what will surely be the crucial mission of my life."

"Have you asked for forgiveness?"

I laughed a little and shook my head. "From who?" I asked. "Who has the power to grant me such a thing?"

He sighed and intertwined his fingers as he fell silent, wrestling with the notion that there were some of us who did not believe in the existence of a world outside the one that we could see with our own eyes.

"I had a wife, too, you know," he said eventually in a quiet voice, and I turned to him in surprise.

"You can become a monk if you were married?"

"Oh, you can, surely. She died, is the thing. Many years ago now. She got a terrible pain in her stomach one day and then it only grew worse and worse over time. Soon she could barely breathe on account of it. And then one night, she was screaming so much, the poor girl was in such agony, that I couldn't take another minute of it. I loved her dearly, do you see, and I knew that she hadn't long left for this world. So I was faced with a choice. I could let her live a few more days in torment or I could take the horror away from her. And I chose the latter."

I raised an eyebrow. "How did you do it?" I asked.

"That's neither here nor there," he replied. "We'll just say that I released her to God's gentle mercy, and that's enough for you to know."

"Is anyone else aware of this?"

"My confessors, of course. I received absolution a long time ago, but I still don't feel truly accepted back on to the path of righteousness. There are days when I'm glad I did what I did and days when I think I should have left it all to God. He gave her the suffering, maybe He had a reason for it, and it was up to Him to take it away again. After that I spent a couple of years living what you might call a life of debauchery before I came here. It's been good for me, this place. I think my life was always leading me toward it and I know I'll never leave Kells. My bones will turn to dust in that graveyard over there. But you don't intend to stay forever, do you?"

"No," I admitted.

"There's more on your mind than illustrating pages of the Great Book, I think."

I said nothing. I had been forming a plan and letting it build slowly in my mind. When the time was right, I would take my leave of the monastery and act upon it. But that time had not arrived just yet.

"You won't tell Brother Finbar the truth, will you?" I asked him finally.

"Not if you don't want me to, no, but something or someone, call it God or call it by some other name, brought me here and it's a place where I've found peace. If you let it, maybe it would offer you the same. But you're using it, I know that. You're using all of us. You're in pain, that much is obvious, but all you're doing right now is hiding away from the world, nothing more. Would you not give it a second chance, no?"

"I cannot," I said. "Not right now anyway. Perhaps someday."

I stood up, not wishing to continue this conversation any further.

"One last question?" he said before I left, and I turned around to look at him.

"Yes, Brother?" I asked.

"There's another name you call out. Hugh. Who is he, if you don't mind my asking?"

I shook my head. "I don't know," I lied. "I've never known a man with that name."

NEPAL

A.D. 862

PERHAPS THE MOST SERENE ASPECT of the monastery was its location in the heart of the Nepa Valley, where it was entirely surrounded by a vast forest of maple trees. As holy men, the monks welcomed any stranger who made his way through the woodland in search of sanctuary, no matter how dangerous or threatening he looked, and acts of violence within the walls were as rare as black swans. Many came and went during my time there, some remaining for several months, others for only a few days, but the focus was always on healing and enlightenment. It was considered indecorous to inquire of another person what had originally brought him to this refuge, but while the most common reasons were grief, loneliness, failure or sin, it proved simpler to remain ignorant of other people's stories.

My wife and son had been dead for eight months, and I had been in Swayambhunath for seven, when Girvesh arrived. He was little more than a boy when I opened the gate at his knock and, upon first seeing him, I did my best to conceal my shock at the sight of the scars that disfigured his slight body, deep, pitted burn marks that marred his forehead, cheeks, neck and arms. Some emerged like pernicious lumps upon his flesh, while others appeared taut, stretching the skin so tightly that it seemed almost translucent. When my eyes made contact with his, he lowered his gaze toward the ground and wrapped his arms around his chest, as if he wanted to squeeze himself into irrelevance. Here, I could tell, was a boy who did all that he could to remain invisible in the world, hiding his damaged countenance from anyone who crossed his path. He had come to the monastery, I guessed, to escape disgusted eyes.

To my surprise, however, before I could even utter a word of welcome, he fell to his knees and threw his arms out before him, a study in entreatment.

"Most revered holy man," he cried, the words tumbling out of him so quickly it was obvious that he had been rehearsing them. "Take pity on a weary supplicant who has been much injured by this cruel world and grant me the shelter of your monastery!"

"I am not a monk," I replied, reaching down to pull him to his feet. "Nor am I revered or holy. Quite a long way from both, in fact." He looked up at me then and, despite his many mutilations, it was impossible not to be struck by the beauty and innocence that lay behind his pale blue eyes. For someone so young, it seemed that he had already suffered untold agonies. "Tell me, though, what is your name?"

"Girvesh," he replied, and after offering my own, I invited him to follow me inside, closing the gate behind us. The sense of relief that emanated from him as he glanced around was tangible, his face filling with delight as he took in the magnificent stupa that stood at the heart of the monks' site and the temples and shrines surrounding it. My intention was to bring him directly to the office of Holy Faneel, as I had once been brought, for it was he who would decide whether Girvesh would be permitted to stay or not, but as I walked toward the entrance of that building, I saw the abbot sitting on the grass nearby in the company of some of the younger monks, all of whom were engaged in sound meditation as a small fountain trickled an endless supply of water into a pond.

I indicated to Girvesh that we should sit together until their prayers were completed and, as we took up the lotus position on the grass, I noted how badly swollen were his feet and wondered how long he had been walking, and from what great distance he had come.

It was a hot afternoon and as the sun beat down upon our heads, a half-dozen rhesus monkeys swung in the trees above us, chattering and whooping cheerfully. I had grown accustomed to their presence, for a large population of these mischief-makers lived peaceably among us in the temple and on the land. When one dropped a handful of nuts on the ground, he leaped down, landing at Girvesh's feet, and stared directly into the boy's face while scratching the underside of his chin, as if he was trying to decide whether this newcomer was worth conversing with or not. Girvesh laughed in boyish delight, turning to me with real pleasure on his face, and in that moment, he seemed even younger than I had originally taken him for.

"How old are you?" I asked.

"I have suffered fourteen birthdays," he replied. "Each one worse than the one before."

"And from where have you traveled?"

He hesitated for a moment before answering, as if uncertain about betraying too many of his secrets to a stranger. "Bharatpur," he said. "In the west. I walked all the way here. It has been a very painful journey, very painful indeed."

I glanced down at his feet again. As well as looking bloated, they were filthy with mud, cuts and blisters.

"I'd also traveled a great distance on foot when I first arrived in this place," I told him. "But in my cell, I have a small bowl filled with a white paste, infused with the scent of lavender and the aloe vera plant, and this will soothe your injured feet and bring the swelling down. After you have spoken to Holy Faneel, I will attend to your wounds."

He looked at me gratefully and massaged his toes with his fingers. A few minutes later, perhaps disturbed by our whispered conversation, Holy Faneel ended his prayers and rose, walking over to us with his hands held wide apart in a gesture of welcome. I stood up, as did Girvesh, and we bowed to each other, as I explained that I had discovered the boy at the gates and that he had come seeking our help.

"Are you running away from someone?" asked Holy Faneel, and the boy shook his head.

"I have no home," he said, a note of anxiety in his tone, for the abbot could be an intimidating figure in his red robe and jewelry, the six entwined peacocks of his shawl proving both daunting and hypnotic.

"Your mother?"

"Dead. The hour I came into the world was the hour she departed it."

"And your father?"

He hesitated now, briefly.

"Killed in the Bharatpur riots," he said. "There was nothing left for me then so I visited the temple and prayed to Siddhārtha Gautama Buddha for advice. Soon, a voice called out to me in the darkness and said that I should come here. To Swayambhunath."

Holy Faneel smiled but raised an eyebrow, looking skeptical. "You heard his voice?" he asked quietly. "The voice of the Buddha himself?"

"I believe so, yes," replied Girvesh nervously.

"Our friend here is skeptical about such things," he said, nodding in my direction. "He's not even convinced that the Buddha truly exists. And yet, when he was encouraged to spend a week alone in prayer to the sage of the Shakya clan for the return of his speech, he emerged able to converse as other men do."

Holy Faneel offered me a half-smile and I had the good grace to look discomfited. After months of feigning muteness, I had taken the opportunity offered by the monks' idea of a retreat of pure supplication to speak again, pretending to have emerged with my voice restored, but I had never been fully convinced that the abbot believed that it had been a gift from the prophet so much as a conscious decision on my part.

"Such a thing happened?" asked Girvesh, turning to me with a look of horror on his face, as if he had never heard of anything quite so heretic.

"It was a miracle," I replied.

"And yet you still question His presence in our lives?"

"I question everything, my young friend. I continually seek answers, as do all here."

"Don't worry, boy," continued Holy Faneel, placing a hand upon his shoulder. "He may not be a believer as yet, but he has been welcomed into our community and is, I hope, benefitting from his time here. You, too, will be welcomed if you feel that our temple has something to offer you. Is that what you want?"

"Very much," he replied.

Holy Faneel nodded, satisfied, and turned back to me, giving me instructions to take the boy to one of the guest rooms, which I did, and where we discovered four more monkeys lying on the empty mattress, enjoying the peace of the afternoon.

"They're considered holy in these parts," I told him as he sat down on the edge of the bed, and I retrieved the mixture I had spoken of, adding some clove oil, sage and mustard seeds, before massaging it into his tender young feet. He sighed in pleasure as the herbs blended into the broken skin, offering some much-needed relief. "So you would do well not to disturb them. They say that when Prince Mañjusri first built this holy place, he grew his hair for two years and two days, and when the lice formed in the roots, they grew so big that they transformed themselves into monkeys, before leaping out to create a colony of their own."

"So we do not eat them?" he asked, looking at each of the monkeys in turn and I couldn't help but laugh. The animals all screeched and gibbered, as if they were suddenly concerned that they might be destined for the oven.

"No," I said, shaking my head. "We do not eat them."

. . .

Holy Ujesh, the oldest monk at Swayambhunath, died later that week and I felt great sorrow at the loss of his companionship. Since my arrival at the monastery, we had slept in adjoining cells and he had offered me solace whenever I woke from my regular nightmares. He was the only person in whom I had confided the story of my life and he had reciprocated by telling me of the crime that weighed on his own conscience, but I knew that he had committed his actions out of love, and that a fair and just Buddha, if such an entity existed, would not condemn him for that.

He had been ill for some time and, in his final days, I sat by his bedside chanting parittas while a statue of the prophet stood next to his head and candles burned on all sides. He held my hand as his soul passed from this world to the next and there was agreement that he would surely be reincarnated in splendor as his samsara, the cycle of his life and death, had been a good one.

When the body grew cold, I washed and clothed it in the traditional monk's attire, ready for the cremation ceremony. Our community gathered as one to chant the Three Jewels—*I take refuge in the Buddha, I take refuge in the Dharma, I take refuge in the Sangha*—and when the fire was lit, I wondered whether his soul would travel onward now to reunite with his wife or whether he might be separated from her for several more incarnations yet. Girvesh, I noticed, was struck by the ceremony, both in awe of it and frightened by it at the same time, but when the stench of burning flesh filled the air, his face grew pale and he ran away, back to his room.

A fourteen-year-old boy repulsed by a cremation? Surely he had witnessed many in his life. His reaction struck me as peculiar and I determined to discover more about him.

· · ·

The path to enlightenment, Holy Ujesh had told me, could come only through the teachings of the Buddha but, despite the fact that I studied the sacred manuscripts in the monastic library, I remained skeptical that a spirit could pass into the body of another after death and continue its journey toward illumination. The books intrigued me, however, with their deceptively simply writing and I was touched by the ornate illustrations that covered each page. I was particularly moved by the curled symbol representing the unity of all matter within the world and often found myself becoming mesmerized by it. I had never had a talent for drawing but I appreciated the skill that had gone into each page, the depths of the eyes, the fantastical creatures, the many-winged dragons, and often found my way back to the library when the weather was inclement or my spirits were low simply to lose myself once again in their beauty.

It was on one such afternoon that I discovered Girvesh seated alone in the corner of the room, a manuscript open before him as he read the words slowly, his fingers sliding beneath each of the words.

"Am I disturbing you?" I asked, and he closed his book before turning to me with a welcoming smile. The scars on his face continued to prove an unforgiving blemish on his skin but, as we had grown close in recent weeks, I hoped that he would not mind me asking about them.

"Were you trapped in a fire?" I asked, and he shook his head.

"No," he replied.

"Scalded by water?"

"No."

"Will you tell me what happened, then? Did someone do this to you?"

Tears started to form in his eyes and when he lifted his hand to wipe them away, I reached out and touched him on the arm.

"I don't mind," he said. "You've been very kind to me. I've never spoken of them to anyone, and perhaps I should. My scars were punishments, you see. A new one given to me by my father every year on my birthday."

"Punishments for what?" I asked, frowning. "What did you do?"

"I killed my mother."

I paused, certain that this was not the case. This boy was not one in whom the spirit of violence lived. "You told Holy Faneel that your mother died in childbirth."

"She did."

"But you cannot blame yourself for that."

"My father did," he told me. "And every year, on the anniversary of my birth, he sat me down by the fireplace, heated a steel rod and burned it on to my skin to penalize me for the loss that I had caused him. In this way, he said, I would feel a small fraction of the pain that he endured every day." He stood up and, loosening his tunic, dropped it to his waist. There were more heavy burns on his chest and, when he turned around, even more on his back. Large ones, small ones. There seemed to be no particular order to them, but they had been inflicted on his body over many years, the flawless skin typical of a boy his age barely visible beneath the disarray.

"Monstrous," I said, recalling how disturbed he had become at the smell of burning flesh. Obviously, the foul perfume had served only to recall these dark moments of his childhood.

"Only this year I decided I would not allow him to do it again. I thought of killing him but knew that I could not commit so heinous an act. And so, I ran away instead."

"Then he wasn't killed in the riots, as you first told us?"

"No," Girvesh said, shaking his head. "I apologize for lying."

"And you are forgiven. But will he follow you, do you think? I have known fathers who take great exception to their children abandoning them."

"No," he replied. "For many years he's been telling me to leave but I was too young to have the confidence to make my own way in the world. My father, may his name be forever cursed, will be only too happy that I've gone."

"You're not Buddhist, are you?" I asked. "Or even from Nepal?"

He shook his head. "I am from much further east," he said. "I had been walking for several months when I arrived here, finding food wherever I could. Begging, when necessary. Stealing, more often. I'd lost track of where I was and when I saw the temple rising above the trees of the valley, it seemed to call out to me."

"For a man to treat his son with such cruelty goes against nature itself," I said. "I was not the son my father wanted either, but he rarely beat me, despite being a man prone to violence. But you mustn't cut yourself off from the world, Girvesh," I added. "This is a place of great peace, it is true, but you are young, with a life yet to unfold. Do not grow old here simply because you're afraid of what the outside world might hold for you."

"But isn't that what you're doing?" he asked.

"For now, yes," I replied. "But not forever. My time here will come to an end one day."

"And where will you go then?"

I thought about it. Other than Holy Ujesh, I had confided in no one my reasons for seeking sanctuary in the monastery, but something about the boy made me believe that I could tell him the truth.

"I had a cousin," I told him. "At least, I thought of him as a cousin. We grew up together and I loved him very much. We were each other's protectors and companions. But he committed an act of betrayal that I cannot forgive, for it resulted in the death of my wife and son. One day, I will find him and I will kill him. I could have done so immediately but decided to wait until I had achieved a degree of peace within myself and he felt confident that he had escaped punishment for his crimes. Until that day arrives I will stay here, but after that he will become my prey, as a lion stalks and hunts a wildebeest. When I find him, his death will not be quick. But it will be a matter of retribution, not of cold-hearted revenge."

"And when will that day come?" asked the boy, and I could see by the expression on his face that he did not want me to leave the monastery. We had developed affectionate feelings toward each other, as an uncle might feel toward a nephew, and perhaps he did not like the idea of being left there with only a group of aging monks as his companions.

"Soon," I said, for although the serenity of Swayambhunath had descended upon me, I'd begun to realize that my quest would begin before much more time had passed. "But not quite yet."

INDONESIA

A.D. 907

W E WERE STILL a few weeks away from completing work on the statue of Shiva that would grace the entryway to the Prambanan Temple when Monk Falang appeared in the courtyard where the effigy stood and, seeking me out among the craftsmen, summoned me to his office. I had never seen him quite so anxious before and, as we made our way along the corridors and staircases at an exaggerated pace, I wondered what had upset him so much.

"Sit," he ordered, indicating the chair opposite him and, lifting a sheaf of parchments from the block of stone at which he worked, handed the top one across to me. "A messenger arrived this morning from Jombang," he said, "carrying this with him. What are we going to do?"

I scanned through the calf vellum on which the message was written in iron gall ink; a simple note informing us that King Balitung would be visiting the temple to mark the unveiling of the statue on which we had been laboring since my arrival almost a year ago.

"But surely this is good news," I said, looking up from the missive. "The statue is almost completed and His Majesty will surely be pleased to see—"

"Read on," he told me. "Look when he proposes to visit."

I turned the pages and understood immediately what was causing his distress. "Seven days from now," I said. "But it won't be ready by then."

"I know," said Monk Falang. "But what can I do? Write back and tell him not to come? He would have my head for it. Tell me, when do you think work might be finished?"

I ran my hand across my chin and considered it. I had hoped for another three weeks before the unveiling, but it was not unreasonable to think that, with a little extra effort on all our parts, it could be completed in two. But seven days? That seemed close to impossible.

"Certainly not by the day he proposes," I said.

"Not even if we found more people to help?"

"I'm using every skilled person as it is," I told him. From the moment that I'd been placed in charge of the project, I had drawn good work from each of the monks, but they had varying degrees of talent. The statue stood at twenty-four feet in height, was burnished in bronze and featured a yogi seated in the lotus position upon a garden of flowers, lost in meditation, and there was still much to be done before we could wheel it to the spot where it would welcome visitors, including King Balitung and his descendants, for all eternity.

"And what if we seek help from the local villages?" he asked. "What then? Might there be skilled craftsmen living nearby who—"

"But Monk Falang," I protested, "you've stated explicitly that work on the statue can only be completed by those who live here, in the temple itself. To corrupt that idea at this late date would—"

"All that was before I knew the King was coming," he said, raising his voice for the first time since I had met him. "You must have heard the stories about his rage?"

I nodded. It was common knowledge that the King was a man of little patience, with a quick temper, and had a predilection for administering imaginative punishments upon anyone who displeased him. It was said that he had taken a thousand heads since ascending the throne eight years earlier.

"I'm sure the King would never behave vengefully toward a holy man," I said slowly, uncertain if I even believed this or was simply trying to reassure him.

"Oh no? They say that he tied Monk Raliappa to a stake in Surabaya and slowly poured hot oil over his skin for three days until the poor man died, and all because he had served some objectionable grapes after dinner."

"Perhaps he thought Monk Raliappa was trying to poison him?"

"I don't know, and I don't care," he said, throwing his hands in the air. "And I certainly don't want to find out. We have no choice; the statue has to be finished. Go into the village and find anyone who can help. I will pay whatever you need from our coffers. If it's not ready by the time the King arrives, then none of us might survive his visit."

. . .

Shiva, if he truly existed, must have been looking down at us benevolently during those days because we managed to complete the statue on time, having employed a dozen or more men from Prambanan who felt, not unreasonably, that the King might hang the lot of them and burn their village to the ground if things were not exactly as he wanted them. As the statue was moved into place, a task that took many hours and resulted in at least three broken limbs that I learned of, I stood back and examined the work I had directed. It looked very fine indeed and even I, who had always been something of an agnostic when it came to spiritual matters, found myself touched by its serenity.

The King himself, when he finally appeared, was a curious creature. Known by some as the Great Walrus of Jombang, he was a man of very wide girth but incredibly short stature, with small, sad eyes, a drooping beard and a heavily lined face. His most defining characteristic was the two canine teeth that protruded from the top of his mouth and hung almost as low as his bottom lip. In the pocket of his robes, four or five legs of roasted chickens stuck out prominently and his retinue included four of his current wives, the first of whom had dark hair, while the second had blond and the third red. Curiously, his fourth wife was not a woman at all, but a young boy of almost feminine beauty who dressed in the same robes of many-winged dragons as his sister-wives and was addressed as Queen Indah. The four queens marched behind their husband in descending order of age and, whenever he stopped to speak with one of the monks, they fanned out so there were two standing on his left side, and two standing on his right.

Our entire monastic community gathered to greet the King and queens and, at the very end of the line, stood Gunadi and I. The boy had apprenticed himself to me since his arrival at the temple and, over time, had become less self-conscious about the burn marks on his face and body. He had grown taller, too, and his work on the statue had added muscle to his previously slight frame. Still, I knew that he had been dreading these introductions, for his disfigurement always came as a shock to strangers and could often provoke unkind remarks.

King Balitung circled the statue of the yogi for a long time, examining its every intricacy, before finally nodding his head in approval. Withdrawing a couple of the chicken legs from his pocket, he ate a few bites from both before tossing them over his shoulder, where the dogs attacked the bones with a vengeance. Making his way slowly among us, he accepted the bows of the monks, offering a few words to some, before coming to a halt in front of me.

"And you?" asked the King, looking me up and down as if I was barely worthy of his attention. "You don't look like these other men. You wear no yellow robe and have failed to cut your hair. Who are you?"

"A pilgrim, Your Majesty," I replied, bowing my head. "Given sanctuary at the temple these last twelve months."

"And you worked on this?" he asked, pointing in the direction of the statue.

"Yes, Your Majesty."

"And who's this boy, your son? What's happened to his face? He looks like something that an animal would vomit on to the street. Caught in a fire, were you?"

I turned to glance at Gunadi, who was staring at the ground, and I could feel his entire body trembling in a mixture of anger and embarrassment as his skin grew even more red with humiliation.

"Not my son, no," I replied, speaking for him. "Another pilgrim. A very fine craftsman. Skilled with his hands. Hardworking. Reliable."

"He may be all those things, but how can you stand to look at him?" asked the King, turning away in distaste as the third of the queens, the one with flame-red hair, stepped toward us and placed the palm of her left hand gently against Gunadi's disfigured cheek.

He looked up, still shaking, but when she smiled at him there was an obvious warmth to her presence.

"Ignore what my husband says," she told him quietly. "He is a man who looks only for outward beauty. There are some of us, however, who have no choice but to search for the inner."

There was a long silence as we each took in the meaning of her words and I noticed how Gunadi held his head high now as he met her eyes. She was not, I thought, very much older than him but, rather than feeling intimidated by this unfamiliar girl, he seemed utterly enchanted by her.

"Was that remark made for my benefit?" roared the King, pushing her back to stand in line with the other queens. "Stupid girl. Take my advice," he said, leaning so close to me that I could smell the remnants of chicken on his breath. "Never marry. I've married dozens of times and every one of my queens has proved more painful to me than the last. Sometimes I think I should have become a monk like these men. I'll stay for dinner!" he roared then as he marched past us. "But first, show me to the bathhouse!"

• • •

The evening went much as expected, with King Balitung consuming his body weight in food while the monks, Gunadi and I sat peacefully at our tables, hoping that our heads would still be attached to our shoulders by the end of the night. When an argument broke out between two of his attendants, the King declared that they would fight to the death for his entertainment but, fortunately, Monk Falang persuaded him that this was a holy place and it would be a sacrilege to sully it with spilled blood.

Throughout the evening I noticed Gunadi staring at the redhaired queen, whose name was Yayachandra, and it was obvious that he was completely unsettled by lust. We had become loyal companions at the monastery but, other than telling him the stories of the two women I had loved and lost, we rarely spoke of matters of the heart and I had not given any thought at all to his own romantic inclinations due to his tender years. But, of course, many boys of his age were already siring children. My own father, indeed, had been married to his second wife by fifteen years old and had probably committed the marriage act with any number of other girls, too. So perhaps I should not have been surprised that, having spent so long in the company of older, celibate men, Gunadi's desires would become aroused in the company of a beautiful girl who had displayed unexpected tenderness toward him.

And Queen Yayachandra was indeed something of an enchantress, as I'd realized earlier in the day when I chanced upon her while walking back from the temple, where, she told me, she had gone to watch the sun set over the head of the meditating yogi.

"I can walk ahead if I make you uncomfortable," I told her, for I did not know whether her position meant that she should not be in the company of men who were not her husband.

"Please don't," she said. "Perhaps when we're closer to the monastery, but not yet."

"The King seems like a . . ." I paused, trying to find the appropriate words. "A wise and gentle fellow."

"Is there not some rule about telling shameless lies at a religious site?" she asked, smiling a little.

"I think Monk Falang would frown upon it, certainly," I admitted. "Although neither he nor I chose to marry the King."

"Do you know many women who have chosen to marry their husbands?" she asked. "In my experience, it is always a thing decided for them by their fathers, by their brothers, by men. If women were allowed to choose, then the world would look very different, I think."

"My wives chose to marry me," I said, and she raised an eyebrow in surprise.

"Wives?" she asked.

"Two," I explained. "Both dead."

"I'm sorry," she replied.

"Thank you, but I came to terms with my first loss long ago. And my time here at Prambanan has been spent trying to make peace with my second."

"And have you succeeded?"

I thought about it. "I feel more serene than I did when I arrived," I told her. "Which means the time for me to leave is fast approaching."

"And where will you go? Back to your home village?"

"No," I replied, shaking my head. "I have a task to undertake first."

My tone must have suggested that I did not want to discuss this in any greater detail, for she asked no more questions as we continued to walk, a little slower now, as if we did not want to arrive at our destination too soon.

"How long have you been a queen?" I asked finally, and she breathed in deeply, inhaling the scent of jasmine sweeping through the air.

"Not long," she said. "Less than a year. Currently, I am the fourth queen. Maharani is first, Permata second, Indah third and then I."

"And Queen Indah," I asked cautiously. "She is—"

"A boy? Yes. The King always likes to have one boy in his marriage harem. Indah is not the first, nor will he be the last. Soon, he will develop the signs of manhood and will be dispatched to the Cave of Snakes."

I looked at her, unfamiliar with the phrase, and she shivered a little, rubbing her arms with her hands.

"A hollow near the palace," she explained. "Enormous, I am told, although, happily, I have yet to make its acquaintance. They say there are a hundred thousand poisonous snakes inside. Vipers, cobras, taipans. An enormous boulder seals it shut but when the King is in one of his tempers, he banishes those who have displeased him inside its dark corridors and, of course, they are never seen again. From what I've been told, it is where all his boy-queens have been sent in the past."

"And how soon will this be?" I asked, horrified for the child, who had surely done nothing to deserve such a ghastly fate.

"Within weeks, I expect," she said. "Only recently, while he was singing, his voice broke a little and he started to cough, and I could see the expression of disgust on my husband's face. I suspect that when we return to Jombang the boulder will be opened once again and the cave will swallow its latest victim."

Ahead of us, the monastery appeared in our sights, and, as if we were somehow in tune with each other's thoughts, we stopped and stood facing each other.

"How old are you?" I asked. "If I may be so bold."

"Seventeen years."

I felt a longing to reach out and touch her cheek. Her skin was very soft and her lips red and plump. But even at that moment, I could not do so. To touch her would have been to soil the memory of my late wife, whose mourning period of a year had not quite come to an end. But still, when she looked directly at me, something passed between us, a moment of understanding, and I said nothing more, simply smiled before making my way back to my cell, where I fell to my knees in a mixture of frustration and shame, beseeching my murdered wife to forgive my faithless thoughts.

All of this ran through my mind as I stood at the edge of the banquet and observed the expression on Gunadi's face. There was desire there, certainly, but also a belief that he could love this girl if she would only afford him the opportunity. I recognized these emotions, for I had felt them three times myself.

First for Larinda. Then for Kalshava. And the third time only this very day. For Queen Yayachandra.

"Are you all right?" asked Gunadi, turning to look at me, but I did not reply, simply placing a hand on his shoulder in solidarity with him, for I was certain that either his heart or mine would be broken—more likely both—over the time ahead.

ARMENIA

A.D. 944

T HE FOLLOWING DAY, I was walking through the heart of the chapel, replacing the burned-down candles, when I heard Father Fahram calling my name. A year had now passed since my arrival at the monastery and during that time there had been many moments when, alone in my cell, I'd found myself almost overwhelmed with grief and rage. At such times, rather than throwing myself from the turrets to the ground below, I had made my way toward this cool stone room where prayers were chanted in low, harmonious voices throughout the day. Seated in a pew, inhaling the incense-perfumed air and the scent of jasmine that drifted through the gaps between the stones, I usually found a way to expel negativity from my mind and return to the state of serenity encouraged by the priests.

Before retiring to bed after the previous night's banquet, however, I had left a note on Father Fahram's desk informing him that it was time for me to leave and that this would be my last day in Tatev. Having spent a year as a welcome member of his congregation, he seemed both surprised and saddened when he came to see me.

"But why?" he asked. "You've been such a help to us in our endeavors. And you've been happy here, haven't you?"

"Very happy, Father," I agreed, bowing my head in gratitude. "Had I not found my way to this place after—" I looked away. Halfway through my time at the monastery, I had told him of the events that had taken place in my village before my departure and he had proved a source of great comfort to me. "I doubt that I would even be alive now, were it not for your many kindnesses and those of all the priests who live in this place."

"Well, we shall miss you," he said, embracing me. "Although I'm sure you won't miss some of the things we are forced to do in order to keep this place alive. I spent much of last night on my knees, praying to the Lord for forgiveness."

I smiled. "It was an interesting evening," I admitted.

"And not one that I would care to repeat," he said. "Although I'll probably have to, sooner or later. Let us pray that Boghos Sanasar does not return to visit us any time soon."

The priests at our monastery were exceptionally devout and many had taken to their beds the previous evening, rather than being forced to spend time in the company of so notorious a sinner. Others had drunk their soup and eaten their meat with expressions of such discontent on their faces that it was difficult not to wonder whether their food had been poisoned. In fact, the only three people who seemed to be enjoying the evening were Boghos Sanasar himself, my young apprentice, Garnik, and I, and we were only happy because we had become entranced by Yayranush.

"All I hope is that when the Lord finally calls me home, He forgives me for entertaining such a man and his harem," said Father Fahram in disgust. "But I did it in His name. Without Boghos's offerings, this monastery would never survive."

"I daresay the Lord will forgive you," I told him.

"And where will you go when you leave us?" he asked, and I gave him the deceptive answer I had been preparing for some days. Father Fahram was a man of goodwill and I knew that if I told him the truth, he would do everything in his power to dissuade me.

"I will travel," I said. "Peace has been restored to me at Tatev and I feel ready to rejoin society."

"You want a new woman, I think?" he said with a smile, and I looked down at the stone floor, blushing a little. My year of mourning might have come to an end, but I felt ashamed to admit that my mind was already turning toward matters of the flesh. "And what of Garnik?" he continued. "Will you take him with you?"

I frowned, surprised by the question. "I hadn't given the matter any thought," I replied. "We're not family, after all. I'm not responsible for him."

"Perhaps not, but you must know that he's devoted to you. He's not a priest and nor does he show any interest in becoming one, so it seems inappropriate for him to remain here much longer. Would you not consider taking him with you?"

I thought about it. While I was aware that the boy saw me as a sort of father figure, I was uncertain about aligning myself to him for any substantial period of time.

"I don't know," I said carefully. "There are things I need to do that might be better achieved alone."

"And what things are those, my friend?" he asked. "I hope you don't mean to pursue your vengeance?"

"It's simply that I have my own path to follow and hadn't thought about looking after a child."

"He's more than just a child."

"Still," I said.

"Just think about it, my friend," said Father Fahram, reaching a hand across and placing it on my shoulder. "That's all I ask. The boy is too young to be cooped up here in the company of old men. You could be helpful to him. He needs guidance. And I believe that you, too, could do with a steadying influence. I see something in your eyes that tells me you do not feel quite the peace that you claim."

I did not reply, not wishing to deceive him any further.

"Well, if your mind is made up, I will not try to dissuade you," he said with a sigh. "When will you leave?"

"Later today," I told him.

"Then you have a few hours yet. I will leave you to consider my question. But think of this: when you first came here, I took you in because I knew that you needed the support of people who could take care of you. And I think the boy still needs that. But only you can offer it to him."

. . .

Although I knew that I would be better off leaving her in peace, I went in search of Yayranush soon after leaving the chapel. I wanted to look on her face one last time before she returned with her monster of a husband to the capital. A part of me longed to invite her to accompany me on my journey but I knew better than to give in to an act of such reckless impulsiveness, particularly when my desire for her was built on nothing more than a single conversation. But no matter how hard I looked, I could not find her, and decided that if there was indeed a God looking down upon me, then perhaps He had kept us apart for my own safety. And so I put her from my mind and made my way to Garnik's room instead.

As Father Fahram had predicted, the boy was deeply unhappy to hear that I was leaving the monastery and immediately asked whether he could join me.

"I don't know where the road will take me," I told him. "And, while I'm fond of you, I'm not sure that I can take care of you."

"I don't need taking care of!" he cried.

"Nevertheless," I said, unconvinced, "it feels unfair to involve you in what I have to do."

"And what is that?"

I hesitated before answering. "If I tell you, do you promise that you won't betray me to Father Fahram?"

"You have my word."

"Then I go in search of my cousin. And when I find him, I will put him to death. Not for anger's sake, but for justice's."

He looked down at the ground and frowned, the scars on his face turning the pale shade of pink they always did when he was troubled.

"You don't have to do it, you know," he said. "You could forget about him entirely and begin a new life."

"I could," I admitted. "But I won't."

"He might already be dead, for all you know."

"He's not. I'm sure of it."

"It won't make you happy," he continued. "Killing him, I mean. Can you really imagine what it must be like to take a person's life?"

"Garnik," I said, ignoring his question as I looked him in the eye. "The truth is, my wife's ghost will lie uneasy until I have put this man to death. Or until I know that he has found his way to the next world by some other means."

He nodded. Perhaps it was not as shocking as I thought. After all, we had been surrounded by killing our entire lives. Which of us Armenians had grown up without regularly seeing heads lopped from shoulders and swords plunged through the breastplates of men?

"If you're sure about leaving, then perhaps it's time for me to go, too," he said at last, looking out beyond the walls of the monastery. "I've been happy here, it's true, but I can't stay forever. I'll travel on," he added with a dramatic sigh. "And see what hardship awaits a young boy on his own in the world. I will probably be attacked. Or murdered. Or forced into the marriage act with a fat old man against my will."

I rolled my eyes and tried not to laugh.

"Fine," I said, giving in, as he knew I would. "You can come with me. But we follow my plans, understand? And if you're not happy with them, then you're free to part ways with me at any time. Is that agreed?"

His face broke into a wide smile, a rare treat, and his eyes shone with happiness.

"Agreed," he said.

. . .

We left in the late afternoon, the priests having given us a pair of horses and a buggy for the journey, as well as presenting me with an old cloak to remember them by and to keep me warm on cold nights. When I brought my few belongings from my room, Garnik was already waiting for me and he reached for my bag, throwing it beneath a canvas sheet that was covering the rear of the buggy, an unnecessary addition, as the weather was fine and we had not seen rain in some months. Using a sturdy sisal rope, he secured the canvas at all four corners.

"I don't think we need that," I told him, nodding toward the covering.

"The weather might turn," he said. "We'll be glad of it then."

"And there may be bandits along the road who think that we're in possession of valuable goods that need hiding. Let us not give them cause for suspicion."

He glanced toward the buggy but turned back with a determined expression on his face.

"Please," he said. "I won't ask anything else of you from here on. But let us keep the sheet."

It seemed a curious thing for him to be so insistent upon, but I gave in, thinking that it couldn't do any harm, and turned around as the entire monastery came out to bid us farewell. I thanked each man individually for the kindness that had been shown to me since my arrival and promised that in the unlikely event I ever found myself saying prayers, then I would be sure to include their names among them. As I climbed into the buggy, I noticed Boghos Sanasar wandering around the top of the monastery with a furious expression on his face. I did not know why he looked so aggrieved but felt happy that I would not have to encounter that dissolute creature again.

Finally, we were on the road and we made our way in a westward direction for an hour or two without much conversation, my intention being to steer us toward Gaul, a place that my cousin had often spoken of as a sort of dreamland. As I had no other idea where I might find him, it seemed as reasonable a place as any to begin my search.

"At some point, we'll need to look for a bed for the night," I said eventually, driving the horses forward. "When the sun sets, we'll search for an inn."

"Are they dangerous places?" asked Garnik.

"They can be," I told him. "My late wife was brought up in just such a place and it was not a happy experience for her. They can corrupt the soul. Although," I added, turning to him with a smile, "perhaps you're hoping to be corrupted, Garnik?"

He laughed a little. "I suppose I might be willing," he said.

I was going to add that I'd noticed the way he'd stared at Yayranush the previous night and, in other circumstances, perhaps I would have said something, simply to amuse myself, but what stopped me was an unwillingness even to acknowledge a potential relationship between the two. She was much closer in age to Garnik than I, so it was natural that she would have been more interested in him. But still, this stung at the vanity in my heart, so I remained silent.

He sneezed suddenly and the sound was so strange, even muffled, that I turned to him in surprise.

"What was that?" I asked.

"Nothing," he said, but as he spoke, the sneeze came again, only not from him. I almost jumped out of my skin in fright. We were alone on the road, there was not a soul to be seen for miles around and darkness was beginning to fall. Were there ghosts on these roads as well as thieves? Should we be afraid of supernatural beings as well as mortal ones?

"Did you hear that?" I asked him, and he shook his head.

"The sneeze?" he asked. "No."

"If you didn't hear it, then how do you know what I'm talking about?"

He opened his mouth to answer but seemed incapable of coming up with a reasonable response.

"Garnik," I said. "What is going on?"

I looked around and, as I did so, I was astonished to see that something was moving in the back of the buggy, beneath the canvas sheet that Garnik had been so insistent upon bringing. I stared at it in fright, then pulled the horses to a halt, jumping down and running to the back, where I lifted the cover a little. A moment later, to my astonishment, a head shot out from beneath. It was Yayranush!

"Is this your doing?" I shouted at Garnik, and it was obvious from the look on his face that it was. His expression made it clear that he was feeling both guilty and a little pleased with himself.

"Don't blame him, please," said the girl, stepping out onto the road and adjusting her dress, her flame-red hair even more striking now than before. "It wasn't his fault. I asked him to do it. I couldn't stay with that pig any longer. You have no idea of the indignities he forces upon us all."

In truth, it excited me that she was there, but I felt a mixture of anger and resentment that she had chosen to confide in my young apprentice rather than me. After all, had she told me that she wanted to hide in the buggy, then I would have planned an escape for her. But no, she had chosen Garnik.

"I have money," she added, reaching into her pocket now and removing a small cloth bag before shaking it so I could hear the jangle of coins. "I can pay my own way, if that's what you're worried about. Just don't send me back."

"Three of us, then," I said with a sigh, nodding my head as I considered how her presence might affect my plans.

"Actually, there's four," said another voice, and I turned around to see another person emerging from beneath the sheet. Idara, the boy-dressed-as-a-girl who Boghos Sanasar had brought to dinner and who, if Yayranush was to be believed, was destined for a horrible end upon their return to the capital. I stared at him, my mouth falling open in astonishment.

"Sorry," said Garnik, Yayranush and Idara in unison and I could do nothing but stare at them, one after the other, wondering where my journey would take me now.

PART 6

MILLENNIUM

ICELAND

A.D. 999

A S SOON AS MY ANNOYANCE began to dissipate, my three companions and I made our way toward the village of Vík í Mýrdal, on the south coast of the island, where we remained for several days with the intention of procuring a boat that might take us to the great lands across the water. But, somewhat unexpectedly, two separate matters threatened to frustrate my plans.

The first was the insistence of the boy, Ími, that the world was going to end a few days hence, when the millennium drew to a close. Ími, who continued to dress in the skin of a bear despite being told that he could wear human clothes now that he was no longer subject to his master's bestial fantasies, sat in the corner of the empty igloo we'd rented, weeping uncontrollably and insisting that he would soon be burning in the fires of hell as he had led such a sinful life.

"What sins could you possibly have committed?" I asked, unconvinced that a person as young as him could have much wickedness weighing on his conscience, but when he told me some of the acts that he and Bógi Saranssón had engaged in together, it was difficult not to appreciate his anxiety. "Still," I told him, hoping to ease his concerns. "You were just a child when he purchased you from your parents. If the gods are going to seek atonement from anyone, it will be from your former master and from them, but not from you."

This seemed to be of little consolation and, as he continued to howl, I wondered whether there might not be a way for us to leave him behind in Iceland. But, as Yanníka seemed utterly devoted to him, and I was so drawn to her, I did not want to do anything that might upset my hopes for romance.

"Can't you just ask for forgiveness from the gods if you're that worried?" asked my young apprentice, Garðr, who had as little pa-

tience for the boy's lamentations as I did. "Not half a mile from
here lives a priest, Stefnir Einarsson, who hears confessions. I met
him on the day that we arrived. Why not go speak with him rather
than sitting here crying all day like a dog that's lost its master?"

"I'm afraid that Stefnir Einarsson was murdered yesterday," I
whispered quietly to Garðr, who must not have been privy to the
latest piece of town gossip. The ongoing war between the pagans
and the Christians was tearing the country apart and Einarsson, a
devotee of Jesus Christ, had been dragged by some of the villagers
to a frozen lake, in the center of which a hole had been drilled,
where he'd been ordered to swear fealty to the gods of the Aesir,
Odin, Frigg and Balder. Seeking martyrdom, he refused and was
plunged head down into the freezing water for half a minute. When
he was pulled out again, his beard and eyebrows were white and,
although he could barely speak, he was once again instructed to ask
for mercy from the eternal gods. Again he declined, so down he
went a second time, only now he was held under for much longer
and, when he was dragged up again, he had breathed his last and
was no longer in a position to ask for mercy from anyone, neither
gods nor mortals, at which point his murderers had simply tossed
him back down into the hole before returning to the village, certain
that they had done the work of Thor.

"Well, I'm sure we can find someone else who will listen to you
confess," insisted Garðr, walking over to Ími and kicking ice at him,
which only made the boy weep even louder. "Stop crying!" he
roared, but to no avail. "Stop crying, you little shit!"

That was the first problem.

The second was the fact that King Óláfr, who ruled over us from
the distant land of Norway, had decreed that no trade would be allowed between our two countries until the contentious matter of
the national religion had been determined once and for all and, that
being the case, all boats had been docked, with sailors and captains
told that the penalty for taking them out would be death.

"I heard a rumor that a holy man is coming here soon," said
Garðr, "sent by the King himself, to lay down a law on how this

country is to pray. The old gods are to be forgotten forever, it seems, and the Nazarene is to take their place."

"He'll be lucky to get out alive," I said. "These old men are lost in the old ways. They believe in the gods of Asgard, not in a single God in heaven."

"And you?" asked Yanníka, stepping so close to me that it took all my self-control not to wrap my arms around her and pull her to me. "What do you believe in?"

"I believe in getting off this stinking island and completing my mission," I said. "Nothing more, nothing less."

"There's no point even trying," said Ími, drying his tears at last. "The world is going to end anyway. We'll all be dead in a few days."

A statement that led Garðr to leap on top of him, Yanníka to jump into the fray to tear them apart, and me to step outside, praying to whoever governed us from whichever heaven to grant me patience with this motley crew that I had somehow inherited. Looking up toward the sky, I thought that if there was no peace to be found on this befouled planet, then maybe there would be some to be discovered up there.

. . .

The following night, with the cold settling into my bones, I donned an old cloak as I made my way toward the igloo of Líus Líusson, who was known to harbor a violent antagonism toward our Norwegian overlords and therefore was always happy to defy their rules and laws. When I called his name and entered, removing my hood out of respect for his seniority in the community, I discovered him cooking fish on a stick and he waved me forward, offering me a seat by the fire.

Líus was an extraordinary-looking man, more animal than human, with skin that appeared so thick that it would have taken the sharpest of knives to penetrate it. He had the darkest eyes I had ever seen on a man and wore a permanent expression of fury, although his countenance belied his personality, for he was surprisingly amiable in conversation. I glanced around at the walls of ice and, to my surprise, saw that they were not pressed flat as most igloo walls were but had become a frozen canvas for carved images of the gods, notably of Tyr, who was depicted carrying a spear and looking outward as if threatening anyone who might challenge his dominion over the hoar frost. Above him, a curious birdlike creature with a sharp beak and eyes that suggested wisdom descended, talons outstretched, poised for attack.

While trying to decide how I could make my exit from the island, I, too, had often found myself using a knife to carve designs into the walls of our frozen hut, images that had appeared in my head unbidden, with depictions that I struggled to make sense of. Monkeys swinging from the branches of a tree. A set of entwined peacocks. A face carved into a stone. My hands seemed to move almost independently of my brain as I chipped away at the ice, and afterward, looking at what I'd created, I experienced a curious stirring across my body, a wave of memory, as if I had woken from a dream but could feel the reverie slipping away from me by the second.

"What brings you here, friend?" asked Líus, tossing the bones of the fish onto the fire, where they sizzled and lent a spicy perfume to the air before charring black and disappearing into the coals.

"I need a boat," I told him. "Can you help me?"

He shrugged. "You have money?" he asked.

"I do."

"Then of course I can."

I smiled and, from the shadows, a small boy appeared. This was Líus's son, who buried his body into his father's greatcoat as he looked at me suspiciously through damp eyes.

"How big do you need it to be?" he asked. "How many will be sailing?"

"Four," I replied with a sigh, wishing the number was half that.

"That shouldn't be a problem," he replied. "You're getting away before the Berserkers come, I suppose?"

I shrugged. Rumors were flying around the village that, along with his holy man, the King was sending an army of Berserkers to Iceland to put an end to the old beliefs once and for all. These warriors were legendary, each one stranger than the next, a group of men who barely belonged in this world at all and who would fight as if they were lost in trances, using weapons, their arms, their feet, their teeth, their heads, anything they could find in order to subdue their enemies. They screamed and roared like lunatics while they fought, putting so much fear into their opponents that many were known simply to run away in terror, but a Berserker never gave up and would run faster, trap them, throw themselves upon the coward's body, before ripping him limb from limb in a great fury of bellicose antagonism. Some didn't believe that the Berserkers were human at all, but I held to none of the old superstitions and preferred to think that they were nothing more than normal men who had lost their minds and returned to the ways of the beasts.

"It's not that I fear them," I said, although I did. Very much. "It's just that I have a mission to fulfill. And I cannot accomplish it here."

"Where will you sail to?" he asked.

"Around the coast of Hibernia," I told him. "Then onward to Iberia."

"A lengthy journey. And a dangerous one. Your mission must be an important one."

"It is," I agreed.

The boy whispered something in his father's ear and Líus nodded, reaching into a bucket next to him and extracting a fish, which, still alive, flopped back and forth in his hands. The boy laid it on the ground then removed a wooden knife with an image of a shark carved into the hilt from inside his coat before driving it directly through the fish's brain. The unfortunate creature shivered for only a few seconds before settling into the stillness of the dead. He slit it down the center then, removing the innards and piercing the flesh that remained with a stick before sitting quietly by the fire and staring at it closely as it started to roast. I watched as Líus observed him with great love in his eyes and felt a sudden pang for my own lost son, who had not even lived to see his second birthday. Anger burned inside me at the thought.

"I need to leave as soon as possible," I told Líus in a determined voice.

"The day after tomorrow," he replied. "I will have something for you by then. Although you may not want to leave on such an auspicious night."

"The end of ten centuries?" I asked, raising an eyebrow skeptically. "If we retain faith in the old gods, then marking time from the birth of Jesus Christ should mean nothing to us anyway. The day after tomorrow will be fine." I handed over my pouch of coins and he took them from me, counting the contents slowly, before putting them in his own pocket.

"And so it is agreed," he said.

. . .

On the night of the millennium, Ími was still refusing to sail, so I made it clear to him that he could either come with us or stay behind, whichever he preferred, but that there were no other alternatives. Yanníka seemed annoyed by my insistence upon this but didn't question my authority, and Garðr, who loathed the boy, clearly hoped that he would choose the second option. In the end, however, Ími gave in, albeit with an expression of abject misery on his face.

I chose to set sail at sunset and, as the sun began to fall and I pushed the boat out into the water, I observed another ship approaching from the east. The flag of King Óláfr could be seen flying from its mast and, as it drew closer to the shore, the strange and discordant echo of screaming men could be heard across the waves.

"The Berserkers," I said as my companions looked in that direction in terror.

I shivered a little as I unfurled the sail and hoped that we would be guided to our destination without incident. The men from the encampment were coming down to the shore now in a large group, awaiting the arrival of these barbarian hordes, and each one was carrying weapons in their hands—spears, knives, shovels, ropes, whatever they could find. As our boat was docked around the curve of a bay, it was a stroke of good luck for us that no one could see us leaving and our boat found its path through the water just as the King's men landed on the icy shores to unleash what I assumed would be scenes of unimaginable violence.

As we drifted further out to sea, we watched in a mixture of fascination and horror as the two tribes let fly at each other. Limbs were hacked off, heads were lopped from their bodies, blood scattered like spray above the waves, and a part of me felt guilty that I had not stayed to fight alongside my compatriots, but our stay at Vík í Mýrdal had only ever been intended as a short one and I had private business to take care of.

Soon, we had sailed out far enough that the sounds of violence would live on only in our nightmares and I took my place at the front of the deck, next to Garðr, trying to ignore the plaintive cries that were coming from our bear-boy, Ími.

"How many days, do you think?" Garðr asked, and I shrugged as I looked up at the sky, hoping that the stars would guide us correctly.

"Two weeks," I said. "And even then, we're relying on the gods not to throw storms in our way."

"I thought you didn't believe in the gods?" he said, smiling at me, and seeing his cheerful expression made me realize that I no longer even noticed the burn marks that had so disfigured him. Had they not been there, he might even have been a handsome boy.

"I'll believe in whatever I have to believe in," I told him. "If it means that I find my cousin. That's the only star that guides my life now."

MOZAMBIQUE

A.D. 1000

M Y DREAMS WERE TERRIFYING.

For days, weeks, I knew not how long, I wandered alone, lost in fantasies of places I had never been, arguing with people I had never met, odd words and scraps of strange conversations floating through my mind.

I woke at random hours, perspiration seeping through my pores and soaking the sheets beneath me, an unpleasant residue clinging stickily to my chest and face. Sometimes, the sun leached through the cracks in the stone wall next to my head, scorching the lids of my eyes. When I tried to open them to make sense of where I was, I could make out nothing but blackness. My body was in perpetual pain and, if I tried to move my arms or legs, the agony grew so intense that it either threw me back into a fitful, unhappy sleep or left me crying out for someone who might put me out of my misery.

A hand placed cold, wet cloths upon my forehead and a soft voice sang unfamiliar melodies as I drifted in and out of consciousness.

Occasionally I would rise from my bed in an attempt to walk around the room, pressing a hand against the walls to keep myself from falling over, but the pain in my ankle was severe and I struggled to remain upright. The chamber itself appeared to have an oval shape and contained nothing but a bed on the floor and a wooden table with a roughly carved top. A door led to a second room and, inside, a fire remained lit throughout the day and night, but if I tried to enter, a figure would stand up and walk toward me, ushering me back whence I had come.

"You must sleep," insisted the voice, a female. "Your strength will return only if you sleep."

She fed me, too. Warm dishes of a distinctive broth, imbued with the flavors of roasted meats and unfamiliar vegetables, the scent of jasmine and lavender infusing my nostrils, forcing me to drink bowl after bowl. So starved was I that I could feel the food making its way through my body, rebuilding my energy, but as soon as I was satisfied, my eyes would grow heavy and I would return to my disturbed slumber.

Sometimes, I could hear music, the sound of strings being plucked and then a voice filtering through the air once again, the voice of an old woman as she sang a lullaby. Her tone was deep and filled with texture, her intonation suggesting that she had experienced more suffering than most.

When I tried to speak, I found the words caught in my throat and she would shush me anyway, as one might a baby, telling me to wait, that all my senses and abilities would return in time, but that I needed to be patient.

I grew to value the woman's presence, feeling safe whenever she was nearby. I tried to ask her name but could not seem to make myself understood. And throughout it all were the dreams, the endless, incessant dreams. Pyramids and sculptures, jewelry and wooden steles. Sandals, amulets and elaborate paintings decorating the hulls of boats. What did I know of any of these things? And yet they seemed more real to me than the solid world that surrounded me.

Finally, one morning I opened my eyes to see the sun breaking through the empty space in the stone that served as a window and across which the old woman would sometimes throw a sheet to block out the light. I lifted myself slowly, sitting up against the wall, and when she entered, I looked at her, my eyes able to focus at last. She was very old and wrapped in a tight body of cloths that hid her ancient form. Her skin was wrinkled, and it was obvious from the whites of her eyes and the manner in which she stared directly ahead that she was blind.

"Where am I?" I asked her. "What happened to me?"

• • •

The storm, it seemed, had broken late on the second night of our journey, and its effects were felt from the southern tip of our land to across the coastal regions. Although my intention had been to sail north toward Dar es Salaam, the head of the mainsail came loose from the mast once the winds began, leaving me to curse Lisula, the man who had sold me such a precarious vessel, and from there we were thrown around the seas at the mercy of an unforgiving God.

My memories were few at first—I could recall sleeting rain, the darkness of the night and our four bodies rolling around the deck every time the boat spun out of control—but these came back to me only gradually as the weeks passed. I had been sleeping in the cabin beneath the main deck when my apprentice, Guvesh, came down to fetch me. The skies were clouding over, he said, and lightning could be seen splitting the heavens in the distance. I could tell by his tone that he was growing anxious but I thought little of it at the time, assuming there would be many such incidents before we reached land but that they would simply test us, not destroy us. When I made my way up the steps, however, I looked around to see Yaya at the helm and the boy Indrus lamenting in a corner.

As I threw myself toward the tiller, Yaya turned back to ascend the grooves in the mast in an attempt to repair the sail that had come loose. As yet, I still believed that we would come to no great harm, that we would surely survive this calamity, but it quickly became obvious that she was struggling to reattach the canvas and, a moment later, the boat slipped further into the heart of the storm, whereupon it began to shake terribly, plunging up and down in the sea before throwing us all back across the deck.

I tried my best to steer but lost my footing in the water that was pouring in on top of us and fell, crashing toward the open door that led to the cabin and then tumbling downstairs, where my entire body slammed against the woodwork. When I pressed my hand to my forehead, it came away red with blood and, although I could feel myself growing dizzy, there was no time to attend to the wound. I ran back up as fast as I could.

Guvesh was at the helm now and when I looked up toward Yaya she was balanced precariously, one bare foot holding tight to a step, the other reaching for the sail, and for a moment it looked as if she might succeed, but then another great wind blew in our direction and I watched as she slipped, lost her footing and plunged into the sea below. I cried out, rushing to the side of the boat, where I saw her emerge from the water momentarily, her mouth open in a desperate gasp for air, before sinking below again, her arm reaching up forlornly. It would have been a fool's errand to dive in after her—she was already gone—but to my horror I saw Guvesh kicking off his sandals and jumping onto the hull.

"Stop!" I roared toward him. "You'll drown."

He shook his head, the foolish boy, and dived in after her, while I did the only sensible thing that I could think of at such a moment, which was to continue to try to steer the boat back to safety, shouting to Indrus to help me.

My eyes clouded with red as the blood poured down my face and, to my astonishment, I felt myself beginning to laugh hysterically. Yaya and Guvesh were certainly drowned, there was no way that they could have survived such treacherous waters, and all I could do now was try to save myself and Indrus.

A great burst of noise from the sky, a streak of lightning to my left, another to my right and then—darkness.

. . .

It took almost a month for me to be on my feet again, having broken my left arm, several ribs and my right ankle, all of which the old lady, who told me that her name was Tozia, had strapped with splints of wood while they healed. She had lived on the beaches of Quelimane her entire life, giving birth to nineteen children there, almost all of whom had either perished in the sea or in the tribal wars that plagued our country. Blind since birth, she had no idea what it was to see a sunset, to look up at the stars or to witness an expression of love on another person's face. Others had described to her what trees looked like, how flowers were shaped, how people were formed, but it was impossible to know whether the images drawn in her mind were accurate.

Tozia had discovered me lying on the beach on the morning that I washed in with the tide, clinging to a piece of the boat's hull, barely alive. Of Yaya and Guvesh there was no sign and I guessed that they now lay together at the bottom of the ocean. Miraculously, however, Indrus had survived and Tozia had taken him to the hut, too, where she had done her best to nurse him back to health, but after a week or so, he succumbed to his injuries. When I was able to walk again, she led me to one of the forest clearings, where she had buried the boy, a simple cross in the ground marking the place where his body lay. She had carved it herself, she told me, using a wooden knife with an image of a shark etched into the hilt, her fingers doing the job of her eyes to see the shapes as they formed before her.

"Did he speak at all?" I asked, imagining how frightened he must have been when he found himself hugging a piece of broken wood and floating in an unknown direction. "Did he know what had happened?"

"He did," she told me as we stood side by side over the place where his bones lay. "And of the two of you, I thought he would be the one to recover, for he seemed to be growing healthier by the day, but then one evening, he began to cough up blood and was dead within the hour. He was broken on the inside, I think. Your wounds were easier to identify and to heal."

"And what did he say?" I asked.

"He told me about his parents," she replied. "How they sold him to a man who treated him badly."

"I met that man," I said. "He forced Indrus to wear the skins of animals when they performed the marriage act."

Tozia turned to the sound of my voice and raised an eyebrow in surprise. "The skins of animals?" she asked. "What manner of insult is that?"

"Some men have very peculiar ways," I told her.

"I've known all types of men," she said, shivering a little. "But I've never heard tell of such a thing before. Anyway, he will be at peace now. Spearthrower Owl will guide him to the next world. And you?" she asked as we stood up and walked away from the boy's grave, making our way back in the direction of the hut. "What will you do now? Where will you go?"

"Onward," I said. "Deeper into the continent. I go in search of—"

"A boy with twisted legs," said Tozia, interrupting me, and I looked at her in surprise.

"Yes," I said. "My cousin, or so I thought of him. And the source of a great betrayal. How did you know?"

She held both hands, palms out, to the sky. "I see more than most men or women do," she told me. "When I was deprived of my sight at birth, I was given different senses in compensation. Also," she added with a mischievous smile, "when you were lost in your delirium, you often spoke of him."

. . .

And so I began again. More companions lost and a journey to undertake by myself. I sat by the shore that night, planning the boat that I would build when I was fully restored to health, a safer vessel than the one that had brought me to this place, and for the first time I wondered whether my mission was even worth undertaking. My cousin deserved to be hunted down for what he had done, of course, but would I derive any satisfaction from killing him, particularly now that it had cost the lives of three innocent people? Would even more be lost before our paths crossed? And then there was the question of whether I would even be able to find him. I could waste years in my quest, years that could be more usefully spent.

In the distance the sun began to set, and I closed my eyes, listening as the sounds of the waves lapping against the shore echoed around me. The truth was, I had no choice; I was not at ease, and would never be at ease, until I stood face-to-face with him once again and made him answer for his actions.

I would continue on. Alone.

PART 7

PLUM
BLOSSOM
MELODIES

BELGIUM

A.D. 1050

T HE BEER TAVERNS OF BRUGES seemed as good a place as any
for me to spend some time while I planned my next move.
My wounds had healed and when I left the blind woman's
home on Haringvliet island to sail the short distance back to the
mainland, it seemed as if the continent was opening up before me
like an oyster, with my traitorous cousin the black pearl lying at its
deceitful heart. While Tesia had been uncommonly kind, saving my
life and nursing me back to health, the deaths of my three companions weighed heavily on my conscience and I felt glad to be among
the noise and bustle of mankind once again, where I could smother
my guilt by taking frequent advantage of the city's inns.

I lost myself in drink for a time and could usually be found in one
hostelry or another, my head slumped over some wooden table
with a roughly carved top, slurring words of regret deep into the
night until either the landlord or another customer dragged me out
and threw me in the gutter. In the evenings, before the drink took
its effect, I might pick up a woman who was willing to offer her favors for a few coins, debasing myself with such transactions.

It was in a tavern called the Bickspitel, however, that I had the
good fortune to encounter my older brother, Jasper, who I had not
seen in several years. When last our paths crossed, we had been staying overnight in a hostelry, he heading south, I heading north, and
he had left early the following morning before I awoke. Seeing him
march toward me now, grinning in delight with his arms open wide,
I felt a wave of delight break over me.

"Brother!" he roared, the words emerging from a face that
seemed more hair than skin. His red beard covered him so thoroughly that only his eyes and nose were visible through the foliage.
He seemed to have grown no older and his body appeared accus-

tomed to combat. I was certain that he could still fell a man for nothing more than looking at him the wrong way.

"Jasper," I replied, standing up to embrace him. "Can it be you?"

"It can and it is!" he said. "I saw a miserable-looking creature sitting over here in the corner, drinking alone, and thought, I recognize that ugly face. What brings you to Belgium?"

He sat down opposite me and when the waitress came over with more beer, he dragged her onto his lap for a few moments before sticking his tongue in her mouth, a liberty to which she offered no objections. Their ardor grew even more intense as his hand wandered up her skirt and when I saw her throw her head back and sigh in contentment at whatever he was doing to her under there, I began to wonder whether he had forgotten my presence entirely. Finally, however, he released her, slapped her on her rear end, and she wandered off to serve someone else.

"What?" he asked when he turned back to me, the rouge from her cheeks feathering his beard. "You don't like women?"

"I do," I replied. "But I usually ask before doing . . . whatever it was that you were doing."

"Your trouble, Brother, is that you were always too polite," he said, slapping his hand on the table before him. "I've never asked permission from a woman in my life and have no intention of starting now. Remind me, Brother, you have a wife? Or you had a wife? I can't recall."

"I had two," I said. "I lost them both."

"In childbirth?"

"The first in an accident, the second to murder."

"I hope you cursed the god responsible for the former," he said, frowning. "And killed the man responsible for the latter."

I gave a noncommittal smile and he grunted, finishing the rest of his beer in one draft before reaching into the middle of the table, where a bowl of roasted chicken legs sat. He gnawed his way through three before tossing their denuded bones over his shoulder, where they landed on the head of another drunk, who looked up in surprise for only a moment before settling back to sleep. A dog sensed his chance, leaped up on the table and grabbed the carcasses before making its way into a corner, where it settled down with its spoils.

"Your accent," I said. "Of course, you've been away from home for many years, but you sound very different. Where have you been living?"

"Scotland," he told me. "Perhaps I've picked up some of its filthy brogue. I've had a good life there, Brother. Sired a bunch of children, although I haven't seen any of them in years and couldn't tell you their names. Some were girls, some were boys, I know that much anyway. I was a farmer for a time, then I set up an inn of my own, much like this one, but I didn't like serving men and cleaning up their vomit when they'd taken too much. So I gave it up and set out on the road once again in search of adventure and before long I found myself in service to the King."

"The King of where?" I asked.

"The King of Scotland, of course, what other king would I mean?" He nodded toward the end of the room, where a crowd of similarly burly men were gathered around a tall, thin man, laughing sycophantically at his every word as if he were the greatest comedian of his age. "That's him down there. Yon weaselly looking fellow with the droopy eye."

I raised an eyebrow skeptically. "The King of Scotland is sitting in a tavern in Bruges?" I asked. "That seems unlikely to me."

"Men have died for suggesting I'm a liar, Brother," he said, pushing his face close to mine. "So have a care with your words, aye?"

"My apologies," I said, bowing my head a little. "It's just unexpected, that's all. And his name?"

"Surely you know the name of the one true King of Scotland?" he asked, sitting back again and looking at me askance. "How ignorant can you be? 'Tis King Macbeth and no other! You were supposed to be the clever one in our family, I thought. Have you no knowledge of any land outside your own?"

"I've been away from the world for some time," I told him, choosing not to enlighten him on my recent activities. "I haven't kept up with politics."

"Well, that's the poor bastard down there anyway. He's been

King these last ten years, aye, since Duncan trespassed into Bothna-gowan and sacrificed his life on account of it. A nice enough man, is Macbeth, if you get him on the right day. A total monster, of course. Brutal and sadistic. But a nice enough man all the same."

"So—forgive me—but what is the King of Scotland doing in an inn in the Low Countries?"

"It's all a lot of nonsense, if you ask me," he replied, leaning forward and lowering his voice. "He's on a pilgrimage, may God bless him for his eternal stupidity. Going to Rome to see the Pope and get the papal blessing, because he knows that'll put the wind up that English prick, Edward, and there's no great love lost between the pair. Perhaps he has a stain on his soul that needs removing. I don't know and I don't much care. He doesn't confide in the likes of me."

I stood up and made my way down toward the piss-pots at the rear of the tavern, taking the opportunity to steal a look at this supposed King when I passed his table. He had a bushy head of dark hair but, unusually for a man of these times, a clean-shaven face. Next to him sat an elegant lady with fine blond hair. When she caught my eye, it was difficult to hold her gaze for too long, for she was very beautiful. Her face bore an inscrutable expression and it seemed that she was determined to stare at me until I turned away and so, finally, I did.

"And the woman?" I asked Jasper when I returned to our table.

"What woman?"

"The one sitting next to him."

He glanced around for a moment as if he were unsure, even though she was the only female in the inn outside of the serving girls and prostitutes.

"Oh, that piece of filthy baggage?" he asked, blowing a sound of distaste through his lips. "The Queen. Granddaughter of King Kenneth as once reigned. Daughter of Prince Boite. Once Lady Macbeth, but that was a little further away from the seat of power than she liked, so she made sure to rise to even greater heights. The power behind the throne, as they say." He sniffed as he lifted both a fresh beer and the skirt of another passing girl, who, unlike her colleague, entertained no such liberties, taking an empty plate from the table next to ours and smashing it down over my brother's head. He took the assault in good spirits, all the same, laughing heartily and pressing the heel of his hand against the cut on his forehead until the blood clotted. "I've had the Queen a few times myself, as it happens," he added. "I'd recommend her to you, Brother. She's a dirty wee mare and knows the kind of tricks that can drive a man to dribble with lust."

A little drunk, I couldn't help but laugh, and he shrugged his shoulders.

"Most of us have been called to her bed at one time or another," he continued. "She likes variety, you see. Tall men, short men, fat men, thin. Ugly men, too, so you're in with a chance there. The King doesn't care. He likes a bit of variety himself and doesn't go a day without finding a little pleasure of his own. It's what you might call a very happy marriage."

"Perhaps he'll have to spend longer confessing to the Pope than he might anticipate," I said. "And you're going on this pilgrimage with him?"

"I'm one of his guardsmen," he replied. "He likes us to be big and brutal, so I fit the bill quite nicely, don't you think? I can't imagine anyone wanting to attack him, though—no one in Europe even knows who he is—but the poor man likes to think he's very important so he surrounds himself with men like me and we get paid handsomely for it. You should join us, Brother! It's a long road to Rome and I could do with someone sensible to talk to. Most of these animals can barely string three words together."

I considered his offer and felt immediately drawn to the idea. I would have food and accommodation, after all, and could ask after my cousin in the towns and villages along the way. For now, though, there was more drink to be had, more memories of the past for us to share, and before I knew it, I was stumbling back to a room above the inn and falling into a deep sleep.

• • •

Like any man, I was accustomed to having dreams of an erotic nature, but that night, I experienced one that felt more real than anything I had known since I was a young boy edging my way toward manhood. A woman was between my legs, her mouth around my cock, and I was groaning in pleasure as she made herself familiar with it. Soon, the dream became so vivid that my eyes opened and, to my astonishment, the woman was no figment of my imagination, but a living, breathing person. I pulled aside the thin sheet that I had thrown atop myself and there was a naked woman, seducing me in my sleep. I cared not who it was, for I was too far gone in my lust to protest and simply lay back with my head upon the pillow, my eyes closed again, while she moved her body up a little and allowed me to slip inside her. When I was spent, I reached down to pull her closer, certain that she would be some doxy my brother had arranged to be sent to my room as a surprise and was shocked to see that this was no common trollop at all but a person of far greater import.

"You're not as big as your brother," said the Scottish Queen in a cool voice when our eyes met. "But I think you might have more tenderness in your soul. And you lasted a little longer. He's more interested in his own pleasure than anyone else's. And he doesn't often take long to achieve it."

"How did you get in here?" I asked, dazed and astonished by her presence.

"There are no locks on the doors."

"And what if the King finds out?"

"The King is otherwise engaged," she said. "Having done to him what I've just been doing to you. There's no reason to worry. My husband is not a jealous man. We have an understanding, he and I."

I frowned. As much as I'd enjoyed the experience, I wasn't sure that I liked being treated in such a cavalier fashion. At the very least, she might have asked first.

"Do you always enter the rooms of strangers in the middle of the night, when they're asleep, and seduce them in this way?" I asked.

"Whenever I feel like it, yes," she replied. "I've never been the sort that seeks permission of others. Anyway, you enjoyed it, didn't you?"

"What if I had a wife?"

"There's no one here with you."

"There could be someone waiting for me at home."

She smiled and shook her head. "I don't know you," she said. "But if I'm certain of anything, it's that there is nowhere in this world that you call home anymore. I saw it in your eyes earlier."

I felt a sharp pain in my stomach at this observation but, after all, she was right and there was no point in my denying it.

"I hear that Jasper has invited you to join us on our pilgrimage?" she continued, climbing off me now and pulling her clothes together as I sat up in the bed and nodded.

"He did," I admitted.

"Are you a person of religious scruple?"

"I'm not, no."

"All the better. Neither am I. And neither is the King, in his heart, but he has a superstitious bent."

"Although I did spend a year among monks not so long ago," I told her. "And found their company stimulating. There was a serenity there that—"

"I don't care," she said.

I laughed, unsure whether to be offended or charmed by her bluntness.

"You know that we're planning an audience with the Pope when we arrive in Rome?"

"Jasper told me, yes."

"Perhaps that would interest you, regardless of whether or not you're a believer."

"Would I be welcome, do you think?"

"In Rome? How should I know?"

"I meant if I were to join your retinue. There wouldn't be any . . . awkwardness?"

She burst out laughing and shook her head. "You're quite naïve, aren't you?" she said. "No, you don't need to worry about any of that. I may want to have sex with you again as we continue our journey, or I may not. Who knows? Don't let it concern you, it'll be up to me to decide either way and you won't have any say in the matter. If you hadn't chanced upon Jasper, where would you have gone anyway? What were your plans?"

"To travel through the bigger cities of Europe," I told her. "I'm trying to track down an old friend and, given enough time, I'm sure I'll be able to find him."

"And this man has done you some disservice?"

"He has."

"So, you mean to kill him."

"I do."

She nodded. "Then you must do so. Some killings are justified."

"I suppose a queen would know that very well," I said, and she threw me a fractious look.

"Don't be impertinent," she said. "My husband came to the throne in the old-fashioned way. Defeating King Duncan in battle. He invaded Moray, which was our domain, so my husband led an army against him. And rightly so. Duncan fell on the field of battle and my husband took the crown. Yes, there was killing involved, but all of it defensible. It's been that way since the dawn of time. It's how thrones are won. Perhaps you're too innocent to understand."

"I'm not as innocent as you may think," I replied quietly. "As it happens, I have the blood of more than one person on my hands."

"Then you're just like everyone else in this scarlet-soaked world," she said, standing up and making her way toward the door. "We have choices in this life. We hurt or get hurt. We betray or get betrayed. We kill or get killed. If you want to survive, then you need to know which side you're on."

"And which side are you on?" I asked, and she smiled, as if the answer were obvious.

"My own," she replied. "Always my own."

· · ·

A few hours later, I descended from my room to the inn where Macbeth, his Queen, and their guards were eating a lavish breakfast, and it was as if nothing unusual had taken place at all.

"Well, Brother?" asked Jasper, taking me to one side and throwing a big, burly arm around my shoulder. "Have you made your decision? Will you join us?"

"For now," I said. "Perhaps not all the way to Rome but, if the offer still stands, then I will join you for some part of the journey and earn my keep."

He slapped me on the back so hard that I stumbled forward, tripping over a chair, and fell to the floor. Jasper burst out laughing and, as he picked me up, I saw the Queen cackling, too, and shaking her head.

"Two brothers back together," he said. "Just as nature intended! Our father would have been a proud man at this moment!"

NETHERLANDS

A.D. 1086

PRIDE AT SEEING HIS TWO SONS reunited would have been one thing, but I suspect our father would have been less gratified to learn that the man we'd been hired to protect was killed by his own brother only a few days later, and we had been unable to prevent this from happening.

Having spent little time in the company of the King, I felt no great sense of loss at his murder, but the effect on Queen Adela was obvious and she deferred to my brother Jannik on what to do next. He advised that we leave our lodgings under cover of night, but still, it was not until several days later, when we reached Enschede in the Netherlands, that any of us began to feel secure.

Naturally, the Queen was fearful that those traitors who had murdered their sovereign would come after her, too, but we were careful to hide our tracks as we rode. Since we were only a small group of seven—the royal party, a lady-in-waiting, Jannik, three other soldiers, and I—we hoped to arrive in Flanders without further incident.

"We shall call it a pilgrimage," the anxious Queen declared as we rode along, and Jannik and the soldiers nodded in agreement, for warriors always preferred to think they were journeying toward a place rather than running away from a fight. "Since I was a girl, I have been told of the beauty of St. Bavo's Cathedral in Ghent and, if asked, I shall say that I want to kneel at the altar there to pray for the soul of my beloved husband."

"You have a spiritual bent, my lady?" I asked as we rode ahead, our conversation muted so that our companions would not hear our words.

"Of course," she replied. "I am an anointed queen. How could I honor that title if I did not feel a devotion to Christ?"

I declined to answer. Despite her mourning, Adela continued to seek me out every night in my chamber. Typically, she would join me as soon as the others had gone to bed, although she never stayed until morning, preferring to return to her own room when our games were over. The woman was insatiable, demanding so much from me that I found myself in a permanent state of exhaustion.

"Did you love him?" I asked.

"Who?" she replied.

"Your husband, of course."

"No, of course not," she said with a laugh. "Don't be naïve. Kings and queens don't marry for love. That's not how the world works. But he was kind enough, in his way. Kinder than many men in his position might be. Obviously, he was an idiot, but that's to be expected from those born to reign."

I must have gasped at such brutal honesty, for she turned to look at me in surprise.

"He was never happy with his lot," she explained in a tone that suggested she was talking to a child. "They never are, haven't you noticed that? The moment a prince ascends his father's throne he turns to a map of the world and asks himself which countries he wants to invade in order to prove how much better he is than the man who sired him. My husband had his eyes on England, did you know that? He considered the English King to be a usurper, but they're all usurpers if you examine the lineage closely enough. Even I could have told him that invading an island nation is a lot more difficult than invading a landlocked one. I did tell him that once, in fact, but he just laughed at me and told me to return to my sewing. Really, if my husband hadn't been struck down on the altar at Odense, then I have no doubt he would have perished on some English battlefield sooner or later. It was only a matter of time. I just hoped that he wouldn't betray his stupidity until our son was old enough to rule. But now look at us," she added with a sigh, signaling the empty road ahead.

"And you?" I asked. "When we reach Flanders, what will you do? Stay in Ghent? Retire to a nunnery?"

She burst out laughing and touched me on the arm so affectionately that surely the men riding behind us could see the intimacy we shared. "Oh, I'm glad you're traveling with us, you stupid man," she said. "You do make me laugh. Do I seem like a woman who was born to take the veil?"

"Well, no," I replied. "Perhaps not."

"I haven't formed a definite plan yet," she continued. "Securing the throne for my son is by far my most important obligation but I can't make that happen on my own. I shall write to my allies around Europe. I'm related to half of them anyway so one will be sure to send help. The idea of that fratricide Olaf sitting on a stolen throne infuriates me and it will test the mettle of other sovereigns. If I have to, I'll go back to Denmark and put a sword through his heart myself. Other than that, I suppose I'll seek out another king to marry. Or a crown prince, if worst comes to worst. There's usually a few in search of a useful alliance to be found scattered around the continent. That's what we do, we queens. We marry, our kings get murdered or die, and then we keep on marrying until our looks fade. But I'm almost twenty-four years of age now, so time is not on my side."

I didn't doubt her intentions for a moment but, as committed as I was to fulfilling my promises and protecting her, I also found that this was proving to be a useful journey for my own purposes. Traveling such a long distance and stopping every dozen miles in order to rest the horses gave me an opportunity to meet people, and while others caroused in inns at nights, I made my way from house to house and table to table inquiring whether anyone might have crossed paths with my false-hearted cousin.

As a boy, I had developed some skills with art, even hoping to pursue this passion as an adult, but all that had been taken away from me after my wife's death. I returned to it now, sketching a fair likeness of Hjalmar on scraps of paper, which I showed to townspeople along the way. So far, I had not discovered anyone who could help. Occasionally, someone might look at the image and display a flicker of recognition and, once or twice, even mention a man who fitted my description, so I hoped that I was at least journeying in the right direction. And when a serving girl spoke of a man who had spent an evening at a hostelry carving eagles into a pair of crutches, my spirits soared, knowing that my trail was a good one.

And then, finally, I struck gold.

. . .

We had stopped for the night in Enschede, where I behaved as I always did, feeding and brushing down my horse before finding a water pump to wash the dirt of the road from my body and then making my way from inn to inn with my drawing. When I entered an inn called the Noskleite Tavern I found it filled with all manner of men and women, carousing as a fiddle player sung songs by a fireplace; I wandered from person to person, asking my usual questions. After receiving negative responses from all, I retired to a table in the corner in disappointment to order some food and beer. A girl with a black eye and a severely bruised countenance served me a bowl of roasted chicken legs and when I asked her to sit with me for a moment, she shook her head, curling her lip in contempt.

"I'm no whore," she said, spitting out the words. "Even if I get treated like one half the time. If you want something to mount, go back to your horse."

"That's not what I'm looking for," I replied, sitting back in my chair and doing my best to look as innocent and honest as possible. "I only wanted to ask you some questions. Nothing more."

She frowned, appearing defensive now. "I've done nothing wrong," she said.

"I didn't say that you had. Here"—I threw a few coins on the table—"if I give you this, will you at least sit with me while I eat?"

She stared at the coins for a few moments before sweeping them up in her hands and secreting them in the pocket of her apron. Sitting down opposite me, she brushed her hair from her forehead, and by the candlelight I could see that her bruises were beginning to heal, for they were already a sickly shade of purple and yellow.

"Who did that to you?" I asked.

"Who do you think?" she replied, nodding toward the bar, where an obese man stood behind the counter, singing along loudly with the fiddle player.

"Your husband?"

"No, thank Christ."

"Your father?"

"My uncle. I work for him. This is his inn."

"And what did you do to deserve such a beating?"

"What do I ever do?" she asked with a shrug. "Said the wrong thing, looked at him the wrong way, spilled a glass of wine. It never takes much to anger him. He enjoys it, that's the truth of it. All you men enjoy hitting women, don't you? You get a thrill out of it."

I shook my head. "Not all men," I protested. "Not me."

She rolled her eyes. It was obvious that she had heard such avowals before and quickly discovered them to be false. "There's not a man in here who doesn't punch his woman when he feels like it," she said, leaning forward. "Tell me you're different and I'll call you a liar."

"Believe whatever you like," I said. "But it's the truth."

"So, what do you want, then? You just enjoy looking at a girl's sullied face while you eat, is that it? Gives you more of an appetite?"

"I'm searching for someone," I told her. "A man. I wondered whether you might have seen him pass this way."

"This is Enschede," she said. "Do you know how busy it gets in these parts? Hundreds pass through every day, thousands probably, traveling in every direction, and very few of them are memorable to me. Sometimes, one might say please or thank you, and that's enough to make them seem special, but I still put them out of my mind the moment they've paid their bill and left."

"The man of whom I speak has twisted legs and walks on sticks," I continued. "An accident from when he was a boy."

She said nothing for a moment, reaching down and taking a piece of meat from my plate before tossing it into her mouth, where she chewed it slowly while tapping her fingers on the table. I sensed from her expression that something I'd said had rung true with her.

"There's men with deformities all over the place," she replied eventually. "Look at him," she added, nodding in the direction of a man a few seats away who had only one leg and also walked on sticks. "He lost his leg when he fell off his horse and the animal tumbled after him, crushing his bones. And him over there with the scars on his face. Branded for sleeping with another man's wife. And do you see him?" She pointed now into the corner of the room where a young man with a pleasant visage was cleaning a table with his left hand, for his right arm had been sliced off at the shoulder, leaving a grisly stump in its place. "Well, I don't even want to tell you what happened to him."

"I'm not interested in any of them," I said, reaching forward to make her look at me again, but she reared back as if I'd been about to strike her. I wanted information, nothing more. "There's only one man who concerns me. Here, look at this."

I removed the drawing from my tunic and handed it across to her. She glanced at it for a moment and raised an eyebrow. Looking around, almost in fear, she leaned closer to me and lowered her voice.

"Well, him, I remember," she said quietly.

"You do?"

"Oh yes. But what's it worth to you to know?"

I took another few coins from my pocket and handed them across.

"He lived here," she said with a smile, gathering them up. "In Enschede, for a few months. There was a . . ." She paused for a moment and, once again, glanced around anxiously. "Wait here," she said, standing up and making her way over to the other side of the room, where she sought out the one-armed boy. I watched her talk with him for a moment but then lost them both in the crowd of people standing up to join in the singing. I considered following her but was afraid that I might lose her entirely and so remained in my seat, trying to keep my excitement at bay. When she returned, I looked up expectantly but, to my disappointment, she shook her head.

"My mistake," she said, handing me back my drawing. "I don't know that man. I've never seen him before in my life."

"But you just said—"

"I told you, I don't know him. No such man has ever passed through here."

"You're lying," I said, standing up and growing angry.

"I'm not!" she insisted. "And, what's more—"

Before she could finish her sentence, however, her uncle arrived at my table. He was wiping drool from his chin and looked to me like a man who was accustomed to getting his own way.

"You're finished eating, friend," he said, lifting my plate and mug and throwing them over his shoulder with absolutely no regard for where, or on whom, they might land. "No charge. You've eaten for free, so it's a fortunate night for you. Be on your way before some damage falls upon you."

"Good evening, sir," I said. "My name is—"

"I have no more interest in your name than I have in the size of your cock. There's nothing for you here. It's time for you to go."

"I don't know why you're getting so angry," I said, growing frustrated now. "I only want to know if—"

"Either you leave quietly or I'll throw you out," he said, stepping forward aggressively, and I gave in, sensing that my time in the Noskleite Tavern had drawn to a close. Several men had gathered around him and at that time of night, with drink coursing through their veins, I knew they would have enjoyed nothing more than to get into a fight with a stranger. Annoyed and unsatisfied, I said no more and left.

It was obvious that Hjalmar had been there at some point but something had made the girl lie to me. I began to walk back in the direction of the tavern where Queen Adela and our party were staying, but had only made it a short distance when I heard the sound of footsteps from behind me and turned, my hand on my blade, fearful that some of the men had decided to follow and cause me some fatal injury. I narrowed my eyes, trying to make out who it was, and felt a burst of relief when I saw that I was not about to be confronted by a gang of drunken thugs, but instead by the one-armed boy, whose attitude suggested that he did not intend me any harm.

"Who are you?" I asked, my words echoing in the quiet of the forest. "What do you want?"

"Alfred of Enschede," he replied quietly, approaching me with caution. "The girl in the tavern, the one you were talking to, she's my cousin. My father is the man who threw you out."

"And what made you follow me?" I asked.

"She told me who you were looking for. She showed me the drawing."

"You recognized him, then?" I asked eagerly.

"His name is Hjalmar," he said.

"It is!" I cried, my excitement building. "How do you know him?"

"How do you?" he asked suspiciously.

"He's my cousin," I replied. "I haven't seen him in a long time and am trying to find him. There is . . . unfinished business between us."

"We were friends," he said, looking down at the ground, and I noticed a small crack in his voice as he spoke. "He lived here in Enschede for a time but left some three weeks ago now."

"And what did he do while he was here?"

"He worked at a forge, creating shoes for the horses. That's where I first met him. My father's horse needed to be shod and I brought the beast to his stable. We started talking. We became friends."

"And?" I asked. "What became of him?"

"He fled," he told me.

"But why?"

"Something happened."

I felt my patience beginning to grow thin. "Just tell me," I said. "What did he do? Did he hurt you in some way? Did he do that to you?" I asked, nodding toward his stump. The flesh at the end was red and seemed tender. It looked as if he had lost it only recently and, although Hjalmar had caused me so much trouble, it would have surprised me to learn that he had turned to violence.

"Hjalmar would never even think of hurting a soul!" he cried, looking up at me now, and I could tell by his tone that he truly believed this. "He was the kindest, most honorable man I have ever known."

I stared at him. There was a time when I would have said the same thing, of course, but no more.

"What took place between you?" I asked, stepping forward now so almost nothing separated our bodies in the night. "Just tell me. I have no interest in pursuing your personal scandals but it's important that I know. Were you lovers? Is that it?"

The boy nodded.

"And what happened? He hurt you in some way?"

"My father discovered us. A fight ensued and, luckily, Hjalmar got away. I never saw him again. If you find him, tell him that he must not come back here. My father says that he will kill him if he lays eyes on him again."

I nodded. "And you?" I asked. "Did your father do this to you?"

"Yes," he said, nodding toward his right shoulder. "First, he chopped off my hand. A week later, he took off my arm at the elbow. A week after that, my arm at the shoulder. It seems he's done for now—I can't clean tables if I have no arms—but he's made it clear that if Hjalmar returns, he will do the same to the other one, then to my right leg, and then to my left. And he will do even worse to him. I am to be married now, it seems. A few days from now. To—"

"But do you know where he might have gone?" I asked, interrupting him. "Hjalmar, I mean. Did he ever suggest where he might go if he was to leave Enschede?"

He shook his head. "Never," he said. "And if I knew the answer to that question, I would not be here now. I would be with him. He's gone forever. No, you'll never find him."

"Everyone can be found," I told the boy, handing him a few coins for his trouble. "It just takes time, that's all. And patience. And fortunately, I have plenty of both."

SWEDEN

A.D. 1133

I T SEEMED THAT I WAS NOT the only member of our party engaged in a romantic interlude, for my older brother, Janne, had
succeeded in seducing Queen Ulvhild's lady-in-waiting, Ulla, and
appeared to be completely smitten by her. I could scarcely comprehend his attachment, for not only did Ulla look as if she were the
product of a forced mating between a camel and a goat, but she
sported a beard that would have made a Viking envious. Added to
this was the fact that she stank to the heavens, for she had a deep
aversion to water.

Before Queen Ulvhild had been forced to leave Copenhagen,
Ulla had somehow become engaged to a Danish count and lost no
opportunity to complain of how she had been robbed of her chance
to be elevated to the aristocracy simply because she'd found herself,
in her words, in service to a Norwegian whore who had once been
Queen of Sweden, then became Queen of Denmark, and was now
returning to Stockholm to become Queen of Sweden once again.

"The stupid woman can't decide which throne she likes better,"
Ulla grumbled when her mistress was out of earshot. "She bounces
between them all, hoping the cushions in each palace will be a more
comfortable fit than the one before. She murdered her first husband, of course—"

"You don't know that for sure, Ulla," said Janne cautiously. "So
have a care with your tongue lest she cut it out."

"I know what I know," she insisted. "And she made King Niels's
life a misery in Denmark. The poor man was probably happy to end
up slain like his brother Canute, although at least his jezebel of a
wife, Adela of Flanders, had the comfort of knowing that her husband was murdered in the Lord's house and not on the streets of
Schleswig."

I had never heard of Adela of Flanders and nor had I ever been to Schleswig, but I felt a shiver run down my spine at the mention of their names, as if a stranger had walked over my grave.

"What's got into you?" asked Ulla, frowning at me. "Adela was dead before you were even born so there's no need to look offended on her behalf. Anyway, where will Ulvhild go if this next marriage doesn't succeed? Should Adeliza of England worry that she'll sail across the water to steal King Henry? Should Isabella of France be keeping a closer eye on King Philip? That woman won't rest until she's bedded the king of every European country and, even then, she'll probably look eastward toward the heathen world."

• • •

"I haven't been with many women, Brother," Janne remarked a little later as we rode together in the direction of Vreta Abbey, where Queen Ulvhild wished to pay her respects to her first husband, the slain King Inge, before marching to the capital to meet her third. She saw it as a pilgrimage of sorts, employing that word as often as possible in order to suggest divine approval for her journey, although there were some in our party who wondered whether it might serve more as an atonement than anything else. After all, there were rumors that Ulvhild herself had served the drink that ended the King's life. "No more than a thousand, I would estimate."

"A thousand?" I cried in astonishment. I could scarcely fathom how a man could be so promiscuous and still have enough energy to get through the day.

"I know, it doesn't seem like that many," he replied, shrugging his shoulders and looking a little humbled, "but it's been enough for me. I'm a man of simple tastes and limited means. How about you?" he asked.

"Fewer than that," I told him, which was quite the understatement in itself. "Far, far fewer than that."

"But still, I don't think I've ever met a woman like Ulla before. She can do things to a man that would make your toes curl and your eyes pop from your head."

"Indeed," I said, not wishing to imagine them.

"And have you ever seen such a beauty?"

"She's . . . unique, that's for sure."

"I like that word, Brother. Unique! She is that!"

"And her . . . her unusual scent?" I asked carefully.

"I know," he replied, his face lighting up. "It's exhilarating, isn't it? I like a woman to smell like meat and beer!"

"I can see why you're so drawn to her, then," I said. "She definitely smells of those. Among other things."

"And you haven't even got to sniff the best parts of her," he added, laughing lustily. "The woman hasn't washed in a year so the smell down there—"

"Brother, please!" I cried, raising a hand to stop him from saying any more, for I felt ill even at the idea of it. That such a cantankerous scold could prove an enchantress in the bedchamber remained bewildering to me. Still, despite his more unwelcome confidences, I was happy for him and pleased that my brother felt comfortable talking to me in such intimate terms.

"And you?" he asked. "You seem to be enjoying the journey."

"In what sense?" I said.

"Don't play coy, Brother," he said, slapping me on the back. "You and Ulvhild. Although you're taking your life in your hands there. She's about to become a queen for the third time, remember. She murdered her first husband, caused the death of her second, and now returns to Sweden to marry the new King. How many more crowns will she steal before her looks fade?"

"She is no murderess," I said. I felt flattered by her attention toward me, of course, and her lovemaking was spectacular, but if I was honest, I considered her an intimidating presence, for she had a way of looking at me that suggested that if I did not perform up to her standards, then she would feel no guilt about slitting my throat and finding someone else to attend to her physical needs.

"Or perhaps you have designs on a crown yourself?" he asked.

I laughed. "There is little chance of that, Janne," I said.

"You don't think so? If she kills the third one and ascends the throne of Sweden, then she'll be looking for a consort. Someone she can keep in his place. This one has been ruled by men for far too long and some say she could wield an orb better than any man alive. Her claim would be strong, too. She might even unite the Scandinavian kingdoms under her own rule if she put her mind to it."

I shook my head. "There's no part of me that wants to be a king," I said. "I'm a simple man."

"That's what everyone with ambition says," he replied.

· · ·

Queen Ulvhild told me that she wanted to enter Vreta Abbey alone. It had been standing for less than thirty years and, while she and her first husband had supported it financially throughout their reign, she had visited on only a few occasions in the past, notably on the night that he had drunk from the poisoned chalice before falling to his death.

Taking advantage of the Queen's absence, Janne and Ulla disappeared into the woods together, she slung over his shoulder like a bag of potatoes. I tried not to picture the antics they would be engaging in within the forest—no doubt she would complain about the roughness of the bark, or the insects on the ground, or the sun being too hot, or not hot enough, or too bright, or too sallow.

While the Queen was in the abbey, I took a walk around the grounds, looking up toward the clock tower, and marveling at the work that had gone into the monastery's design, feeling a pang for the artistic ideals that had once been such a part of my life, and wondered why I had abandoned them. For a moment, reading the inscriptions in the stonework, I questioned whether I should abandon my quest for Hasse entirely and return home, set up a workshop and return to the things that I had once loved. Reaching out now to touch the carvings, my fingers connected with the stone, and, in that same moment, a burst of lightning sounded from the sky above, but when I looked up, the weather was clear and the sky was blue. My companions did not seem to have heard it, despite the intensity of the clamor, for they were talking among themselves and seemed undisturbed. The lightning sounded again and now my hand appeared to be stuck to the wall for, no matter how I tried to pull it away, it would not move. What sorcery was this? I asked myself, and only the sound of weeping nearby pulled me from this strange reverie. I snapped out of it at last and my hand came free from the wall.

I turned around, feeling deeply unsettled, and watched as a young woman dressed in the white habit and veil of a postulant made her way around the corner before sitting down on a bench, a set of rosary beads clasped between her hands. She was weeping silently and, intrigued, I stepped closer toward her. As I approached, I coughed a little, so as not to startle her, but when she looked up, she did not seem like someone who would be easily frightened.

"Who are you?" she asked, and I bowed before her in order to show that I meant her no harm, offering my name and telling her that I had arrived in service to Queen Ulvhild.

"I saw her inside," said the woman. "I tried to greet her, but she waved me away as if I was a fly. They say that the last time she was here she poisoned her husband. She's kneeling on the altar now, praying for forgiveness, I suppose."

"Or praying for the safe repose of his soul," I suggested. "For who knows the truth of what went on that night? And who are you, if I may be so bold? Will you tell me your name?"

She looked me up and down for a moment, as if deciding whether or not she wanted to continue this conversation. "Signy," she said finally.

"And you're a nun?"

"Not yet," she replied, shaking her head. "But I will be one day, I'm told."

"You're told? Have you not chosen this path for yourself, then?"

She shrugged and looked away.

"May I sit?" I asked.

Again, it took her some time to decide whether or not she would grant me this honor but, eventually, she nodded, and I took my place next to her on the bench, keeping as respectful a distance between us as I could.

"How long have you lived at the abbey?" I asked.

"Six months," she replied.

"Something tells me that you did not come of your own volition."

She smiled ruefully and turned, the tears drying on her cheeks now, and there was something musical in her voice when she spoke again. "I'm nineteen years old," she said. "And a woman. Do you really think there is anything that I do that is of my own volition?"

"No," I said, shaking my head. "I expect not."

"It is the way of the world," she said.

"Your family sent you here, then?"

She smiled a little. "Not quite," she said. "It's a long story and not one to go into on such a beautiful day as this. Particularly with a stranger."

"Perhaps you'll tell me why you were crying, then?" I asked.

"Because today is an important one for me," she said. "It is marked deeply in my heart."

I nodded. I knew enough not to inquire any further.

"And you?" she asked. "You will be here at the abbey for long?"

"We ride on when the Queen is finished praying," I told her. "The Swedish king is preparing to make her his bride."

"I hope he has someone to taste his food," she said, and, despite myself, I laughed. As I did so, I looked up and saw Ulvhild standing by the entrance to the abbey, watching me with a curious expression on her face. I jumped to my feet, ready to go as soon as I was bidden, and turned to Signy to say that it had been a pleasure to meet her, but she had already departed, her feet taking her quickly back in the direction from which she had appeared.

My eyes followed her, even when the Queen called me, and called me again, until I at last obeyed and walked toward her. When I stood before her, she slapped me hard across the face, her ring catching against my lip and drawing blood from the corner of my mouth.

. . .

As it turned out, we did not ride on immediately after the Queen's prayers, for the abbess, Mother Pernilla, invited Ulvhild to stay for dinner and pass the night at Vreta before continuing to the capital the next day. Seated next to each other over an insubstantial plate of potatoes and dry meat, and drinking a glass of wine, the Queen was still annoyed with me, but I refused to acknowledge her irritation and spoke as if nothing unusual had taken place at all. Finally, she laid down her cutlery and turned to me with an expression of pure fury on her face.

"I will not be made a fool of," she said, and I continued eating, uncertain why she was telling me this. "Are you listening to me?"

"I can hear you, certainly," I said. "But I don't know what you're talking about."

"You and that girl earlier. In the gardens."

"The nun, you mean?"

"The postulant."

"A nun by any other name."

"You were trying to seduce her."

I shook my head. "I am many things," I said. "But a seducer of nuns is not one of them. If I have displeased Your Majesty in any way—"

"Just remember what happened to my first husband," she hissed. "Here in this very place." She reached forward for the flagon of wine that sat on the table before us and poured a glass before handing it to me. I stared at it, momentarily paralyzed, but then lifted it and drank it down, placing the empty glass back on the table and returning to my food. I did not intend to be intimidated by her. If death was to come for me, then let it come. I had faced more frightening ordeals.

"I didn't realize that you had feelings for me," I said. "I assumed ours was a purely physical relationship."

"Don't flatter yourself," she said. "I don't have any stronger feelings for you than I would have for a dog in the street. But if it's my dog, then only I get to play with it. So don't make a fool of me, do you hear? We only have a few more days together and, after that, perhaps I will want you to remain at the palace for longer. My next husband is not a handsome man, they tell me, and I will need entertaining."

CHINA

A.D. 1191

F I FELT ILL-USED that my life had become subject to the whims and caprices of the Empress Li Fengniang, it was nothing compared to the subordination experienced by her husband, our Imperial Ruler, the Emperor Guangzong, who, despite being the Exalted One and the Son of Heaven, suffered greatly from his poor choice of wife.

Weeks after accompanying this toxic creature, this serpent of the lake, this foul-tongued harridan, back to Lin'An after her pilgrimage to the Shaolin Monastery, I now completely regretted having joined the royal party at all for, as I discovered, once welcomed into the imperial household, it was almost impossible to be released from it again.

Traveling back from Henan Province, the insatiable Empress insisted that I provide her with pleasures of the flesh, and while my brother Jiao-long was amused by how exhausted I grew, he advised that I would do well to end relations with Li Fengniang as soon as we reached the imperial court. Others had fallen under her spell, he told me, and had grown to regret such an awkward alliance. It was advice that I was minded to heed but, once we arrived in the capital, the Empress refused to permit me to return to private life, despite my best entreaties. I even confided in her the truth about my past and my ongoing search for my errant cousin, Hai, hoping that such honesty would burrow its way into that hidden part of her soul where goodness lay, but, to my disappointment if not my surprise, my words fell upon deaf ears.

The Emperor himself was a weak man, controlled by his mother, the Grand Empress Dowager Wu, and by Li Fengniang herself, the two women locked in mortal combat for dominion over his soul.

Wu frightened me even more than her daughter-in-law, for she was known to order on impulse the execution of anyone who displeased her. The most trivial offense was grist to her murderous personality—not bowing at the correct elevation when the imperial presence passed; possessing a speaking voice that was offensive to the imperial sense of harmony; wearing a color that displeased the imperial eye—and I made sure to steer clear of those parts of the palace where she was known to spend most of her time, for I valued the bond between my head and my shoulders and had no desire to break it.

The position that was thrust upon me at court was one from which, in other circumstances, I might have derived great pleasure, for I had been a dress-maker by trade before the murder of my wife and son and had spent much of my youth designing lavish robes for the ladies of my village, my colorful sashes being a particular mark of my style. Being put in charge of the imperial wardrobe, with forty seamstresses under my command, would have been a welcome challenge, were it not for the fact that I longed to be elsewhere.

Li Fengniang came to my room without warning most nights, offering detailed instructions on how she wanted me to pleasure her, vile perversions that she had read about in the forbidden books. If I diverged from her desires by even a jot, she would complain and beat me about the head with a stick, using words like "fox spirit," "rabbit whelp" and "mallard's orphan" to diminish me, but at tender moments she would cling tightly to my body, claiming that no man had ever given her the satisfaction that I did, a compliment that might have appealed to the vanity of proud men but which served only to prolong my stay in Lin'An.

On one such occasion, having performed the sort of unspeakable acts upon which even a farmyard animal might have turned its back, I sat on the corner of my bed, lost in despair and shame and, looking across at Li Fengniang, who was sighing in contentment, decided to plead my case once again.

"Perhaps if Her Imperial Majesty, the most sparkling diamond in the shimmering tiara of the world, would permit me a year away from the capital, I might be permitted to continue my journey and—"

"No," she replied, interrupting me and waving her hand in the air as if she were swatting away a fly.

"The Daughter of Heaven, the most gracious Empress Li Feng-niang, will remember that when I first joined her retinue on the invitation of my older brother, honored Jiao-long, it was with the intention of continuing with Her Imperial Majesty's train only as far as Lin'An so that I might inquire of people along the way whether they had encountered my cousin."

"We've had this conversation," she said, rolling her eyes. "Many times. The answer each time has been no, and it remains no."

"Your humble servant is flattered that the most precious jewel in the diadem of the heavens enjoys the company of one so unworthy as I," I continued. "But I have it on good authority that many of the young men in the palace find that they become almost blind with adoration when Her Imperial Majesty, the brightest pearl in the heart of a glorious oyster, passes their way. Many would die happy if they could spend a single night in her company, satisfying her every need."

She yawned heavily and looked at me as if she wasn't sure whether she wanted to commit the marriage act with me for a fifth time that day or have me beheaded.

"It's kind of you to care so deeply for my gratifications," she said. "But the fact is, I have tried engaging with other men on the nights that I am not with you, but none pleases me quite as you do. You're not the world's most handsome man, it's true, but you have a certain something that remains delicious to me. No, you will remain here at my pleasure and feel honored to do so. I may tire of you at some point—you will grow old and withered, you will no longer be able to perform as men should—and when that day comes, I will either have you thrown in the river or give you leave to quit the palace. Or, perhaps, you might choose to kill yourself from the shame of displeasing me."

I soon grew to realize that the more I begged to leave, the more determined she was that I should stay, and as the weeks passed, I grew so frustrated that I found myself cursing the bad luck that had led me to this place. Time was moving on, after all, and Hai would undoubtedly be moving further away all the time. I considered leaving without permission but knew that, if I did such a thing, she would send hunters who would track me down and return me to her clutches before I could get far; the skin would be peeled from my body in a public square, one slice at a time, as she watched and laughed.

And so I was left with no choice but to remain at her command and hope that, someday, something might happen that would see my fortunes change.

. . .

For all her own infidelities, Li Fengniang hated the fact that her husband maintained a harem of concubines in the palace who served at his pleasure with just as much dedication as I served at hers. Most of these young women were quiet but friendly and I had grown close to one in particular, a girl named Shun, whom I had first met soon after my arrival in the city, when I discovered her alone and weeping in the gardens of the palace. Since then, we'd enjoyed several pleasant encounters and I found her an intriguing presence, although she seemed cautious of revealing too much of herself to me. As yet, all I knew of her story was that she had been brought to Lin'An as a concubine when the Emperor had been passing through her village and happened to see her standing at the roadside. Enamored, he'd instructed one of his soldiers to take her to the capital and, of course, like all his subjects, she had no choice but to obey.

There was another girl, Huang, who had a certain authority to her bearing, for it was well known that Guangzong favored her above all others. Certainly, she was a great beauty with a tender singing voice, so perhaps it was no surprise that the Emperor enjoyed her company. Every night as the sun began to set, Huang would stand on the balcony that overlooked the central courtyard and sing Plum Blossom Melodies, ostensibly to the province but, in reality, to the Emperor, who would sit by the fountain, lost in pleasure as he allowed his beloved's voice to seep into the depths of his soul.

"The Empress loathes her," Shun told me one afternoon as we took a tour of the formal gardens together. "She tolerates the rest of the concubines because she knows her husband would barely notice if any of them lived or died but she despises the fact that Guangzong has an emotional attachment to Huang that he has to none other."

That part of the palace where the concubines lived was ruled over by Ui, a noblewoman who, for some time, had been engaged in an inexplicable romance with my brother. I found Ui to be difficult company, for she had a dispiriting nature and rarely washed, her malodorous nature proving an inexplicable aphrodisiac to Jiao-long. She and I, along with Jiao-long and Shun, were seated by a fountain in the gardens one afternoon, the wind blowing in a westerly direction so Ui's stench floated toward my brother, who was sniffing at her like a dog investigating its next meal, when she recounted just how much the imperial couple loathed each other.

Although she professed to hate gossip, Ui was one of its greatest practitioners and told us of an incident that had taken place that morning when Li Fengniang had come into the Emperor's bed-chamber while the concubine Huang was still present and flown into a rage. The girl had run naked from the room, weeping like a child, while Ui, listening at the door, overheard the Empress insisting of her husband that he abandon his concubines forever and live a faithful life.

"A ridiculous idea," he laughed. "Every emperor in the history of our country has taken concubines to his bed. Why would I be the first not to follow in this tradition?"

"Because I cannot stand to be anyone's inferior!" she roared.

"You have your men," he told her. "Why should I not have my women? We cannot be left to sleep with only each other, surely? You loathe me, and I cannot bear the sight of you."

"You make a good point, Husband," she replied, considering this. "But it's one thing to fornicate with concubines. Another to fall in love with one."

"Fall in love?" he asked, laughing. "And with whom am I supposed to have fallen in love?"

"Huang!" she screamed. "Don't treat me like a fool. I don't like her, and I don't trust her. She fails to treat me with the respect to which my position entitles me. All the court knows how you sit in the gardens every evening listening to her croak her dirges. It's a humiliation to me."

The Emperor shook his head. While he gave in to both his wife and mother on almost every matter relating to the court, this was one area where he was determined to remain master. His encounters with Huang, after all, were the happiest moments of his days and he was not prepared to give them up for anyone, least of all a wife who treated him with such contempt.

"So what would you have me do?" asked Guangzong, infuriated by her pointless jealousy.

"Chop her head off!"

"Never!"

"Pluck her eyes out and sever her ears!"

"No!"

"Refuse to see her!"

"Impossible!"

"Send her back to her people!"

"I will not!"

"You would defy your wife?"

"I would!"

At which point Li Fengniang flung herself on the bed and wrapped her hands around the Emperor's throat, throttling him, leading Ui to run into the room, followed by four of Guangzong's bodyguards, who dragged his angry wife away, leaving him nursing his bruised neck and weeping like an infant girl, a humiliation that only made Li Fengniang burst out laughing.

"Fine, Husband," she declared, brushing away the men who were doing their best to restrain her. "If you will not take care of this matter, then I will do so myself."

"And what did she mean by that?" asked Jiao-long, nuzzling his face into Ui's fetid shoulder.

"Who knows?" replied Ui. "That woman has no more sense than a grasshopper. She's liable to do anything to get her way."

"I pity the Emperor," he replied, shaking his head. "Being spoken to like that, and by a woman, no less! And I feel great sympathy for you, Brother, being forced to satisfy that she-wolf's desires whenever she demands it."

I glanced toward Shun, who blushed at his remark. I supposed that it was common knowledge that I was regularly summoned to the Empress's bed, but it was not something that I liked to speak about.

. . .

A few nights later, to my astonishment, Li Fengniang suggested that I might be permitted to leave Lin'An after all.

"I've been giving it some thought," she said, relaxing on a window seat that was decorated with symbols of fire, earth, wind and water, as she tapped a painted nail against her chin. It was clear that she was enjoying the power she wielded over me. "I realize that I'm being a little unfair to you. It's true that when you first joined my entourage you were clear about your plans so you'll have to forgive me if I became so attached to you that I didn't want to lose you. But I see now that I've been selfish."

I stared at her, waiting to see whether she was playing some cruel trick on me or whether she actually meant it.

"Daughter of Heaven!" I exclaimed, dropping to my knees and kissing her feet. "The brightest beam from the morning sun! Your generosity is extraordinary. I am most profoundly grateful to you and when I find my malignant cousin, Hai, and end that longstanding relationship between his head and body, I will sing your name forever in eternal glory."

"Of course," she continued, holding a hand in the air to still my gratitude. "For me to let you go is a great sacrifice on my part. And I hope that you will show your gratitude to me in return."

"Without delay," I replied, standing up to undo the buttons of my trousers. I had already lowered them to my knees when she shook her head, laughing, and instructed me to stop.

"Not that," she said. "At least, not now. No, I have a far more important request to make of you."

"Anything, Exalted One. Speak your words and I shall fly to my task with the speed of one thousand horses."

"The rooms at the top of the palace, where the concubines live," she said. "You are familiar with them?"

"I know where they are, of course. But I have never visited them. They are forbidden to me."

"But you've stood below and looked up toward the rooftop?"

"I have, Magnificence."

"Then you will know the balcony where that daughter of a mountain goat, Huang, stands every evening to sing the foul lullabies that pollute the air and draw blood from the ears of innocent souls. They extend across the grounds of the palace and my husband, Guangzong, fool that he is, sits by the fountain, listening as she serenades him, his expression embarrassing all who look in his direction."

I nodded. I had often hidden in the shadows myself at those times, for it was a pleasure to hear Huang, a skilled songstress, give voice to some of our ancient melodies.

"The railing on that balcony," she continued. "I would like it to be loosened. For some of the nails to be pulled from the walls."

I frowned. "But if that were to happen—"

"If that were to happen, all it would mean was that a railing had come loose, nothing more. The man who loosened it would not be responsible for any calamity that might later befall a person who happened to lean against it. You are anxious to leave Lin'An and to pursue your quest for vengeance, are you not? Well, this is how you can achieve your goal. Can I rely on you to do this?"

I felt my heart sink within my chest as my good angels did battle with my bad, but finally I shook my head. "No," I said. "If I were to do such a thing, and if someone were to fall, then I would surely be as responsible for that person's death as if I had pushed them myself."

"It wouldn't mean anything of the sort."

"With respect, Radiance, it would."

"How disappointing," she replied with a sigh after a lengthy pause. "But, on the other hand, it does mean that I will get to enjoy the pleasures of the flesh with you for many more years to come. Perhaps for the rest of our lives? We can grow old together here. Wouldn't that be a wonderful thing?"

"Please, Greatest Star in the Firmament," I protested, dropping to my knees.

"Silence!" she shouted. "I make one simple request of you and yet you refuse me. So why should I grant your wishes? No, we will forget this conversation ever took place and you and I will return to our previous arrangement. Undress immediately, dog. I have a peculiar fantasy that I want to share with you. It might sound a little distasteful at first, even contrary to the laws of nature, but it rather excites me."

• • •

And so, to my eternal shame, I decided to do what she asked of me. Two mornings later, when the concubines were partaking of the baths, I ascended to the top floor of the palace, stealing along the corridor to the great room where they sat at their sewing in the evenings before the Emperor summoned some to his bedchamber. My heart pounded in my chest in a mixture of fear and self-loathing, but I told myself over and over that I was doing nothing more than loosening a few screws and that whatever happened afterward was outside of my control.

The balcony was very easy to access and the view that it offered across the palace grounds spectacular. Looking down, I could see where Guangzong sat every evening as he listened to the voice of his favorite concubine and, taking care to ensure that my work was completed quickly, I did as I had been instructed, removing some of the screws entirely while loosening some others. Putting them in my pocket, I made my way back out to the corridor when, to my dismay, I heard a voice calling out from behind me. A familiar, if unpleasant, stench drifted my way.

"What are you doing here?" cried Ui, the Mistress of Concubines, who was standing before me now with a frown on her face.

"I was lost," I said.

"Lost? Here? An unlikely story. I hope you weren't trying to ingratiate yourself with one of the concubines. You know what the penalty for that is, don't you?"

I nodded, muttering an apology, and perhaps out of loyalty to my brother, she dismissed me with a contemptuous flick of her wrist, saying that we would speak of it no more, and walked away, turning into the corridor out of sight. Removing the screws from my pocket now, I stared at them, finally appreciating the gravity of what I had done. I was desperate to leave the capital, of course I was, but surely an innocent girl's life was too high a price to pay for my freedom? Crying out in frustration, I released myself from the curse that Li Fengniang had put upon me and marched back toward the concubines' room, then out to the balcony once again, determined to secure the railing. However, I had barely started upon my repairs when I heard noises coming from outside the room and, looking around, I saw the concubines, fresh from their baths and wearing clean robes, walking through the door. They stopped as one in surprise, for a man was almost never admitted to these quarters, putting their hands to their mouths as they wondered whether they should laugh or scream.

I bowed, begging their forgiveness for invading their sacred space, and unfortunately for me, Ui chose this moment to reappear, ushering me out as she roared that this was my last warning, and the next time she discovered me there, she would report me to the head of the Imperial Guard, who would have no hesitation in removing my eyes from my head.

"Wait," I said, for I knew that the balcony was still unsafe. "You must tell Huang not to—"

"I'll tell no one anything," she said, pushing me toward the staircase. "Be gone, you debauched creature, or you might not live to see the morning."

• • •

An hour later, I stood in the shadow of the trees watching as the Emperor took his usual place and stared up, waiting for his beloved Huang to appear. When she did, I held my breath in anticipation, hoping that the railing might hold until I could return the following day to complete my repairs. When the girl finished her first song and leaned forward, looking out across the city, all seemed well and I breathed a sigh of relief.

Her second song was even more beautiful than her first and when she came to an end, she looked down, smiled, and blew a kiss toward her beloved Emperor. Typically, she sang only two songs, but tonight he called up, asking for one more, and as her voice rose in melody once again, I noticed another figure appear in the courtyard, on the opposite side to me, looking up with as much anticipation as Guangzong or I. It was the Empress, of course, my despised lover, and she didn't flinch when the songbird began her tune.

At that same moment, a crack of lightning sounded from above, the concubine startled, the balcony shook, the railing fell forward and she toppled after it one hundred feet, her body crashing immediately to the ground, her broken limbs splayed at unnatural angles from her body, her blood spilling at the feet of the Lord of Ten Thousand Years.

GREECE

A.D. 1223

SPENT THE FOLLOWING WEEK alone in a small, dark cell, starving and dehydrated, with only a family of rats for company, cursing both my inexcusable selfishness and my inexplicable stupidity. As my brother's patron, Gergo Aquilo had welcomed me into his villa and I had abused his hospitality by allowing his wife to seduce me and become part of her plot to kill his mistress.

Perhaps traveling with such destructive and murderous ambitions in mind had caused me to forget my true nature, but if I felt a deep sense of shame over my actions, it was as nothing compared to the anger I felt toward Lieke. My waking hours were devoted to pacing my cell, cursing her name and influence, and it was only at moments of profound self-reflection that I was willing to take responsibility for my actions and accept that I had no one to blame for my downfall but myself. I now had the deaths of four people on my conscience. How had I allowed such a thing to happen?

Gergo, the wealthiest spice trader in Greece, had been good to me from the start, even rewarding me for keeping his wife safe on her recent pilgrimage by commissioning me to create a mosaic on the wall of his house. And while I had been desperate to leave, the work had pleased me, for it had been a long time since I'd had the opportunity to indulge my passion. I created an image of the twelve classical gods of Greek history, using tiny pieces of fractured glass and stone to bring them to life.

"Tell me, Master Craftsman," Gergo said only a few days before my imprisonment as I worked on a standing figure of Dionysus, the god of the grape harvest, whom I depicted in the act of feeding his produce to a prostrate Demeter, "how does a man with such skills end up roaming the countryside when he should be spending his days devoted to his art?"

"It is a story of some length and complication," I replied, understating things considerably. "Suffice to say that my life has been a mixture of the simple and the problematic. Thrice I have loved and thrice I have lost. Grief has been an all too familiar companion to me and there are stains upon my soul that are difficult to cleanse."

"You married each of these women?"

"Only two."

"You had children with them?"

"Yes, but none have survived."

"Lieke and I were never blessed with sons or daughters," he told me, looking down at the ground with a sorrowful expression on his face. "I wish it had been different. My mother has always blamed my wife for this. Perhaps you've noticed they are not the best of friends."

I declined to answer, assuming the statement was rhetorical, but yes, it had been obvious to me since my arrival in Athens that Gergo's mother and wife were locked in an eternal battle to see who could assert the most control over him. I added a piece of turquoise glass into the bunch of grapes and felt a burst of guilt at how I was making a cuckold of this unfortunate man, for I liked him and he had been good to me. From the villa nearby came the sound of singing as a young woman accompanied herself on the kithara and Gergo lit up, for it was his beloved Hermione, with whom he was infatuated and whose death I would facilitate before the sun had risen and set many more times.

In my cell now, I wondered whether Lieke was experiencing similar pangs of guilt. She was being held in the room next to my own and spent her hours wailing, screaming or so quiet that I wondered whether she had taken her own life. Had I the means, I might have done so myself.

• • •

I did not see sunlight again until I was being dragged in chains along the streets of Athens while the locals huddled together in groups, cursing my name, spitting at me and throwing rotten fruit at my head. Having spent a week of confinement in such a small cell, I found it difficult to walk at first, but I knew that if I tripped or fell, the horses would simply drag me along, and so I had no choice but to keep moving.

If they were furious with me, however, the Athenians reserved their worst condemnation for Lieke. They accepted that men were weak creatures, too easily swayed by a woman, but expected a wife to behave with more loyalty. My erstwhile lover was walking a third of a mile behind me and I could hear the jeering that was being aimed in her direction, and knew how deeply she, who had always prized her status, would hate this public shaming.

As we approached the center of the city, I saw my brother Jorgen standing with his beloved Ulyssa, and next to them was Shura, the young woman with whom I had developed an affectionate relationship. She was weeping, as she had been when we first met, and I hoped that she did not despise me too badly for what I had done.

Othon de la Roche had been Lord of Athens for many years and was well known to be that rarest of creatures, an uxorious man. He and his wife, Isabella, had been married since the start of the century, producing ten children together, all of whom miraculously lived. The couple were inseparable and it was rumored that they had even been observed holding hands at a public event, an unprecedented intimacy. While this might have suggested that they were kind and considerate souls, I guessed Othon's fidelity would work against Lieke and me, for if there was one thing that a man who loved his wife enjoyed, it was castigating those who brought shame upon the institution of marriage.

The lord was seated impassively upon a painted throne, his hands resting regally upon the arm-supports, and when I was unshackled from the horse, I fell to my knees, in relief as much as pain, while a bucket of what I hoped was dirty water but smelled like piss was thrown over me to wipe some of the dust from my face. A moment later, I glanced to my right as Lieke, also bruised and bloodied, slumped to the ground next to me, looking so unkempt that I almost felt sympathy for her. Her hair had been chopped short, she bore cuts on her lips and across her face, and I dreaded to think what other indignities the jailers might have inflicted upon her during her imprisonment, for they were brutal fellows.

The crowd fell silent now and we looked up to see Isabella, the lady of the city, joining her husband on the dais, while, seated on a chair a few steps lower, was the cuckold himself, Gergo Aquilo, looking wounded and miserable. I hoped that he would not turn in my direction, for I could not bear to feel the weight of his disappointment upon me. To my relief, he spent most of our trial staring down at his sandals, only occasionally throwing a glance toward his errant wife.

"You have been brought here today to answer charges of murder," cried Othon, raising his arm now like an old Roman emperor. The last voices were silenced as he stared down at us. "You, Lieke, wife of Gergo Aquilo, claim that this worthless creature kneeling next to you was responsible for the death of the songbird Hermione. He, on the other hand, insists that it was you who loosened the rocks above the area where she sat to play her kithara, hoping that they would fall and kill her. As they did."

"He's lying!" shouted Lieke. "I would never do such a cruel thing! I am an honest and faithful wife, as God is my witness! This man tried to seduce me on many occasions, but I always resisted him out of loyalty to my beloved Gergo. He seeks to denounce me now out of bitterness, nothing more."

"And you?" asked Othon, unmoved, turning his gaze to me. "How do you respond to such an allegation?"

"I admit that Lieke and I have enjoyed those pleasures that are sacred to a husband and wife," I replied, my voice catching in my throat, for it had been some time since I had used it. "But I did not unsettle the stones. She begged me to do it, yes, but I refused. So, either she took it upon herself to complete the task or she found another."

Of course, this was a lie. Lieke had asked me to commit this act of folly in exchange for my freedom and I'd even begun to do it before reconsidering and restoring the stones to their original places. But there had not been enough time for them to settle correctly and a crack of lightning had seen the stones tumble from their perch, killing Hermione even as Gergo watched from the courtyard of his villa.

More questions were asked and Lieke and I contradicted each other at every step until, at last, it became clear that neither of us was going to admit any guilt.

"Then there is no way for me to decide who is telling the truth and who is lying," announced Othon finally. "So I will leave it to God to decide."

The crowd cheered in delight; they had been hoping all along that this would be the verdict. The greatest and most vicious spectacle of all.

Lieke and I, however, looked around in terror, for this was what we had feared the most. Hanging would be bad, and having our heads lopped off would be equally objectionable, but this? This was the worst of all possible punishments.

"We shall have a trial by ordeal," declared the Lord of Athens. "And may God instruct us on who is at fault here and who is blameless!"

. . .

No one in the history of our great city had ever survived a trial by ordeal. Despite the pretense that the outcome was a result of divine providence, there was really only one possible verdict, and, accepting that I would fail and forfeit my life, I did my best to make peace with my situation, hoping that I would be reunited with my loved ones in the next life. I put the question to Jorgen as I waited for the trial instruments to be set up, doing my best not to look in their direction, for they were fearsome tools, capable of striking terror into even the hardiest of souls. Lieke had screamed in panic when the large pot was wheeled into the courtyard, and the smell of boiling lead was already beginning to grow pungent in the air.

"This is a question that I cannot answer, Brother," he replied sadly, and I noticed, to my astonishment, that he had tears in his eyes. "A thousand women await my presence in the next life and I don't know how I'll choose between them either." A hand flew out, slapping him hard across the face.

"My apologies," he said, turning to Ulyssa.

"You'll be waiting for me, Jorgen," she snapped. "I will outlive you and then you will remain chaste until I arrive to join you."

"Of course," he said. "I meant that I never played favorites in the past. Obviously, now . . . now is different."

Ulyssa reached across to kiss me now and I wondered whether I might ask her to embrace me again when the terrible moment came, as her scent might cause me to pass out entirely, but I was touched to see that she seemed upset by my upcoming torment. She had not admitted her responsibility for telling Gergo Aquilo that she had seen me lurking among the fatal stones earlier on that terrible day, but I guessed that it was she who had betrayed me. Still, I did not blame her; she had been fond of Hermione and my actions had been my own.

A great horn sounded from the platform and, intertwined with the ecstatic roars of an excited populace, Lieke screamed once again as my stomach dipped in fear. I had never considered myself either particularly brave or cowardly, but the idea of what was to come was almost too much for me. Had there been a word that I could have said to bring life to an immediate end, I would have happily uttered it at that moment.

"Good luck, Brother," said Jorgen, throwing his vast body around me. "Tell our father how much I have always regretted my lengthy absence from his life."

Before I could wrap my arms around him, too, one of the soldiers pulled me away, dragging me to the dais, where I stood next to Lieke, who was visibly shaking. I glanced at her and started to say something, but she cut me off by raising her hand and I assumed that she was trying to reconcile herself with what was to come, too, and needed silence. Respecting that, I looked away and held my tongue.

A moment later, Othon de la Roche stepped forward, holding out his arm once again as the crowd fell silent. At the corner of the dais, an executioner stood with an axe and block, ready to end the life of whoever God decreed was guilty.

"These two wretched creatures are accused of taking the life of an innocent girl," he declared. "They both claim innocence, so God shall decide their fate. Behold!"

He pointed toward the enormous steel pot that stood in the center of the platform, decorated with symbols of fire, earth, wind and water. It was filled with lead, which, scalded by the flames beneath it, had returned to liquid form and was bubbling ferociously, great gurgles of darkness eager to swallow us whole. Stepping forward, he opened his palm to reveal a stone, which he held over the center of the pot. I narrowed my eyes, as it seemed to have a face carved into it, but it was impossible to know whose. The Lord of Athens displayed it to the crowd for a moment before dropping it into the cauldron.

"All that is asked of you," declared Othon, "is that you reach into the pot and retrieve the stone. If you can do so without suffering any injury, then you will be declared innocent and will walk free this very day. If, however, your arm is lost to the lead, then you are found guilty, and will be beheaded. First, the shameless wife."

Two soldiers marched forward and dragged Lieke toward the vessel. She struggled with them, doing her best to pull away from the fumes and heat of the boiling lead, but they were too strong for her.

"Retrieve the stone," repeated Othon. "If you refuse to try, you will be lowered in slowly, head first."

Lieke closed her eyes for a moment, her lips moving soundlessly, in prayer perhaps, and then she offered a half-smile, as if she had given up on this world entirely, and plunged her arm into the horrible liquid, sinking it down all the way to the shoulder.

Her scream was like nothing I had ever heard before. It was a shriek as the clouds might have made when they gave birth to the storms that first created the world. The crowd cried out, too, in a mixture of horror and delight, and, although I wanted to look away, it was impossible not to stare as she fell to the ground, her arm missing, a horrible, boiling stump at her shoulder.

"Guilty!" cried Lady Isabella, leaping up from her throne. "God has declared it so!"

"He has," agreed Othon, nodding toward the soldiers, who lifted the unconscious woman from the dais and dragged her toward the block. She came back to life for a moment but seemed dazed by what was going on. She was thrown down, her head pressed against the wood; the executioner lifted his axe and, without a moment's delay, it fell upon her, severing her head from her body, a great stream of blood pouring from the corpse. Looking away in terror, I caught Gergo's eye and could see that he was deeply upset. I suppose he had loved her once.

"And now you," said Othon, and I stepped forward, determined not to be dragged by soldiers but to show some courage in death. I looked into the lead, hoping for a miracle, then thrust my arm out, feeling the heat of the pot rise against my skin, before allowing it to sink down as deep as it would go.

There was no immediate pain. But there were visions. Curious visions. Before my eyes, the world turned a multitude of colors and the audience seemed to grow silent, as did the person of Othon de la Roche standing next to me. I saw a boy tending to another, pressing a damp cloth against his forehead. A man sailing away from a shore on a block of ice. A group of monks bent over their manuscripts. And then, as if by common consent, the crowd parted, leaving an aisle in the center, and an elderly woman dressed entirely in black walked slowly between them, ascending the steps to where I stood, her eyes completely white. It was obvious that she was blind but when she stood before me it was as if she could see directly into my soul.

"It doesn't burn," I said.

"It does," she replied. "But you cannot feel it. Do not give in, son of Makira."

"Am I dead?" I asked. "Has the lead killed me?"

She shook her head. "Do you want to live?" she asked.

"Of course," I said.

"Where?"

I thought about it. The words emerged from my mouth without my even understanding what they meant.

"Among the stars," I said.

"And you will," she replied, turning her back on me then, walking away, and as she disappeared in the distance, I heard a great swell of noises and, blinking, was astonished to see the people of

Athens restored to their places, looking at me and crying aloud in delight. Some were even crying.

"Your arm," said Othon, and I looked down. I was no longer reaching into the pot but was holding the stone that he had dropped into it earlier. I stared at it in astonishment. The moment had come and gone so quickly that I could scarcely believe what had happened.

"You are innocent," he declared. "God has decreed it! And you may go free."

The crowd cheered again, and I opened my palm to look at the stone itself. Someone had used a chisel and hammer to chip away at it, for there was a rough portrait of a man carved into the front. Had the idea not seemed absurd, I would have sworn that the face belonged to my father.

PART 8

THE
REFUGE OF
THE WORLD

PORTUGAL

A.D. 1267

AFREE MAN ONCE AGAIN, I made the decision to travel eastward from Lisbon toward Évora, intending to make my way
through Spain and Italy as my quest continued. I did not,
however, journey alone. Serafina and I had developed a friendship
from the day I encountered her weeping silently in the duke's courtyard, and when I was preparing to leave the city, having somehow
managed to keep my head attached to my shoulders, she took me
aside to ask whether she might accompany me.

My brother João found a pair of horses for us and, after an emotional farewell, we began our ride cross-country, occasionally conversing but more often content to be left alone with our thoughts.
On our second evening, however, when we stopped at a hostelry in
search of food and rest, I saw a more determined side to her character than I had observed so far. Earlier that day, we had visited a
new cathedral that stood in the center of the city and while I had
been content to stroll around the nave and transept, marveling at
the work of the stonemasons, Serafina had knelt in one of the pews,
her head bowed low in prayer. It seemed that she was not praising
God, however, but asking for His help, for with every movement of
her lips, her body arched forward a little more in desperate entreatment.

The inn where we spent the night was one of the most modern I
had ever encountered, with separate tables for smaller groups and a
washroom outside that was connected to a well. One simply pressed
down on the arm of the pump and the water flowed out, as if by
magic! I would have thought that witchcraft was involved, had a
fellow traveler not explained to me the simplicity of the operation.
And then, before our meals were served from an enormous steel
pot, we were each handed a small knife, no bigger than my middle

finger, and a steel implement with two tines at the end, which, we were told, should be used to pierce our food before bringing it to our mouths. Why we could not simply use our hands as nature intended was a mystery to both of us, but, happy to engage in the customs of this strange new world, we did as instructed, even though I feared that I might perforate my tongue with two neat holes as I separated the meat from the steel.

"Do you recall the afternoon when we first met?" I asked as we ate. "You were drying tears from your cheeks."

"I remember," replied Serafina.

"You told me that it was a special day for you but did not say why."

She nodded but offered no explanation and I wondered whether I was perhaps intruding too far on a private matter. Before I could ask anything more, however, a man came over, quite drunk, and slumped down next to us, leering at my companion, who looked back at him coolly as she continued to eat.

"How much?" he asked, turning to me with a wink.

"How much for what?" I asked.

"For her. Ten minutes. I'll be quick, I promise. And I don't have any diseases, not like most of this lot," he added, pointing toward the other tables. "I'll get her back to you much as you gave her to me."

As if his boorishness wasn't bad enough, I doubted his honesty, for his body stank and his hair was so thick and matted upon his head that I felt certain a legion of lice must have set up camp there. His nails were blackened, too, and those few teeth that remained in his head were an unsettling shade of yellow.

"Friend," I said, trying to control my temper, "remove yourself from these seats before I do you an injury."

He raised an eyebrow, apparently more surprised than offended by my reply, and shook his head. "I have money if that's what you're worried about," he said, extracting a pouch of coins from the pocket of his coat and letting a few fall into his grubby palm.

"I don't care how much—"

"I'm not for sale," said Serafina, interrupting me as she reached across, enclosing the man's hand in her fist. Like a kicked dog, he yelped in pain and surprise as his skin cut against the edges of the coins, pulling back from her with a curse.

"Do you always let your whore behave to honest men in this way?" he asked me, massaging his wounded hand with the other. "If she was my woman, I'd whip her till she learned the natural order of things."

I stood up and reached for his collar, ready to defend Serafina's honor, but he had had enough by now and moved away, cursing us as he went.

"I'm sorry about that," I said as I sat back down, and she shrugged.

"Why? You didn't do anything."

I lifted my fork again, wondering whether I might return to the question of what had been so special about the day we met when, to my surprise, she leaped up from the table, marched across the room and, clutching the knife the innkeeper had given us to carve our meat, pressed it against the throat of the man who had tried to pay for her. The entire room fell silent, staring across at her in astonishment. A woman attacking a man! Such a thing had never been witnessed by any of us before. But she had the better of him, that was for sure, and there was nothing he could do to escape her clutches. Leaning her head down, she whispered something in his ear before standing back up, releasing the knife and returning to our table. The room remained still, looking from her to the man and back again, and the unfortunate creature who had dared to insult her stood up now in humiliation, an expression of terror on his face as he made his way quickly from the room, to the laughter of the patrons.

Serafina looked down at her knife and examined the blade before turning to the astonished innkeeper.

"I might need a clean one of these," she said.

. . .

The following morning, when we rode on, I felt as if we were both making a point of ignoring the events of the night before. It was not that I was unaccustomed to women behaving violently—my own sister had hardly been a peaceful creature—but until now, Serafina had struck me as one in whom gentility reigned over ferocity.

"Were you married?" I asked her after the lengthy silence between us began to grow awkward.

"Is it so obvious?"

"Only a woman who has been badly mistreated by a man could harbor such mercilessness within her soul. It was either a husband or a lover, I know that much."

"A husband," she replied.

"Does he yet live?"

"He does. But he will die soon."

"We will all die soon."

"Yes, but when my husband's time comes, it will be at my hand. The last face he sees will be my own. The last words he hears will come from my lips."

"Will you tell me about him?" I asked, wondering what monster could have inspired such terrible resolve. "Who is he? Where does he live?"

She rode on ahead for a while and I assumed that she did not want to discuss this matter any further, but in time, she slowed down and we were alongside each other once again. When she spoke, her tone was carefully controlled, as if she was determined not to give in to her rage.

"He is called Victorino," she told me, "may his name be forever cursed. And that spawn of the devil still lives in my home village."

"With another woman? He betrayed you and cast you out?"

"He betrayed nature itself. To my dismay, our daughter, Beatriz, remains under his roof."

"You have a daughter?" I said, surprised by this admission. "It is unusual for a mother to be separated from her husband and child, is it not? What happened to bring about such a peculiar estrangement?"

She turned to look at me and I shook my head in apology.

"I'm sorry," I said. "It's not my place to ask such questions. If you would rather that I hold my tongue, you need only say so."

She did not reply but pulled her horse to a stop. We had arrived at the Temple of Évora, a monument to the Roman Emperor Augustus, which stood in ruins before us. Serafina stepped inside and I followed, but when I reached out a hand to touch the stone carvings, something made me pull back, as if to touch them would be to desecrate the monument in some way. I sat next to her and was disturbed to see tears rolling down her cheeks, as they had been on our first encounter, but she wiped them away quickly and took a deep breath, as if she did not want to give in to any form of weakness.

"You don't have to talk about it, of course," I told her.

"Until now, I never have," she replied. "Can I trust you?"

I nodded. "I hope so."

She remained silent, considering this, before turning and looking me directly in the eye. "Tell me," she said. "Your search for your cousin. You are determined to kill him, isn't that true?"

"Yes."

"And do you think that you will feel better afterward? When he is lying cold in his grave, your wife and son will still be lost to you. Do you truly believe that his death will lay to rest whatever demons torment you?"

I looked up to study the architraves of the temple that had not suffered the ill effects of time and the carvings of the gods that were the work of subtle craftsmen. "I have so much blood on my hands already that it shames me," I told her in a quiet voice. "My actions in the past weigh deeply on my conscience and I fear that I will one day be condemned for them. I have always believed myself to be a decent man, Serafina. Truthfully, I consider myself a man of peace and art. And yet look at the destruction that I have brought about during my years on this flat plane we call Earth. The unforgivable loss of life. And still I am determined to kill my cousin, after which I hope to return to a peaceful existence, if such a thing is even possible. And I will feel better for my act of vengeance. I'm sure of it."

"We are both driven by anger," she said.

"As mankind has always been. The world changes constantly, you must recognize that? There are always new inventions, new explorers and new ideas. Consider the exhilaration that man must have felt when he invented the wheel. When the compass allowed us to find our way to and from other lands. When the calendar helped to define our days. Once, the Romans mixed pozzolana with water and created the Colosseum. A man from China designed a mechanical clock. Only last night you and I were given new implements for eating, shown novel ways for washing our hands and faces. Who could have predicted such things, even a generation ago? Someday, we may build towers taller than the eye can see, fly through the sky on wings, even live among the stars. But I know this much; the things that surround us may change, but our emotions will always remain the same. A man who lost his beloved wife a thousand years ago suffered the same grief that I felt when I lost mine, no more and no less. A woman who discovers her child is being mistreated a thousand years hence will experience the same levels of murderous fury that you feel today. Love does not change, anger never varies. Hope, desperation, fear, longing, desire, lust, anxiety, confusion and joy; you and I endure these emotions just as men and women always have or ever will. We are a small people in an ever-changing universe. The world around us might be in a state of constant flux, but the universe within?" I shook my head, both admitting and accepting the weakness of man. "No, Serafina. None of these will ever change. No matter how long this world continues."

We both remained silent for a long time, considering all that I had said, and I hoped that I had not given her cause to despise me or, worse, to be frightened of me or think me a fool.

"I am not a monster," I said finally in a plaintive tone. "I realize that you might think me one but—"

"Killing is sometimes necessary," she said, interrupting me. "We live in violent times, we are a passionate species, and few men I have known are unstained by blood. How can I criticize you when I plan on killing two people myself?"

I raised an eyebrow in surprise. "Two?" I said. "So your husband is not your only intended victim?"

"No."

"And who is the second?"

"His mother."

"For what reason?"

She reached down and lifted a fistful of sand, letting it pour slowly through her fingers. "Something terrible happened," she said. "Something in which that malevolent creature was complicit. A little over a year ago, I noticed that my daughter, Beatriz, was beginning to change. In the past, she had always been an outgoing girl, filled with life and song, cheerful in all respects, but the joy that had once defined her character began to disappear. I thought perhaps it was nothing more than a result of her age—she was twelve years old then—and guessed that she was finding her transition from childhood to adulthood to be more difficult than expected."

"Was she ill?" I asked.

"No," she replied. "Her health remained good. But then one day, her actions turned violent. Where she used to play with her friends, now she assaulted them, starting as many fights as she could. The other mothers, they came to me and said, 'Serafina, we cannot permit Beatriz to play with our daughters anymore. Look at how she mistreats them!' I was shocked by her behavior and sat her down to ask what had happened to make her so unhappy, but she would not tell me. I feared that an evil spirit was growing inside her, some spiteful imp that was becoming more troublesome by the day. I consulted a priest, but he only laughed at me and said that it was of no consequence. Beatriz, he told me, was only a girl, nothing more, and she would surely marry one day and fulfill her duties as a wife. Her happiness should not be a matter of importance to me or to anyone else. But I was not satisfied."

She stopped talking then and I did not push her to tell me more. Instead, she stood up and walked over to the side of the temple, leaning against one of the columns as I watched her, wishing that I could do something to take her pain away.

"I spoke to my husband's mother, Débora," she continued, staring into the distance, in the direction of Évora itself, where we intended to pass the next night. "And she, like the priest, told me that I was worrying over nothing. I expected nothing more from her, of course, for we had never been friends. She adored her son, treating him as if he was still a child who could do no wrong. On one occasion, when she overheard me exchanging cross words with Victorino, she spoke harshly to me, calling me the daughter of a sea-snake and insisting that a wife should always treat her husband with respect, no matter what he might have done. When I asked whether he should not behave in the same fashion toward me, she slapped me across the face, kicking me when I fell to the ground, and were I not so surprised by her unexpected burst of violence, I would have fought her in the streets and shamed us both."

"What kind of man is your husband?" I asked. "Did you love him when you married him?"

She considered this for a moment. "I liked him, certainly," she admitted. "When first he made known his interest in me, when first we were introduced, I was flattered, but I was naïve and impressionable. He's a great fighter. A leader in our village. A man who commands the respect of the townspeople. In my vanity I enjoyed the idea of being married to him."

"How old were you when you wed?"

"Only fourteen," she said. "And he was twenty-five. I was not his first wife, of course. There had been three others, and they had all died in mysterious circumstances when they failed to give him a child."

"You were very young to take a husband."

"Too young. But my father desired the match and, of course, I had no say in the matter. A woman never does. But Victorino was kind to me for a time and I thought myself lucky to be under his protection. However, after a few years, he grew bored with me and his attentions began to wander. What could I do? This is the way of men, I know that, and I have always accepted it, even if I am not certain why I should, and Débora continued to insist that I never complain. And perhaps I wouldn't have, perhaps I would have made my peace with my circumstances, were it not for the fact that as Victorino grew older, the girls he liked, the ones he seduced, remained the same age. Little more than children. Sometimes even younger than I had been when he first took me to the altar."

I closed my eyes, dreading what I was sure would come next.

"Your daughter?" I asked, and she nodded her head slowly but, rather than weeping, her face took on a grim determination.

"I discovered them together," she said. "One afternoon when I returned home early. Débora was in the kitchen and when she saw me come in the door, she grew pale and told me that we should go outside and sit together. I didn't want to. I had come from the marketplace and was carrying fresh fruit and vegetables. I was hungry. I was tired. I wanted to prepare food. But Débora was so insistent that I grew suspicious. And then I heard cries of pain emerging from the next room and I brushed past her. When I went inside . . . when I went inside—"

I stood up and walked toward her, taking her hand in mine, but she pulled away. This was not a woman who needed a man to comfort her. Her consolation came from her own resilience.

"Your husband's mother knew, then," I said. "And yet she did nothing?"

"She believes that her precious Victorino should be allowed to do whatever he wants, whenever he wants, to whoever he wants. I, on the other hand, lost my reason, screaming the place down, breaking dishes and pots. I took a poker from the fireplace and dashed it down over my husband's head, thinking that I had killed him and caring little if I had, but no, the damage was not severe and he recovered quickly, ordering me to leave town that very day or face the authorities, who would surely condemn me to death for trying to murder him. In that moment, despite how much I longed for my daughter, I had no choice and had to go. The day that you and I first met was the thirteenth birthday of Beatriz. I haven't seen her in more than a year now and dread to think of what she has been put through since my banishment. She must hate me, believing that I abandoned her to such a terrible fate. And so I go back there now," she continued, "with the intention of killing both my husband and his mother for what they have done. I intend to kill him first and force her to watch. And then I will take my daughter in my arms and leave that place forever."

A long silence ensued. Nearby, the horses whinnied, restless for more exercise, and a cold wind blew toward us from the west.

"It would seem," I said eventually, "that we are both guided by the spirit of vengeance."

"It is as you said," she replied. "We are all alike, men and women. As we were at the birth of time, and as we will be at its death."

NORTH KOREA

A.D. 1301

ALTHOUGH THE CITY from which Sun-Hi had been exiled stood on the banks of the Taedong river, her husband, Vi-Shik, presided over it from a grand Romanesque villa situated at the top of a nearby hill, from which he enjoyed excellent views of the surrounding towns and villages. Dismounting our horses at the city boundary, Sun-Hi told me how Vi-Shik was the third member of his family, after his father and grandfather, to control a Korean province, having been among the leaders of the invading Mongol armies when they took control of the country during the last century. Once the people were conquered and Vi-Shik had set himself up as their new ruler, a group of twenty young girls, barely out of childhood, had been brought before him, stripped naked and studied as potential brood-mares while he made his choice of wife. She, of course, had been the unfortunate victor in that contest but, in some ways, fortune had been on her side, for at least she had enjoyed the benefits of a public marriage while many of her friends were taken without their consent and kept as part of his harem, subordinate to his pleasures whenever the mood seized him. Vi-Shik himself was a tall, unusually thin man, she said, with prominent teeth and a hump on his back so pronounced that, in private, he was often referred to as the Great Camel of Kisong.

Sun-Hi's husband was a darughachi, the term ascribed to those who administered a province, and his power meant that he was both feared and honored in equal parts. He made grand gestures of munificence when it suited him to do so, throwing coins to the beggars in the streets when the sun shone on his temper, but when his mood turned irritable, he would round up a handful and hang them from the gallows for their indolence. Justice, such as it was, was dispensed from a court that stood in the center of the market square and, if the evidence in a particular case proved uncertain, he harked back to the old Greek system of trial by ordeal, deciding on a person's guilt by forcing him—or her—to fight one of his champions to the death.

There were some crimes, however, for which he had particular punishments. A thief would lose his hands. A liar would forfeit his tongue. An unfaithful wife would be imprisoned for a month in a hut where any boy or man could take his pleasure with her unrebuked. An unfaithful husband, on the other hand, suffered no consequences for his duplicities, the rules governing the behavior of men and women being very different.

On the morning of our arrival, Sun-Hi and I took great pains to avoid the attention of others. Although I, of course, was a stranger in these parts, she had grown up there and was wary of being recognized, and so covered her head with a shawl, keeping her gaze firmly on the ground in order to escape the notice of anyone who passed us by. It concerned me that we were rushing to this place, having not yet agreed upon a plan for the rescue of her daughter, Bong-Cha, and I was keen to do so, but Sun-Hi insisted upon seeing the girl with her own eyes first in order to reassure herself that she was alive and healthy. Content to give in to such a natural desire, I followed as we made our way by side streets toward the school building where the wealthier children of the ruling class studied every day.

Taking our place at a table across the street, we ate kimchi and bibimbap from a street stall, watching as mothers, grandmothers and servants arrived to leave their children before continuing on to the marketplace to purchase meat, fish and fresh vegetables. I tried to engage my companion in conversation, but she was lost in thought. When she let out a small cry and put a hand to her mouth, I turned around, assuming that the child walking down the street must be her daughter, but she shook her head, her eyes filled with pity.

"That was Hwa-Young," she told me. "A friend of Bong-Cha. I've known her since she was a baby. Her mother, a friend from childhood, gave birth to seven daughters. After each one was born, her husband beat her fiercely, for he wanted a son. When Hwa-Young, his seventh disappointment, was born, he dragged my friend to the river and drowned her, taking a new wife later that same day. She gave him three sons in as many years and died as she was delivered of a fourth."

"And he was permitted to commit such an act?" I asked, horrified by this wickedness. "He was not hanged for taking the life of another?"

"Hwa-Young's father is also a darughachi," she told me. "And darughachis can do whatever they like, they are above the law. I remember once when—"

She stopped suddenly and I followed her gaze across the street. An older woman had just turned a corner, wearing a dark red duru-magi over her clothes, an ostentatious item for such an early hour and one that was clearly intended to signify her importance. Next to her walked a young girl of about twelve years of age, pretty, with dark hair and a clean complexion, dressed in a pale green hanbok.

"That's her," whispered Sun-Hi, the words catching in her throat. "That's Bong-Cha."

"And the woman with her?"

"Despised wretch Dae, the mother of my husband."

I looked at them as the child glanced in our direction but did not see anyone she recognized. Sun-Hi, her face still covered, rose to her feet and I grabbed her by the arm quickly, shaking my head.

"Not yet," I said.

"I have to go," she insisted. "I have to talk to her. I have to let her know that I have come back."

"No," I said. "Not in a public place like this. It's too soon and we have yet to form a plan. If you are to be reunited with your daughter, then this is not the way. Trust me, Sun-Hi, we have to bide our time. You will be reunited soon, but you must wait a little longer."

• • •

Sun-Hi knew that Dae liked to visit her sister every afternoon for lunch, so we waited until noon, when the house was sure to be empty, before making our way there. Stepping inside, I noticed how Sun-Hi seemed both frightened to be in this place again and strangely drawn to it. We looked into each of the rooms in turn and, from the condition of the bedroom, it seemed that Vi-Shik had taken another woman since disposing of his wife, but quite how old that unfortunate creature might have been, we could not guess.

Most upsetting to Sun-Hi, of course, was Bong-Cha's room, in which there was no evidence of her mother at all. Instead, the walls were decorated with painted portraits of the child's father and his ancestors. Sun-Hi lay down on the mat where the girl placed her head every night, inhaling her scent, and I watched her silently, empathizing with the pain that seeped from every pore of her body.

The depth of her maternal love was almost palpable and made me think of the children that I might have raised to adulthood, too, had fortune favored me. Most days, I tried not to spend too much time thinking of my murdered son, En-Su, not because my love for him had diminished in any way but because to remember him was to endure the most extraordinary pain. When he forced his way into my daydreams, however, I pictured him scrambling across the floor of my workshop, his arms outstretched, Kyung-Soon encouraging him as he learned to walk, and how my beloved wife would clap her hands in delight when the boy made it from one side of the room to the other without falling over. Perhaps, one day, he might have even followed me into my trade and we could have built a work-shop together.

To my surprise, I felt a hand upon my face and, drifting unwill-ingly from my reverie, I realized that Sun-Hi was pressing her palm against my cheeks.

"You are crying," she said. "What is it that upsets you?"

I shook my head, unable to find the words at first, but then I spoke of the many losses that I had suffered. Without intending to, I lifted my hand and wrapped it around hers, feeling the soft skin of her palm against my fingers. A moment later, my lips were pressed against hers. I could feel myself growing aroused and, rather than being embarrassed by such predictable weakness, I leaned into her and, for a moment, she reciprocated, her body pressing back ur-gently against my own but then, without warning, she pulled away, shaking her head.

"Forgive me," she said, placing her hands together now in an attitude of prayer. "But I cannot."

"Do you worry that someone will return and discover us?" I asked, torn between confusion and desire. "If so, then we could always find—"

"The vows I made to my husband remain in place," she replied. "And while he yet lives, I will not betray them. I am sorry if this causes you pain."

I shook my head and turned away. In truth, I respected her unwillingness simply to fall to the floor with me and felt ashamed of my clumsy attempts at seduction.

. . .

Toward the rear of the property stood an old well that, Sun-Hi told me, had dried up many years before. A boulder lay across the top to prevent anyone from falling in and it took all our strength to move it out of the way. When we did, I stared down into the mysterious darkness, lifted a handful of stones from the ground and dropped them inside. It took a few seconds for them to sound against the shallow layer of water that sat at the base and I guessed that the well was perhaps twenty or thirty feet deep.

While we waited for Vi-Shik's mother to come home, we devised our plan and Sun-Hi hid out of sight, masked by a small copse of trees, while I remained in the garden, making sure that I remained visible so Dae would notice me the moment she returned. I felt somewhat nervous at the idea of what lay ahead and wondered whether it was this anxiety that was causing me to perspire so much. My arms and legs felt unstable, too, but then I'd been feeling unwell since earlier in the day. Growing nauseous, I sat down upon the grass next to the well, placed myself in the lotus position and breathed slowly, trying to distract my mind from my bilious stomach by examining the carvings of the gods inscribed into the stone. When I continued to feel dizzy, I placed my hands on the ground on either side of me and was about to rise and force myself to be sick when I heard a voice cry out in a mixture of surprise and anger.

I opened my eyes and looked up as an elderly woman, Dae, marched toward me. She wore a ferocious expression on her face, furious that her property had been invaded by a stranger, and lifting a stick from the ground, she waved it in my direction, as she might to a dog.

"Vagrant!" she cried. "Tramp! Beggar! Be gone from here before I do you an injury. You trespass on the grounds of the darugha-chi of Kisong!"

I pulled myself to my feet but remained silent and when she roared at me again, I shook my head and babbled some nonsense about having permission to be there, that this was the home of a dear friend of mine.

"What do you want?" she asked, her face close to mine now. "What are you doing here? Don't you know that you could be put to death even for daring to trespass in this place?"

Knowing that she was standing exactly where I needed her to stand, I smiled and continued to mutter quietly to myself so that she might relax and feel that I presented no danger to her. Frowning, she barely had time to register the sound of footsteps running behind her and when I stepped out of the way she turned, but not quickly enough to prevent herself from being pushed into the well by Sun-Hi. The old woman cried out in terror as she fell to the bottom and then, a few moments later, we heard the sound of groans ascending from below.

Sun-Hi breathed heavily, her face illuminated with pleasure as she looked down into the cavernous opening. The sun appeared from behind a cloud at this moment, allowing us a better view of what lay below. Next to the scurrying rats, lying prostrate in the puddle of foul water, was Dae.

"Gracious Mother!" she cried. "You appear to have fallen."

"You!" came the voice from below, but it had little strength in it, for Dae must have been badly wounded in the fall and sounded both frightened and disoriented. "You daughter of a she-goat! You were told never to come back here!"

"And yet here I am!" shouted Sun-Hi defiantly. "Did you think that I would abandon my daughter to you or to that monster you raised? You of all people know what it is to love one's child and to put their interests ahead of everything and everyone. You should have known that it was only a matter of time before I would return."

There was a long silence from the floor of the well and then the voice came again, but in a more beseeching tone this time. "Please," she said. "My leg. I think it's broken. And blood seeps from my forehead. You have to help me."

"Help you?" cried Sun-Hi. "So you can steal from me again? Think yourself lucky that I'm not pouring a pot of boiling lead over your miserable body and letting you burn to death—"

"Beloved Wife," said a voice from behind us, and I spun around to see the Great Camel of Kisong himself standing a few feet away, looking from one of us to the other with a half-smile on his face. "My mother might have believed that you would remain in exile, but I knew otherwise. You have the bravery of a lion and the stupidity of a monkey."

"I've come for only one thing," said Sun-Hi, doing her best to sound as if she had the ferocity of the former, but her tone was panicked now and lacking in conviction. "I want my daughter, that's all. Then I will leave, and you won't see me again."

"Bong-Cha belongs to me," replied Vi-Shik, shaking his head. "She is much more . . . accommodating than you ever were, Wife." He smiled again, displaying his yellow teeth. "It would be too painful for me to let her go. Not for another couple of years, anyway. Perhaps when she's a little older? You could come back for her then if you like. She won't interest me as much when her youth is just a memory."

The three of us stood in silence for a few moments, taking in the monstrous nature of his words, before Sun-Hi threw herself at him, her fists turning into claws that ripped at his eyes. He was caught off guard and stumbled, but recovered quickly, and even though Sun-Hi did her best to gain the upper hand he was far too strong for her and, with one savage blow, he punched her in the face, and she fell to the grass, unconscious.

I watched in horror, the sickness inside me growing ever greater now, and my stomach began to turn in revulsion. I wanted nothing more than to lie down in a cool, dark place and expel the contents of my breakfast into a basin. Vi-Shik cocked his head to the side a little as he looked at me, perhaps wondering why I was not being more physical in defense of Sun-Hi, before walking toward the well and leaning over to look inside.

"My son!" cried Dae from below, her tone filled with relief. "You have come for me. I knew you would."

"I think they meant to push us both in there," he replied. "Well, I'll get you out and then we can send my wife and . . ." He looked at me uncertainly. "Her lover? Is that what you are? We can send them down there to spend eternity together." He glanced toward the boulder that we had removed, and I knew that it was his intention to seal us inside, just as it had been ours to bury him and his mother within its cavernous walls.

Turning around now, he made his way toward me and I moved slowly, trying to escape him. He was bigger and stronger than I, however, and in my current condition, there was simply no possibility that I could best him. From the corner of my eye, I could see Sun-Hi rousing herself and groaning on the grass, trying to lift herself, but she was too weakened by the punch that he had inflicted on her to be of any help.

"Who are you anyway, stranger?" he asked casually, as if this were nothing more than a pleasant conversation with a new acquaintance. "You lie with my wife? And now you come to steal my daughter? Is that it? Perhaps you want to lie with her, too? Do your tastes converge with mine? But she belongs to me, you must understand that. They both do. And I do not tolerate thieves."

I stepped back toward the well and, when I moved my feet, I came close to stumbling in. Opening my mouth to protest, I found that words failed me. At that same moment an unexpected sound caught my attention. Looking past Vi-Shik, I watched in astonishment as a figure came running across the grass, moving faster than I had ever seen a person run in my entire life.

It was a girl. The same one I had seen walking to school with her grandmother that morning. Vi-Shik turned in surprise as she ran toward him, and, at that same moment, I stepped aside so that when her arms flew out, pushing him hard in the chest, he could not stop himself from falling into the well.

"One of two," said Bong-Cha, turning to me, but before I had a chance to ask what she meant by this curious phrase, I felt my legs give way beneath me, my weakened body finally giving in to whatever illness had beset me, and I tumbled to the ground. After that, the world turned black.

NORWAY

A.D. 1349

STRUGGLED TO SEPARATE the real world from the nightmares. As monsters from the deep snapped at my heels, eagles descended in a fury from the sky, breathing fire while they tried to capture me in their claws. Ogres surrounded me, threatening to crush my body into the dust. I saw a man march from house to house, pulling babies from their parents' arms. The boys had their throats cut while the girls were returned to their screaming mothers. Wherever the man went, cries of terror followed in his wake. Flames from the ground licked at his feet, an army of the dead reaching up to drag him to his new home in the underworld.

My mother, Flavia, sat on my left-hand side, sewing a dress using thread the color of blood to run along the hem, a pattern that reflected the flow of a great river. My aunt, Noria, sat on my right, crafting shoes and tying laces into the leather. At the end of the bed, near a painted portrait of his ancestors, stood my father, Magne, staring down at me with a fierce expression on his face as he chastised me for being weak.

A shadowy figure appeared in the background, but I recognized her immediately as my sister Ablu, a great stain spreading across the front of her tunic. She cried out, pressing her hands against it to stem the flow, but they came away scarlet, the blood running down her legs and from her hairline into her eyes.

"My own brother," she whispered, "and you murdered me."

I tried to speak but the words caught at the back of my throat. My body was a temple of pain, sores weeping, pus pouring from open wounds. And then, finally, the sound of sticks making their way toward me, a blurred figure at the back of the room, banging on the stone floor as he hobbled into the light. My cousin, Hakje.

He narrowed his eyes when he saw me, then smiled through yellow, rotting teeth.

"You thought you could kill me, Cousin?" he asked. "It seems that you will be forced to make your peace with God before I."

Behind him, my wife, Kateryna, appeared with our son, skeletons carrying the skin that had been stripped from their bodies, screams emerging from gray bones. On the wall behind them, painted portraits of the child's father and his ancestors. Now I cried out in terror, too, and tried to sit up, but a hand pushed me back down.

"Rest," said a voice. "You must rest."

"Will he recover?" asked another, much younger, and if there came a reply, I was too insentient to hear it.

. . .

I had started to feel ill shortly after arriving in Vossevangen, where we had traveled in order to kill Signe's husband and retrieve her daughter, attributing my nauseous stomach to some bad food that I had eaten near Beate's school. Only now that I was lying in my sickbed, beginning to recover from my lurid hallucinations, did I realize what had actually caused my illness.

A few days earlier, in Bergen, I had been offered employment at the dock unloading the cargo ships that arrived on the merchant trade routes and, in need of money if we were to continue our journey, we decided to stay for a week until our purse was full. The work was dull but tolerable, with ships arriving every day from England and the continent of Europe laden down with fabrics, food, spices and tea. I was not much accustomed to manual labor but found it refreshing to be outdoors alongside honest working men.

On the third day, however, a curious event took place. Wherever he went, the harbor master, Rudiger, carried a list of the ships that were due to dock in our port and, typically, somewhere between four and eight would arrive between dawn and dusk. On that particular afternoon, however, all the ships we had been expecting had arrived and been unloaded. The sailors and captains were busying themselves with eating, drinking and whoring around the town when, over the horizon, we spotted another boat sailing in our direction.

"Perhaps it's one of tomorrow's ships, arriving early?" suggested Oddleiv, one of the workers who toiled alongside me and with whom I had grown friendly. Like me, he was a frustrated artist, but his main interest lay in the design of buildings.

"That would be unusual, would it not?" I asked. "I understood that boats were more likely to arrive late than early?"

He nodded and we grew captivated by the boat's approach, for it was charting an unsteady course, a strange zigzag through the water that no serious navigator would ever consider. Ten minutes lurching port, ten more starboard, so bizarre were its falterings that most of the men, including the harbormaster, remained where they were rather than returning home, watching and wondering what inept, foreign crew would bring a boat into dock in such a bizarre manner.

"The captain must be either a drunk or a Frenchman," declared Rudiger, shaking his head as the ship drew closer. "Or both." At one point it looked as if it was going to crash onto the rocks of the islands to the east of Bergen, but somehow it managed to right itself as we called out, trying to guide it in a straight direction, before it achieved a steady path with the tide into the harbor itself.

However, as it approached, the ship neither slowed down nor dropped anchor and it became clear that it was going to crash into the stone wall that divided the sea from the land. We ran back in fright as it collided, with a cacophonous breaking of wood and iron. When it was finally forced to a halt, no one moved and we simply stared at it, waiting for the crew to appear, but, no matter how long we stood there, not a single person made themselves known.

"This is a peculiar business," said Oddleiv, scratching his beard and looking, like the rest of us, a little unsettled. "Should we go aboard, do you think?"

Rudiger cried out to the ship, hoping that someone on the deck might make themselves known, and when no one did, two of the men brought over a ladder and a half-dozen of us decided to make our way across. The deck, however, stood empty, without even a man to guide the helm, and we looked around us in bewilderment.

"A ghost ship?" asked Rudiger, shivering in fear, for superstitions like this were always rife in harbors and there was no one more superstitious than an old sailor. They spoke of the *Daraman*, which spent its nights sailing around the northern tip of Denmark, and the *Laramie*, which had washed up on the shores of Ireland without a soul to be found. They sang songs of spirits, banshees and poltergeists.

"There's no such thing," I said. "They're just myths made up to frighten the nervous and the gullible."

"Then where are all the men?" he asked. "It can't have set sail on its own."

It was a good question, but one that I could not answer. A moment later, a cry came from one of the hands who had made his way belowdecks and we moved to follow him. Before we could descend, however, he emerged from the cabins, running as fast as his legs could carry him toward the harbor, crying, "Scatter! Scatter if you value your lives!" We stared after him, one or two following him in fright, but the rest of us remained where we were out of pure fascination. It was all quiet now and a crowd had gathered on the harbor, for rumors had already spread that a ghost ship had docked in Bergen.

I stood at the door to the staircase that looked down into the darkness, considering my options. A foul stench rose from below, but name me a ship that did not stink in its nether regions and I'll name one that has not yet spent a day at sea.

"Don't!" cried Oddleiv, putting a hand on my arm to stay me, but I stepped forward, a fool to curiosity, and made my way down the steps, my hand pressing against the wall in search of candles. When I located one I reached into my pocket, struck a match against the woodwork and lit it, holding it out before me.

What I saw was a sight that I had never imagined in all my life. The hammocks were all in place but on each one lay a dead man, his arms or legs hanging over the side. I spoke some words aloud, hoping that one might wake and answer, but was met only with silence. Stepping carefully into the center of the boat, I lifted my candle and looked down at one of the bodies.

It was a horrific sight. The man's face had been transformed by sores and blisters, his lips turned black, his hands and fingers charred as if they had been lost in the frosts of the Arctic regions. As my breath caught in my throat, I knew what I was looking at, for I had heard tell of a plague spreading across Europe, but had never thought it would reach this far north.

I turned on my heel and, like the man before me, ran back upstairs toward the deck.

"The Black Death!" I cried. "The men are dead of it!"

The dockers stared at me in horror and then, realizing the danger they were in, charged back to the ladder and to the shore as the crowd rushed about with cries of "The plague! The plague!" I, too, ran, desperate to get away from that cursed ship and back to our inn, where I threw myself in a bath of scalding water and scrubbed myself clean. Through the window, I could hear the sound of the ship burning and guessed that the townspeople had poured whale-oil across the deck and set it alight.

As I washed, I thought of the stories I had heard of this terrible disease. It had been brought from the Asian countries, we were told, by fleas that lived in the fur of diseased rats. As ships were notorious for being more populated by vermin than men, and the merchants refused to see their coffers diminish by docking their vessels until they were scoured clean, the boats made the perfect transport for the disease, becoming a plague on the people of Europe. Survivors were few and most who grew infected were dead within days.

Standing naked in my room, I examined my body from toes to head but could see no sign of any unusual markings, saying a silent prayer that I might be spared the fate that had befallen so many. And for a few days more, indeed, it seemed so. It was only as we reached Signe's village that I had begun to feel ill, and by then I had already forgotten about the so-called ghost ship, assuming I had just eaten something that was past its best.

But clearly I had been wrong. The pestilence had infected my blood and I opened my eyes to see Signe sitting over me, a scarf wrapped around her face to prevent herself from inhaling any of my corrupted breath. I believed that my moment had finally come and that it would not be long before I stood before the face of God and admitted that yes, my last act on this Earth had been to participate in the murder of a man and his mother, two more souls added to the list of those whose deaths already weighed upon my conscience. When I reached out a hand, expecting her to pull back in fright, she took it in her own and I felt a burst of tenderness toward her that I had not experienced since before my wife's death.

. . .

But somehow, I survived. And when I did, Signe was still there.

"How long have I been ill?" I asked, and she smiled, pressing a cold, damp cloth against my forehead.

"Almost three weeks," she replied. "But you're improving by the day. Most don't. Your fever has broken, and the sores have begun to heal. You may have some scarring, but you can live with that."

"And Beate?" I asked.

"I didn't let her in here," she said, shaking her head. "Her physical health is fine. She wasn't affected by the plague."

"And outside of that?"

"I'm not sure. She's not quite as I remember her, but perhaps that's no surprise. It will take time for her to recover. But she is young, and the young are resilient. As, it seems, are you. No matter how close you were to death, you kept pulling back. Although you said the strangest things in your sleep."

"Such as?" I asked, hoping not to have uttered anything too vulgar or lurid.

"Where are the Temples of the Sun and the Moon?" she asked, and I frowned, for I had never heard of any such places.

"I don't know," I replied. "Did I talk of them?"

"Yes, and the Avenue of the Dead."

"The delusions of a man under a fever," I told her. "And your husband and his mother?"

"Beate and I rolled the boulder back above the well. They will be paying for their crimes in the next world by now."

I nodded, feeling no sympathy for them.

"Thank you for staying by my side," I said, reaching for her hand. "I daresay that I would be dead now if it weren't for you."

"And I would not have my daughter with me if it were not for you."

The door opened behind Signe and I glanced over her shoulder. Beate was standing there, looking in at us, but the sun was shining on her in such a way that I could not read the expression on her face. And yet, for some reason, I sensed that she was not smiling.

INDIA

A.D. 1385

TIME PASSED, my health recovered, and events of a personal nature overtook my desire for revenge. When Shanthi and I married, I said a prayer to Brahma, pleading that as long as they should live, no harm would come to my third wife or any children we might have. Not a hair on their heads should be pulled without permission. Not a scratch should disfigure their perfect skin.

I tried my best to be a father to Shanthi's daughter, Bhavna, but it was a task that was proving more difficult than anticipated. Bhavna was now fourteen years old and a quiet girl, prone to introspection, which was not surprising, considering the many tortures she had endured at the hands of her cruel father. Sometimes I would discover her hidden away in the corners of our home, tears falling down her cheeks, which she tried to hide from me, for she did not like to be seen as weak. She would frequently fly into an extraordinary rage under little provocation, behaving so badly that I grew concerned for the well-being of her mind. And while she seemed to like me well enough, I knew that she was uncomfortable with any attempts on my part to offer physical comfort, so I showed my affection toward her only through words. Her relationship with her mother, on the other hand, was even more difficult, and it bothered me how little she seemed to trust Shanthi, departing rooms whenever her mother entered, or remaining but staring at her with an expression of controlled fury on her face. Although I never voiced my concern aloud, I worried what the future might bring for them both.

Our marriage, however, was a day of great festivity, and when Shanthi and I promised our lives to each other, I was happier than I had been in many years. The ceremony was brief and the celebration even more so, for we had few friends in this part of India. At one point, we even considered venturing toward the ancient lands of the Persian Empire, but neither of us had ever left our country and felt no urge to do so now.

Ravi was conceived on the night of our wedding and Shanthi's pregnancy was an uncomplicated one, the boy coming into the world with the minimum of pain and providing joy from the moment he appeared. He ate when he should eat, slept when he should sleep, and was apparently content to sit and watch us during his waking hours, attuning himself to this remarkable universe of which he was now a part.

The decision to postpone my search for my cousin, however, was a difficult one, but I did so at the request of my wife, who made it clear that she did not want me abandoning her on what might prove a fruitless quest when we had a new baby to care for. Anxious to make our marriage a success, I agreed to her terms but knew that I would look for him again in the future, when time proved more providential. Still, this temporary abandonment of my mission weighed heavily on my conscience, for I owed a debt of justice to those whose deaths he had caused, and I was not ready to insult their memory by forgetting this.

And so, for now, I established a workshop in Jahanpanah, returning to labor on the terra-cotta pots that I had always enjoyed crafting in my youth. Arriving early most mornings, I worked all day, singing songs to myself as I created my designs and, when I had built up a good supply of pots, Shanthi took them to the marketplace, where she quickly attracted buyers. Within months I found that I had to commit to long hours in order to keep up with the demand. My youth had been built around my great desire to be an artist and it was a joy to be at this work once again. Looking around me at the life I had built, I reveled in that rarest of sensations: contentment.

· · ·

Here, in the refuge of the world, we were surrounded by thirteen fortified gates, each designed to ward off invaders, and it was through the largest of these that I wandered one warm afternoon, having grown weary of sitting alone in my workshop. Making my way into the marketplace, I carried Ravi in my arms and when he saw his mother seated on a mat, my pots laid out before her, he struggled to be allowed down. I placed him next to her and his hands reached out for the vessels, although they were far too heavy for him to lift. We watched him, smiling at his Herculean efforts, and she told me that she had already sold seven pots that day, a number that astonished me, for we rarely sold more than four.

"You may have to think about taking on an apprentice," she said, an idea that did not fill me with delight, for I had allowed novices into my life before, with unhappy results.

"Or I could simply continue production at my current rate," I suggested. "And if demand continues, we can increase our prices. After all, my work will be more valuable if it is harder to obtain."

A great commotion sounded from the stalls nearby and a boy charged past me, his arms filled with stolen fruit that tumbled onto the street as he fled his pursuers. Two burly men ran after him. "Have we lost anything in this way?" I asked Shanthi, and she shook her head.

"Fruit is a lot easier to steal than terra-cotta pots," she said. "Also, you can eat it."

I glanced around at the market traders, who had gone back about their business after the moment's excitement. I noticed a crowd gathering in the distance, close to the mosque. Another boy, aged no more than ten or eleven years old, was seated on the ground next to an older man who was summoning an audience to witness what he called a most extraordinary performance. Upon the ground, between man and boy, stood a wicker basket filled with rope. Intrigued, I joined the group of bystanders and watched as the man raised his hands, which were covered with sores and blisters, and called for silence. We stilled our conversation as he reached into the basket, taking the end of the thick rope in one hand while, with his eyes closed, he muttered incantations over it. When his prayer came to an end, he threw the rope in the air and, to no one's surprise, it fell back down, landing on the ground at his feet. Some of the men jeered but, as anyone who has ever witnessed a street show knows, this was only a prologue to the main entertainment. He asked for silence once again, repeating his earlier mantra, but once again the rope fell, this time landing around his head. More laughter from the crowd, and I wondered whether I was wasting my time on such folly but decided to give him one more chance to prove his skill, and this time, to my astonishment, when he threw the rope up, it remained aloft, pointing into the sky.

There was a gasp from the crowd and some applause before he reached into the basket to pull out another length of the sisal, feeding it upward until it was difficult to see where the rope ended and the sky began. He took a bow, clapped his hands, and the boy, who had been seated all this time in the lotus position with his eyes closed, praying quietly to himself, stood up and marched toward it. He was short for his age but handsome, with clear skin and bright blue eyes, and wore a vivid yellow dhoti with a green belt holding it in place around his waist. On each of his fingers he wore a different-colored ring and on each of his toes he had tied a multi-colored string. Approaching the rope, he glanced back toward his ustad for a moment and then the man clapped again, the sharp strikes indicating that the performance should begin.

Taking the rope in both hands, the boy pulled at it a little and it appeared to be solidly locked into the sky. Leaping from the ground, he ascended four or five feet in the air, holding it tightly between his hands, his legs wrapped around the base. The crowd cheered in delight, as did I, for I had heard of such tricks, of course, but never witnessed one myself. The ustad pointed toward the heavens and the boy, the jamoora, shook his head with a fearful expression that was so poorly acted it was difficult not to laugh. Reaching into a bag, the ustad then withdrew a large Talwar sword, a beautiful foil with a star-shaped emerald as its centerpiece, and waved it in a threatening manner in the direction of the jamoora. To even more laughter, the boy began to scurry up the rope like a squirrel escaping the attention of a hungry dog. We watched as he ascended higher and higher until, finally, he rose so high that he seemed to disappear into the sky itself.

The entire crowd broke into applause and the ustad bowed, accepting the tributes of the audience, before clapping once again and, looking up, we all expected the boy to reappear. But no one came. He clapped again and, this time, with a performance almost as poor as the boy's earlier, he shook his head, returned his sword to its scabbard and began to ascend the rope, too. Soon, we could hear raised voices from the skies and then, astonishingly, something fell from above. It was an arm, each of the fingers wearing a ring, and then another arm, followed by a pair of legs, a torso, a head. Each fell quickly and cleanly into the basket and no one dared approach it until the man descended the rope, the cord unrolling itself behind him so that at last, when he was standing on the ground once again, it lay on the ground beside him. He stared into the basket and reared back, feigning disgust, before lifting the lid and placing it on top. Then, turning the basket around in a full circle, he removed the lid and the boy jumped out, fully intact and healthy, and grinning from ear to ear.

The crowd cheered as the boy took a pan and wandered among us, accepting the coins we offered for the entertainment. When he reached me, I patted his head as I threw my offering in on top of the others.

"What's your name anyway?" I asked, and he bowed deeply at the waist.

"Deepak," he said. "The Amazing, Incredible, Astounding, Fantastic Deepak."

I smiled at his superlatives and, as the crowd began to disperse, felt pleased to have witnessed the trick. Returning to Shanthi, I described to her what I had witnessed.

"Magic?" she said, shaking her head, for she was a superstitious sort and did not like meddling with matters that seemed contrary to nature. "That is best avoided, Husband. It is the work of the devil."

. . .

The following morning, when I arrived at my workshop, I was surprised to discover the door slightly ajar. I was prone to forgetting to lock it at night but, as yet, no one had ever bothered to steal anything from within. Opening the door cautiously, I glanced inside, but it was still dark and so I reached for a candle, striking a flame for the wick. I could hear the sounds of shuffling toward the rear of the room and cursed under my breath, for I thought that rats had broken in through the night. Stamping my sandals upon the floor, I hoped that this would scare them into fleeing, but the expected rush of tiny feet did not appear.

My heart thumping faster in my chest now, I made my way slowly toward the rear of the workshop, where I discovered someone huddling in fear in the corner. As I turned the candle in his direction, I was surprised to see that it was the boy from the market, the one who had supposedly ascended the rope toward the heavens.

"What are you doing here?" I asked, and he shook his head, holding his hands out before him in a gesture of supplication.

"Please," he said. "I didn't take anything. I just needed somewhere to sleep, that's all."

He posed no threat to me and I ushered him to his feet, leading him to the center of the studio, where he stood before me, hanging his head in disgrace.

"It's Deepak, isn't it?" I asked, and he nodded.

"Yes," he said dolefully. "The Amazing, Incredible, Astounding, Fantastic Deepak."

"And where do you normally sleep?"

"In the hut with my master."

"The ustad?"

"Yes."

"And he's thrown you out?"

"He says that I've grown too big to climb the rope. He has a new boy, two years younger than me, who he's trained to take over from me. Yesterday was my final appearance before the people of Jahanpanah. I am no longer a jamoora. I am destitute."

"And your parents?" I asked.

"I don't have any," he told me. "My master took me in when I was a child."

"So what do you mean to do now? How will you live?"

He shook his head and I could see tears forming in his eyes. "I'll find a way," he said. "I may become a beggar. I think I would make an excellent beggar. My master always said—"

"Stop saying 'my master,'" I told him. "None of us are slaves."

"My ustad, then. He always said that I would make a good beggar because I have a pleasant face."

I laughed a little. He did have a pleasant face, it was true, but I wasn't sure that it would be enough to make a living on the streets, nor did I think that this was the only goal he could set for himself.

"Is that really all you want from your life?" I asked. "To be a beggar? You don't hope for more?"

"Oh no," he said, shaking his head. "My master always said that I was a perfectly useless boy and that it would be better for all if I were ground up for horse meat."

"You managed the rope trick quite efficiently," I said. "Tell me, what's the secret behind it anyway?"

He looked up then and, when he smiled, his teeth were astonishingly white. "Don't you know," he said, "that a good magician never reveals his tricks?"

ARGENTINA

A.D. 1430

LTHOUGH WE WERE NOT related by blood, I soon began to think of Diego as a son in all but name. When he came to live with us as a member of the Selk'nam tribe, I introduced him to Sofia, Bonita and Rafael and they were surprised at first but soon welcomed him into our home as part of our family. And in time it fell to me, as the person who had presented him to our community, to lead him toward his initiation ceremony.

In those early months, I worried that Diego might be cursed with an evil spirit, for he spent much of his time performing strange, unholy entertainments for Bonita and Rafael that seemed to me to be the work of the devil. Reaching behind their ears, he would discover an acorn where no acorn had previously been. He could make objects disappear from surfaces using only mirrors and sleight of hand. And, most disturbing of all, he would occasionally perform a trick that saw him levitate from the ground and float in midair, held there with no apparent means of support. While such distractions delighted the young people, I disapproved of them, concerned that the gods would punish us for such imprecations, and ordered him to stop. Had the elders of our tribe learned of his magical ways, I feared they would fear he was bringing a profane element into our world and that he might even be asked to leave. For a time, he obeyed me, but I suspected that when I was not present, the children would beg him to perform his tricks and, like anyone who enjoyed the attentions of an audience, he would find it impossible to disappoint them.

Still, for all the strangeness of his character, I enjoyed his company and had grown fond of him, for he had a pleasing manner and frequently made me laugh with his buffoonery.

Since his birth, I had looked forward to the day when Rafael would be old enough to learn the craft that I had spent many years perfecting—I was regarded as the most talented maker of quivers on the archipelago, even if some of the men rejected my creations as too ornate, more suited for a woman than a man—but as that day was still some years off, I decided to train my new ward in the skill. I had designed my first quiver when I was just a boy, a gift for my father, but had made the mistake of decorating the leather pouch with colored fabrics stolen from my mother's design box. He considered such gaudy additions an affront to his manhood and ripped them off, belittling me and throwing the rich fabrics into the fire. He continued to use the plain quiver for many years afterward, however, even when he took to the mountains to await the arrival of the invaders, for it had an integrity to the design that even he, who had a revulsion for beauty in inanimate objects, could not deny.

Of course, even now I forced myself not to go quite as far with my designs as I would like, as I needed to trade my products with hunters and they preferred arrows with no extra frippery or adornments. I made exactly what they wanted, plain belt or back quivers, the occasional ground quiver, but sometimes a tribesman might quietly suggest that he would be willing to carry something a little more elaborate across his back and I would embrace the freedom that such a commission could bring, sewing pieces of broken glass or ornamental stone into the leather, crafting a fur trim to set off the design, a green belt stitched around the base.

Try as I might to train Diego, however, he was entirely lacking in artistic skill. Yes, he could make half my tools disappear with a dexterity that irritated me and then point across the room to a buffalo hide in the corner of my workshop, under which I would find them, but when I attempted to teach him the art of sewing and cutting, his fingers were worse than useless things. I finally gave in, hoping that my own son would one day show more agility with his hands than this foundling.

Still, we were affectionate toward each other and I enjoyed his presence in the workshop during the day, his idle chatter and his tales of life among the Yaghan people of the Southern Cone.

And then, one day, seeing how his body was changing before my eyes, I realized the time had come for him to be initiated into manhood and I spoke to the elder of our tribe, Qui'ho, who agreed that Diego should be initiated into the Selk'nam people, despite the otherness of his birth, an honor that was rarely afforded to outsiders. But the boy had ingratiated himself among us and we were happy to call him one of our own.

. . .

The initiation, which we called hain, took place in the largest hut at the edge of our village and, in preparation, a dozen men arrived dressed as spirits of the underworld, settling themselves in different parts of the darkened room while I dressed Diego in a tanned animal hide and led him toward the place of ceremony. I could tell that he was nervous about what was to come but impressed upon him the importance of undergoing this rite if he was to become a true member of our tribe and eventually be permitted to take a wife.

"At what age must that happen?" he asked, and I was surprised to hear anxiety in his tone rather than excitement. Most boys of his age looked forward to the moment when they might lie with a woman for the first time.

"Within the next year or two," I told him. "I myself was married for the first time when I was not much older than you are now."

"Must I marry?" he asked me, his voice low and tremulous.

"Of course," I said. "It is the natural order of things."

"But might I not live alone? Or with one of my friends?"

I turned to him with a puzzled expression on my face. No man who came of age ever lived alone or in the company of other men. What strange thoughts appeared in this boy's mind, I thought, choosing to ignore his question and putting his curious nature down to his Yaghan upbringing.

The hut appeared before us now and he hesitated.

"What will happen to me in there?" he asked tremulously.

"I cannot tell you that. You must enter and discover for yourself."

He stepped forward, opened the door and, taking a deep breath for courage, walked inside.

I moved away, sitting on the ground in the shade of an ancient tree, and recalled my own hain many years earlier. The men were terrifying in the way they had roared about me, sweeping down as they whispered curses in my ears. They had poked me with heavy branches, whipping them hard against the back of my legs, and whenever any light appeared through the gaps of the stone, I was frightened by the ghoulish masks they wore upon their faces. Soon, however, I came to understand that each spirit could be tamed if I simply threw myself upon them and pulled their masks away. They were not demons at all, of course, only men, and men who would retreat to the corner of the hut when their true nature was exposed. When each one had been unmasked, they gathered in a circle around me, lighting sticks of incense, and spoke of how the world had been created and the small part that I played in its current incarnation. And then, at the end, the leader of these men, the Great Elder of our tribe, took his place behind me and whispered in my ear the legend of Spearthrower Owl, who had been venerated by the Mayan people a century earlier and whose image as a leader of men had been inscribed into the hieroglyphs that could be found upon stones in this part of the world. Spearthrower Owl was always among us, the elder whispered, sending shivers down my spine. He lived inside our souls, determining our destinies, watching every move we made. He was our great Overlord and the one who would ultimately decide whether we had lived our lives with honesty or shame.

Hours later, when Diego reappeared, I could see how altered he was by what he had experienced. He walked like a man now, not a boy, and in his eyes was a portion of the wisdom that each of us, as Selk'nam people, had acquired across the centuries. I felt a burst of pride to know that I had brought him to this place.

He bowed low when he approached me and I placed my hands upon his shoulders as the men from the village emerged from the hut, ready to embrace our newest tribesman.

"It's over now?" asked Diego quietly, and I shook my head.

"Not quite," I said, for there was one more part of the hain to come, one that involved a quick and unwelcome burst of pain. I had not spoken to him about this before but I felt certain that, looking around him at the men of our village, and comparing their bodies to his own, he must have known that there was one further initiation rite left. I pulled the animal hide from around his waist and, reaching down, took his manhood in my left hand. He flinched as I removed a sharp knife from my belt. As his father figure here, it would be my responsibility to perform the cut. "Look toward the heavens," I instructed him. "The men will hold you tight. Breathe slowly and evenly. It will be quick, I promise. And then you will be ready to marry."

I could see the panic in his eyes, the same panic that every boy who had gone through this ceremony had felt since the dawn of time.

"But I told you," he insisted, shaking his head. "I don't want to marry."

. . .

Happy though I was with Diego's initiation into the Selk'nam tribe, I continued to be concerned about the relationship between my wife, Sofia, and her daughter, Bonita. The girl had become deeply introverted since returning to the care of her mother, a state of mind I put down to the twin traumas of being used in a bestial fashion by her father and the fact that she had been partly responsible for his death and the death of her grandmother.

Daughters of our tribe never spoke to their elders with anything other than respect, but Bonita was that rarest of creatures who said what she wanted when she wanted. It was obvious that she resented Sofia for having abandoned her in the first place, even though it had been explained to her time and again that this was not her mother's fault. With me, she was more polite, and with her younger brother, she was friendly; it was only the relationship with her mother that caused problems.

"I am considering taking her on the Great Walk," Sofia whispered to me one night as we lay in our cot. "Just the two of us. It might be good for her."

I turned to my wife in surprise. I knew of only a few people who had completed the Great Walk and each one had been a man. It could take many weeks, even months, to complete.

"You would be the first females to undertake such a journey," I said.

"Would the elders object? Would they stand in our way?"

I considered it and shook my head. "Not if I gave my consent," I replied. "And if you wish it, Wife, then you must do it. Where would you go?"

"To the southern tip of the archipelago," she replied. "And then we would sail to the islands beyond and complete our expedition on the rock that lies at the very end of the world. If she and I look into the water there and pledge our souls to the gods, then perhaps I can exorcize the demons that lurk within her soul."

I felt a growing anxiety. Such a trip would surely prove dangerous and I feared any harm coming to her.

"And what of Rafael?" I asked. "Who will take care of the boy while you are gone?"

"You," she replied, smiling at me, and I touched her nose in a moment of love. Who had ever heard of a man looking after a child? I would be mocked so deeply by the tribe that I would never be able to show my face again. But still, he was too young yet to be left alone. "We may be gone for three months," she told me. "And if we are, then you must take another woman in my place."

I shook my head.

"I would never do such a thing," I said. "I am not my father. I do not live by his values."

"But you have needs, Husband," she protested. "And if I am not here—"

"Then I will await your safe return," I replied. I was unusual among the men of my tribe in that I did not long for the affections of multiple women. I would remain chaste until she came back to me, as I had done after the death of my first wife and, for a time, after the murder of my second.

And so, a few days later, my wife and adopted daughter left our hut together, with provisions enough only to see them through till nightfall. After that, their destinies would lie in their own hands. Rafael wept and even Diego looked moved, but I held my head high and wished them both good fortune on their quest. Bonita was a damaged girl, but one who had never asked for that trauma to be inflicted upon her. It was right for her mother to help her in this way.

PART 9

THE
SHADOW OF
MY SHADOW

NAMIBIA

A.D. 1471

A YEAR TO THE DAY after Shakini and Beka left our village to journey through the mountain ranges in the west country, it occurred to me that I was probably the only person who still thought of them and believed that they would return safely someday. Our son, Rafiki, never spoke of his mother anymore and, if he sought a maternal figure at all, they were innumerable within our tribe, while Dembe, the foundling I had taken into our home, knew better than to mention her name. Once, he made the mistake of saying that he prayed she had met her end in a peaceful fashion and I struck him so hard that he fell sprawling to the ground, the only act of violence I had ever inflicted on him, and the wounded expression on his face as he looked up at me only intensified the shame of my actions.

"Adopted father," he said, tears streaming down his cheeks. "I apologize for my insensitivity. I only meant that when death came for her—"

"Death has not come for her," I insisted, striding toward him in such a fury that he scuttled back toward the wall. "If she was dead, I would know it. I would feel her loss within my blood."

"Of course," he replied, nodding quickly. "And she will most certainly appear again over the hills someday when her journey is completed."

I could tell from his tone that he did not believe this for even a moment, and later, when my temper had calmed, I regretted my brutality but repeated that I was certain both were still alive and that they would find their way home eventually. He never made the mistake of referring to my wife in the past tense again.

My grief, an emotion all too familiar to me, was almost overwhelming. Twice before I had suffered such loss and twice I had survived, but I was not sure that I could endure a third ordeal. Unlike when my first two wives had been taken from me, however, I could not spend my time wallowing in self-pity, for there was Rafiki to think of. The boy was four years old and a happy presence in my life. I could not fail him. I had no choice but to remain strong.

Each morning, I made my way to my workshop to craft masts for the trading ships that docked in or departed from our ports, but before leaving our tent, I would stand outside and turn my head slowly in all directions, listening for Shakini's voice, hopeful that this would be the day when I saw her walking along the flatlands in my direction, but each morning, I was disappointed. I repeated my actions at night, standing alone until the sun went down and the winds forced me back indoors. When I slept, my dreams were filled with disturbing images of the woman I loved being savaged by lions or taken away as a slave.

It did not help when one of the elders from our village, Vital Quihozo, came to see me and made a proposal that I could not possibly accept. Vital Quihozo was an old man, the oldest in our tribe, the skin on his face so lined with the passing of time that it resembled a ghoulish mask. Still, he remained in good health and, only recently, the youngest of his wives had given birth to his latest son. No one knew for certain how many children he had fathered—I was acquainted with at least twenty of his offspring, and they were only the ones who continued to live in our village—and it seemed at times as if his direct descendants outnumbered every other family group. Still, I admired and respected him and his presence in my tent was a great honor.

"Your sorrow is writ large across your face, my friend," he said, sitting cross-legged on the ground opposite me, wearing only the white loincloth that signified his superior status. "I witness you making your way toward your workshop every day, looking as if God has cursed you."

"He has," I told him, trying to keep the bitterness out of my voice, for he knew as well as I the suffering that I had endured across the years. "Sometimes I wonder what I ever did to displease him so."

"You have suffered your share of calamities, it is true," he agreed, nodding his head. "But then which of us has not? I have lost wives and children. Some whose names and faces I cannot even recall. That is the way of the world. Old women of thirty lose their husbands and find themselves with no one to marry or provide for them since their beauty has faded and they look like beasts from the forest. Should we tear at our hair and skin or should we continue about our daily business? Tell me, my friend."

I bowed my head but remained silent.

"You must take another wife," said Quihozo eventually, reaching across and placing his hand upon my forearm, and I looked back at him in dismay.

"Shakini advised the same of me before she left," I replied. "And I refused. I will not betray the promise I made to her."

He frowned, for a promise made to a woman was a comical thing.

"But this is not healthy, what you are doing," he insisted. "A man must spend his juices." He pointed to my loincloth and, despite the fact that this was all that any of us men wore, I felt suddenly self-conscious of my nakedness. "You must plant your seed in fertile territory. I have a daughter—"

"Please, Vital Quihozo—"

"Hear me out, my friend. I have a daughter, Okapi. She has seen only sixteen summers and has yet to find a husband. She will bear you many children, should you take her as your wife."

I was familiar with Okapi, an arrogant girl who never tired of complaining. She marched around the village arm in arm with her friend Quesa and, once, I had stumbled upon them in the bathing pool, where they were engaging in unholy acts with each other. At the time I had considered telling her father what I had observed but decided against it, for he would have certainly seen her stoned to death for such wickedness and I had enough deaths on my conscience already.

"I cannot," I told him, shaking my head. "Your offer is generous and any man would be delighted to be given the chance to marry Okapi, but while my heart still belongs to another, it would be unfair to your daughter."

"But she grows old," he replied with a sigh. "And I worry for her."

"Of course. But I would not make her a good husband. She deserves better than me."

He seemed disappointed, and Dembe, to his misfortune, chose this moment to return to the tent. When he saw that I was not alone, he looked regretful that he had come in, for he was nervous of the elders, particularly of Vital Quihozo, who had been suspicious of the boy ever since he saw him performing a trick for children that involved him pulling a many-colored snake from each of their ears.

"My apologies," he said, bowing and backing away.

"Don't leave," said Vital Quihozo, beckoning him forward. "Sit down. Tell your guardian that I am right."

"I am sure you are right in everything you say," he replied. "So I am in full agreement with you."

Vital Quihozo narrowed his eyes, uncertain whether the boy was trying to be humorous.

"And you, Dembe," asked the elder, standing up. "How old are you now?"

"Fourteen summers, Vital Quihozo."

"And you are healed?"

Dembe shrugged. Unfortunately, when I had initiated the boy into the Ovambo tribe some months earlier, the incision had not gone quite as smoothly as I'd hoped. Perhaps the knife had been unclean, for a disease had spread to the boy's manhood, turning it an unhealthy shade of green, and I feared that it might fall off altogether, but in time, it seemed to have returned to normal.

"Yes," said Dembe. "Perfectly healed."

"Show me."

"Must I?" he asked.

"Show me," insisted Quihozo, and, reluctantly, the boy removed his wrap, displaying a perfectly healthy member.

"A good size," remarked Quihozo, nodding in approval. "Then it is decided. You are young and restored to your powers. You will marry my fourteenth daughter, Okapi, in three days' time."

Dembe's eyes opened wide and, if he had regretted entering the tent a few minutes earlier, then it was nothing compared to how he felt now. I looked away, afraid to catch his eye, for I had not anticipated this turn of events.

"But I do not know her," he said. "We've never even met."

"That is not important," said Quihozo, laughing a little at the boy's foolishness. "Okapi is growing old; she is sixteen years of age and remains unwed. You, too, have yet to know the pleasures of a woman. It is time for her to take a husband and bear children. Three days." He turned to look at me and raised an eyebrow as if seeking my approval, which was not something he needed.

"Three days," I agreed, for although I was behaving badly by leaving my foundling as the unhappy groom, I preferred the idea of him marrying Okapi than being forced to do so myself. When the elder left our tent, I turned to the boy and, by the expression on his face, it seemed that there was one magic trick he wished he could do above all others: make himself disappear.

. . .

Okapi, it seemed, was even less eager than her prospective husband for the marriage to proceed. On the morning of the wedding, while Rafiki and I were painting Dembe's body in streaks of white and gold, the foundling confided in me that he had had an illicit meeting with her the night before, after messages had been passed from young person to young person and an encounter set for the edge of the forest at sundown.

"And?" I asked, trying not to sound as duplicitous as I felt. "Is she as beautiful, witty and intelligent as they say she is?"

"I hated everything about her," he replied. "And she hated everything about me."

"How can that be?"

"Firstly, she's ancient."

"She's only two years older than you," I sighed. "She's little more than a girl."

"And she's ugly. She has more hair on her chin and cheeks than I do."

"It is true that she takes after her father in some respects more than her mother."

"Her nose reminds me of a mandrill's."

"I believe she fell from a tree some years ago," I said, for it was true that her nose was not her finest feature. "She landed on her head. The accident caused some . . . disfigurement."

"That's probably why she's stupid, too. Her conversation is dull and her mind uninspiring. Also, she has these horrible enormous . . ." He searched for the word but couldn't even bring himself to say it, instead making cupping signals before his chest.

"Most boys would consider that a good thing," I said, but he shuddered in distaste.

"They're vile," he said. "She ordered me to show myself to her and then laughed when I did. She said she'd never seen anything as ugly as what hangs between my legs."

I was uncertain how to respond to this. There was a part of me that envied Dembe for the adventure that lay before him, hoping that he would grow to care for his new wife in time. The companionship of marriage, after all, was something that I deeply missed.

"She says that if I ever try to touch her, then she will stab me in my sleep," he continued. "And I told her that I would rather rub myself against a tree until my member fell off than put it anywhere near her. I don't want to marry her and I don't see why I should."

"Because Vital Quihozo has decreed it," I said. "And if you wish to remain a part of the Ovambo people, then you must abide by his wishes."

He looked as if he was about to burst into tears, knowing as well as I did that his only alternative to the match was to leave the tribe entirely. But where else could he go? Even if he chose to wander away in search of a new life, the disappearance of Shakini and Beka had put an end to any such ideas. The outside world, after all, was full of predators.

Rafiki watched these proceedings with a wide smile on his face, for he enjoyed seeing the boy he thought of as his brother being painted in such lavish colors. He asked whether he might be painted as well, but I shook my head.

"On your wedding day," I told him. "Then your mother and I will paint you for your bride."

He frowned and it hurt me to recognize that he showed no interest in her return—she was virtually a stranger to him, after all—but I said no more of it for now.

On the way to the ceremony, which was to take place outside Vital Quihozo's tent, we passed by my workshop and, trying to put Dembe's mind at ease, I invited him inside to see a particularly ornate mast on which I had been working for several weeks. He studied it for a few moments and, his eyes lighting up, seemed to come to life.

"Watch," he said, placing both hands at the top of the mast and then rolling them down the front of the wood. As he did so, all my etchings disappeared, and I was left with nothing but the piece of wood that it had been before I started work. I gasped in horror.

"What have you done?" I cried out. "This needs to be ready in a few days' time."

He laughed and shook his head, then repeated the gesture with his hands and my work reappeared. I closed my eyes in bewilderment. I had never understood the secret to his tricks and, in truth, they frightened me a little, for I knew that there were some who believed he should be drowned in the river for acting like a god.

"Come," I said, leading him back outside toward the center of the village, where a dais had been set up for the wedding. The entire tribe had gathered to watch, each person adorned in the ceremonial clothing of our people. When Dembe took his place at the front, Okapi appeared with a furious expression on her face, and only when Vital Quihozo roared at her did she pretend to smile. Standing next to the girl, he tried to take her hand, but she brushed him away as another of the elders stepped forward to raise the rain-stick over their heads and sing the incantations. When it was over and hands had been placed on both of their heads, the two young people bowed to each other and were married. I had never seen such misery on the faces of anyone before and, had it not been such a terrible thing to witness, it might almost have been funny.

Stepping off the dais, Dembe marched straight over to a friend of his, a boy with whom he spent more time than I thought healthy, while Okapi ran over to Quesa, who threw her arms around her, the pair collapsing on each other's shoulders in tears. It was the most extraordinary thing to witness and I tried not to laugh, turning to my wife to ask whether she had ever seen something so bizarre before, but of course Shakini was not there and whatever good humor had resided in my soul disappeared now as I was left to confront my loneliness.

SPAIN

A.D. 1492

ON A BRIGHT, SUNNY MORNING in early August, a few weeks after my young ward's calamitous wedding day, I stood by the harbor in Huelva, overseeing the installation of the sails on the three ships that were soon to set off for the Indies in the hope of finding a new and faster route to the Orient. As the ships were old and had been refitted for a journey that many considered a fool's errand, the designs had proved more complex than I'd originally imagined, but I enjoyed my work and was being well compensated for it. King Ferdinand and Queen Isabella had agreed to fund the explorer's travels and, true to their word, had been extremely generous, although perhaps this was not an act of pure selflessness or philanthropy on their part. After all, they knew that if he was to succeed, and the new trade routes fell under the control of Spain, the benefits to the kingdoms of both Castile and Aragon would be immeasurable.

Deago was with me, as he often was in those days, for he sought any opportunity to escape the attentions of his wife, Olallo, and I feared that he was irritating the workmen more than entertaining them with his sleight-of-hand tricks. His dear friend, Timo, was lurking nearby, too. This did not surprise me, for wherever one was found, the other was never far away, just as whenever I spotted Olallo around the town, I could be certain that her friend Querida would be walking next to her. Sometimes I thought the two pairings would have preferred to have married each other, had such an idea not been an abomination.

"And how is married life?" I asked him as the sailors extended the sails on the first of the three ships, making sure that the square rig fitted perfectly against the masts. The breeze was light, which helped in the task.

"Horrible," he replied. "I had the misfortune to witness something last night that made me want to pluck the eyes from my head."

"And what was that?" I asked.

"My wife in a state of undress. Once seen, it is emblazoned upon the memory like a regretted tattoo. She removed every stitch of clothing before climbing into bed and her naked body gave me nightmares. Also, I vomited. Twice. Once so unexpectedly that the contents of my stomach discharged themselves onto the bedsheets."

I stared at him in bewilderment. It was true that Olallo had the personality of an ill-tempered mule, but her proportions were fair and her countenance pleasing. I found it difficult to understand how the boy's feelings toward her could be so lacking in sensuousness.

"But the . . ." I struggled to find the right words as I didn't want to embarrass either of us. "The marriage act itself," I said. "Everything . . . works in the way that it should?"

He rolled his eyes, a new affectation of his that implied I was being foolish beyond words. "If you're asking whether we've been rutting like farmyard animals since being forced into this unhappy union, then no, we haven't. I can't think of anything more repulsive, to be honest. I tried, I will admit. Once. Out of politeness more than anything else. But trying to enter her sacred bordello was like trying to force a sleeping worm through a keyhole."

"Good God!" I said.

"I know for a fact that there's nothing wrong with me, for I spend most of the time in a state of tumescence. It's only when she appears that the great letdown happens. The fact is, she looks like a cabbage down there. How could anyone find such a thing attractive?"

"Most men do."

"Then they must be suffering from a disorder of the brain."

"And has she complained about your lack of ardor?"

"On the contrary, she told me that she'd cut my member off with a pair of scissors if I ever tried to come near her again."

His indifference confused me, for I had always delighted in the

marriage act with each of my wives and, since the mysterious disappearance of Santina, I found that I missed it tremendously. Occasionally, I availed myself of the services of the girls in the taverns,
but never found it a satisfying experience. Without love, the act
seemed much less enticing.

"And what about children?" I asked.

"What about them?"

"How can you hope to father a child if you do not engage in
relations with your wife?"

He stared at me and frowned, as if I was speaking in a foreign
tongue.

"You do understand that it is a prerequisite for the creation of
babies, don't you?" I asked.

"In what way?" he replied. I sighed and explained the nature of
conception to him in as simple terms as I could master and the
more I told him, the more disgusted he looked.

"Is that how we are created?" he asked finally, shaking his head.
"I often wondered and heard rumors that it involved something as
ghastly as what you have described but had always assumed that
there must be more to it. How disgusting!" He shivered, a great
chill running through his bones. "Honestly, if that's what it takes,
then I'd prefer never to be a father," he added. "The whole idea
repulses me."

Happily, this conversation could not be continued any further, as
the captain of the three ships was marching along the dock toward
us, appearing both excited and apprehensive as he looked across at
his small fleet.

"Well, Master Sailmaker," he roared, placing a hand upon each of
my shoulders in delight and grinning from ear to ear. "It seems that
you have excelled yourself. Those sails are fine things indeed and
will guide us speedily toward our destination."

"Thank you, my friend," I said, nodding graciously, pleased that
he was satisfied with my work. "Deago," I said, turning to the boy.
"You have not met Señor Cristóbal Colón yet, have you? The captain of these three vessels."

Deago bowed at the waist in the manner of a popinjay, one hand pressed against his back, the other offering a flourish, and then, to my irritation, he reached forward and pulled an egg from behind the captain's ear. Peeling the shell away, he revealed it to be hard-boiled and devoured it in three quick bites before smiling content-edly at both of us. I turned to Colón, wondering what he would make of such childishness, but to my relief he burst out laughing and reached around to the back of his head, checking that there were no further eggs to be located there.

"A fine trick," he said. "Although one that could see you burned for witchcraft, lad. The Inquisition does not look kindly on such games."

Deago's smile fell.

"Still, we could use a clown like you on board to keep the sailors entertained on dark evenings," he continued. "What say you? Would you care to explore the Indies with us? Do you have the legs and stomach of a seaman?"

For a moment, it seemed as if Deago was considering the offer, perhaps as a way to escape the ministrations of his new wife, but then he shook his head and replied that he did not think a sailor's life was the one for him. Colón merely shrugged his shoulders, as if he could not quite believe why any young man would pass on such a glorious opportunity, before returning his gaze to the boats.

"Shall we go on board?" he asked, and I followed the captain as he stepped across the gangplank onto the *Santa María*, the only carrack, or three-masted ship, in the fleet, for both the *Niña* and the *Pinta* were caravels, with only two. He looked around, strolling along the deck with his hands on his hips, and breathing in deeply as if he were trying to become one with the woodwork. "What do you think of her?" he asked, and I nodded my head in appreciation.

"Very fine," I said. "A worthy vessel for your adventures. Will you captain this one or—"

"Yes, this one," he replied. "The Pinzón brothers will take charge of the other two, under my command, of course. By my reckoning we should arrive in Japan in a little over a month's time and then I will have proven that there is a faster route for the spice trade."

"A worthy goal, Señor," I said.

He reached out and took a handful of the sail in his fist, before pressing his face into the fabric and rubbing the material along his cheek as if it were the nightgown of his lover. "You've done a fine job," he told me. "You worked well with the mast-maker?"

"Yes," I replied, for I had been in constant communication with the man who'd designed the wooden masts, which were mostly smooth and unornamented, except for one, which had the design of a many-colored snake carved into the wood. My sails had an artistic bent, too, with various intricacies in place around the hems. I had used my needles to inscribe images of other lands into the cloth, places that lived not only in my imagination but, I assumed, in the imaginations of explorers such as Señor Colón.

"Well, it's fine work, fine work," he agreed. "And you will come to the palace tomorrow evening for the farewell party?"

"I was honored to have been asked," I said, for an invitation had come from Queen Isabella herself and I was looking forward to it immensely.

"Good," he replied, dismissing me and Deago now. "Well, I'll let you both return to shore, Master Sailmaker," he said. "I have some more inspections to complete before being satisfied that we are ready to depart."

Deago and I bowed, making our way back across the gangplank while, in unison, all three ships extended their sails and a great sea of white appeared before us decorated with the scarlet emblems of Castile and Aragon. It was a tremendous sight to behold and it thrilled me to imagine another sailmaker in Japan, a fellow craftsman, examining my work when the ships arrived at their destination.

• • •

Returning to my workshop, I discovered my son, Rafe, seated in a corner, apparently lost in thought.

"Are you well?" I asked, surprised to see him there, for he preferred to spend his afternoons drawing and playing with his abacus.

"I wanted to ask you something," he replied. "About someone."

"Who?"

"My mother."

I nodded, both surprised and pleased that she remained on his mind.

"You haven't spoken of her in a long time," I said.

"I've been afraid to," he replied. "When I think of her, I feel very sad. So, more often than not, I try not to think of her at all."

"It's natural," I told him. "You're growing older. You miss her. A boy needs his mother."

"Will you tell me what happened to her?"

I sat down next to him. I had been expecting this conversation to take place someday but, nevertheless, felt ill prepared for it.

"What would you like to know?"

"Was your marriage a happy one?"

"Very happy," I said, nodding my head. "When first we met, there was no hint of romance between us, but we became friendly quite quickly. And, in time, something more blossomed."

"So she didn't leave because you did not love her enough?"

"No," I replied. "I loved her very much, and she knew this."

"Then why did she go?"

I hesitated for a few moments before replying. "Do you remember her daughter, Beatrisa?" I asked.

"A little," he said. "She was nice to me, I remember. But she had dark moods."

"Yes, she was a troubled girl, but she had suffered much ill treatment in her life. Santina took her away to see whether they might be able to find some peace for her tortured mind. They were expected to be gone only for a few months and when they didn't come back—"

"You didn't go in search of them?"

"No."

"Why not?"

I sighed, for I had asked myself this same question many times. "I wouldn't have known where to start," I told him. "And you were still so young that I had to take care of you. Deago is a fine lad, but he is also an idiot. I could not trust him with a jewel as precious as you."

"You could have brought me with you?"

"And risk harm coming to you? No, my son, I had already wasted many years of my life searching for someone who caused me pain and suspended that odyssey in order to settle down to family life. I couldn't go on another crusade. Not yet anyway."

He looked up, apparently intrigued by this story. "And who were you looking for then, Father?" he asked.

"Someone I knew when I was much younger. Someone who hurt me very badly."

"And you never found him?"

I shook my head. Although I didn't think of my cousin very often these days, I was sure that our paths would cross again one day.

"You didn't . . . you didn't kill her, did you?" asked my son.

"Who?" I asked.

"My mother."

My mouth fell open in surprise. "Of course not!" I cried. "How could you even think such a thing?"

"There are rumors that you have the blood of many people on your hands."

"The blood of some, yes," I admitted. "We live in a violent world and there are people who would still be alive today had our paths not crossed. Some I regret, some I don't. But this was all a long time ago and, I promise, I would have cut my hand off before I used it to injure your mother. You must believe me when I tell you that I loved her very much."

He stood up, walking toward the door, apparently unsatisfied by my answers, and I suspected that this was a conversation we would return to again before he grew much older.

"Maybe when I'm a man I can go in search of her," he said, and I nodded.

"Maybe," I said. "But that time has not come just yet."

He smiled, considering this, and stepped out the door, looking left and right to see where his adventures might take him next.

• • •

The following evening, at the palace, I found myself in conversation once again with Captain Colón when an elderly priest named Father Rodríguez hobbled toward us wearing an expression that combined determination and fury. He was at least sixty years of age, with a crooked nose and a handful of long white hairs on his head that he dragged from one ear to the other in order to give the illusion of youth.

"You are the captain that is setting sail tomorrow?" he asked, pointing a gnarly finger at Colón, who smiled and bowed deeply at the waist.

"I am," he replied. "Cristóbal Colón."

"And who are you?" he asked, turning to me.

"Nobody," I said.

"Nobody is nobody. You must be somebody."

"The sailmaker, nothing more."

"Then you're the one responsible for sending this man and the men who sail with him to their deaths?" he asked.

"I don't see how that follows," I replied. "I've been making sails for many years and my work is of the highest quality. They will guide them safely in all weathers. I would stake my life on it."

"You make your way toward the Indies, is that right?" asked the priest, dismissing this as he turned back to Colón, who nodded. "But you are sailing westward?"

"Yes. To discover a faster route."

"But, my ignorant friend, the world is flat," insisted the priest. "It is a disc, nothing more. When you reach the end, you will simply fall off into the great abyss." He leaned forward, looking around and lowering his voice as if this were too great a secret to be shared with others. "There be dragons there," he said. "And they will swallow you whole."

"Those myths have been debunked," said Colón, laughing and shaking his head. "The world is neither a disc nor a flat surface. Nor is it held in the arms of Atlas or upon the back of a turtle. Consider, Reverend Father, when you observe a ship sailing into the distance. It disappears bit by bit as it reaches the horizon, does it not? That is because the Earth is spherical."

"If you believe that, then you are a fool and a heretic," said Father Rodríguez.

"I may be a fool," replied Colón, his expression becoming grim.

"But I would have thought that a priest would know better than to refer to any man as a heretic in these dark times. Such words can lead an innocent soul to the burning palisade."

The priest waved his hands in the air, turning back to me in the hope that I might take his side, although in truth I had no firm convictions on the subject. I had certainly grown up assuming that the world was flat, but in recent times I had begun to doubt whether this was the case. And what Colón had said made a certain amount of sense.

"And what about you?" he asked. "Will you be going on this voyage, too?"

"No," I said. "I remain here to continue my work. There are many more ships departing Huelva than Señor Colón's and they all need sails."

"Good. Then you will not fall off the edge of the world."

"I feel like I already have. Several times, in fact. But not this time, no. And not in the *Niña,* the *Pinta* or the *Santa María.*"

A messenger interrupted our conversation, whispering something in Colón's ear, and he nodded quickly and put his glass down.

"Their Majesties are in the state room and have summoned me," he said. He turned to walk away, then seemed to think better of it and looked back. "Master Sailmaker," he said, "would you care to meet them?"

"The King and Queen?" I said, opening my eyes wide. "I would be honored. Would I be permitted an audience?"

"Of course. King Ferdinand is particularly interested in the design of the ships. Come with me," he said. "He will be pleased to make your acquaintance."

I said goodbye to the priest, who seemed annoyed not to have been invited to join us, too. Even as we walked away in the direction of two enormous gilded doors, I heard him cry out in our wake:

"It's flat, you mark my words! And you shall fall off and be devoured by dragons! I promise it!"

VATICAN CITY

A.D. 1512

J UST BEFORE THE GREAT DOORS OPENED, my patron turned to
me, placed a hand upon my shoulder and looked me directly in
the eye. I looked into his pale and drawn face, the creases on his
skin pockmarked with fragments of paint and plaster, and wondered
how a man so devoted to his work could remain on his feet for so
long every day.

"Remember," he whispered. "Do not speak until he addresses
you. Do not interrupt him. Do not contradict him. Do nothing at
all, in fact, unless he asks it of you. Pretend that you do not exist,
that you are nothing more than the shadow of my shadow."

"With so many conditions attached, Master, perhaps I should
leave you to go in alone," I suggested. "After all, I was not invited
and he has never laid eyes upon me. He may not welcome a stranger
being so presumptuous as to enter his presence without permission."

"Perhaps not," he said, smiling a little. "But I prefer to bring
someone with me for such meetings. It helps if there is a witness to
any conversations that might afterward be . . . how shall I put this?
Forgotten. Or misremembered."

I nodded and tried to keep my anxiety under control as four
members of the new Swiss militia that had been created by the Pope
a few years earlier stepped away from the doors and we walked into
the receiving chamber. I expected a great crowd of priests and bish-
ops to be gathered in entourage, but no, to my surprise, the only
people waiting for us were the Holy Father himself, Pope Julius II,
and a handsome young priest who stood in attendance upon him.

Michelangelo and I bowed deeply, and the artist stepped forward, kneeling before the Pope and kissing the ring of the fisherman on his right hand. I followed suit and the old man placed his

palms atop my head, muttering something incoherent, a blessing of sorts I supposed, before I made my way to the corner of the room, determined to follow my master's instructions and remain silent until I was addressed.

"My friend," said the Pope, addressing Michelangelo, and sounding anything but friendly. "We are happy with you and we are unhappy with you. Twin emotions that cause discord in our mind."

"Please, Holy Father," replied Michelangelo, spreading his arms wide in an act of subordination. "In what way have I distressed you? Allow me to rectify the situation before I die of unhappiness."

"We visited the Chapel yesterday," replied the Pope, "and looked up toward the paintings that you have created upon the walls and ceilings. They are very fine and gave us much pleasure."

"Thank you, Holy Father."

"It has been almost a year since we last visited, of course, and there is no question that you have accomplished much in that time."

"With the grace of God, yes."

"And lying on your back every day. This cannot have been easy. It is the work of whores, no?"

He spat out a laugh and I raised an eyebrow in surprise, for I had not expected a man of divine grace to speak in such earthy terms.

"Actually, Holy Father, I work standing up. Although yes, my neck has, on occasion, suffered unhappy agonies."

He rotated his head a little, the better to demonstrate the injury, but His Holiness waved away his complaints as if a mortal man's discomfort were of no consequence to him. "We all suffer," he intoned. "But we will receive our bounty in due course when we are granted eternal reward in our Father's kingdom. And the more suffering we endure in this world, the greater the reward shall be in that one."

"Speaking of rewards," began Michelangelo, and, sensing that he was about to be asked for money, the Pope turned to look in my direction before summoning the priest over and whispering something in his ear. The younger man looked across at me with a contemptuous expression on his face before speaking in a surprisingly loud voice, as if I were hard of hearing.

"The Holy Father should like to know the identity of the man you have brought into his sacred presence, uninvited."

"One of my assistants, Your Holiness," replied Michelangelo, introducing me then by name, and I bowed again, wondering whether I should say something now or remain silent.

"And what has been your role in this project?" asked Pope Julius.

"Each morning, I prepare the plaster for the frescos, Holy Father," I replied. "A certain mixture that prevents mold from forming on the ceiling of the Sistine Chapel."

"You are an artist, too?"

"I have tried to be, yes," I told him. "I had a workshop of my own in Florence. It was there that I first met the Master and was fortunate enough to be invited to accompany him to Rome."

"The Master," he said, shaking his head and looking displeased by the honorific. "There is only one master, young man, and He does not reside in this temporal world."

"Of course, Holy Father," I said, lowering my eyes. When I dared to look up again, I studied him more closely as I waited to see whether our dialogue had come to an end or whether he was going to chastise me further. He was very old, one of the oldest men I had ever encountered. At seventy years of age, his eyes were sunken into the back of his head and the papal robes hung off his frame loosely, suggesting a thin man beneath the mantle, unlike his predecessor Pius, who had been fat, or the Borgia pope, who had been so obese that he was known as the Great Whale of Rome by those who did not value their lives. He wore a long white beard and the skin on his hands, when I kissed them, had been paper thin, the blue veins almost breaking through their tender surface. I suspected that it would not be long before the Lord called him to his own reward, and perhaps he sensed this himself, for his next complaint related to the subject of his own mortality.

"We are unhappy, so-called Master," he continued, looking back at Michelangelo, "with the condition of our tomb."

"Your tomb, Holy Father?"

"We visited it this morning and it is far from ready. How many years has it been since we commissioned it?"

"Eight years!" said the priest, shouting again. "The Holy Father gave instructions for the completion of the tomb in 1504. That's eight years ago, Artist, and still it is not finished!"

"Of course, it has been an ongoing project and—"

"It was supposed to be ready by 1510!" roared the priest.

"And fortunately, the Holy Father has not required its services," I said, ignoring the directive I had been given earlier, and Michelangelo turned, offering me a look that was difficult to interpret. "His Holiness appears in great health," I continued, growing a little flustered now. "And, with the grace of God, he will surely remain on his throne for many years to come."

The Pope looked at me and his face contorted in pain, as if even the sound of such lies were too much for his tender ears.

"Who is this fool?" he asked, turning to the priest again.

"An assistant to the artist," said the priest. "He told you a moment ago."

"I don't remember," said the Pope, waving him away. "All I know is that our tomb is nowhere near completion. We asked for forty statues to be built around it and by our count there are only half that number."

"As the Holy Father will be aware," said Michelangelo, "I have been distracted from the work by other commissions that you have since honored me with. The Sistine Chapel, for example, was no easy task and—"

Again, he dismissed this, now shaking both hands in the air as if he were drying them. "A simple job," he grunted. "Any halfwit could have done it. Which brings me to my second concern. The nine panels at the center of your fresco."

"Yes, Holy Father?"

"You begin on the right-hand side, with God creating the water, the sun, the planets. He divides light from darkness on the right and you finish the sequence on the left with the story of Noah."

"Your Holiness is most observant," said Michelangelo with a polite bow.

"But in the center there are three panels, are there not?"

"Yes, Holy Father. First, we witness the creation of Adam, then the introduction of Eve, and in the third piece, their temptation by the serpent, followed by their disgrace and banishment from the Garden of Eden."

"But you chose to place the creation of Eve as the centerpiece, not the creation of Adam?"

"Yes, Holy Father."

"A woman!" he roared, slamming his fists down on the armrests and making me jump in surprise. He leaned forward dramatically in his throne now and the priest blessed himself, as if evil spirits needed to be exorcized from the room.

"Yes, Holy Father," repeated Michelangelo.

"It seems most strange to us that you should consider a woman worthy of such an honor."

"But Adam was created first," I pointed out. "Eve was taken from one of his ribs. It says so in the Old Testament."

The Pope turned and glared at me. He seemed to know who I was now and was not even slightly interested in my opinions. "We are talking to the master!" he shouted at me. "Not the servant!"

"My apologies, Holy Father," I replied. I tried to distract myself from his anger by directing my attention toward the frescoes that adorned the walls; an island of palm trees, an image of the Madonna, a three-masted ship sailing through the sea.

"My assistant forgets himself in addressing His Holiness in such a disrespectful fashion," said Michelangelo after a careful pause. "But, despite his insolence, he is correct in what he says. I could not paint Eve before painting Adam. It would make no sense."

The Pope seemed unimpressed by this answer and stared down at his hands for such a long time that I wondered whether he had fallen asleep or died.

"We want our tomb completed as soon as possible," he said finally, returning to life.

"Of course, Holy Father."

"We may have need of it before many more days have passed."

"May God prevent such a catastrophe."

The Pope looked at him and rolled his eyes before dismissing us. Back outside, I realized that my clothes were sticking to my back with perspiration. Michelangelo looked at me with a mixture of amusement and annoyance on his face.

"I warned you not to say anything," he said.

. . .

My first encounter with Michelangelo had come some months earlier, in Florence, when our paths crossed on the banks of the Arno. I had just delivered a set of figureheads of the gods Neptune, Poseidon and Apollo to the captains of three boats that were making their maiden voyages into the Ligurian Sea and he stopped to inspect them. So impressed was he by my work that he asked one of the sailors for the name of the artist responsible and was directed toward my small workshop. When he stepped inside, I was examining a piece of marble that had been delivered from Rome a few days earlier for a new commission and, looking up, felt a little overwhelmed to be in the presence of such a great man.

"You designed the prows of the boats that set sail today?" he asked, looking around at my other sculptures, and I struggled to find words at first, for I had seen the Divine One, as he was known, in the city many times but had never, as yet, had the courage to approach him. The crucifix that he'd designed for the Santo Spirito church had thrilled me in its execution.

"I did, Maestro," I replied, introducing myself, and he wandered around, inspecting the work that was scattered across my shelves. Deangelo, my ward, was sweeping dust from the corner of the workshop, wearing his usual miserable expression, but when he saw our visitor, he cheered up considerably, strolling over with a small ball of marble in one hand and three cups in the other.

"Witness," he said, placing the cups upon a table and the marble beneath one of them, before stepping back for a moment. "The ball is hidden from view. Now watch." He reached down and swapped the center cup for the one on the left. Then the one on the left for the one on the right. This went on for a half-dozen more moves, at which point he invited Michelangelo to select the cup under which the marble sat.

"That one," said the artist, pointing to the center, and Deangelo's face fell as he lifted the cup to reveal the ball. "So, I assume that you will give me a coin now?" asked Michelangelo, and reluctantly, the boy reached into his pocket to remove one, but the older man shook his head and waved him away. "Keep your money," he said. "I am not easily fooled."

"Forgive him," I said, walking over to join the artist. "The boy plays these tricks to keep himself entertained."

"He is your son?"

"My ward," I said. "Although he is married now, so my duties should have long come to an end."

"And how is married life?" asked the artist, turning back to Deangelo. "You look young to have taken a wife."

"Each day feels as if I am slowly descending into the eighth circle of hell," he replied. "Each morning I wake to look at the face of a hideous troll whose bed I am condemned to share. I tell her how much I loathe her and she spits in my face. And each night, when I return to that cursed bed, I am reminded of how much her body repulses me. How any man can stand to live in bondage to a woman is beyond my understanding."

Michelangelo stared at him a few moments in surprise, before turning to me and then looking back at the boy. Clearly, this had not been the answer he had anticipated.

"Can she cook, at least?" he asked eventually.

"She can," replied Deangelo with a shrug of his shoulders. "I'll admit that much."

Michelangelo shook his head in wonder, before asking whether he could see some more of my work.

"You have great skill," he said at last. "I have need of a man of such talent."

"You cannot want to commission a piece from me?" I asked in astonishment. "It would be my honor to—"

"No, not that. But you are aware that I employ a number of assistants who help me with my work?"

"I am."

"I need another man. Would you be interested?"

It took me no time to reply in the affirmative, knowing that I could learn from him and improve my own proficiency. And so I went with him that very day, traveling to Rome with my ward and my son, and living within the walls of the Vatican, where I mixed the plaster that the Master used and created rough sketches for his panels. I had also fashioned the busts of slaves that could be placed upon the tomb of Pope Julius. Naturally, I felt fortunate to have found such a position but there were moments when I longed to be recognized for my own work. To that end, I had begun to design a bust that I tentatively called *The Plague of Rome*.

For many years I had been intrigued by the history of my country and particularly by the first three centuries under the Caesars, the Antonines, the Severans and the Gordians, creating several marble sculptures based on these events. And while most of my time was spent working under Michelangelo's direction, I found a few hours every night to complete my own projects, and this one was a particular favorite.

I worked from an idea that, thirteen hundred years earlier, a plague had descended upon Rome, carried back to the streets of the capital by soldiers returning from the ongoing wars in the Far East. Thousands were dying every day and there was talk of the city being abandoned entirely. My piece depicted the Emperor Commodus when he was just a child, lying in the arms of a young friend who was tending to him after he had been laid low by the plague and was in danger of death. It was, I believed, one of my better works.

When it was finally ready, I decided that I would show it to Michelangelo, in the hope of earning his approval. If he liked it, after all, there was always the chance that he might incorporate it into one of the areas of the Vatican still awaiting statues. This push for immortality might not have shown great humility on my part, but I was, after all, only human.

ENGLAND

A.D. 1599

CARRYING THIS NEW WORK in my hands, it was with a sense of trepidation that I stepped through the doors of the theatre and looked around in search of my patron. The playhouse was busy, as I guessed it would be, for tonight marked the first presentation of his new drama, *Julius Caesar*, a tragedy that William had been working on for several months, and there was much excitement in the air. Most of his plays so far had concerned themselves with English kings or been lighthearted, trivial fantasies that would quickly be forgotten and I thought it a brave choice to step back in time to the Roman age, although I felt reasonably sure that he would prove himself worthy of the endeavor and the audience would be entertained. He was not untalented, after all, and I for one considered him among the twenty best playwrights in England.

The Globe, finally completed after much hard work, was an impressive structure, with three levels of seating for the mob and a pit at the front where the groundlings could sit. In total, three thousand stinking Londoners, a pretty number, could enjoy the evening's entertainment as a relief from the drudgery of their miserable lives. Most of the materials for its construction had been salvaged from Burbage's playhouse in Shoreditch and moved here, to Bankside, after an almighty row had seen the place close down. Burbage had in fact produced three of my own plays over the years, but we had fallen out over money, for he was a thieving swine, and it was my hope that William would be interested in producing my most recent one in this wonderful new space.

I spotted David, my young ward, standing on the stage. He had found employment helping with the pyrotechnics that would allow Caesar's ghost to appear to Brutus in the fourth act, on the eve of the Battle of Philippi, warning the assassin that they would see each other again e'er long. David had rigged a series of wires in the eaves that meant the ghost could glide on and off effortlessly while his dear friend, Timothy, was not far away, for he had been cast in the role of Calpurnia, Caesar's wife. I worried that David's wife, Olivia, would feel even further estranged from him, as the two young men were utterly inseparable and their work in the playhouse only increased their proximity, but, as she preferred to pass her days in the company of her bosom friend, Queenie, the arrangement seemed to work rather well.

"My friend!" cried William, approaching me through a huddle of costume-makers. "You've arrived!"

"Of course," I said. "I wouldn't miss it for the world."

"What do you think?" he asked, looking around. "A fine theatre, is it not?"

"Very fine. It will inspire all of us to create great plays."

"And you've brought another copy of the script," he added, noticing the pages in my hand. "Good. It will do us well to have a spare copy backstage. I believe we might have need of a prompter tonight, for there are one or two of my cast who have not fully committed to their lines, the worthless dogs. It grieves me and I would as soon dismiss them from the company than mark their presence, but who, at this late stage, could fill their roles? No, a prompter it must be." He thought about this for a moment. "You!" he said, grinning from ear to ear. "You have no commitments this evening, I hope?"

I shook my head. "Only to be here," I told him. "And to watch the play."

"Then watch it from the wings, my friend, would you do that? And be prepared to whisper any words that these asses forget."

I nodded. I was happy to do so, for this was a role I had fulfilled many times in the past and I quite enjoyed watching the action from the side of the stage rather than from the seats, for the good people of London had a stench to them that would make one fear the pox. And as for sitting among the groundlings? Why, one could barely hear a word of the performance for their tittering and boorish behavior. It was said that at least one child a night was conceived in the pit of the average London theatre, and I did not doubt it, for these were saucy types and strangers to modesty.

"However," I said, "I will need to find another copy, for the manuscript in my hands is not, in fact, a transcription of *Julius Caesar*."

"It's not?" he asked, frowning. "What is it, then?"

"A copy of my play. My *new* play, that is. I wondered whether you might take a look at it for me when you have a chance? Perhaps it's something that could be staged when yours has run its course?"

He took it from me and glanced at the title page. " '*The Most Terrible Calamity of Spearthrower Owl, of his descendants and kin, as related by the playwright in this, the forty-first year of the reign of her most gracious majesty, Elizabeth, Queen of England, France and Ireland, Defender of the Faith, etc.*' Catchy title, my friend!"

"*Spearthrower Owl* for short," I said.

"A spirited name! And what is it, a comedy? A tragedy? A farce?"

"It is a play," I replied. "No more, no less than that. But it has, I hope, a deal of excitement and adventure within its scenery."

"Does anyone die?"

"Several people of both a goodly and indifferent nature."

"Does the main character suffer a cruel betrayal of punishing depth?"

"He does."

"Is there a dog?"

"One or two."

"A Jew?"

"A few."

"A lady of scandalous morals?"

"Several."

"A lady of goodly chastity?"

"Here and there."

"And are there jokes?"

"Unfortunately, I have not found room for humor. My hero endures suffering more than laughter throughout his life."

William shook his head in disappointment. "Your last two plays were filled with jokes. That's why people enjoyed them so much.

They proved a nice change from your earlier work, which, if I recall, was always so sad."

I nodded, for his assessment was true. I had been writing plays since childhood and longed to devote more time to the craft but had become distracted time and again by unexpected events. Only now, when my grief at the disappearance of my wife and her daughter had finally started to diminish, did I feel that I could return to my writing and, with this new play, I hoped I might at last reach the wider audience that a performance at the Globe could guarantee.

"I look forward to reading it, my friend," he said, slapping me about the arm and putting the pages under his. "But I must press on. There is still much to be done before tonight's performance gets under way. Fly to the wings before the games begin and I shall reacquaint myself with you there anon."

"Which part are you playing?" I asked as he walked away, and when he turned back, he offered a surprised smile, as if he could not believe that I was so naïve.

"Why, the title role, of course," he said. "What else would be worthy of my talents?"

. . .

Later that afternoon, as we dined in our modest dwelling, Richard asked whether he might accompany me to the Globe that night. The boy was nine years old by now and had never shown any particular interest in my work before, so I was rather glad when he said that he would like to visit the playhouse.

"Of course," I said. "I shall ask William to secure you a seat in the middle level. The best views are from there."

"Is that where you'll be sitting?" he asked, and I shook my head, explaining to him the role that I had been offered earlier in the day. "Can't I watch with you, then?" he asked. "I won't be any trouble and I'll remain silent."

I thought about it and could see no reason why not. Richard was a well-behaved boy and would surely remain silent as the actors performed their parts. While we ate a light supper of swan stuffed with pigeon stuffed with vole, I found myself glancing in his direction from time to time, noticing how much he was beginning to resemble his mother, Sarah. They shared the same shy smile and deep blue eyes and, as it had been with my wife, to be in his company was to feel completely at one's ease. I allowed my mind to wallow in memory for a few moments. Like all who had known her, I had come to accept that Sarah and her daughter were dead, assuming that when they had left London to travel toward Land's End, they had encountered thieves, murderers or Welshmen along the way.

"Father, you're weeping," said Richard, and I put a hand to my face, surprised and embarrassed to discover that my cheeks were damp with tears.

"It is the weather," I said. "Nothing more. The summer air has placed a curse upon my eyes."

He looked at me, unconvinced, and returned to his food.

"Did you finish the play you were writing?" he asked after a moment.

"I did," I replied, nodding. "I gave it to Master Shakespeare earlier. If all is well and he approves of it, perhaps I will be able to stage it in the new year. A new century approaches, my boy! A happy way to begin, don't you agree? With a triumph upon the London stage?"

"Perhaps I could perform in it?" he asked, and I sat back in surprise, for he had shown no leanings toward an actorly life before and, in fact, had always seemed a rather shy child, nervous of any attention.

"You?" I said. "You have aspirations toward a theatrical life?"

He shrugged his shoulders, a new gesture of his that I found intensely irritating. "I'm not sure," he said. "I like the idea of transformation. The thought of becoming someone else entirely intrigues me."

"There's nothing wrong with you as you are."

"I don't know. My mind is filled with numbers and some say that I am a strange boy."

I considered this. It was true that Richard had an obsession with mathematics and could often be found drawing strange objects in his vellum pads. Once, he drew the world itself, and the moon, and a series of unusual shapes surrounding the planet where he said men might live someday. It was an amusing idea but I had encouraged him to keep his nonsense to himself, lest others think he had lost his reason and send him to the madhouse.

"Perhaps I would have more friends if I partook of the entertainments?" he continued. "Is there a part for me, do you think? In your play, I mean."

In fact, there was. A boy who journeyed with his father to the top of a mountain in order to learn the art of war. I could very easily imagine Richard performing the role, assuming he had the skill to transform himself from a nine-year-old Londoner to a third-century native of Switzerland.

"First we must get approval for the production," I told him. "And then, if all is well, we could certainly see about you appearing within it."

He smiled and seemed content with that. It was a most surprising conversation but then, if I had learned anything during my life, it was that despite thinking I understood what went on in the hearts and minds of those who surrounded me, more often than not they held secrets.

· · ·

The mob was already gathering in the theatre when Richard and I arrived backstage a few hours later, ready for the opening night. I had yet to see the play from start to finish but had been present for some of the rehearsals and it seemed a very fine piece, one that might still find an audience a year or two later if luck was on William's side.

Before long, the playwright himself appeared nearby, standing next to an image of the Madonna that someone had placed upon a wall, and he was arguing with David's friend, Timothy, who was dressed in Calpurnia's flowing robes. The quarrel appeared to be over Timothy's facial hair, for the boy had recently grown a neat mustache and William had given him strict instructions earlier in the day to shave it off before the curtain rose.

"I won't!" insisted Timothy, stamping his foot with the petulance of a child. "It took me four weeks to grow it and I won't give it up for anyone, not even for you. Who do you think you are, Christopher Marlowe?"

"Marlowe's dead," cried William. "And if he weren't, he'd hold you down and shave it off himself."

"I think it looks wonderful," said David, who had wandered over from his ropes and was staring at his friend's upper lip with an adoration that seemed excessive to me. "It makes you look so handsome."

"I will not go onstage with a wife who has better whiskers than me!" said William, who had shaved his own beard off to play Caesar. "You may remove it, young man, or you may return home. The choice is yours."

Timothy continued to protest but William's ultimatum stood, and in the end he had no choice but to return to the dressing room and look for someone with a knife who might rid him of his pride and joy.

"And you," added William, turning to David. "Back to your ropes, and not another insolent word or I shall send you to the ghost world myself."

Soon, the lights went down, and the play began. Only the actor playing Cinna gave me cause to whisper forgotten lines when, in the early part of the second act, he stood in Brutus's orchard with his fellow conspirators Cassius and Trebonius. Timothy, however, caused some confusion for the audience, for when he recounted to Caesar the ill portends he had witnessed—a lioness whelping in the street, graves that opened up to yield their dead, fiery warriors within the clouds—blood began to seep down his chin from a wound inflicted by the unsteady hand that had shaved him earlier. Every time he wiped it away, the cut reopened, the blood refusing to clot, and Calpurnia's robes soon grew stained. I could sense the bewilderment from the pit. Was the bleeding of Caesar's wife a metaphor for something that they did not understand?

Finally, in the fourth act, David's great moment came, and he operated his levers and pulleys to send William onto the stage, now playing the role of the ghost of the murdered dictator. The theatre had grown quiet by now and, having no need to prompt, I found myself entirely lost in the action, as frightened by the entrance of the specter as either the audience or Brutus himself, for David was a skilled magician and had proved himself more than worthy of his position.

I felt a darkness grow around me as Brutus spoke of a sleepy tune and a murderous slumber. I could see nothing but the ghost on the stage and, as the audience shivered in fear, I felt a curious unsettling within my mind and bones.

A sound from the opposite side of the stage distracted me, and a figure, dressed entirely in white, stared in my direction, then raised a hand. I could not make out her features and wondered what strange vision this was. But as Brutus and the ghost conversed, the figure began to walk slowly across the stage, barefoot, toward me, passing by the actors without either of them appearing to notice her. She was clad only in a simple nightdress and, although it had been many years since I had laid eyes on that face, I recognized her now as Laura, my first wife.

"Can it be you?" I asked, rising to my feet as she approached me, her face placid, her expression neutral, and I would have reached out to touch her, were it not for the fact that a second figure had started to make her way across the stage now, too. Another woman dressed entirely in white, who, to my horror, I acknowledged to be Katherine, my second wife.

"Both of you?" I asked, wondering whether it was the weakness of my eyes that had shaped such monstrous apparitions. "Art thou women?" I demanded, raising my voice. "Some angels or some devils? Speak, damn you! Tell me what thou art!"

"Husband," whispered Laura, reaching out to touch my face, and Katherine repeated the word as she rested her hand upon my arm.

"Can it be you?" I asked of them. "Both of you? Together?" I felt no fear, just wonder, and my heart seemed to slow down within my chest as I glanced across to the opposite side of the stage, waiting for my third wife, Sarah, to appear. But, of her, there was no sight. "You are alone?" I asked them. "But where is your third sister? If two shall venture forth from the grave, then why not three?"

The ghosts smiled at me, saying nothing, then closed their eyes in unison and separated, leaving a gap between them. The theatre was silent and still; I heard neither words from the actors nor gasps from the audience, just the distinctive sound of sticks banging against the wooden floor as they performed their job of aiding a man with twisted legs to make his way toward me. The echoes grew louder, and I looked around me, filled with fear, praying for this illusion to end.

"Harry?" I cried, for surely this was my cousin returning to torment me, too, but no, although the sounds of his sticks grew clearer by the moment, and the echoes were monstrous insults to my ears, no vision took shape between my wives. Instead, the women opened their eyes wide and the sounds grew so loud that I had no choice but to press my hands against my ears until, as one, they screamed a single word aloud:

"Vengeance!"

I cried out and fell backward, tumbling over some chairs that had been laid out for actors in the wings, and when I looked up I thought at first that the ghost was on top of me, but no, it was only the playwright himself, Master Shakespeare, exited from the stage now, the ghost's appearance completed.

"Quiet," he hissed, putting a hand over my mouth. "I know the scene can be frightening, but you, my friend, should not be so overcome. I expect professionalism here at the Globe." I sat up and looked toward the stage. The apparitions were gone and, in their place, the actors playing Brutus and Lucius were now in conversation. Richard was staring at me in fright.

"Did none of you see them?" I asked, looking around me in dismay. "Did none of you hear them?"

"See what, Father?" Richard asked. "Hear what?"

And I did not dare to say, lest I was accused of losing my reason. Had this been a fantasy, I wondered? A waking dream? Or had my wives truly visited me from the other-world? These women who were so familiar to me and had seemed so real, as real as the noise those sticks had made against the stage.

A thought occurred to me now, one that had never passed

through my mind before. Was it possible that my once-beloved cousin had had some hand in the malicious dealings that had cost me my third wife and her daughter? Had that been the meaning of the visitation, to tell me that Harry had, for reasons unknown, spirited the pair away? Or had it been nothing more than a strange malady of the brain?

Whatever it was, I realized at that moment I had put off my promise for far too long. Years earlier, I had promised to hunt him down and make him pay for what he had done to my wife and son. And, by setting this undertaking aside, I had betrayed them both. It was time to stop living a fantasy life in the playhouse and hold a blade against his neck.

It was time for justice to be served.

PART 10

A
DEVIL'S
PROMISE

BRAZIL

A.D. 1608

AND SO, MY SEARCH BEGAN once again in earnest. I left a tearful Ricardo in the care of Dami and his reluctant wife and made my way toward the coastal town of Macapá, where I encountered a group of men, some two dozen of them, dining in an inn as they sought a native to guide their craft along the Amazon. Approaching them, I volunteered my services, and when they asked what experience I had in the navigation of vessels along the river, I explained that I had traveled most of its distance from Peru in the west to the tavern where we currently sat. I could scarcely recall a day, I claimed, when I had not spent my time upon the water and doubted whether there was a man alive who was more familiar with its dangers, surprises and trials than me. A lie, of course, or an exaggeration at best, but I felt confident that men so ignorant would certainly mistake familiarity with skill.

"Robert Thornton," said the captain, extending his hand and looking me up and down, as if I were a horse he was considering buying. A tall man, he wore a neat mustache on his upper lip but his cheeks were startlingly gaunt, and I could make out the shape of his skull beneath the skin, the long fingers of his hand appearing more skeletal than human. He informed me that he came from a place called "England," a land of which I had never heard, and he seemed shocked when I remarked upon this.

"Come, come," he said, staring at me in utter disbelief. "Never heard of England? It can't be possible. It is the very center of the world!"

I shrugged my shoulders.

"Well, what about London?" he asked. "Or Norwich? Plymouth, certainly?"

"I'm afraid not," I replied, shaking my head.

"And what of King James? You can't tell me that you're a stranger to his name, too?"

"I know the chieftains of my own land," I told him. "They are many and they take up much space in my head. I have little room left for the chieftains of yours, too."

"But King James is more than just a . . . a chieftain," he said, spitting out the word as if it were a sour fruit. "He is a great sovereign. The most beloved and powerful on Earth."

"And he sent you here?"

"Well, no," Thornton admitted, looking a little chastised. "For all his glory, the master of my terrain has little taste for exploration. In fact, I was hired by his cousin, the Italian King, Ferdinando of Tuscany. It is his intention to establish a settlement here in the years ahead."

I considered this. The word was unfamiliar to me but, somehow, like a dog who can sense evil in a stranger, I did not like the sound of it.

"A settlement?" I asked. "I don't understand what this means."

"Italy has much need of wood," he explained. "For their ships, for their houses, for their marketplaces. And your country, this uncivilized and brutal land, populated by savages, is rich in forestry. King Ferdinando intends to send many of his people here to erect a colony over which, with God's grace, he will rule. Once it is established, the settlers can begin the process of chopping down the trees and sending the wood back across the ocean."

He spoke very slowly. At first, I wondered whether he thought I was hard of hearing, but it soon became clear that no, he simply assumed that I was stupid. Some in my position might have felt insulted, but I was happy for him to continue under this delusion if it gave me free passage along the river.

"You have spoken of this matter to the tribesmen you've encountered along the way?" I asked, and he raised an eyebrow in surprise, glancing across at his men, but they were paying little attention to our conversation as they gnawed on lamb bones. "You have sought their permission to build this settlement?"

"No," he replied, laughing a little, as if I had suggested that he seek consent from a cow or a donkey. "Why in God's name would I do such a thing?"

"Because it is their land."

"Until we discover it, yes. Then it becomes ours."

"But it is already discovered. We live here. We have lived here for generations innumerable. Indeed, since the dawn of time and the birth of mankind itself."

"I don't think you fully understand," he said, placing a hand upon my shoulder and looking at me with the benevolence of one who offers treats to a child while all the time planning how to get him alone. "You are savages, you see. Godless men. We have come to help you. To educate you, indoctrinate you and rule over you. Nothing more."

"And you do this by invading our land and cutting down our trees?" I asked, shrugging away his touch. "If my people were to send a craft across the water to your country with plans to establish a fort there before stealing from your forests, would you not expect us to ask permission first?"

"But we don't have any forests," he said, smiling. "That's why we've come here."

I held my tongue, willing to humor him for now. Since my father's time, there had been much talk of fine people who arrived on ships with decorated masts and sails, landing on shores that were not their own but laying claim to them nevertheless, as if these places did not already have tribes of their own whose blood was interred with the soil. They claimed that they were bringing "civilization" to us, but all they brought was bloodshed and domination. They called themselves "explorers" but the name was as false as a devil's promise. My people had explored our land thoroughly across many generations and were familiar with every cave and every tree. It would take him and his kind a thousand years to know it as well as we did. It did not need any further discovery. No, these were nothing more than thieves and it was the sworn duty of every native to kill such men when they had the misfortune to chance upon one. But I had no intention of drawing my blade just yet.

"How far into my country do you plan on venturing?" I asked.

"As far as we need," replied Thornton. "Once we find land that is open enough for a settlement to be built, I will claim it in the name of the King for Italy and—"

"You will claim it," I repeated under my breath, staggered by the man's arrogance.

"That's right. And then I will leave half my men behind to begin preparations while I return home to inform His Majesty that we can start transporting those lucky volunteers to their new abode."

"And those men who remain behind after you are gone," I said. "You expect them to still be here upon your return? Still healthy? Still breathing? Their heads still attached to their shoulders?"

"Of course. Why would I expect otherwise?"

"Because some might not take well to an occupying force seizing our land."

He dismissed my concerns with a wave of his hand. "It matters not; the claim will have been made for Italy, for Tuscany, and you'll have no choice. It's the modern way, my dark friend. The law of the white man. This is a new world and it is the responsibility, nay the birthright, of Europeans to take whatever they can find. The truth is, you people are not enlightened enough to govern yourselves. You need a guiding hand. And that is what we offer. Don't think of us as an enemy, think of us as overlords who wish only to humanize you. It is God's work that we perform. So will you guide us down the river or not? There'll be payment, of course, at the end. When our journey is completed. I won't see you left short for your services."

I nodded. "Yes," I said. "Yes, I will help you."

• • •

My cousin, Hernán, had often spoken of traveling deeper into the country, following the path of the Amazon, and I guessed that this would be where he might be found. It was my intention to make inquiries of the people I met as to whether they had seen him. If he had passed through this region, then I was sure that he would not be easily forgotten.

While I remained quiet through most of our sailing, doing little more than identifying different species of fish, offering the names of animals that stared at us from the riverbanks and pointing out which were more dangerous than others, I grew friendly with one of the colonizers, a man named O'Hara. He seemed more respectful of the terrain and the people than most of his shipmates and, because of this, we fell into an easy companionship. O'Hara was from a place called Ireland, he told me, another land whose name had not, until now, reached my ears.

"Is it in Italy?" I asked, and he shook his head. He had a thick red beard, ginger eyebrows and the whitest skin I had ever seen. It was hard to believe that such coloring could even exist on a living creature and I found myself staring at him, wondering whether he was even human. Was it a curse of some sort, I asked myself? Had he angered God and been poisoned in his mother's womb to be left so repulsively pale?

"No, it's far enough away from Italy," he told me. "Closer to England. They'd be our nearest neighbors, although we've been at each other's throats this long time. That's where the captain's from, of course. England. They despise the Irish and we despise them back on account of how they took our land from us. He only hired me for this voyage because I can read the stars better than any lad alive, but he knows that if I had more shillings at my disposal, then I'd as soon stick a knife up my own arse than do anything to help him. But a man has to earn his keep and so here I am."

O'Hara had brought a musical instrument with him, he called it a fiddle, and in the evenings he would play tunes on it, horrible discordant melodies that made me want to stick leaves in my ears, but the men would dance to give their legs something to do.

"Will you remain here to build the settlement?" I asked O'Hara one evening as we lay back in the rear of the boat, looking up at the stars.

"We Irish don't colonize," he grunted. "We get colonized. We're just a small country, that's the problem."

"But here, we are a big country," I said.

"So stop them. Don't let them in."

"How do we do this?"

"Fight them. Fight them until every man, woman and child is

dead on one side or the other. Then fight among yourselves a little longer, just to be on the safe side. There'll always be a few traitors that need weeding out. The enemy within."

I nodded. I cared about my land, of course, but the tribes in my country had stopped warring with each other a century or more earlier and we had been happy when the wars finally came to an end. We were a peaceful people now and saw no reason to live anything but nonviolent lives. But while my mind was focused on my own revenge, I worried about what the future might bring, should we allow these Europeans further ingress into our dominion. I did not understand how they could come here and simply assume that what was ours could suddenly become theirs.

"And you," he asked me. "Did you leave a family behind when you took on this voyage?"

"A son," I said. "But I left him in the care of someone I trust."

"You need the money, I suppose? Sure we all need the money," he said, answering his own question.

"It's not about money," I told him, choosing my words carefully, for I had told no one on the boat about my true intentions. "I go in search of someone."

"A woman, I suppose?"

"No, a man. Someone I used to call a friend many years ago."

"Did you fall out with him, is that it?"

I frowned, uncertain what the phrase meant.

"Did you have an argument, the pair of you? Did he do something dastardly to you?"

"He committed an unforgivable act," I said. "And I mean to hold him to account for it."

"You do right," said O'Hara, lying back and glancing warily at the heads of the alligators that were making their presence felt in the waters around us. "I had a friend once and he went in for a kiss with my wife and I took the head off him."

"You decapitated him?" I asked, my eyes opening wide.

"No," he said, laughing. "It's just a phrase. I meant I beat the shit out of him, that's all."

"Oh," I said.

"And is that what you plan on doing?"

"No," I replied, shaking my head. "No, I mean to literally take the head off him."

. . .

After sailing for more than a week, stopping at dozens of villages and encountering hundreds of my countrymen and -women, I grew to despise Captain Thornton, who liked to treat everyone he met as if they were barely human. At every stop, however, I would leave him to attend to his inhuman intentions while I sought out villagers old and young, taking them to one side and asking them my familiar questions.

"I travel in search of a man."

"His name?"

"Hernán."

A shake of the head. "I know no Hernán."

"He's not from here but grew up on the other side of the country. About my age but with twisted legs. He walks on sticks."

"This man has hurt you in some way?"

"He has."

"Do you mean to kill him?"

"Will my answer affect your memory?"

But I had no success. Some would claim that they might have seen him but wanted money to reveal what they knew and I could tell that they were simply inventing a tale for a reward. Some seemed to know more but were reluctant to tell me anything, as if they feared the earthly consequences for my cousin. I began to despair that my search would once again prove fruitless.

But then, one cold evening, as we docked our vessel at one of the larger villages along the river, luck finally came my way. The elders came out to welcome us and the women placed garlands of flowers around our necks. The timber there was very fine and it irritated me to see Thornton examining it, carefully slicing some off with his knife and chewing it between his yellow teeth, then making notes in his journal as if this might be the place that he could obliterate for the sake of increasing the felonious Italian king's wealth.

I was making my usual inquiries when I heard the sound of chil-

dren playing in the distance and wandered in that direction, happy
to be separated from the world of men for a time in favor of the
solace of the young. There were perhaps seven or eight of them,
boys and girls running around at their games, each one overflowing
with energy, but I took particular note of a girl sitting alone by one
of the huts, not taking part in the activities but just watching, and
made my way toward her, sitting down next to her in the dust.

"You aren't playing with your friends?" I asked, and she turned
to look at me, not even slightly frightened to find a stranger addressing her.

"No," she said.

"Don't you feel the urge to run around as they do?"

She shook her head before nodding toward the wall, where I saw
two sticks with handles at the top balanced against the woodwork,
sticks similar to the ones that Hernán used.

"I cannot run," she told me. "My legs don't work as other people's do. I can only walk with the help of those."

I reached over and picked one up. It had been fashioned from
the wood of the local trees and was very fine. Hernán himself had
always designed his own sticks, fashioning new ones every few
months when he'd grown a little taller, the old ones proving no
longer fit for purpose. As a craftsman myself, I'd always admired the
detail he put into each one. His signature was an elaborate *H* at the
end of each stick, where the vertical lines of the letter were grooved
into the wood in the shape of snakes. To my knowledge, he had
never created one without adding this adornment to the base and,
turning the girl's stick over in my hands now out of habit, I was
taken aback to see that same symbol there. I felt excited, frightened
and horrified all at once.

"Where did you get these?" I asked, turning to her, and she
looked a little intimidated now, perhaps by the force in my voice.

"My sticks?" she asked.

"Yes, you didn't make them. Who made them for you?"

"A man," she told me.

"Which man?"

"I don't know his name. He was here a few weeks ago. He arrived on a boat. He needed new sticks and used the wood from here to make them. I sat and watched and thought they were very beautiful. I asked whether he might make some for me and he said yes. Until now, my own had been nothing more than heavy branches of trees that cut into my palms, but he used his knives to make something better, something smoother, then he taught me how to make new ones when I grow."

"He created these for you?"

"Yes. He was very kind."

I could scarcely believe it. After all this time, I was finally closer to Hernán than I had been in years.

"And is he still here?" I asked, looking around and hoping against hope itself that I might see him hobbling around in the distance. "Did he remain in the village?"

"No," she said. "He left some weeks ago."

"Which way did he go?"

"West," she said, pointing toward the horizon, where the sun was beginning to set.

I stood up and handed her back her stick. West was the direction in which Captain Thornton was heading, too.

"And was he alone?" I asked. "Was the man with the twisted legs traveling on his own?"

She thought about it for a moment, before shaking her head. "No," she replied. "He had a woman with him. And a girl."

NEW ZEALAND

A.D. 1642

THE NEXT MORNING, it was the Irish sailor, O'Brien, who first caught sight of land, and we immediately set course for the shore. Arriving at a beach, we looked around in awe at the beauty of this new territory and there was not a man among us who did not think that we had discovered paradise on Earth.

"Completely unspoilt," remarked one of the sailors.

"For now," I replied.

"What was that, sir?" roared Captain Tasman, who seemed capable of hearing every word that any of us said, whether it was spoken aloud, beneath our breaths, or existed as nothing more than a random thought passing through our minds.

"I said it's unspoilt for now, Captain," I replied, less confidently.

"And I suppose you think that I'm here to spoil it," he said with an unpleasant smile. "Because I'm such a scoundrel, taking land that isn't mine to take. You have a comment for everything, don't you, sir? Anyone would think that you weren't being paid to guide us."

"I only meant—"

"I know what you meant, sir, and I reject the charge. I reject it utterly. So spare me your sermons, as I have little patience for hypocrisy."

It was hard to argue with this assessment. I could hardly condemn his actions, after all, when I was happy enough to profit from them.

"Where do you suppose we are, Captain?" asked O'Brien, and Tasman drew in his breath, looking around at the mountain, the forests, the golden sand.

"You know the story of Columbus, I suppose?" he asked.

"A little."

"Spanish sailor. Left Madrid in 1490 to chart a new course for the Indies in the hope of finding a faster route to the Orient. Only he bumped into the Americas instead and claimed it for his King. The luckiest mistake a man ever made."

"He was Italian," I said, the words coming out of my mouth before I could consider the wisdom of aggravating him further. "And it wasn't Madrid that he departed from. It was Huelva. In 1492."

Tasman glared at me—the man hated to be contradicted—and I would have been more concerned about his retribution, had I not been wondering how I had come to know these facts in the first place, for I had never read or heard much about Christopher Columbus and yet seemed to know the details of his voyage as if I had been standing on the dock to wave him off.

"Just testing, sir, just testing," the captain replied, grinning through his yellow teeth as he put one of his meaty hands down the front of his trousers and gave his nether regions a lengthy and apparently enjoyable scratch. "My point being that Señor Columbus discovered something unexpected on his travels and we might have done the same thing. We'll claim it as our own anyway. What do you say, lads? And we'll put a name to it later."

"Could it be the Province of Beach, do you think, Captain?" asked one of the men.

"Do you see any gold hereabouts, Mr. Harkin?" roared Tasman. "If you can, then you have better eyes than me, for all I can see is sand and mountains."

"But it may be further along," said another, Meijer. "Hidden in the center of the island. Out of sight from here."

The captain considered this. "Aye, it might be," he agreed. "It very well might be."

A silence descended on us then as we wondered whether we might soon be rich men. When the Dutch East India Company had commissioned Abel Tasman to explore this part of the world, one of their objectives was to discover the famed province described in Marco Polo's work, where gold, he said, was so plentiful that only those who laid eyes on it could believe that it existed.

"Has anyone ever wondered," asked O'Brien, "how we'd get it all back home in our ship anyway? The weight of it would sink us, surely?"

All heads turned toward him, for it was not an unreasonable question, but the captain said that we would put all our tenders out to sea and fill them with our haul, dragging them back to Europe with the sun sparkling off their burnished surfaces, and this seemed to put the minds of the men at rest.

Our mood shifted a few minutes later, however, when a group of men and women emerged from over the sand dunes, perhaps one hundred of them, barely dressed but with their skin covered in the most elaborate tattoos, and each one carrying a fine-pointed spear in his hand.

"Stand easy, men," said Captain Tasman quietly. I glanced in his direction as he stood his ground, holding a determined arm in the air and waving it back and forth as he beckoned them forward in a gesture intended to signify friendship. The group moved toward us in a similar formation to a flock of birds in the sky, with one of their number leading the way and the rest spread out behind him so they resembled an arrowhead ready to pierce our core.

When they came closer, Tasman bowed his head and introduced himself, extending a hand, but the chief of these people, who we were later to discover were called Māori, simply stared at it, uncertain what was expected of him. The captain continued to talk, explaining our reasons for being there, but it was a fool's errand since none of them spoke our language and they seemed as baffled by his words as we were by their replies. He reached back into the tender and removed a handful of trinkets and jewels and instructed me to distribute them among the natives. I did so carefully, for I did not want to be perceived as a threat and pierced with a spear, but they seemed delighted by the baubles, hanging them around their necks and grinning broadly. Finally, I had only one piece left, a colorful necklace that I handed to the chieftain, who, from the way he spoke and pointed at himself, appeared to be named Kalawai'a. He snatched it from my hands, examined it and placed it around his neck and, although he wore a smile, he still seemed uncertain whether he approved of our landing or not.

Tasman made some indications that we would like to rest on the beach for the evening and the chief understood, for he nodded and indicated that we might go where we wished, before turning and leading his people back in the direction from which they had come.

"Savages," Tasman said to their retreating backs. "Absolute savages."

The chief turned then and stared at him before continuing on his way. Of course, he could not possibly have understood the word but clearly the man was no fool and he recognized the insult embedded in his intonation.

. . .

It had been a long time since I had last slept with a woman, but I did so that night, betraying my wife for the first time since she went missing. The girl's name was Laka'sha and she approached me while I was sitting alone in the sand dunes, staring out into the vast expanse of sea. She wore only a thin cloth around her waist and her breasts were full and rounded, so much so that I found myself instantly aroused by her presence.

I told her my name, pointing at my chest as I said it, and she tried to pronounce it but the syllables proved too complicated for her tongue and she could not repeat it back to me with any proficiency. And then, to my surprise, she took my hand and placed it on her heart. I had heard stories among sailors of how friendly the native women in these parts could be, but little imagined that I would find myself in such a situation. As I lifted my other hand to touch her, she looked me in the eye, leaned forward and pressed her lips against my own.

Soon we stood up and made our way toward a clearing that was surrounded by rushes and, when she lay down, I found myself intrigued by the many tattoos and piercings that adorned her body. While she was nowhere near as elaborately ornamented as some of the men I had seen earlier, there was still an extraordinary amount of ink embedded in her skin. Each image fascinated me and I couldn't help but run my fingers along the designs. They revealed ideas and images that only the members of her tribe could fully understand but somehow I felt moved by them. She ran her fingers along my body, too, as if she could scarcely comprehend how a grown man's pelt could remain a blank canvas; I suspected that the only times she had seen such unmarked flesh was on the skin of babies and small children. What elaborate ceremonies and initiations did these people have to go through, I wondered, in order to mark their transition from childhood to adulthood?

Her piercings were also a source of fascination. She wore hoops through her ears, another through her nose and, to my utter astonishment, another in that most private of places on her body. I had never seen or imagined such a thing before, but it excited me.

Later, we walked along the beach together and I drew an image in the sand.

"Have you seen this man?" I asked her, pointing to my drawing, and she seemed confused by what I was asking. "This man," I repeated pointlessly. "I know him. We were friends once. I believe he has passed this way. Have you seen him?"

She looked down then and cocked her head a little to the side. She was concentrating hard on the drawing itself and, after a few moments, she looked back at me and nodded.

"Where is he?" I asked.

She didn't answer but, next to the picture that I had drawn, she drew another, this time of a woman. It was a rudimentary image but I guessed what it might signify.

"My wife," I said. "I believe he has taken her. Which way did they go?"

She turned around and pointed into the distance, past the curve of the mountains.

"That way?" I asked. "How long ago? When were they here?"

She pulled me to her then and I could tell that my questions were too confusing and that I would get no further answers. And so what else could I do but head back toward the dunes, where I lost myself in her illuminated body once again.

. . .

A few nights later, the Māori people invited us to feast with them, and the entire crew, along with Captain Tasman, sat entranced, and a little nervous, as a group of about twenty men and women performed a ritual dance in our honor. They chanted words that we could not understand and moved their bodies in curious and contortionate ways, sticking their tongues out and allowing their eyes to bulge from their heads as they stamped on the ground and beat their chests. When one of our number, inebriated by the native drinks, stood up to join in the revelry, he was roughly pushed back to his place by the leader of the dancers, who seemed to interpret this as a great insult to their ceremony.

Afterward, we dined on an enormous roasted boar and did our best to communicate with our hosts through simple hand gestures. Throughout it all, I kept a close eye on the chieftain, Kalawai'a. There was something in his expression that told me it would be a mistake to cross him.

To his left sat his daughter, a young and pretty girl, and I noticed how Van der Berg, one of the youngest members of our crew, kept his eyes focused on her throughout the night. Van der Berg was not popular on board, behaving as if he were a cut above the rest of us. His father was one of the wealthiest spice traders in Amsterdam so the boy had grown accustomed to a life of luxury until, after some minor indiscretion, his family decided that he needed to earn some knowledge of the world and sent him abroad on this expedition. He loathed being among common sailors, however, complaining of the heat in our confined quarters, the stink of our bodies and the lack of education that we shared, and sought any opportunity to express his superiority.

When the festivities came to an end, I watched as he made his way over to the girl to attempt a conversation with her. She was beautiful, there was no question about that, with large brown eyes and an expression of innocence on her face, for she could not have been any more than fourteen years of age, and as he talked to her, she looked around anxiously for her father, who marched over and took her by the arm, pulling her away as he threw furious looks in the direction of the young man.

Returning to where I stood, Van der Berg shook his head and laughed.

"You'd think she'd be grateful for what I was offering."

"And what was that?" I asked.

"A night with me," he said. "A civilized man. I expect the poor girl is only accustomed to these illustrated barbarians."

I gave him a contemptuous look. "She's just a child, Van der Berg," I said.

"She's old enough," he replied. "Anyway, I'll have her yet. See if I don't."

He marched away and I thought little more of it for now but, early the following morning, even before the sun had fully risen, I woke to a great commotion as the sound of angry voices filled the air. I had been sleeping on the beach and, as I stumbled to my feet, I watched as the rest of our crew ran toward me, the Māori warriors following with spears in their hands, led by their chieftain, who was dragging his daughter behind him by her hair. There seemed to be even more of them than had been present the night before.

"What's going on?" I asked O'Brien.

"Bloody Van der Berg," he said. "He took the girl without her permission. So the daddy there wants to skewer him on his pike."

I looked out toward the small tender that had brought us to shore and was not surprised to see Van der Berg climbing into it like the coward he was, a look of humiliation and terror upon his face, as Kalawai'a stood in front of Captain Tasman, arguing with him as he pointed toward the young sailor.

"Very slowly," said Tasman, looking around at our crew and maintaining a relaxed smile, "every one of you get into the boat. We'll be leaving now."

We did as he ordered while he continued to try to calm the temper of the furious chieftain, but there was no soothing the man and Tasman reached into the tender, taking out some more jewels and handing them across as a token of our regret, but the chief brushed them out of his hands, tossing them into the waves. With a shrug, Tasman boarded the boat himself and gave instructions that we set sail.

The moment our craft began to depart the shore, Kalawai'a turned to his own men, roaring an invocation at them, and soon, spears were flying through the air and we were forced to row faster and faster, the muscles of our arms burning, in order to reach our ship with our lives intact.

The following morning, when I had eaten, the sailors were gathered together on deck. I hung my head in shame for I, too, had disgraced myself. Looking around to see whether he recognized his part in this calamity, my eyes searched for Van der Berg, but he was nowhere to be found.

"Captain," I said, raising my voice. "Where is Van der Berg? Is he belowdecks?"

A search began, but there was no sign of him. It seemed a most cryptic affair until I chanced upon four of the sailors later in the evening, particular combatants of the young man who had often been on the receiving end of his cruel remarks, and the conversation turned to our missing colleague.

"Do these mysteries often happen at sea?" I asked them, and the men simply shook their heads at my naïveté.

"There's no mystery," replied Meijer. "If a man gives offense all day, every day, to his fellows, then behaves in such a manner that they come close to meeting their deaths on an unfriendly island, why, there's every chance that late at night, when that young fellow is standing on his own at the prow, another fellow might come up behind him and tip him over the side."

"You drowned him?" I asked in surprise.

"Us?" asked Harkin, looking around with an innocent expression on his face. "Oh no. I'd say it was just a strong wind took him, nothing more. But rest assured, we've seen the last of that young prick. He'll be at the bottom of the ocean now or resting comfortably in the belly of a shark."

CANADA

A.D. 1694

BADE FAREWELL to my companions shortly after our boat arrived at Lake Ontario, having made the long journey from the St. Lawrence River through the narrow Lac Saint-Pierre and past the many small islands that formed part of the terrain. Saying goodbye to Captain Talaman, I thanked him for allowing me to join the voyage but explained that my mind had now turned to the Iroquois settlement village of Bead Hill, where my cousin might be found. He was none too pleased to see me go but grudgingly paid me the money I was owed.

I rested overnight at an inn called the Pyramid of the Sun and was seated, enjoying a flagon of beer and a beef stew, when I noticed an unpleasant scent wafting through the air, as if a group of farmyard animals had been granted entry to the dining hall but been encouraged to roll around in their own filth first. Had I not been so hungry, it might have been enough to put me off my food but, starving from weeks on the river, I did my best to ignore the vile stench. Finally, when I felt someone pushing past me, it grew so overpowering that I was forced to turn around to locate its source.

To my astonishment, this malodorous perfume was emanating from a woman and when I saw her face, my heart lifted in delight even as my stomach churned in nausea.

"Ursula!" I cried.

She stopped and turned to look at me, offering something approximating a smile.

"Well, look what the cat dragged in," she said, placing her hands on her hips. "We've often wondered what became of you."

"We?" I asked, turning around and searching the busy room with my eyes. "Is my brother here, too?"

"He's over there," said Ursula, scratching herself in her most private place before examining her hand, palm and front, and wiping it on her deeply stained dress. "In the corner. Go over. He'll be glad to see you."

I lifted my plate and mug and marched across the room in delight, catching my brother's eye as I approached him, and he let out an enormous roar of pleasure. He appeared older than I remembered and it seemed that he had not trimmed his hair or beard since our paths had last crossed. He was more mountain animal than man.

"Brother!" he cried, wrapping his arms around me and lifting me, momentarily, off the ground. "As I live and breathe!"

"Jonah," I said, releasing myself from his grip and sitting down opposite him at the table, summoning the waitress over to order two more beers. "Well, this is fine fortune! What brings you to Canada?"

"Whalin'," he told me. "I've spent the last couple of years toiling my bollix off on one of them whalin' ships, and I've had luck on my side, for I've only gone and made a pretty fortune! I'm rich, Brother, richer than I ever imagined I'd be!"

"Rich?" I said, for no one in our family, least of all me, had ever been blessed with wealth. "From whaling?"

"You'd be surprised how much money there is in it," he said. "I learned the craft, bought my own ship, hired a crew, and God must have been looking down on His faithful son with benevolence in His eyes, for since I saw you last, I've become one of the most successful whalers in North America. Where other men have pennies in their pockets, I have trinkets and jewels."

"Well, I'm very glad to hear it," I said, both impressed and surprised by his good fortune. "And Ursula?"

"She comes with me to cook for the crew. We're married now, if you can believe it."

"Really?" I said, although I don't know why I was so astonished. After all, this unlikely couple had been romancing each other for many years now and he seemed completely indifferent to her unpleasant aroma. If anything, he seemed to find it an erotic charge.

"Oh yes. The sailors love her cooking so much that they encourage her to stay below deck all day long, making her stews and pies. If she even tries to come up and sit with them, they refuse to have her, sending her back down below! She's very flattered, of course. It makes her feel valued."

Ursula rejoined us at that moment, declaring that she had just been to the toilet, to which intelligence I had no response.

"My beloved," said Jonah, pulling her onto his lap and planting a kiss on her lips that went on so long and with so much passion that I had no choice but to look away.

"And what are your current plans?" I asked when their amorous display eventually came to an end. "Do you have another voyage due to set sail?"

"No," he said. "We're taking a break. Might as well enjoy some of the good luck I've had. We'll sail again in the spring, no doubt. And you, Brother?" he asked. "What brings you into this territory?"

"You remember I told you before about my cousin, Henry?"

"I remember," he said. "He betrayed you, if I recall correctly. Cost you your wife and child."

"And, I think, my third wife, too."

"You married again?"

"I did."

"Joyous news!" said Jonah. "Is she here with you?"

"No, she disappeared some years ago."

"Disappeared?" he asked. "And how does a person do such a thing?"

"I believe the two stories may be connected and that Henry had a hand in it. If God is on my side, though, I shall find out the truth soon enough and make him pay for his villainy."

"You don't have much luck with your wives, do you?" asked Ursula, looking at me as if I were the author of all my own misfortunes.

"Not much, no," I admitted.

"And where is the bastard?" asked Jonah. "Does he live nearby? If he does, let's go and kill him tonight!"

"I have it on good authority that Henry can be found in Bead Hill."

"Well, that's not far," said Jonah. "A few hours' ride at most. Shall we go? I'm happy to mount a horse right now, if you are."

"No, I'll wait until the morning and leave in search of him then."

"And you will kill him, of course?" he asked.

"When I find him, then yes, I will kill him," I said.

"Excellent," said Jonah, slapping his hands hard on the table now. "I haven't been involved in a good killing in a long time. I'll come with you! Let's finish this man off once and for all so you can resume your life! But for now, let us drink more! When brothers are reunited, it goes against God and nature for either of them to retire to bed sober!"

. . .

To my great relief, Ursula decided not to join us as we traveled toward Bead Hill the following morning. As we rode, Jonah entertained me with stories of his whaling adventures but, when I grew quiet, it must have become obvious that my mind was troubled.

"Your thoughts are elsewhere, Brother," he said.

"I'm thinking about what lies ahead," I replied.

"You've killed before, though, haven't you? It doesn't frighten you?"

"I have, yes," I admitted. "But never with so much forward planning. The deaths that linger on my conscience have always sprung from moments of anger or when I've been under the influence of others, but I've been tracking Henry for many years now. This is the first time I'll have done something so premeditated."

He grunted in approval and we remained fairly silent for the rest of our journey. The Iroquois had set up a settlement in Bead Hill a few years earlier and, as we rode into the town, I was struck by the number of shops and inns that were dotted around the streets. Canada was changing, it seemed, and barely resembled the country in which I had grown up. They called this the New World but I wondered whether that referred as much to attitudes and people as it did to places on a map.

The most successful businesses in the town dealt in the fur trade and there were large storehouses displaying their goods while merchants wandered to and fro with carts laden down with the skinned hides of animals. Jonah purchased a coat for Ursula and it smelled so bad that I dreaded to imagine how it would feel to be in her company when she wore it.

We made our way to an inn and I spoke to the owner, showing him a sketch of Henry, but to my disappointment, he shook his head and claimed that he'd never seen the man. I wandered through every building, every outhouse, every store that I could find, asking the same questions. I even entered the whorehouse and spoke to the working girls but they insisted he had not partaken of their pleasures. As Jonah and I ate dinner later, I thought about the son I had left behind and wondered whether I might not be better off devoting my life to his care, rather than building my world around a single moment of revenge.

I took the drawing out for the final time and placed it on the table between Jonah and me and stared at it for a few moments.

"Should I give up?" I asked him.

"Give up your search?"

"Yes."

"After all these years? When you've tried so hard to track him down?"

"It won't change the past," I said quietly. "And his will be just another death on my conscience."

"But your wife? Don't you—"

"If we could recapture her, then I could take her home and leave Henry on his own."

Jonah looked at me and shook his head.

"You need blood, you know you do."

I thought about it and nodded. "Perhaps you're right," I said. "I never thought that would be the type of man I would become, though. In my heart lies a great yearning for justice. For retribution. But time passes."

A shadow fell over the table and I looked up to see a man standing behind me, staring down at the picture.

"Can I help you, friend?" I asked. He had the look of someone who had endured more than his share of troubles, with pockmarked skin and a deep scar that ran from his left eyebrow down his cheek and toward his chin.

"You're searching for him?" he asked without preamble, tapping a filthy finger against the drawing.

"I am," I said.

"Why?"

"It's a private matter."

"Then I can't help you."

"You know him?" I asked, standing up. "You've seen him?"

The man looked me in the eye and spent a long time considering my question. "Answer me this," he said, poking me in the chest, "and answer me true because if you lie, I'll know, and then I'll walk away."

"All right," I said.

"When you find this man," he said, "do you mean to help him or harm him?"

I hesitated. I took the man's warning on board, certain that I could not afford to lose this opportunity. "I mean to harm him," I said, and he smiled.

"Good," he said. "Then yes, I can help you."

"I was told that he was here," I said, relieved that my honesty might pay dividends. "In Bead Hill. But I've looked everywhere and asked everyone and—"

"He's not here," he said, shaking his head. "You may have been told that he was living in one of the Iroquois settlements, and that's true enough, but it's not this one."

"Which one, then?" I asked.

"Teiaiagon," he said. "Not far from here, only a few miles. The next one westward, in fact. He's a fur trader there. Has been for a few years now. Made his fair share of money, too, and the fair share of others' alongside it. But he's brutal with it and isn't a man known for charity. They say he keeps his wife under lock and key and never lets her out in daylight on account of him not wanting any man to lay eyes on what belongs to him."

"You're sure it's him?" I asked. "You're certain that he lives there?"

"No question about it, friend," he said. "I've bought and sold off him for a while now. I was always honest in my dealings with him, but he wasn't honest with me. Gave me this for my troubles when he thought I was overcharging him on hides." He touched the scar on his face. "Or rather, he got one of his men to do it for him."

I turned to Jonah in delight. Finally, this was the news I had been waiting for. I reached into my pocket and took out some banknotes but the man pressed his hand against mine, closing my fist over the money.

"I don't need nothing," he said. "Just you get yourself along to Teiaiagon tomorrow and sort out this business once and for all. If I ride through there in a few days' time and hear that he's dead, then that'll be reward enough for me."

. . .

We rested well, breakfasted heartily and then waited until the late morning to leave Bead Hill, making our way toward Teiaiagon without engaging in much conversation. I was preoccupied with what might lie ahead of me and Jonah respected my silence. How could Henry hate me so much, I wondered? All this loss, all this bloodshed. Suddenly, our whole lives as children and young men seemed so futile and fraudulent.

When we arrived in the town, we rested our horses at a local stable for the night and, pulling our hats down low over our heads, walked in the direction of the local inn. Not wanting to give him any advantage over me, I was wary of Henry seeing me before I caught sight of him. We sat at a table near the door with a view over the street but hidden away from the glances of passersby. We talked, drank, ate a little and, as the sun began to set, I heard the distinctive sound of sticks approaching the tavern from outside. I felt a combination of excitement and biliousness, my heart pounding faster inside my chest, but remained where I was, waiting as the tapping grew louder, and then, walking toward the door, I saw him.

I glanced at Jonah, who looked back at me, and I nodded slowly. He strained his neck to get a better view and I prayed that my cousin would not enter the inn but continue along. Despite the length of my odyssey, I was not quite prepared for what I was going to say or do. I felt a sense of relief when, rather than entering the tavern, he continued on his way, and watched as he reached the end of the road before turning to his right and ascending a staircase to a small house, opening the door and walking inside.

Once we were sure that he wasn't going to reappear, Jonah and I made our way out on to the street and followed in the same direction. Standing outside, I looked up toward the first floor and, in the window, I watched as some candles were lit and the familiar shadow of a woman stood by the glass. I let out a cry of delight under my breath but, before I could rush up the staircase and race inside to reclaim my wife, my brother touched me on the arm and pointed to the corner of the garden, beneath a willow tree, where a tombstone stood. I crouched down to read the words inscribed upon the monument and, without warning, the ground began to feel unsteady beneath my feet, for there, carved into the rock, was my wife's name.

I let out a cry and turned toward the window again. If that was not Sara up there with Henry, then who was it? Only when she turned and I saw her profile did I understand why I had made such a simple error.

Of course, it wasn't Sara at all. It was her daughter, Beatrice.

JAPAN

A.D. 1743

HAVING FINALLY TRACKED Hachirou down, I wanted nothing more than to march into his home and terminate that longstanding relationship between his shoulders and his head. However, my honored brother Junpei, calmer and wiser than I at this moment of pain, persuaded me that I should first afford my mind and body the opportunity of rest before approaching this terrible business in a more rational frame of mind the following day. We repaired to our lodgings, a small travelers' rest house where an elderly lady by the name of Mitsuki lay some tatami mats on the floor of one of the guest rooms for us.

Mitsuki's granddaughter, a rather shy young girl named Nanako, knocked on our door shortly afterward, her head held low so as not to catch my eye, carrying a tray with two bowls of hot water to wash our hands and faces, along with some miso soup to fill our stomachs, and while Junpei fell asleep almost immediately after eating, I lay awake for many hours, drinking a flagon of beer, worried that somehow my prey would sense my presence in the town and flee in the middle of the night.

I was troubled by my stepdaughter's presence in his house, wondering why she had allowed herself to remain his prisoner, particularly since he had, I assumed, murdered her mother, for whom my heart grieved. A third wife lost to me.

Eventually I dozed off but woke only a few hours later, just as the sun began to rise, and made my way into the kitchen, where our hostess, Mitsuki, was already standing by her oven, preparing food for the day ahead. She bowed when she saw me, placing a light breakfast of grilled fish, two dashimaki eggs and a chawan of rice on the table.

"You have traveled far?" she asked, sitting down opposite me as I ate. She had a kindly face, but a patch of skin on her right temple where no hair grew and the skin was deeply scarred suggested at least one violent encounter in her past.

"Across most of Japan," I told her. "From Sendai to Niigata, Osaka to Hiroshima, and Fukuoka to Kumamoto. I have seen our country in ways that I had never anticipated."

"You must be a man with a great interest in the world."

"Given the choice," I said, smiling, "I would have remained in my home village, father to a large family, crafting chashaku and chasen, my chosen profession. But circumstances stood in the way of my plans."

"This happens," she said, nodding her head. "I myself had ideas for how I wanted to live my life but perhaps I was born in the wrong time or the wrong country. But if you have traveled so far unwillingly, then I must assume that you are searching for something?"

"For someone. But I have found him here in Kyoto."

She poured some tea and watched as I drank it. "Today will be a day of violence, I think," she said quietly. "I can tell from the expression upon your face."

"What expression is that?"

"You appear determined. And a little regretful. But, above all, frightened."

"Frightened?" I repeated, frowning. "I don't think so."

"You are frightened that you have turned into a man that you never expected to be. Tell me your name, honored guest."

I told her and she smiled. "That is not the name of a man who enjoys the spilling of blood. And today, there will be bloodshed, yes?"

"There will."

"May I ask whose?"

I looked away, uncertain whether it was safe to confide my plans in her. But she was very old and did not seem likely to threaten them.

"A man named Hachirou," I said.

"The fabric seller?" she replied. "He who carries himself upon sticks?"

"The very one. You know him, then?"

"He is well known by all here. A man without honor."

I raised an eyebrow. "How long has he lived here?" I asked.

"Not long," she replied. "A few years at most. He came with money and bought the largest machiya that he could find. Three floors, as if anyone needs so much space. Soon, he bought other buildings around the city and began to rent them out to people who could scarcely afford his exorbitant rates. When they default, he makes them pay penalties. He is feared, of course, but also despised. He has hurt you in some way?"

"He has," I admitted.

"Then perhaps his moment has come. We must all bid farewell to this life at some point."

A vein in her temple, close to the area of bare skin, pulsed a little as she said this and, seeing the direction of my eyes, she placed her hand against the scar, covering herself for a moment.

"My husband did this to me," she said. "A cruel man. The type who is excited by violence against women."

"Does he yet live?"

"It is said that he left Kyoto with a young girl, his lover, many years ago under cover of darkness," she replied. "But in truth, he is buried beneath this very house. I took a knife to his throat one night while he was sleeping. Perhaps, after I am gone, they will find him there. It will be too late to punish me, though."

I stared at her in surprise until, smiling, she placed a hand upon my shoulder for a moment and stood up to return to her cooking. I took her hand in mine before she could move on. "Tell me, Respected Elder," I said. "Did you ever know a woman named Sanyu?"

She nodded and sat down again. I could see tears forming in her eyes, but she wiped them away. "A beautiful creature," she said.

"Can you tell me anything about her? About what happened to her, I mean?"

Mitsuki sighed. "She arrived with him," she told me. "With Hachirou. And with a girl. Her daughter, I think."

"Bashira."

"A strange girl. A troubled girl."

"Her life has been difficult," I said. "Scars lie deep within her soul."

"Sanyu hurt her in some way when she was a child?"

"No, her tormentor was her father."

"And yet her anger, as far as I could see, was aimed toward her mother. She screamed at her in the street, behaving with no respect. She brought shame upon them both with her rage."

"Sanyu was permitted outside the house?" I asked in surprise, for I had heard that she had been locked indoors, out of sight of other men.

"Sometimes. Although on those rare occasions, Hachirou would accompany her wherever she went. He tied her arm to his with some sisal rope to prevent her from running away. When asked why he treated her in such a degrading fashion, he said that she had tried to kill him once, to stab him in the back with a kaiken, and so he kept her on a leash as punishment, as one might keep a temperamental dog. The men, of course, thought the situation amusing and none would ever have intervened. As for the women, well, there was nothing that we could do about it if we wanted to keep our heads. The world is not ruled by mothers, more's the pity."

"And when did she die?" I asked, the word catching in my throat as I uttered it.

"Perhaps a year ago," she replied. "In the most mysterious of circumstances. I saw her myself earlier that same morning at the marketplace, where she had gone to purchase fish. She appeared healthy. But the next day she was carried from Hachirou's home and buried in a plot of land next to it. It is assumed that he murdered her, perhaps she tried to kill him again, but of course he was never held to account for it."

"Not yet, anyway," I said. "Believe me, that will change today."

She rose again as Junpei entered the room, bowing toward him before returning to the kitchen to prepare a second plate. "When you kill him," she said as she departed, "make sure that he suffers. And if you need a place to bury his body, let me know. I have some experience in these matters."

. . .

Breaking into Hachirou's home proved easier than expected. The door was unlocked and, unlike most of the wealthy merchants who lived in the city, he stationed no guards outside. Stepping inside, I was impressed by the elegance of the house. Its long rooms were separated by translucent paper shōji while the water features connecting the living area to the opulent gardens beyond were very beautiful. It was obvious that my cousin had thrived in the years since fleeing our village. Stepping outside and walking beneath the cherry trees, I examined the statues that had been erected, marveling at the hands that had crafted such beautiful art. Pressing my fingers against each one, I felt as if I had known this stone before, as if it were familiar to me. Lost in my reverie, I barely noticed when Junpei appeared by my side.

"It is what you imagined it to be?" he asked.

"I never gave much thought to his circumstances," I replied. "My mind was always so focused on my search that I never really considered what he might have done in the intervening years. But he has done well for himself, that much is clear."

"Well, I hope he enjoyed it, because he won't be able to take any of it with him where he's going."

I nodded and turned to look at him, placing a hand on each of his shoulders. "I must thank you, Honored Older Brother," I said, "for your willingness to join me in this quest. And for your many kindnesses whenever our paths have crossed."

"Of course," he said. "I hope it makes up for how cruel I was to you when we were children. And the disservice I did to your respected mother."

"It does," I said. "I forgive you for all of that and, were she here now, my mother would forgive you, too. The past is behind us and I am grateful for all that you have done since. But now, however, I must ask one last favor of you."

"Name it."

"I must ask you to leave."

"To leave?"

"Yes," I replied, looking him directly in the eye. "What happens next must be down to me and me alone. No one else can be involved. I will wait for Hachirou and, I hope, save Bashira, as Sanyu would have wanted me to do, but I must do all of this without assistance. Now that it is here, I need to confront it alone."

He considered this for a few moments before nodding his head. He knew that what I said was true and honorable. I had brought my long sword with the curved blade—my katana—and he removed his own tantō sword from his belt so that I now carried the traditional samurai weaponry of daishō, one large and one small sword, about my person. He embraced me and departed without another word while I remained in the garden, testing both swords by moving them cleanly through the air as I grew accustomed to their weight in my hands. So lost was I in my practice that I did not hear the sound of sticks coming through the house or the approach of the man I had come to kill. Only when he spoke my name did I turn around in surprise, both swords still held aloft in a threatening fashion.

"Hachirou," I said.

• • •

He had changed, of course, but then so had I. Where once he had been strikingly handsome, now his face was lined and dark bags hung low beneath his eyes. His hair, once dark, had thinned and what remained was scattered with flecks of gray. The hands that held the grips of his sticks seemed to tremble slightly, the blue veins visible in a way that my own were not.

"I knew you would come eventually," he said, stepping out into the garden, sitting down on a bench and laying his sticks on the grass next to him. The sound he made as he sat seemed like that of a much older man and, for a moment, I wondered what trials he had endured over the years. "It was inevitable. Every morning, I've woken wondering whether this would be the day that you would appear."

"And did you dread it?" I asked, laying my swords down, too, as I took a seat on a second bench, which was positioned at a right angle to his. Despite how many years it had taken me to find him, I did not want to end his life just yet. I wanted to speak to him first, to understand his actions, if possible. He considered my question for a long time before answering.

"I dreaded it happening too suddenly," he replied at last. "I didn't want to wake some night to find you leaning over me with your katana in your hand, the blade tearing at my throat before I could even speak a word. I hoped that when you came, you would come like this. Alone. In the light of day. And that we could talk first as cousins, as we once did."

"Do you intend to beg for your life?"

"No," he said, shaking his head, a half-smile on his face. "No, I won't waste my time or yours doing something so futile. But perhaps you will let me explain. And then you will do whatever it is you came here to do." He let out another sigh and shrugged his shoulders. "Or you will leave and we will never see each other again. I don't know which."

"You betrayed me," I said, feeling that old, familiar rage in my blood. "We knew each other our entire lives and you betrayed me. We treated you as part of our family. What did I ever do to deserve what you did to me? What did Katsumi do? Or Eito? He was just a child! How can you justify what you did to him?"

"You may not believe me when I tell you this, Cousin," he said, looking down at the grass and speaking quietly. "But I never meant for them to die. I was so full of bitterness toward you that I almost lost my mind. I blamed you for what I had lost. He was killed, did you know that? When he returned to his village, somehow word of our affections traveled with him and his people sliced his throat open the moment his feet touched the dirt outside his minka. Had you only allowed him to remain as your apprentice, everything would have been different."

"But I did not kill him!" I protested.

"No, but you sent him away. He would not have died, had you allowed him to continue in your workshop."

I turned away, my gaze taken by a small stream of water that flowed down a series of rocks in the corner of the garden. A judgment all those years ago that the integrity of my art was more important than the welfare of a stranger had led to so much misery and death. It was true. I could have allowed him to remain under my charge. I could have trained him.

"When I wrote to your wife's father," continued Hachirou, "I had no idea of what he would do when he found her. I thought that he would simply come and take them both away. That you would then suffer as I had."

"As if I had not suffered enough," I said. "You saw how I was after my first wife died. You were there."

"It is true," he replied, closing his eyes. "You had already lost someone you loved. But I was too racked with self-pity even to consider this. Still, you must believe me when I tell you that writing to Katsumi's father was not entirely my idea. It was suggested to me by another."

"By whom?" I asked, although I could already guess the answer.

"By your sister Aiko. It was she who told me where he lived. Without this information, I would never have been able to contact him."

"She hated my wife from the start," I said. "She was jealous of my love for her."

"And Aiko?" he asked. "She is—"

"Dead," I told him. "I killed her that same night. While you were riding through the night like a coward, her body was growing cold on the floor of her genkan."

He swallowed and closed his eyes. "And now you have come to kill me," he said.

"And after you had hurt me so much," I said, ignoring his question, "why take Sanyu, too? And Bashira? What injury did they ever do to you?"

"I knew you were looking for me," he explained. "I knew that you were intent on hunting me down."

"How?"

"Cousin, you have traveled across the breadth of Japan in search of me. I have money. I have resources. There are many men who want to be in my good graces and they bring me information. Did you not think that I would find out?"

"I hoped that it would bring you out into the open."

"Instead, it simply made me wary of you. I had men keep track of you and you were always a lot easier to find than I was. Temples, monasteries, at the kabuki theatre. I was aware of your movements at all times. When I found out that you had a new woman, I thought that if I took her, one day I would be able to bargain for my life."

"But you killed her instead."

"No, Cousin," he said, looking up and shaking his head. "I did not kill Sanyu, I swear it. I would never have done such a thing. In fact, I have never taken a life with my own hands."

"Of course you haven't," I replied. "You get others to do it for you. Such is the way of those who lack courage. You think that I would believe you simply because you say it? You're just hoping that I make your death quick and painless."

"You may believe whatever you want. I can't control that. But it is the truth."

"And if you did not kill her?" I asked. "Then who did?"

"Me," said a voice from behind, and I spun round in surprise. Again, so lost had I been in our conversation that I had failed to hear footsteps coming through the house as a familiar figure stood by the fusuma leading onto the garden.

Bashira.

• • •

"You?" I asked, standing up slowly and looking across at her. She, too, had aged since I had last seen her. She was very beautiful now, almost a replica of her mother, but there was a coldness in her eyes that had never been there with Sanyu. "But why would you do such a thing?"

She stood very still, looking from me to Hachirou and back again, her expression so ruthless that I began to wonder whether she was ever going to speak. I had not known Bashira well during the short period that she had lived under my roof but I had tried my best to be a father to her. She had been receptive to kindness from me but had treated her mother with a mixture of disdain and contempt. Of course, I had understood this, putting her disfavor down to the traumas to which she had been subjected at the hands of her father, and had been certain that one day, when time had placed a salve upon her wounds, relations might improve between the pair. But clearly, that day had never arrived.

She stepped out into the garden now, standing across from us both, and I saw that she was carrying a yumi longbow across her back as well as a kaiken dagger around her waist. I reached down and lifted my swords and stood up to face her.

"She left me alone with him," said Bashira, her face an emotionless mask. "She abandoned me."

"She didn't," I told her. "Your father exiled her when she discovered what he was doing to you. And your grandmother even assisted him in his foul deeds. It was their fault, Bashira. Not Sanyu's. She would have taken you with her if she could."

"She could have come back," she snapped, raising her voice now, and I could see the fury growing behind her eyes. She reached down to her belt and removed her kaiken, holding it in her right hand while her left thumb stroked the blade like the skin of a lover. Blood began to drip onto the grass beneath her feet, but she appeared immune to it. "Instead, she stayed away. She left me to his ministrations."

"The day I met your mother, do you know what she was doing?" She blinked but did not answer, her expression unchanging. "She was crying," I continued. "I discovered her weeping as she sat in a garden much like this. I asked her what was wrong but she would not tell me. It was your birthday, I discovered later. She was inconsolable because she missed you so much."

"Then she should have returned for me!" she screamed, turning her dagger around and pointing the blade in my direction. "Instead she left me alone with that monster. Do you know what he did to me?"

"I do," I said. "And I'm sorry for it."

"I was a child."

"It wasn't her fault. She would have swapped places with you in a heartbeat, had such a thing been possible."

She laughed bitterly and shook her head. "You were there the day that I pushed my father into that well," she said. "Don't you remember what I said afterward?"

I threw my mind back to that fateful afternoon in Yokohama, shortly before I had fallen ill. It was a long time ago but yes, now that she asked me, I did remember. I hadn't understood it at the time, but it made sense now.

"One of two," she repeated. "My father was the first and I knew that one day my mother would be the second. They're both dead now. Both punished for their crimes."

"But you remained here," I said. "After you killed Sanyu. You stayed with him," I added, nodding in the direction of Hachirou. "Why? Why not just leave? What hold does he have on you?"

She shrugged. "Where else would I go? He takes care of me. He gives me money. He used his influence to ensure that I was not investigated for my mother's death. Do you want to know what I did to her? I cut her head off!" She started to laugh now. "I cut her head off!" she repeated, shouting now and dancing around in a circle so that it seemed as if she had lost control of her senses. "And I enjoyed it. She knew that I was going to do it, too. I tied her up, then I told her my plans and I made her wait. She begged for mercy, but I did not give it. Instead, I simply—"

I did not hear what happened next, for I had already raised my sword and, without any preamble, I drove my katana into her heart while using my tantō to separate her head from her body. It rolled to the ground at Hachirou's feet and he let out a cry, stumbling to his feet and reaching for his sticks, darting away from the horrible artifact. The girl's body fell to the grass, the blood quickly spilling from its neck, and I could feel my own body begin to tremble in response to what I had just done.

When I turned around, I saw that Hachirou had picked up the dead girl's kaiken and was holding it in his hands. I frowned, wondering whether he really meant to fight me. When I looked into his eyes, I saw something of our shared boyhood there and, to my surprise, my anger began to dissipate. Perhaps, I thought, there was a route toward forgiveness after all. A dead girl lay at my feet. A girl who had never deserved such an ending. Perhaps enough blood had been shed. Perhaps it was time to forgive.

"Hachirou," I said, but before I could utter another word, he turned the kaiken to face himself and plunged it deep into his abdomen, before dragging it across his stomach from left to right. A wound opened, the blood flowed, and yet he stood still for a few moments, a half-smile on his face, before collapsing to the ground.

PART 11

GOOD AND
BAD ANGELS

GERMANY

A.D. 1790

MY CELL WAS SMALL, no more than twelve feet in length by six feet in width. A cot with a hard mattress was pressed along one wall while a pail that served as a toilet sat in the corner. Beyond that, there was no extra furniture. Some prisoners were lucky enough to have a view through the bars but mine overlooked a courtyard and, when storms blew, the wind was often so strong that it left me huddled in my bed, my arms wrapped around my body for warmth, the threadbare blanket a poor defense against the cold. I knew that on the other side of the building, prisoners could see a series of rocks in the corner of the garden and I longed for such a simple pleasure. Still, I was fortunate that I had the cell entirely to myself, for many of the inmates of Hohenasperg Prison were forced to share, with the more fearsome one taking the bed and the other reduced to a spot on the floor. Anyway, I preferred isolation to company, particularly when the potential for violence in such a claustrophobic environment was high.

The daily routine never changed. Each morning we were woken at six o'clock by the sound of gongs and made our way in single file toward the large dining hall on the ground floor, where we were handed a bowl containing a stale bread roll, a lump of hard cheese and a cold sausage, along with a mug of some hot water that might have once had a passing acquaintance with tea leaves. This was not food as I understood the term and it took a long time for me to grow accustomed to the pangs of hunger that made my stomach ache. Sometimes, when a rat passed through my cell, I imagined how it would feel to trap it, skin it and roast it over a flame.

In all weathers we were taken outside to the yard after breakfast, where we paraded around in silence for an hour before returning to our cells for the rest of the morning. Most of the men had perfected the art of sleeping at will, in order to make the time pass faster, but this was not something at which I was particularly skilled and I usually remained awake, working on my poems. In the midafternoon we marched again and, occasionally, the guards would play music so that we could dance, which allowed us a better opportunity to stretch our legs and increase our circulation, even though we must have looked ridiculous from the outside. I had read that the captains of British naval ships encouraged their sailors to do likewise on deck every evening for the same reason and, while it felt strange at first to be performing a Zwiefacher or Ländler with a bunch of murderers, thieves and rapists, I soon got over any discomfort and learned to get on with it. In fact, I joined a group of five other men—an arsonist, a pedophile, a thief and two men who had murdered an old woman for her pocket watch—in perfecting the Schuhplattler, which we performed to the delight of the other prisoners and guards equally, standing in a circle and repeatedly hitting the soles of our shoes, thighs and knees in the traditional Bavarian style.

Later in the day, we were given another plate, which the guards humorously referred to as dinner, usually an impenetrable stew with dumplings that could crack teeth and more stale bread on the side. Why the bread was always stale, I never did find out. It seemed to me that we were constantly using yesterday's baking when surely it would have made more sense to discard one day's produce entirely and start from scratch every morning. I suggested this one day to the governor and he simply stared at me before bursting into laughter and patting me on the arm, as if I had been sent to lighten his day. Which was ridiculous, as I was German, had never left my homeland, and jokes were not my specialty.

Once a week we were brought to the basement of the prison, where we were forced to stand naked in rows of ten while the guards turned the hoses on us. Although we were soiled and stank to high heaven, it was a painful experience for anyone stuck at the front, as those hoses had the most extraordinary pressure. I welcomed the pain, however, and always brought myself to the fore, stretching my arms wide and allowing the water to pound against my filthy skin.

The evening that followed was the only time of the week when I felt close to being clean.

Afterward, I would continue to read or write before all candles were extinguished at nine o'clock. The routine was the same, seven days a week, and I had long since lost track of what day of the week it was. It didn't matter anyway. Nothing ever changed.

. . .

I might have been able to make good my escape from my cousin's house were it not for the fact that, only a minute or two after Heinrich shot himself in the heart, his maid, Magnilda, arrived to begin her daily chores. Stepping into the garden, she discovered not only the body of her employer sprawled on the grass but also the corpse of Bathilde, with half her face blown away, and a stranger—me— standing between the two, holding a gun in my hand. I heard a cry from behind and spun round to see the unfortunate girl's face turn pale, no doubt believing that she would be my next victim. Walking quickly toward her, I hoped to persuade her to let me flee without punishment, but she turned and ran, letting out such an ear-piercing scream that even the deaf must have wondered what horrors had taken place behind those doors.

Running howling from the house, she charged down the street, telling everyone who would listen of the murders, and before I could find a place to hide, the police arrived to arrest me. I was taken to the local barracks and held overnight before being brought before a magistrate the following morning, where I was told that I was being remanded for trial.

I thought long and hard about whether I should confess to my crimes and ultimately decided to do exactly that, hoping that if I threw myself upon the mercy of the court, then they might spare my life. I recounted for the judge the story of my unhappy journey through adulthood, recalling the various losses I had suffered and explaining my reasons for hunting my cousin down. I swore that I had never intended to hurt Bathilde but that she had made a grave error in taunting me over the murder of her mother. I insisted, too, that Heinrich had taken his own life in remorse for his actions, although it seemed obvious to me, even as I told the story, that no one believed me. In the end, I was found guilty as charged and sentenced to ten years in jail.

Hohenasperg Prison was a dispiriting place in which to be exiled. Located near Stuttgart, it overlooked the town and had, at different times in its history, been a parliament, the seat for a feudal lord and a garrison, before being turned over to the government, who adapted it for its current usage. It held about two hundred prisoners in total, all men, and the guards and prison staff numbered a further thirty.

The cell next to mine was occupied by a prisoner named Niko Kalawai'a, of Tasmanian birth, and as the walls between us allowed the slightest sounds to pass through, we often talked to each other to relieve the boredom, recounting the misadventures that had brought us to such a desolate place. I was unfamiliar with the part of the world from which he hailed but he enlivened my evenings with stories of his early life on the beaches and in the forests of his native land. It turned out that he had been an outlaw, a gang leader, and been convicted of the murder of a policeman in Cologne and was now languishing in Hohenasperg Prison awaiting death while his lawyer continued lengthy court proceedings in an attempt to commute his sentence. I sometimes read to him from the verses I composed, and he listened in silence, occasionally asking me to repeat a favorite phrase or stanza.

"I never much saw the point of poems," he told me one night, his voice carrying through the gaps. "Give me a good story any day over rhymes. A hero to root for. A damsel to dream about."

"My father felt much the same way," I replied. "He said that poetry was the domain of women and feebleminded men."

"Seems to me that a poem never says what it means to say. There's always something hidden behind the words. Why not just come out and say what you want in the first place? Call a brick a brick. Ideas don't always need dressin' up in fancy clothes, do they, like they're on the way to Sunday school?"

"Not always, no," I said. "But if it makes the reader think about the world in a different way—"

"I mean no offense, friend," he grunted. "But I'm living in the same corner as your father on this one. Give me a good honest story," he repeated. "That'll do for me."

"I think you and he might have got along well," I said.

"Was he a tough man?"

"Oh yes. A soldier. He did not suffer fools."

"Mine was much the same," said Niko. "He spent a fair amount of his time in jail, too, for his villainy, the poor bastard, so the apple didn't fall far from the tree in my case. How did yours die?"

"Old age."

"Well, that's the best way to go, they say. Mine met his maker only a few days after being released from jail. Go on, then, read us another poem. I'll see if I can make sense of it. And if I can't, maybe it'll send me to sleep."

Over time, my pages increased in number. I composed poems about my mother, about each of my wives, about my children, about the towns and villages that I had visited during my travels. And then, occasionally, I found myself writing poems about places that came to me in my dreams, people and situations that I had never known or visited. And while these often proved to be among my most original work, I sometimes wondered from where these strange imaginings had come. When I read them to Niko, he told me that I must have lived other lives in other lands, but I dismissed this idea as fantastical.

• • •

Once a month, my brother Johan came to visit and we would sit for an hour in the visitors' room discussing family matters. He brought me books to read, another month's supply of paper and pens, and in return I entrusted him with all the work that I had produced in the intervening time for safekeeping.

I could hardly sleep the night before one particular visit, as I was anxious to discover whether he had fulfilled a request I'd made of him the last time he came to Hohenasperg.

"Well?" I asked when he sat down, barely giving him a moment to inquire after my health. "Did you find him?"

"Have you heard about this?" he said, ignoring my question as he placed a copy of the *Wiener Zeitung* before me and tapped his finger on a news story. "An English naval captain suffered a mutiny on board his ship last year and now, twelve months later, he and some of his crew have shown up in England when they were all presumed dead, having traveled three and a half thousand nautical miles in a small launch. Isn't that extraordinary?"

"Why should I care about such a thing?" I asked, frowning as I glanced at the article. A young cabin boy by the name of Turnstile was recounting his story to the reporter with great dramatic flourishes. I hoped the child was being paid by the word, as he could earn a pretty penny for such a narrative.

"Well, you were in a shipwreck once, weren't you? When you lost—"

"I remember," I said, nodding my head. "I don't need reminding of that terrible night. Three people died, after all."

"Of course," he replied. "I just thought—"

"Rikard," I said, more insistently now. "Did you find him?"

"I did. And I'm pleased to say that he's now safely living with Ulli and me."

I breathed a sigh of relief. My greatest concern throughout both my trial and incarceration was for the welfare of my son and, after my conviction, I asked my brother to take him in and act as his guardian.

"And how is he?"

"He's quiet," he replied. "Doesn't say much. He misses you, that's for sure. He doesn't seem to get along with Ulli, for some reason. If she tries to pull him in for a kiss, he screams. What do you suppose that's about?"

"I have no idea," I said, even though I could offer a fairly educated guess.

"But other than that, he's a good-humored boy," Johan added. "We've put him into the local school, although he's struggled to make friends. His head's always in the clouds."

"And his reading? His writing?"

"He's good at both. He takes after you in that regard. But he excels in mathematics and the sciences."

He reached into his satchel and removed my monthly supply of pages and ink and I handed across my most recent set of poems, which were on the subject of icebergs, despite the fact that I had never seen this phenomenon with my own eyes. He glanced at them for a moment and shook his head, as if he couldn't quite understand why I would waste my time on such scribblings.

"What should I do with all these?" he asked me. "Do you want me to see if I can get a printer to publish them for you while you're in here?"

"No," I said. "Just hold on to them, that's all. When I'm released, I'll decide what to do with them. Perhaps I can make my career from it yet. I'm not too old to start over, I hope. Especially now that I'm no longer chasing Heinrich."

"A career as a poet?" he asked skeptically.

"Yes."

"Well, there are worse ways to earn a living, I suppose. I can't think of any off the top of my head, but still."

"And what about Dieter?" I asked.

"Dieter?"

"When you found Rikard, wasn't he being looked after by a young man?"

"Oh him, yes," Johan said, shaking his head and laughing. "He's a peculiar one. He made Ulli disappear before my eyes so I punched him in the nose. He won't make that mistake again."

"But was he well?"

"Very well. He has a strange household, though."

"What do you mean?" I asked.

"So, this Dieter, he lives in a house with a friend of his, Tilmund, while his wife, Olaia, stays next door with her friend, Quira. How can a marriage thrive under such strange circumstances?"

I shook my head. "They're a peculiar couple," I admitted.

"They seem to loathe each other. They came out to say goodbye to the boy when we were leaving and barely even looked at each other. Anyway, Dieter said to wish you well and to thank you for all that you have done for him. He's making a living as a magician now and said that he would never have been able to do it, had it not been for your help."

Before Jonah left, I asked him whether he might bring Rikard to see me sometime and he looked down at the floor, as if he didn't want to hurt me by answering truthfully.

"I asked the boy that myself," he said. "Only he seems frightened of coming to a prison. Perhaps not quite yet, but one day in the future? When he's a little older?"

I nodded, but felt a great depth of sorrow. I longed to see my son but, of course, I did not want to upset him by bringing him into such an awful place. At least I knew that while I could not fulfill my obligations to him as a father just now, he would not be short of love.

SCOTLAND

A.D. 1832

A COUPLE OF YEARS into my sentence at Bridewell Prison, Glasgow, I no longer felt intimidated by my fellow prisoners, but the boredom remained. Even Johnny's monthly visits did not make up for the tedium I felt at being trapped within these four walls and I longed both for my freedom and to see Richie again. Although my son still declined to visit, he wrote to me regularly and I treasured each of his letters. Displaying a higher than average aptitude for his studies, he had been transferred to a school in Edinburgh and I was pleased to know that he was receiving a good education. It showed from the manner of his writing, which was formal and composed with a careful hand. He wrote a lot about the sciences, a subject of which I knew little but in which he had a particular interest, and he could spend pages detailing facts and suppositions about the planets and the constellations of the night sky.

Having grown up immersed in Scottish literature, I had always hoped that one day I might finally write a novel. I took particular pleasure in reading the adventure stories of Walter Scott. Knowing my passion for the man's work, the warden allowed me to keep copies of *Ivanhoe, Rob Roy* and *Quentin Durward* on my shelves. Even Kelman, the Australian incarcerated in the cell next to mine, enjoyed me reading aloud from them at nighttime, although he maintained that a true writer specialized in composing verse, a talent that I had never been able to call my own.

Since my confinement, I had been working on a novel, my first attempt in many years. It told the story of an itinerant musician. Eventually he settles in the home of a wealthy merchant who employs him to play in the evenings, whereupon he falls in love with the man's wife. There's a great hullabaloo, of course, and I included three duels within its pages as well as a lot of swordplay and ladies swooning. The hours in my cell were so long that I found the words flowed. Taking my heart in my hands, I decided to write to my literary hero and ask whether he might be willing to read it.

My dear Sir Walter Scott

Forgive the intrusion of an unsolicited letter from a stranger, but I hope it finds you in the devil of good health. I will not lie to you, sir. I am currently bound in the Bridewell in Glasgow, taken in for a ten-year stretch on account of the fact that I did kill a young girl. She was asking for it, though, I won't pretend otherwise, for she did me some wrongs that I will relate to you on another occasion, should you give me the opportunity, but believe me, if her ghost was to pass your way as you read these lines, I would hope that she would have the honesty to say, Aye, he's not wrong, I was asking for it. *Anyway, here I am, paying the price for my crime, as that's what the courts decided and there's little point in me crying over what cannot be changed. (I might add that I am also charged with the murder of a man, a cousin of mine, but of that accusation I assure you that I am wholly innocent.)*

I write to you now as one who has read all your books and think them to be among the greatest stories ever told. I have nurtured a lifelong desire to be a writer myself and, while counting the days away in here, have composed a novel that I hope might be of interest to you. It tells the story of a musician and has a motley cast of characters in it, and a deal of adventure, fighting, misunderstandings and bloodshed.

I have also included a humorous section related to a boy who does magic tricks. I knew such a fellow once and have stolen some of his artistry for the chapters that include him. I don't know if this is proper. Perhaps you can advise.

I'm sending it to you here, Sir Walter, and it's the only copy I have so take care with it, if you please. Would you be interested in a read?

Until I hear from you again, so—

And here I signed off with a lot of "your most humble servant" and "always in your debt" lines, and handed it to Johnny when he came a-visiting, who in turn promised to send it along to Sir Walter's publisher in Edinburgh. I was right happy, I don't mind telling you.

• • •

My neighbor, Neil Kelman, was drawing closer and closer to the day of his hanging and I knew that I would surely miss him when he was gone. No sooner had I dispatched the letter and manuscript off to Sir Walter than he started to tell me the story of his own life through the gaps in the wall and I began to wonder whether there might not be a story in there, too.

He described a curious childhood in southern Australia, where, he told me, his father had been a career criminal. When the man died only a few days after being released from prison, Kelman was still just a boy, but it was left to him to look after his mother and sisters, and so the family emigrated to Scotland in an effort to improve their prospects. Once he was out of short pants, he suffered any number of arrests, for he was always on the lookout for a way to take something that wasn't his by rights and served a few sentences in the jails of Scotland during those years. But then, when he was in his early twenties, he got involved with a rough bunch. When the police came to his house to arrest him, things went awry and he tried to kill one of them and got away without capture. Later, though, he learned that his mother had been arrested in his place, and wasn't he sick with horror at the thought of such an injustice, and it wasn't long before he, along with his associates, went on a killing spree, their victims being policemen all.

"I don't take any pride in the blood I've spilled," he admitted. "But I was young, that's all. And stupid. And full of passion. But you don't take a man's mother and lock her up when the poor creature has done nothing to deserve such a fate, do you?"

"No," I admitted. "No, you don't. Not if you have any common decency about you anyway."

As it turned out, Kelman and his associates managed to steer clear of capture for a few more years because, for some peculiar reason, the people of Scotland were following their adventures as if they were reading a pictorial weekly. Cheering them on, they were, for there was an element of the Robin Hood story to their tale, only with a lot more bloodshed involved. When he and his gang tried to ambush a police train near Aberdeen, it went badly wrong for them and every lad was killed, save Neil himself, who was captured at last and brought to trial and thence to the Bridewell with the intention of a noose being placed around his neck as soon as was legally possible.

But he'd built up such a following by then among the good people of Scotland that a whole group of them got together and signed petitions for his execution to be commuted to imprisonment. Not a chance, said the Prime Minister and the Home Secretary in unison, and it was thought that the matter was even raised with Queen Victoria herself, who acted like she'd swallowed a bee when she was asked to be merciful.

"So that's how you found yourself in here," I said to him one evening when he completed his tale. "It's a sorry story."

"Aye, it is," admitted Kelman, who remained stoic in such matters. "But such is life."

"Would you let me write it?" I asked.

"A history book, do you mean?"

"No, a novel."

"But it all happened, my friend. In what way would it be a novel?"

"I could take the events of your life," I explained, "and write them as if they were part of a great story. Telling the facts when I knew them and inventing at other times. Putting words into your mouth and those of your gang. It would be a way for people to remember your name."

"People will have forgotten about me by the time they've thrown me in my coffin," he said with a sigh. "I'll be discarded like a lump of hard cheese. But if you think you can make a book out of it, then you have my permission. I can't imagine it'll sell very well, though."

"Maybe not," I said. "But I have another sheaf of pages in here and enough ink to be going on with for now. And I need something to get me through the time ahead or I'll go mad."

"Then my life," he replied with a wide smile, "belongs to you."

. . .

To my surprise, I received a visitor one afternoon who was neither my brother nor, as I continued to hope, my son. During my period of incarceration I had never been asked to meet with a stranger and, as I entered the cold room where such encounters took place, I stared at the fellow, wondering whether he had made a mistake in coming here at all.

He looked to be a middle-aged man of considerable means, aged somewhere between forty and fifty, with graying hair and a friendly complexion. When I first entered the room, I disturbed him in the act of reading a newspaper, which he folded up upon seeing me and placed inside his leather satchel.

"I think you might have the wrong man," I said as I sat down opposite him. "I've never seen you before, friend, but as I rarely get to enjoy a conversation with anyone who isn't a fellow inmate, I'd be happy for you to stay a while, if you don't mind."

He shook his head and consulted a notebook, asked me my name and, when I offered it, smiled.

"Then you are indeed the right man," he said. "You are the fellow who wrote to a particular friend of mine, Sir Walter Scott?"

I stared at him in astonishment, saying nothing for a few moments. Was this a trick that the guards were playing on me or something truer?

"Forgive me," he said, extending his hand. "I should introduce myself. Matthieu Zéla."

"Pleased to meet you, Mr. Zéla," I said, shaking it. "What class of a name is that, if you don't mind me asking."

"French," he told me. "I was born there. Some years ago now."

"I've never much held with the French," I said. "No offense, Mr. Zéla."

"Matthieu, please. And no offense taken. You've visited my country, then?"

"No, never."

"Then might I ask the cause for your complaint?"

"Aye," I said. "Well, truth be told, I don't like the cut of their jib."

"I see. A well-constructed argument."

"And what brings you here?" I asked. "You don't look like a man who spends very much time in Her Majesty's prisons."

"As it happens, I've seen more than my share of these sorts of places," he said. "I have a nephew who occasionally finds himself in need of bail. But I haven't come here to talk about myself, but rather to talk about you."

"About me?"

"Yes, and this novel that you wrote. Sir Walter read it."

"No!" I said, for Sir Walter Scott had always seemed a person of almost mythological existence to me. To think of him sitting in his armchair turning the pages of my manuscript was almost over-whelming. "That's very kind of him. And you know him, you say?"

"Oh yes," replied Zéla. "We've been friends for quite some time. I attended a talk he gave once in Edinburgh and we indulged in refreshments of an alcoholic nature afterward, passing the hours with a discussion over the nature of fiction. He's a fine fellow. He would have come himself, only he's traveling at the moment. His publishers have taken him to London, where he's to offer a series of talks and readings to the paying public."

"I see," I said.

"So he sent me in his stead. He admired your book a great deal. He said that it is not without flaws but these could easily be reme-died with a little more work on your part and a little advice on his. Indeed, he has given me some notes to pass along to you. I hope they won't cause you any offense?"

He reached into his satchel once again, this time retrieving a half-dozen pages, on which a small spidery handwriting could be seen. "It's mostly to do with plot, the passage of time, that sort of thing," continued Mr. Zéla. "Sir Walter is very good on that so I'm sure his advice will be well worth taking."

"And I'm most grateful for it," I said, accepting the pages and looking through them quickly, although I knew I would pore over them when I returned to my cell later.

"One thing he wanted to know, though," he continued, "is whether you are a musician yourself?"

"Me? No. Why do you ask?"

"Your central character is a musician, isn't that right?"

"Aye. A fiddle player."

"And you don't play the fiddle?"

"No."

He scratched his chin and considered this.

"Is that a problem?" I asked. "Would it be better if I did?"

"A little," he replied. "There have been some people of late writing letters to the literary pages complaining of authors who do not share the same experiences with their characters."

I considered this. "If they did," I said, "would that not be an autobiography?"

"It would, yes, and their argument is entirely fallacious, of course. But it's gaining some ground. Recently, another writer of my acquaintance was spat at in the street for writing about a Russian, when he himself is English."

"I've never heard such nonsense," I told him.

"And a lady novelist has been brought up on charges for employing a male narrator for her latest book. The shops have refused to stock it, such is the uproar."

"But she has met men, I would assume," I replied. "She knows what a man is?"

"Of course."

"So she's using her imagination, you might say, to create his voice."

"Yes."

I laughed and shook my head. "Well, take her out and stone her in the streets," I said. "The woman must be insane!"

He smiled. "It's ridiculous, I know. But the letter writers will get overheated about the smallest things. One can only imagine the levels of fury that go into every scratch of pen on paper as they're composing their missives. Still, if it gives their life some purpose and keeps them out of the lunatic asylums, then it's a boon for society. In the meantime, if anyone asks whether you are a musician, we can simply say that you embrace all forms of artistic expression."

"So Sir Walter thinks that my book might be published?"

"Oh, my dear fellow, he'd like to publish it himself," explained Mr. Zéla. "In a little magazine that he edits. In serial form, that is. Perhaps over twelve issues? He can offer a small fee, but due to your current"—he searched for an appropriate word—"circumstances, Sir Walter feels that it might make more sense for him to hold the money on your behalf and offer it to you upon your release. The public might not take kindly to a prisoner being in receipt of money they spend on their leisure magazines. And for that same reason, he thinks it would make sense for you to employ a pseudonym. So no one can trace your writing back to the Bridewell."

"That's fine," I said. "I'm very grateful to Sir Walter for giving me this opportunity. And to you."

"No need to thank me," he said, brushing this aside. "I'm just the messenger, that's all. But I can come back in a week's time to collect the first rewritten installment, if that would give you enough time to complete it? Just the opening chapter about the narrator's youth in Rome. Tell me, have you been to Italy?"

"No," I admitted.

"Well, again, let's not tell anyone that. They might accuse you of having an imagination, too. Until next week, then?"

"Next week," I agreed, standing up to shake his hand.

AUSTRALIA

A.D. 1880

ON THE NIGHT BEFORE he was due to be executed, my neighbor and I stayed up late, talking quietly to each other through the walls. There was a melancholy to our conversation as we knew it would be the last time that we would have an opportunity to enjoy each other's company. So we spoke of nostalgic matters, of our childhoods, our families and the women we had loved throughout our lives.

"Do you regret any of your deeds?" I asked him, and he considered this for a long time before answering. The prospect of a noose, I found, made a man contemplative.

"I'll admit that there are some deaths that weigh more heavily on me than others," he admitted. "Them coppers were only doing their jobs and I daresay they had mothers and sisters and wives who miss them. If they'd only let me alone to get on with things, then there wouldn't have been any need for killing, would there? But they had to throw their noses in. Leave a man alone to get on with his business, that's what I say."

"There are those who would suggest that robbery is an immoral business," I suggested, adding a hint of humor in my tone so he would not think I was being cruel.

"And maybe they're right," he conceded, laughing a little too. "But it gives a man purpose, don't it, taking a thing that ain't his own. It did me, anyway. There's plenty have too much and there's plenty don't have enough. Share it out, that's my view on it. Them judges, they don't like killing, that's what they always say, but they don't seem to have any concerns about sentencing a man to death. That's a thing that ain't never made much sense to me. My way is honest, at least. Give a man a gun, give his opponent a gun, a few bullets in each to make things fair, and let's see who's still standing at the end of the conversation."

"An eye for an eye," I said. "Biblical, I suppose."

"Or maybe it's the numbers that count," he replied. "I've got so much blood under my belt that my keks have turned from white to red. At least you've only got that one girl in Sydney on your conscience, am I right? And they're not even killing you for that, are they? They just gave you ten years a-laggin'. What was her name again?"

"Betty," I said. "My wife's daughter."

"I knew a Betty in Brisbane once. She had some tricks up her sleeve, I don't mind telling you. But then she'd lived her younger years in Paris and they do things there that would make a man's toes curl."

"I take no pleasure in her death, though," I insisted. "She had been through so much in her life and for it to end in such violence was undeserved. But I acted rashly. In a temper. Had I controlled my fury, Melbourne Jail would have had one less inmate right now."

"Count yourself lucky that you're not following me to heaven or hell tomorrow morning," he told me. "I'm not afraid of death, but I'm no great fan of it either."

"The truth is," I admitted, "if they knew everything about my past, then I'd probably be going to the scaffold, too."

"The truth?" he asked. "And what truth might that be, then?"

I wondered whether I should divulge some of my darker moments, but a man like him would sooner cut his own throat than dog on someone to the screws and, even if he had been the type to spill my secrets, he wasn't long for this world anyway.

"Betty isn't the only person I've killed," I told him. "There were four others."

"Four?" he repeated, surprised. "I wouldn't have taken you for someone with a bloodthirsty streak."

"I'm not," I protested. "At least, I don't think I am. The truth is, I'm not sure how I ended up with so many deaths on my conscience. The first was a boy who attacked my sister when she was young. I thumped him over the head with a statue of Minerva."

"That's the worst kind of crime," he said, and I could hear him spitting his phlegm on the ground in disgust. "His, I mean, not yours. Only an animal would do something like that. He was better off being sent to hell. I never took a woman who didn't want me, nor did any of my gang. If I'd heard of such devilment, I'd have shot the fella's todger off."

"Then there was a man who tried to marry my sister against her will. Abby had a hand in that one, too, though. She forced me to do it."

"No one forces a man to kill," he said calmly. "Don't fool yourself on that, friend. If you did it, you did it."

"Then there was my sister herself," I added. "She caused me no end of trouble but I was angry and stuck a knife in her belly without thinking. If I could take that strike back, then I would. And then a girl, an innocent girl whose death I facilitated. I don't mind telling you, that crime weighs heavy on me. There's a couple of others who would still be alive, too, were it not for my actions but who I did not personally kill. And finally, Betty. The irony is, the only person I ever wanted to kill—my cousin, Heath—is the only one that escaped my wrath. He took his own life in the end."

"But you would have killed him, had you been given the chance?"

"Probably," I said. "But I'm not so sure anymore. Maybe I would have let him live. Who can tell what might happen from the moment you strike out in anger? Something might have stopped me from shooting. The trouble is, my good angels have often been in conflict with my bad. And I've never been able to pull the two apart."

"I don't think there are many good angels in Melbourne," he replied with a grunt. "Not so many as I've seen anyway."

"At least I know that I will never kill again," I said. "All that trouble is behind me now. There'll be no more anger, no more acts of revenge in my life. For once, I feel relatively at peace. Or as much at peace as a man can be when he's trapped within these stone walls."

I stopped talking when I heard the sound of keys unlocking the cell next door. From the other side of the wall I heard Governor

Castieau's voice and as I stood up to look through the bars, I saw two officers standing on either side of him, along with a priest who was carrying a leather satchel.

"Ned Kelly," he said to my neighbor, his chest puffing up with the solemnity of the moment. "It's time."

. . .

The inmates of Melbourne Jail stood proudly in the front of their cells as a mark of respect when Ned passed them by as he made his way along the upper corridor for the last time. He was permitted to bring a friend for company on this final march and he chose me, saying that he might as well have a friendly face nearby when the terrible moment arrived. I looked into the eyes of the men as we passed; some were openly weeping, these brave, strong souls, as they watched their hero passing into myth before their eyes. Some simply stared at him, as if they wanted to commit this moment to their memories, a story they could tell their grandchildren, if they were ever released from this godforsaken place. Others just watched him with curious expressions on their faces, as if they almost envied the fact that his pain would soon be over. One thing we all shared, however, was a belief that he was achieving immortality in this world when the rest of us, most likely, would be forgotten before the last breath left our bodies.

At the end of the corridor, we were taken into a small holding room where Chaplain Donaghy asked whether Ned had anything that he wanted to confess to the Lord before he began the journey to meet Him.

"I'll wait outside," I said, turning away, but Ned called out to me and asked me to stay.

"At a moment like this," said the chaplain, "it would be best if you spoke to God without an audience."

"And what are you, then?" he asked. "You invisible or something?"

"I'm nothing more than a conduit," explained the priest, smiling as he opened his hands before him.

"A conduit who'll sell my words to the Argus before my body's even turned cold, I'd wager. No, anything I have to say to God, any man can listen to. I've no secrets. You know what I've done and I've never denied it. Stay, friend," he added, looking across at me and, for the first time, I saw a certain vulnerability in his expression. He didn't want to be alone with the chaplain or with God. The former didn't interest him much and the latter, well, there'd be plenty of time for that before many more minutes had passed.

"Tell me this, are you sorry for your crimes?" asked the chaplain, and Kelly shrugged his shoulders.

"I'm sorry for those I hurt who didn't deserve to be hurt. I ain't sorry for stealing. I ain't sorry for punishing those who laid hands on my mother. This all started with how they treated her and any man who says otherwise is a born liar. Actions have consequences, tell them I said that when you're talking to them reporters, Chaplain, tell them that Ned Kelly said that actions have consequences and if you lock up an innocent woman who never did any harm to man, woman, or dog in her life just to try to catch hold of her son, then you're lower than a snake in the grass and don't act surprised if that same son comes knocking on your door late one night with the intention of putting a bullet in your head."

"You may regret words like that when they come for you shortly," replied the chaplain, who had grown red in the face now. He'd tried to counsel me on a number of occasions, too, but I'd never given him much quarter.

"Ain't a man ever gone to his grave without a few regrets," muttered Kelly.

The chaplain sighed and opened his prayer book; it was obvious that he was not going to convert Ned in his final hour. "Perhaps we could say a few prayers together, then?" he suggested. "Something to give you comfort?"

"Send one of those doxies standing outside on Russell Street in here to me and give me ten minutes alone with her. That'll give me comfort enough."

"Or I could read some verses from the Bible?" he continued, ignoring this last remark. "Something for you to think about as you prepare to meet your maker?"

"He's the one for reading," he said, nodding over at me. "He writes stories, did you know that, Priest? He even sent some to one of them famous writers. Who was it again?" he asked me.

"Marcus Clarke," I told him.

"Marcus Clarke?" asked the priest, turning to me with a look of utter disgust on his face. "Why, that fellow is a ruffian of the worst order. Why would you communicate with such a degenerate?"

"He read some of his stories out loud to me," continued Ned. "On account of me not being good with words, I mean. All about the men who got sent over on prison ships from England for crimes they didn't commit and they end up seeing the worst of humanity in the way they're treated when they arrive here in Australia. They weren't too bad. He can put a yarn together when it suits him."

"I can't believe the guards permit you to write such appalling things," said the priest, looking at me with an indignant expression on his face.

"Well, believe," I said.

"I hope you're not telling tales about prison life," he continued, pointing a finger at me. "And saying that you're treated worse than you really are, just to play the victim? Nothing good ever came from writing stories, I can tell you that."

"Then what about that book you're holding?" I asked, pointing toward the leather-bound volume in his hands that looked as if it must have cost a pretty penny.

"This is a Bible, you blasphemous cretin," he said, his face now growing even redder than before. "This is the word of the Lord."

"If you say so," I replied, rolling my eyes. "He only had one book in him, though, didn't he? Couldn't write another?"

Ned burst out laughing but the chaplain simply closed his eyes and breathed heavily through his nose.

"Keep talking like that," he said, "and I'll make sure that not a single pencil or piece of paper reaches your cell again. I'll stop your brother visiting altogether. You should be using your time in here in a more productive way, communing with Jesus Christ, our Savior. It's not as if Marcus Clarke will ever write back to you."

"Actually, he sent a friend of his to talk to me," I told him. "Reckons he wants to publish one of my stories in this magazine of his."

"Disgraceful," the chaplain replied. "You're in here to pay your debt to society, not to form even worse habits than before."

He glanced up at the clock then and both Ned's and my eyes followed. It was five minutes to ten. And, as if our very actions had willed it to happen, the doors opened at that precise moment and there was the governor once again, standing proud and excited, like a fat man at a buffet.

"He's made his peace with the Almighty?" he asked, nodding in Ned's direction.

"As much as he's ever going to," replied the chaplain with a sigh. "I don't think there's much chance of the two meeting any time soon."

"All right, then," said the governor as the officers walked forward and lifted my friend from his seat, taking an arm each in their own. "Time to pay the piper."

• • •

Ned remained thoughtful as we made our way along the final corridor to where the scaffold had been set up. It was a frightening thing to lay eyes on this instrument of death for the first time. A sisal rope had been slung across a steel girder that stretched from wall to wall and a well-tied noose hung from the end of it. We were standing on the first floor of the jail, removed now from the other prisoners, and a gate opened before us from where the condemned man could either jump or be pushed.

A half-dozen guards had gathered to watch, as well as a few reporters from different newspapers who'd been admitted to watch Australia's most famous criminal breathe his last. They gave a cheer of encouragement when they saw the man who sold more papers than anyone else appear before them, probably wondering who they could use for stories once his neck had snapped. He turned in their direction, a frown on his face.

"What the hell you all cheering for?" he shouted, shaking his head and, even at this moment, when there was no chance that he could hurt them, they looked a little shame-faced.

The governor read out a legal document to state that Ned had received a fair trial and been convicted of numerous murders and that sentence had been passed by Sir Redmond Barry on the nine-teenth of October in this, the year of our Lord 1880, in the city of Melbourne, in the state of Victoria, in the great commonwealth of Australia, and that this would now be carried out according to the demands of the law.

I stepped forward to shake my friend's hand and, although he took it, it seemed at that moment he almost didn't recognize me. His eyes were focused instead on the rope swaying a little before him. He was a brave man, there was no doubt about that, but faced with imminent death, there's not one of us who would not feel a moment of trepidation, question how we've lived our lives and whether we might face salvation, torture or an eternal silence once the last breath had left our bodies.

"The hood?" asked the governor, holding out a black cowl that Kelly could choose to wear if he wanted, but he shook his head.

"No point letting the world go dark until it has to," he muttered.

"Your choice," said the governor, tossing it aside. He nodded to the hangman, who stepped forward without a word and placed the noose around Ned's neck. "Any last words?" he asked, and Kelly glanced at him for a moment while his hands were manacled behind his back to stop him from struggling too much with the rope when he fell.

"It's come to this anyway," he said with a shrug of his shoulders and, a moment later, before I even knew what was happening, he was gone over the edge. Fortunately for him, the manner of his tumbling must have cracked his spine, broken his neck and killed him instantly, for he didn't struggle, not even for a moment, simply hung cleanly in the air as we all watched silently, uncertain who should speak or what should be done next.

"Cut him down," said Governor Castieau finally. "There's a box waiting for him in the prison yard."

PART 12

THE SUN,
THE MOON AND
THE STARS

FRANCE

A.D. 1916

WAS TWO YEARS AWAY from completing my sentence at HM Prison Shepton Mallet when Governor Caster brought me into his office to inform me that I was being offered a choice: I could remain where I was and see out the next couple of years of my sentence under lock and key, or I could sign up to the war effort, in which case I would be released immediately and shipped off to France.

"The truth is," he said, looking me directly in the eye, "you have more chance of survival if you stay here, so you should consider this very carefully before making a decision. A lot of the boys on the front line don't even make it past a couple of days. At least here you stand a good chance of getting out alive."

I didn't have to think it through, although I knew why he was encouraging me to stay, for Caster had been father to three sons, each of whom had already died in the trenches, so he was not well disposed toward the war effort. He was a considerate governor, though, one who didn't treat the men under his care with any form of cruelty. Being locked up was bad enough, he always said, without having to be treated like an animal, too.

We had our share of feather men in Shepton Mallet, lads who'd said no to the fighting on religious grounds, social grounds, or maybe just because they didn't like the idea of pointing a gun at some chap they'd never met before and who'd never done them any harm in the first place. I respected their bravery at sticking with their convictions but hadn't done much to stand up for any of them when they came to grief at the hands of the other inmates. The fact was, many of the prisoners were a lot older than me and had sons who were either still fighting in Europe or had already been lost in combat. To see some strapping twenty-year-old march through the gates telling all and sundry about peace, civility, man's inhumanity to man and the philosophy of Bertrand Russell, well, it set their teeth on edge. Most of these boys had the wind kicked out of them quick enough. One, Joe Patience, a decent enough sort, was almost killed and the guards did nothing to find out who had inflicted his terrible injuries. Prison simply wasn't a safe place to be if you were a conscientious objector. Me, I didn't much like the idea of war, but if it meant that I could feel the sun on my face again, even if I was busy dodging bullets while I looked at the blue sky, then I was happy enough to sign up.

On the evening that I boarded the boat for France, decked out in my uniform, I experienced some of the excitement that the other soldiers were feeling, although my thoughts were very much on my father, who would have been proud, if a little surprised, to see me now. Later that night, as we sailed toward Calais, I passed one of the soldiers who I'd met earlier and who had introduced himself to me as Will Bancroft. He wore an irritated expression on his face and, although I tried to speak to him, he brushed past me without a word. Looking ahead, I saw another of our group standing alone by the prow and made my way toward him, introducing myself as we stood together in the moonlight.

"Tristan," he replied, shaking my hand. "Or Sadler, I suppose. We're meant to use surnames now, aren't we? Will says it dehumanizes us. Makes us feel less concerned about killing."

"Bancroft, you mean," I said with a smile, and he nodded. "I just passed him on my way down here. Looked as if he wanted to punch someone."

Sadler shrugged and looked out toward the dark horizon. He offered me a cigarette, which I declined, then lit one for himself.

"I don't know you, do I?" he asked, glancing at me for a moment as he exhaled his smoke. "You weren't at Aldershot."

"No," I replied.

"So where did you train?"

I thought about it. Would it matter if the men discovered the truth about my past? "Nowhere," I told him. "The truth is, I've been in prison for some years now. At Shepton Mallet. They told me I could get out early if I was willing to do my bit for my country."

He breathed in through his nostrils, shaking his head. "That's a difficult choice to make," he said. "But I think you've done the right thing. What were you inside for, if you don't mind my asking?"

"Breaking the law," I replied, and he laughed, nodding his head.

"Fair enough," he said.

"Sorry. But it's probably best if—"

"You don't have to explain yourself. We all have secrets, I imagine. I know that I do."

We stood in silence, elbows resting on the railings, lost in thought.

"Did he say anything to you?" asked Sadler after a while. "Will," he added. "I saw you talking to him before you joined me."

"We weren't talking," I said. "He just marched past me, scowling. Why do you ask?"

"No reason."

"Is he all right?"

"In what sense?"

"Is he a fellow to be trusted? I imagine we'll all have to watch each other's backs where we're going."

He considered this for a long time. "I think so," he said. "I hope so. We don't know each other very well, to be honest. Will and I had cots next to each other in Aldershot, but other than that—"

"You don't have to lie to me," I said. "I don't care."

"What makes you think I'm lying?"

"Something happened between you, didn't it?" I asked, and he spun around and looked at me in shock. Had it not been so dark, I imagine that I would have seen his face grow pale. "It's not unusual," I added. "We must each find comfort where we can. A man, a woman, there's not much difference when it all comes down to it."

"Why would you even suggest such a thing?" he asked in bewilderment.

"It's just an impression I got, that's all," I said with a shrug. "Don't misunderstand me, it doesn't matter to me in the slightest.

I don't much care what other people get up to when they're on their own."

He said nothing but I could feel the tension emanating from his body.

"It's a damnable thing to say," he responded finally, although without a lot of conviction in his tone.

"If I've offended you, then I apologize."

"A damnable thing," he repeated.

We remained where we were for some time. I got the sense that he wanted to speak further of it.

"I should go back up," he said eventually.

"Look, I'm sorry if I upset you," I replied, placing a hand on his arm, and he looked at it for a moment before shaking it off.

"You didn't," he said. "You haven't. Only . . . don't say things like that to anyone else, will you? Especially not to Will. He might take it the wrong way, that's all. He's rather tricky, you see. Prefers his privacy."

"I won't say a word," I promised, and he nodded and scurried back toward the staircase that led belowdecks. I turned around and looked back out to sea. I imagined that every man on board had a secret to tell and a story to share. And most of them, most of us, would surely never get to tell them.

• • •

Three days in and I was sitting in a muddy trench somewhere near Lille. It wasn't a bit like I'd read about in the papers. It was worse. Far worse. The soil beneath me was nothing but pure sludge and, no matter how often we tried to put new stakes in the ground to act as a dam to stop our roughly made edifices from collapsing around our ears, there was always a part of the trench that was falling apart and needed stitching back together. Was this the army, I wondered? If so, warfare was a filthy business. Things had been a lot cleaner back in Shepton Mallet, that was for sure, and that place had been no great bastion of hygiene. You could catch a disease there just by opening your eyes in the morning.

Still, after so long living on my own in a small cell, it was a plea-sure to be among men again and I did my best to make friends.

Sadler and I remained sociable, although he held on to a certain reserve after our conversation on deck, while Taylor, Attling and Bancroft proved amicable enough types. We palled around together, playing cards in the dirt when we were bored, and some nights, when we found ourselves on duty together, our cigarettes held low around our knees in case the enemy caught sight of a red tip and sent a bullet flying in our direction, we ended up in the kinds of conversation that you have with other men when there's a good chance that you're all going to be dead before you get to worry about what you might have said twenty-four hours earlier.

Attling had a wife at home, he told me, even though he was no more than twenty-one years old.

"Got her in the family way, didn't I?" he explained. "So what could I do but the decent thing? I'm nowhere near as frightened of the Hun as I was of her old dad anyway. The banns were read out a few days later in the parish church and then we were married within a month. The baby didn't even live, that's the sadness of it. He died while he was still inside her. Or she. I never knew, never wanted to know. But still, I was upset about it. I'd got used to the idea of being a dad, you know?"

"I know very well," I said.

"You've got kids, then?"

"A son," I said.

"And where's he? Fighting, too?"

"I haven't seen him in a while," I told him. "But I understand he's working at the War Office. He's a smart one. Much smarter than me. All mathematics and the sciences with my boy. They took him in on account of his brains."

Attling nodded. "Just the one lad, then?"

"I had another once," I said carefully. "But he died. It was a long time ago now. He was just a child at the time. And, like you, a couple more that never made it to their first breath. Still," I added, "you don't forget them. You never forget them."

Bancroft didn't have a wife but he had a sweetheart, he claimed, a girl back home by the name of Eleanor who he planned to marry. He told me that she wasn't conventional and I wondered about his choice of word, what he meant by it, and in the end, I took it to mean that she let him take liberties with her. Bancroft seemed surprised by my being there, on account of me being much older than the rest of the troop, old enough to be a father to some of them, almost as old as Sergeant Clayton himself, who gave us all a rum time of it, but I told him the truth about my life, too, about how I'd been released from prison to be a part of this caper.

"I bet you wish you were back there now," he said, and I shook my head. I wished for nothing of the sort. "Or is the camaraderie much the same?"

"No, it's different," I told him. "In prison, it's every man for himself. You never know when someone's going to come at you with a knife for no other reason than you looked at him funny over breakfast, or maybe he just woke up with a pain in his head and thinks it will only go away if he draws someone's blood. It's a cold place, is prison. A nasty place."

"You can't find this comfortable, though?"

"No," I admitted. "But at least I feel like we're all in it together. None of us are fighting our own private wars."

"I don't know about that," he said under his breath.

"Well, we march as a group, I mean. We fall into these trenches as one unit. We stand guard in indivisible pairs. If we're going to win, then that's how we'll do it."

"You don't think the enemy feel the same way? Act the same way?" he asked. "And I'm not even sure that I know what winning even means anymore, are you?"

I thought about it. He was a young man, but he had something about him, that was for sure. Always thinking. Always philosophizing about right and wrong. "No," I said. "No, I probably don't."

I liked most of the boys, but there was one, Milton, who rubbed me up the wrong way. He had a rough side to him, a sadistic side. Almost everyone felt a certain sympathy for the young lads on the other side of no-man's-land because we were smart enough to know that they'd been dragged from their homes just like we had, only in their case it was by a kaiser, not a king, a pair of cousins who would be dining in their private dining rooms and listening to concerts every evening while the only music any of us heard was the sound the bullets made as they flew past our ears.

Milton liked to describe the terrible things he wanted to do to the Germans, the tortures he wanted to put them through, and it occurred to me that he'd probably been one of those boys who had pulled the wings from butterflies before pinning them on a card.

Attling, Milton, Sadler and Bancroft were ultimately involved in an incident that led to any number of difficulties for us all. We'd made it forward a few miles and achieved something of a triumph over the enemy when they were sent out to make sure that the trenches were clear on the other side. They were, for the most part, but it turned out that there was one soldier left, a German boy who'd had the unfortunate luck of staying alive while his fellows were all killed, and they'd dragged him out and Milton shot him in the head when he should have been brought back as a prisoner of war. It had been a cowardly act on his part and one that contravened all the rules of war, such as they were.

Bancroft, who I took for something of a thinker by this point, was up in arms about the whole thing and spoke to Sergeant Clayton, who shrugged it off as just another casualty of the front, but the boy wasn't having any of that nonsense and I was there one evening when he nearly attacked Sadler, accusing him of cowardice, saying that he'd been present at the incident, that he'd seen what Milton had done and needed to back him up. If the sergeant heard two accounts of the same story and they lay true with each other, then he'd have to do something about it. He'd have no choice.

"It was cold-blooded murder," Bancroft insisted, and Sadler said that he supposed it was but that he'd seen worse, a lot worse, and what did it matter anyway? Then Bancroft accused him of being all bent out of shape, saying that he was lying not to protect Milton but because he wanted to get back at him for something, and I took that to mean that whatever understanding they'd shared had come to an end.

"Can't we just be friends when we're lonely and soldiers the rest of the time?" asked Bancroft, but Sadler was having none of that and caused a great bloody storm. Anyway, Bancroft ended up putting his guns down and saying that he wouldn't take part in any more advances until something was done about what happened to the German boy and because of this he was put under court-martial before being sentenced to death as a coward and a traitor.

It was a miserable morning and I was glad I wasn't called upon to be in the firing squad that took him down. But Sadler was. They offered Bancroft a black cowl, but he preferred to look directly at his killers. And afterward, Sadler was a totally different person. All the life went out of him. All the energy. All the self-belief. He started to shake and tremble. When I tried to talk to him, he would barely say a word. Once, I found him sitting with his back to a tree, his pistol in his mouth, and it took me the best part of an hour to convince him that he shouldn't pull the trigger, that his life was still worthwhile. Finally, when he put the gun down and I grabbed it away from him he looked at me with an expression of utter self-loathing on his face.

"I don't think I could have done it anyway," he said quietly. "I'm a terrible coward, you see."

Anyway, the war went on. Some days we gained a little ground. Some weeks we stayed put for what seemed like a hundred years. Dispatches came and went. Men died, new men arrived who looked just like the ones we'd lost, and somehow, I stayed alive till the final day. The war to end all wars, they were calling it and, true enough, it didn't seem like things could ever get much worse. But still, I never regretted my decision to go to France instead of remaining locked up in Shepton Mallet. It's not a lot of fun being shot at all day. Your body isn't your own. You're covered in maggots and lice and you'll never be clean again. But then again, once in a while, something good might happen. A bird might appear out of nowhere and land on one of the ladders that took us all up to no-man's-land. Snow might begin to fall and we might throw our heads back and open our mouths to allow the snowflakes to land on our tongues. At moments like that, at least you could sit there and think, I'm free. At least I'm free. And soon, one day soon, this might all be over and I'll sail back across the water, make my way to a train station and find my way home at last.

CZECHIA

A.D. 1939

BUT HOME, when I finally returned there, seemed an unfamiliar and far less welcoming place than it had once been. Arriving in Prague, there was a palpable sense of fear in the railway station as I disembarked, and the rush of people attempting to board the train as it continued on toward Western Europe surprised me. I could feel the apprehension all around me, could see it in the faces of my countrymen, could smell it in the air. On the journey, everyone on board had been feverishly reading newspapers, all of which featured articles about President Hácha and the German Führer on their front pages. Looking around anxiously now, it was hard to see through so large a crowd but, thankfully, my brother Jezek stood out. He towered over everyone else, both in height and build, and his extraordinary red beard appeared fuller and more luminous than ever. When he fought his way through the throng, he wrapped his enormous arms around me, practically lifting me off the ground.

"So many people," I said as we made our way toward a taxi rank. "But everyone seems to be boarding trains to leave, as if the city is emptying entirely."

"Because they're afraid, Brother," he replied. "They want to get as far away from here as possible. There's talk that the Luftwaffe are preparing a bombing campaign for Prague and will put it into action if Hácha doesn't capitulate. What do you expect them to do, sit around listening to concerts every evening?"

"Will it come to that?"

"I don't know," he said with a shrug. "Most of us think he'll give in any day now. And then we'll wake up the next morning to find German jackboots marching across Wenceslas Square."

The idea of my country being overtaken by our once-peaceful

neighbors would have seemed preposterous only a few years earlier. Now, any other scenario seemed equally unlikely.

"And Radek?" I said. "How does he feel about all of this? Does he want to get away, too?"

"No," he said, laughing a little. "If anything, he seems oblivious to most of it. Your son's head is full of numbers, nothing more. He sits in his office at the university all day long, working on mathematical equations, staring at the sky, making notes about the sun, the moon and the stars, and barely even noticing what's happening in the world around him. I doubt he even knows who Hitler is."

"Still, I'd prefer that he lose himself in academia than join the Resistance," I said. "How does he feel about my coming back anyway? Has he said anything?"

"He's looking forward to seeing you," said Jezek, with a note of caution in his tone. "But remember, it's been many years and he's changed a lot. He's not one to display too much emotion either, so don't expect any great shows of affection. That's not the type of boy he is."

I nodded, feeling a sense of guilt mixed with anxiety. Jezek and his wife had been good enough to take care of my son while I was in prison but he had pointedly refused to visit during that time. The truth was, he could walk past me in the street and I wasn't sure that I would even recognize him.

"And you are well?" I asked. "And Ulva?"

"We're fine," he said. "My guns are loaded and I'm ready to shoot anyone who even tries to set foot in my apartment uninvited."

"Your wife hasn't tried to dissuade you from such actions?"

"On the contrary, she's the one who bought the bullets. And she's a better shot than I am."

We got into the car and Jezek named a café on the banks of the Vltava, near the Jiráskuv Bridge. As we drove along, I felt reinvigorated to see the streets of the city once again. It had been so long since I had been here that it felt like coming up for air. At last, my adventures and misadventures could be put behind me. All I wanted now was to rebuild a relationship with my son and settle down to a

quiet existence. I only hoped that Herr Hitler would not do anything to threaten that.

When the taxi pulled up outside the café, Jezek paid the fare then
threw his arms around me once again, handing me a key to his flat
and telling me that he would see me later.

"You're not coming in, too?" I asked in surprise.

"I think not," he said. "It's probably best if the two of you talk
without me."

I glanced through the window. It was lunchtime and busy inside
and I didn't see anyone who immediately resembled my son.

"But—" I began, turning back to him, but he cut me short.

"No, Brother," he said. "This is something you must do alone.
Don't worry. He's a good boy. He has more in common with you
than with me or our father. You'll be fine."

I watched him as he trundled down the street. Before I could
step inside the café, I was almost knocked over by a family carrying
six suitcases and doing their best to hail a taxi, although each car
that drove along the street passed without stopping. The woman
had tears streaming down her face.

Taking a deep breath, I placed my hand on the door and pushed
it open. Looking around, I scanned the faces of all the young men
until, finally, in a corner by the window, I noticed one sitting alone,
his head bent low over some textbooks, and I knew that it was him.
I kept still, watching him for a few moments, wanting simply to
observe my son while remaining unobserved myself. Only when a
waitress approached to offer me a table did I make my way over and
stand before him.

"Radek," I said, and he looked up, propping his spectacles up
along his nose, and stared at me with an expression of bewilderment on his face, as if he had forgotten that I was even coming.

"Father," he replied eventually. "My apologies, sir. I was lost
in . . ." He indicated the books and jotters that lay open before him.
"All of this. Please," he said, nodding toward the chair opposite
him. "Sit down. You're most welcome to join me."

I hesitated, the formality of his tone surprising me. I had expected him to stand up, to embrace me or to allow himself to be

embraced, but no. He remained exactly where he was, clearing some of his things to one side but, I noticed, glancing at one of his pages before making a quick note and turning it over. Only when the waitress poured us both some coffee did he smile and give me his full attention.

"You've grown," I said, taking him in. He looked to be of average height with a slim build. He was quite handsome, with blond hair and prominent cheekbones, his face reminding me a little of his mother and a lot of my father.

"Well, of course," he replied. "It's been ten years. It would not be natural if I had stayed the same."

"No," I said, smiling, only it seemed that he was not trying to be humorous, for his face remained solemn.

"Well, it's very good to see you," I said.

"And you," he said. "I've thought about you often."

"Your letters meant a lot to me. When I was in prison, they kept me alive."

"Of course. I thought it important to keep up communication with you, for I assumed that we would meet again one day and it would be ridiculous to try to catch up on ten years of stories. Now we don't have to."

I stared at him, uncertain how to respond to this.

"You were working?" I asked, indicating the books lying on the table.

"I was," he replied. "Mathematics. As I think you know, it's my field."

"What is it about it that you enjoy?"

"The order that can be found in numbers," he said without hesitation. "Every problem has a solution and it is the job of the mathematician to make that solution as elegant as possible. Numbers never surprise you. They hide their secrets, but a good investigator can always decipher them. They don't change or let you down. They never abandon you."

"I was never very good at mathematics," I said, ignoring this last remark. "I was always more of a creative person."

"I remember," he said.

"Perhaps I'll be able to return to my craft soon."

"Now that you're free, you mean?"

"Now that I'm free," I agreed.

He smiled and took a sip from his coffee. "And you think you'll be free here?" he asked. "That's rather naïve of you, don't you think?"

"But why not?" I asked. "Prague is my home. If I cannot be free here, then where else can I go?"

"They're coming," he said. "The Germans, I mean. They'll be here very shortly. And it is likely that we will all lose our liberty."

"I don't think it will come to that," I said. "The President has said—"

"The President has suffered a heart attack," he told me. "And he has betrayed us all. Anyway, we shall see," he continued, waving a hand in the air and dismissing this. "That said, we don't have as much to worry about as some. The Jews are in the most danger. They would all be advised to leave as soon as possible."

"And you've been living with Jezek and Ulva?" I asked, changing the subject abruptly. I did not want to get too involved in politics, preferring to discuss our family life.

"I have, yes."

"They've been good to you?"

"Very kind. They've treated me as if I were their own son."

I nodded. I was glad to hear it but, still, the remark stung a little.

"Do you want to know why I did it?" I asked.

"Why you did what?"

"Why I killed that girl?"

"I know the story," he said. "And, in my opinion, you were right to kill her. She murdered my mother so her life should have been forfeited in return. I admire you for what you did."

"You shouldn't," I said. "She did not deserve such an ending."

"Well, it can't be changed now."

"You're so . . . serious," I said, leaning forward and lowering my voice. "Are you angry with me?"

"Not at all," he said, shaking his head and attempting a smile. "I've been told this before. That I'm serious, I mean. People find it off-putting. They believe that I'm unfriendly but I'm not. It's just my manner. It's deceptive."

"Very different to when you were a child, though. You were quite lighthearted then."

"Indeed," he admitted. "But I'm not a child anymore. And these are not lighthearted times. You missed out on the years between then and now. I'm not the same person as I was."

I nodded and looked away, tapping my fingers on the table. I had hoped for some cathartic moment between us, some exchange of words of love, but it felt as if he was simply welcoming me back into his life while barely recognizing that I had ever left it.

I glanced at his books and tried to find a subject upon which we might connect. "Your mathematics," I said. "What particular branch are you interested in?"

"Rocket propulsion," he said.

"I'm sorry?"

"Rocket propulsion," he repeated.

"And what is that exactly?"

He sighed, as if he couldn't quite believe my ignorance. "It's the process that uses force to move a heavy object, such as a rocket, off the ground and into the atmosphere," he explained. "I'm working on concepts that combine the fuel and the oxidizer in different ways. I'm trying to understand how to move something faster and heavier than an airplane while maintaining its ability to withstand the gravitational forces of the universe."

"To what end?"

"So that, one day, we might be able to send a man into space."

I stared at him, wondering whether he was joking. "But that's impossible," I said.

"Nothing is impossible," he replied. "A hundred years ago, no one would have believed in aviation, but now that's become a fact of life. It's perfectly credible that one hundred years from now we'll be traveling between planets as we now do cities."

"How astonishing," I said. Although I used to express a desire as a child to live among the stars, I had never truly imagined that such a thing would ever be possible. "And how long have you been interested in this?"

"For as long as I can remember," he said.

"I seem to recall you asking me questions about the stars when you were a child," I said, reaching back for a long-hidden memory. "And outside of your work?" I asked. "Is there a woman in your life?"

"There is a girl with whom I have sex," he replied, stating this in such a matter-of-fact fashion that I almost spat out my coffee.

"All right," I said. "That wasn't quite what I was asking, but—"

"It's simply a human need, nothing more," he explained. "I visit her once a week and that's enough for me. I don't see her outside of that."

"You don't even take her to dinner? Or for a drink?"

He shook his head. "That wouldn't interest me," he said. "Or her. We're happy as we are. We meet, we engage in sexual activity and then we say goodbye. Outside of that, I'm far too busy with my work. I have no intention of ever marrying."

"But Radek," I said. "What about children?"

"Yes, I've considered them," he replied. "I don't think I'd be a good father. However, if one day I have a child, I will do my best, of course. Until then—"

"You speak very plainly about your life," I said. "So let me ask you this, are you happy?"

He sat back and frowned. I suspected that no one had ever asked him such a direct question before, nor had he ever asked it of himself. "I'm happy when I'm working," he said. "That alone gives me pleasure. Why, are you happy?"

"Not really," I said. "I hope to find happiness now that I'm back in Prague but, in my life, whenever I have found contentment, it has always been snatched away from me."

"You do seem to have been unfortunate in love," he said. "Three wives, all of them dead."

"Yes," I said, looking away. Was it my fault that he was so cold? And yet he didn't seem angry with me, he just spoke as if we were strangers. Which, I suppose, we were. "Anyway, I think that part of my life is over. I've not brought any luck to the women with whom I've been involved. I'll go back to my artistic endeavors and hope to find satisfaction there."

"Then I wish you well with it, Father," he said. "And where will you live?"

"Actually, that was something I was going to discuss with you," I said. "Jezek has said that I can stay with him and Ulva until I find somewhere for myself but I thought I might look for a flat. With two bedrooms. You could live with me again. If you wanted to, that is. If you're happy as you are, of course, I won't be offended."

He looked down at the table and considered it, before nodding his head. "That would be acceptable," he said. "I've imposed upon my uncle and aunt for too long as it is. Yes, Father, I will live with you."

"All right, then," I said, trying not to laugh. What a strange boy he had turned into. Still, I was delighted that he had agreed to join me and felt certain that, in time, our bond would strengthen. I was about to suggest that we could start looking that afternoon but the sound of shouting from the street outside distracted me.

"What's going on?" I asked, looking through the window and craning my neck to see what was making people run so fast through the streets. "What's going on out there?"

"It's the tanks," said Radek with a sigh, gathering up his books and placing them carefully in his satchel. "They've arrived. It's started."

RUSSIA

A.D. 1961

AFTER TWO YEARS OF SHARING an apartment in the Sokol-niki district of Moscow, Radomir and I had established a routine that worked well for us both. I rose at around half past six every morning to prepare a simple breakfast of kasha and boiled eggs, before tapping on my son's door to wake him. When he appeared in the kitchen thirty minutes later, showered and dressed, he was always wearing one of the five suits that he alternated from Monday to Friday. The suits were of a similar cut, had been made by the same tailor and, in color, might have been almost indistinguishable to the human eye. I had been looking at these same suits for so long now that, were I to forget the day of the week, the answer lay right before me.

Before saying good morning, he invariably stepped out onto our small balcony to stare up at the sky, observing the passing clouds, before smiling to himself, as if they'd shared a great secret with him. He would then sit down at the table, where he would eat what I had laid out for him while reading one of his science magazines.

Occasionally, I would try to engage him in small talk, but my attempts were rarely successful, for he was not much of a conversationalist, unless we were talking about his beloved space program, although due to the secrecy of his work he could tell me very little about it. The things he knew, the work in which he was involved, was a matter of such confidentiality that to reveal anything could lead to serious trouble for us both.

"Busy day ahead?" I might ask as I poured coffee, and he would look me up and down as if I were preparing to inform on him to the KGB.

"No more or less than usual."

"Anything interesting going on at work?"

"Interesting to some, perhaps. Boring to others."

"What are you working on at the moment?"

"Oh, this and that."

There was really no point in trying to draw any further information out of him. All I knew was that he left the apartment at eight o'clock precisely and returned at six, when our conversations would run along the same lines as those we had enjoyed over breakfast. His workplace was only a two-mile walk from our apartment and the people there were engaged in trying to put a man into space and, more importantly, doing it before the Americans could. It seemed like a ridiculous enterprise to me, a lot of money being spent on something that would surely never be possible, but it made him happy and that was fine by me.

• • •

Since my return to Moscow after so many years away, I had reestablished my bookbinding business, setting up a small workshop on a bohemian street near Ostankino. I had built an excellent reputation as a young man, of course, but knew that I would have to work hard to rebuild it after spending ten years in a Siberian gulag. To do this, I began by investing in a series of large medical textbooks, each containing seven or eight hundred pages, and removing the covers before creating different forms of binding, all of which I could display in the window of my shop. I used leather on some, bamboo on others, the hides of animals on others again. I attended various literary salons, introducing myself to publishers and writers and, soon, readers came my way, usually elderly bibliophiles who thought nothing of spending a small fortune to give their collections an appearance of elegant uniformity.

For several days, I had noticed a young man wandering up and down the street outside wearing a long trench coat with a hat pulled low over his ears. One morning, he stepped inside, the small bell over the door ringing to alert me to a new customer. We eyed each other warily and he examined some of the books that I had on display, picking them up and running his fingers along the spines. I was crafting a leather-bound copy of William Shakespeare's *Julius Caesar* at the time for a gentleman who brought me a different play every month and, although Shakespeare generally left me cold, I sometimes glanced through them and had found this play to be particularly engaging, having spent the previous afternoon reading it and feeling the most curious chills in the fourth act when Caesar's ghost appeared to Brutus before the Battle of Philippi.

"Excuse me, Master Bookbinder," said the young man, stepping toward the counter now, his eyes darting back and forth nervously. "May I ask whether you work here alone?"

"I do," I said.

"I suppose a man who works with books has a certain . . . artistic side to him," he said.

"I'd like to think so," I replied. "Although, of course, I don't write the books myself, you understand. I simply bind them. Still, as you can see from some of my efforts, I try to maintain a certain creative—"

"Yes, yes," he said, dismissing all of this. "I have a book that I'd like you to take a look at. But first, I suppose my question to you is this: Are you a trustworthy man? Does what takes place between these walls have the same secrecy that one might expect from a doctor's surgery?"

I had experienced moments like this before, where a person arrived in possession of something that the Party might find questionable. I asked no questions, other than for a description of the binding the customer requested, and simply got on with my work. I had never, as yet, had cause to report anyone and knew that it was unlikely that I ever would, no matter what they gave me.

"I keep a very private business here," I told him, nodding patiently. "If I did not, then I would lose all my clients within the week. I give you my word that you can trust me with whatever you have."

He breathed heavily through his nose and seemed to make a decision, for a few moments later he opened his satchel and removed a wallet, a notebook and a key to his flat before extracting a sheaf of five or six hundred loose pages.

"This book is very sensitive," he said. "As you can see from the title page."

I took the manuscript off him and was not surprised to see that this was a book that was forbidden in the Soviet Union. It had been smuggled out of the country a few years earlier to Italy, where it had been published in translation, and then the Americans had taken it up, where it had proved an enormous success, much to the fury of the Politburo.

"*Doctor Zhivago,*" I said. "Where did you get this? I've never held a copy in my hands before."

"It was a gift," he said. "From the author. I want it bound, that's all."

"You were a friend of Boris Leonidovich?" I asked, impressed, for despite attending many literary events in the city since my return, I had seen the novelist only once in person, a few months before he died, and even then he was surrounded by so many people that it was impossible for me to speak to him.

"Not a friend as such," the young man replied. "But I knew him a little. My friends and I, we do our best to smuggle volumes of high art in and out of the country. Please tell me that I can trust you," he added, beseeching me with his eyes and tone, and I nodded quickly.

"You have nothing to fear," I insisted. "I will guard this with my life."

"Thank you. It will be the first anniversary of Boris Leonidovich's death in six weeks' time and we plan on leaving fifty copies of the novel in prominent places around the city to mark the anniversary."

"Fifty?" I asked, holding up the sheaf of pages. "But you've only given me—"

"There will be more to come. Every few days I will bring you more. Can you produce fifty by the end of May?"

I considered it. I had other jobs on, of course, but it was possible, if I did not use a binding that was too ornate. Indeed, I would have to use materials that I had never employed before or they could be easily tracked back to my workshop.

"For such a large quantity, in such a short timeframe, they will need to be very simple," I said. "A clean binding. Nothing fancy."

"That's all we need. But with the author's name and title embossed on both the cover and the spine. We want there to be no hiding what this book is and who wrote it."

"How will you do this without getting caught?" I asked.

"We'll distribute them at night. There's enough of us to take three or four each and leave them in the appropriate places. By the following morning, the city will awaken to the news that literature is available once again in the Soviet Union. And perhaps others will then imitate our endeavors. The more editions that are out there, the better."

"All right," I said, putting the pages under the counter. "I'll do as you ask. Fifty copies. And I wish you luck. If you're discovered, however, you know what the punishment will be, don't you?"

"I know," he said, smiling at me. "But it seems a small price to pay for something so precious, does it not?"

• • •

As it was a Tuesday, I knew that Radomir would be returning home with his girlfriend, Zhenya, who was every bit as uncommunicative as him, but they had a standing appointment on this day every week, when they would retire to his bedroom for precisely one hour, during which time I took a walk, regardless of the weather. Upon getting back, they would have emerged from their tryst, a little red in the face, before shaking hands and saying their good-byes. It was not, I thought, the great romance of the ages.

When they arrived that evening, however, there was something different in their attitudes. Instead of being sullen and uncommunicative, they both seemed excited, and when I asked what had happened, Radomir looked at me as if he could scarcely believe that I didn't know.

"Haven't you heard the news?" he asked.

"What news?"

"You weren't watching television?"

I glanced over to the set in the corner of the room and shook my head. I had spent all afternoon reading *Doctor Zhivago* and promising myself that, from the next day, I would have to stop turning the pages and start binding if I was to get all fifty copies completed on time.

"Your son is a genius," said Zhenya, and for a moment, I thought there was something approaching a smile on her face. "He will soon be a national hero."

"No," he protested. "Not me alone. The entire group will be. We will remain nameless, which is only proper."

"What's happened?" I asked, for I felt buoyed by such unexpected enthusiasm on their part.

"Today," said Radomir, placing both hands on my upper arms and looking me directly in the eyes. "Russia won the Space Race!"

"How?" I asked.

"We put a man in space. Yuri Alekseyevich Gagarin. His spacecraft completed an entire orbit of the planet and he has come back down to Earth safely."

I stared from one to the other in amazement. I could scarcely imagine that such a thing had proved possible.

"And you were a part of this?" I asked.

"A small part," he said.

"A big part," said Zhenya. "Your son is one of the finest mathematical brains in the space program. He may receive an honor from Chairman Khrushchev yet! Can you believe it?"

I walked over and switched on the television news and, sure enough, everything they were saying was true. The presenter was talking about how the USSR had changed the world today and how the Americans, despite their hollow congratulations, would be humiliated by what we had done. A picture came up on the screen of a smiling young man in uniform.

"That's him," said Radomir. "That's Yuri Alekseyevich."

"Extraordinary," I said. "I'm very proud of you."

"Thank you, Father," said Radomir, bowing a little, and for once I saw something approaching emotion in his eyes. He rarely gave in to such feelings and it pleased me to see that he was not made entirely of stone.

Lying in bed later, I looked up at my ceiling and wondered how it must have felt to have been on the Vostok, the vessel that had taken our brave cosmonaut around the planet. The fear, the excitement, the ability to see the world as no man had ever seen it before.

It was a thrilling notion. And yet, when I fell asleep, I did not dream of other planets and alien creatures, but of Doctor Zhivago and his Lara. My son might have contributed something incredible to the advancement of human enterprise but still, in my small way, I could wake the next morning and feel that I was helping to advance ideas and culture, which had always been my passion.

After all, I still had forty-nine more books to bind.

UNITED STATES OF AMERICA

A.D. 2016

RAYMOND WAS LATE coming home from work, which meant that I was left on my own with his girlfriend, Zoe, who was sitting on the sofa, stuffing Doritos into her mouth and intently watching the television. I'd hoped that she would remain in her own apartment so I could watch the returns in peace, even though I didn't think that the evening would last very long. It seemed pretty obvious that the result would be confirmed by nine o'clock at the latest and that would be the end of that. This long national nightmare, this carnival of intolerance and bigotry, this celebration of rank stupidity over intellect that had played out across our country over the previous eighteen months would finally be brought to an end and Donald J. Trump would be dispatched back to that gaudy monument to bad taste that he'd constructed on Fifth Avenue, where he could blind himself with his grotesque golden pillars and leave the rest of us in peace.

I didn't know whether she was deliberately trying to annoy me or not, but Zoe was wearing a T-shirt with an image of her favorite troglodyte grinning while making the thumbs-up gesture, along with her MAKE AMERICA GREAT AGAIN hat. I wanted to whip it off her head and set fire to it.

We watched a rerun of some news from earlier in the day when Trump had gone to vote and told reporters that things were looking good, looking very good, and it was difficult not to laugh at his delusions. I assumed he didn't really believe he was going to win—there was more chance of *me* being elected President of the United States, and I wasn't even on the ticket—but that he was simply sticking with his braggadocio until the end. Then the cameras switched to a videotape of Hillary voting in upstate New York.

"Lock her up," muttered Zoe through a mouthful of chips. I

glanced across at her and wondered whether she even realized that she had said that or whether it had become some sort of Pavlovian response to seeing the former First Lady on television.

"What was that?" I asked her, eager to test my theory.

"What was what?" she replied, not even turning to look at me.

"I thought you said something."

She shook her head and seemed genuinely mystified. "No," she said.

I picked up the remote and rewound the live television pictures by a minute. "What are you doing?" she asked me.

"Sorry," I said. "I missed something. I just want to see that again."

Trump bragging, Clinton voting.

"Lock her up," said Zoe.

I pressed the stop button on the remote and let it return to regular time.

"You've got four years of fury ahead of you," I said. "Four years of watching Hillary make the laws, appoint the judges, clean up the environment. How will you cope, do you think? Do you think your head might just explode in anger?"

"I'll cope perfectly fine," she replied. "Because it's not going to happen. Mr. Trump is going to win."

"I know you want him to win," I said with a sigh. "But come on, be realistic. He hasn't a chance."

"Mr. Trump is going to win," she repeated. "And when he does, he'll kick all the Muslims out, build a wall so the Mexican rapists can't attack women, and make America great again."

"That's all it's going to take?" I asked.

"Well, it'll be a start."

I said nothing. I had long since stopped trying to figure out how my otherwise sensible son could be attracted to this miserable creature who'd somehow entered our lives and seemed determined to stay there. It was simply more than I could comprehend.

The doorbell rang and I buzzed my brother and his wife in. Joe was beaming and carrying two six-packs of beer under his arms, one of which he placed on top of the copy of *Doctor Zhivago* that I was reading, which made me wince. He was holding his own MAKE AMERICA GREAT AGAIN hat in his hands because his head was too big for it, and his wife, Unwin, was waving the Stars and Stripes while grinning from ear to ear.

"You people," I muttered, shaking my head.

"How's our guy doing?" asked Joe, looking across at Zoe, and, as ever, she refused to take her eyes away from the screen when she answered.

"Great," she said. "He's going to win."

"Of course he is," said Unwin. "God is on his side. Jesus Christ Himself put Donald Trump on this Earth to sort out our problems. It's His will that he be elected president."

I rolled my eyes. "You can't honestly believe that?" I asked.

"I do believe it," she replied. "Just like I believe that climate change is an invention of the liberal left and that Saddam Hussein organized the attacks on the World Trade Center. I know you refuse to accept the truth, but that's because you've been brainwashed by the mainstream media and by the elite. Trust me, in a few hours' time, Mr. Trump will be our president-elect."

"You've seen the polls?" I asked.

"Polls mean nothing. People are ashamed to admit that they're voting for him."

"And do you ever wonder why that is?"

Joe smiled and wrapped me in a bear hug. "We're not going to fall out over this, Brother," he said. "We've got through almost two years without arguing over the greatest man ever to stand for election in our country and we have only a few hours to go. Then it'll all be history."

"Thank God for that," I said, turning around as I heard a key in the door, and Raymond stepped inside. He marched past us all and stared at the television without saying a word before turning around and looking at us, one after the other.

"Father," he said. "Uncle Joe. Aunt Unwin. Zoe."

"Hello," we replied in unison. Raymond always made a point of greeting everyone in the room individually. It was one of his many quirks.

"I forgot the election was on," he said.

"You forgot?" I asked. "How on earth could you forget? It's all anyone's been talking about for months. Sit down, okay? And Joe, hand me one of those beers. I want a drink in my hand when our country does the right thing and elects the most qualified candidate in the history of the United States to the highest office in the land. Instead of, you know, an illiterate racist."

"You say that like it's a bad thing," muttered Unwin.

"Sorry, I was busy at work," said Raymond.

"But you voted, yes?" I asked. "You didn't forget that, I hope?"

"I voted early," he said. "Last week."

"Good," I replied.

"Why aren't we watching Fox News?" asked Raymond.

"He refuses to turn it on," said Zoe, nodding over at me.

"Because it's an oxymoron," I said. "Like koala bears. Or the Pont Neuf in Paris."

"What's wrong with the Pont Neuf?"

"It's actually the oldest bridge in the city."

"That's not true."

"It is."

"That's just liberal bias."

I stared at her. "How on earth—?" I asked, but before I could finish my sentence, Zoe interrupted.

"You voted for Mr. Trump, right?" she asked, turning to Raymond.

"Of course I did."

"You did *what?*" I asked.

"I voted for Mr. Trump."

I stared at him. I hadn't had many conversations with my son about the presidential election because his mind just wasn't in that particular game. Still, I assumed that he had a brain in that head of his somewhere. He was a rocket scientist, for Christ's sake. How dumb could he be?

"But why?" I asked. "Why would you do something like that?"

"*I* voted for Trump," said Zoe belligerently.

"And me," said Joe.

"And me," said Unwin.

"I know *you* all did," I said, throwing my hands in the air. "Because you're all morons. But him? He's my son! I expect better from him."

"NASA's budget got slashed under the Obama administration," he told me with a shrug. "Mr. Trump wants to put people on other planets."

"He can start with himself," I said. "I'd pay for him to move to Mars."

"Obama didn't like the space program because he's a Muslim from Ethiopia," said Unwin.

"Okay, first off, he *isn't* a Muslim from Ethiopia," I said, "so you already lose your argument by saying that. And anyway what you meant to say is that he's a Muslim from Kenya, but he's not even from Kenya, he's from Hawaii, which, last time I checked, is part of the United States. And he's not a Muslim. But even if he *was* a Muslim from Kenya or Ethiopia, which he *isn't,* why on earth would that prejudice him against the space program?"

"We don't know the answer to that yet," she replied. "It'll have something to do with the Illuminati, I expect. Mr. Trump will find out once he's in the Oval Office. He's going to dismantle everything Obama ever did and kick out the immigrants."

"His own *mother* was an immigrant!" I shouted. "And if he hates immigrants so much, why the hell does he keep marrying them?"

"He's promised to increase our funding," said Raymond. "He's a man of ambition. Under him, we could go anywhere."

"Great," I said. "So he's going to make Jupiter great again, too."

"It's perfectly possible," said Raymond.

"We're taking back our country," said Unwin.

"From who?" I asked. "The nasty black man?"

"And all his Muslim friends."

I looked around the room. There were five of us there and only one, only I, had voted for Hillary. For a moment, I experienced a quick burst of concern. The country couldn't possibly be as insane as the people in my living room, could it? But I shook my head, laughing at my own stupidity. No, of course not. The idea was crazy.

Hillary came on the screen again.

"Lock her up!" they shouted in unison.

. . .

The election had come at the end of a difficult few months for me. The publishing house where I worked as an editor had released a novel earlier in the year by a gay Muslim woman and, although it hadn't received a lot of attention at first, it had gone on to win a prestigious literary award, leading to an organization calling themselves the Coalition for Traditional American Values announcing a boycott of any bookstore that stocked the novel, saying that it was insulting that a prize should be denied to an American author and given instead to an immigrant with "questionable ties" to "a troubling organization in Syria," for which there was, of course, absolutely no evidence.

On the campaign trail, Trump himself had been asked about the controversy and he'd remarked that it was the kind of novel that Crooked Hillary would probably take with her on vacation. Asked whether he'd read it himself, he shrugged and said, "Look, I've read all the books, okay? There's probably no one who's read more books than I have so I know all about this," which didn't really answer the question, but that didn't appear to matter to anyone.

A week later, at a reading in a bookstore in Philadelphia, an obese red-hatted man had walked in, pulled out a gun and taken a shot at the author—missing her, fortunately, but destroying a display of Maude Avery reissues and a tall pile of Danny Angel novels—before being wrestled to the ground and arrested. Again, Trump had been asked to comment and he'd nodded and jutted out his lower lip like a petulant child before saying, "From what I understand, he's a very good man. And I think maybe the writer herself has made some provocative statements in the past. So I don't think we should be too quick to judge him."

Naturally, the publishing house had put out a statement condemning what the candidate had said, but this had, in turn, led to a backlash in middle America, with people threatening to burn all our books in the streets, while the author herself, a mild-mannered lady whose novel was an inoffensive tale of caring for a relative with Alzheimer's, had been forced into hiding, with the FBI stating that a number of serious threats had been made against her life.

And this was just a minor incident compared to everything else that had been going on in the country. I was pretty sure that, by this point, everyone was exhausted. The right and the left. We just wanted all of this to be over. None of us could take any more of the tweets, the vulgarities and the name-calling. Even the right-wing commentators looked as if they were looking forward to the result being called. Peace would, at last, be restored. Sanity, too. And we'd never have to deal with such a vile human being again. Trump and his like would be sent into exile and the world could return to a semblance of normality. We just had a few hours to go.

* * *

"I'm almost sorry now that I didn't go to New York," I said, as I watched Kellyanne Conway pursing her lips and insisting that Trump had never had the support of the Republican infrastructure. Well, of course he didn't. The Republicans might have been nuts but they weren't crazy.

"Why?" asked Joe.

"It would be nice to be at the Javits Center tonight," I told him. "To watch Hillary's victory speech live. It's history in the making."

"It would be a wasted trip," said Zoe. "She won't be making any speech. Other than a concession speech, that is."

I sighed. "You keep telling yourself that if it makes you happy," I said.

A few minutes later, the first polls closed and the news anchors burst into life. After hours of speculation, they could stop repeating themselves endlessly and share some hard news. Trump had taken Kentucky and Indiana, while Hillary had won Vermont.

"Two–one," said Unwin.

"Well, they're not surprises," I said. "Everyone expected him to win those states. Kentucky hasn't gone blue since Clinton in '96 and Indiana went for Romney last time."

"Still," said Joe. "It's a good start for our guy."

"Your guy," I said.

Not long after that, West Virginia also went to Trump.

"Also not a surprise," I said.

"MAGA," said Zoe.

"MAGA," replied Joe.

"MAGA!" shouted Unwin.

"MAGA," declared Raymond, and I glared at him.

"I'm sorry!" he said, shrugging his shoulders. "But I'm part of the space program. I want funding!"

"But isn't that the problem here?" I asked. "This is what that idiot wants. People to vote based entirely on self-interest. With no thought for the rest of the country. It's always about putting the individual ahead of the community."

"MAGA," said all four together.

"Christ on a bike," I muttered, shaking my head.

Another hour passed, more states closed their polls, and I breathed a sigh of relief as Hillary took Massachusetts, Maryland, Delaware, New Jersey and the District of Columbia.

"Ha!" I said, and the rest of them just looked uninterested.

"You know she's at the center of a pedophilia ring, don't you?" said Zoe. "And that she has personally murdered children? And she shot Vince Foster? And she burned a flag? And she speaks fluent Klingon? And she has six fingers on her left hand? Also, she's never said where she was on the day that Kennedy was shot."

"Well, since she was about sixteen years old I'd imagine she was in school," I said. "And none of those things are true anyway. I mean, there must be millions of photographs out there of her hands, for one thing, and she has the regulation number of fingers."

"That's what people like Donna Brazile and Barack Obama and Valerie Jarrett want you to believe. But the truth is, she has six."

"She has five."

"Actually, she has four," said Raymond. "Four fingers and a thumb."

"It's going to be so great when all the Mexicans are thrown out," said Unwin, tucking into the burrito she'd brought that was helping to mask her own peculiar fragrance. "They're just awful people."

"Why?" I asked. "Why are they awful people? What have they ever done to you?"

"They're killing us economically," she replied. "The US has become a dumping ground for everyone else's problems. When Mexico sends its people, they're not sending their best. They're not sending you. They're sending people that have lots of problems, and they're bringing those problems with them. They're bringing drugs. They're bringing crime. They're rapists." She paused for a moment to pull a piece of corn out from between her teeth. "And some, I assume, are good people."

"You're just quoting him!" I yelled. "You're quoting him directly from that first day when he rode the escalator down to say he was running for President."

"I have eighteen of his speeches memorized," said Unwin proudly. "When he gives his inaugural address, I'm going to get it tattooed onto my back."

"Well, you'll have a bare back, then," I said. "Because he won't be giving any inaugural address."

But then the anchors started to talk about Florida. How could it be so close there, they wondered? The candidates seemed to be tied at the moment and it was looking like Hillary really needed to win Florida, especially now that Trump had just taken Tennessee. And how the hell had Arkansas gone for the ignorant baboon? Arkansas, of all states! After everything she'd done for them!

Hillary took Illinois and New York. Trump took Texas, Wyoming, Kansas and the Dakotas. I didn't like the look of this. Shouldn't it have been clearer by now that she'd won?

And then things started to shift. He took Missouri. And Ohio. She took Colorado, but no, no, no, he won Florida.

"MAGA," said Zoe.

"MAGA," said the other three.

"Oh shut up," I snapped.

North Carolina. Georgia. Utah. Iowa. Pennsylvania. Wisconsin. Michigan. All went to Trump.

It was over.

The end of civilization as we knew it.

"Told ya," said Zoe.

· · ·

Hours later, I found myself standing on the balcony alone with the lights turned low behind me, drinking a beer. I could sense the disbelief emerging from the streets below me, could hear the howling and the tears from the disenchanted and frightened people as they wandered home.

Raymond came out and stood next to me.

"Happy?" I asked.

"For NASA," he said. "For the space program."

"And that's all that matters, is it?"

He said nothing but offered a small shrug.

"And what are you going to do with the money anyway?" I asked. "Now that he's in. Even if he gives you what he promised, which he probably won't, because I assume that he won't fulfill any of the promises he made during the campaign, I can tell you one thing for certain: Mexico is never going to pay for any wall. The man doesn't even know when he's lying. So what will you do with the money if it actually comes your way?"

He pointed up toward the sky.

"Put people up there," he said.

"But you've already done that. Man has landed on the moon; astronauts go into space all the time. What more can you want?"

He broke into a wide smile, something he almost never did.

"Colonies," he replied.

EPILOGUE

SPEARTHROWER OWL

A.D. 2080

WHEN THE FIRST SETTLERS ARRIVED HERE, they numbered seven hundred and fifty, but since then, two hundred and sixty-eight people have died while four hundred and forty-seven have been born, so our population has risen to nine hundred and twenty-nine. I have fathered a child myself, Xavier, whose mother is a Chinese biologist named Qinyang. Our relationship is based solely on friendship and mutual respect—no one on any of the space stations adheres to the traditional moral constructs of the home planet anymore—but we are compatible beings and when she decided that she wanted a baby, she asked whether I might assist in the conception, and I was happy to say yes.

One of the great advantages of our new world is the changes that we have made in the social paradigm. There are no men or women, no boys or girls, no transgender or intersex people, and no one refers to themselves as binary or gender fluid. Instead, we are simply Beings, some of which are able to create life within their own bodies, some of which are not. I have read many of the history books and am aware that, in the past, there were those who would engage sexually with only half the population. This strikes all of us as most peculiar, for we no longer limit ourselves in any such way. If a Being is in need of tenderness, or comfort, or sex, it is a simple thing to ask another Being whether it would like to partner in this activity. It is no different than asking whether it might like a cup of tea or to take a stroll around the garden deck. Our lack of prudishness makes life very simple and we are a happy tribe here on *Spearthrower Owl*, as the station was named by the Designers, content to live out our days in a harmonious and peaceful fashion, all the time sending data back to the home planet, which continues to evacuate the young as quickly as more stations can be built.

For decades, there were innumerable signs that Earth was reaching its final days, and while some attempted to change the manner in which humankind lived, the truth was that it was already too late. It was only a matter of time before it could no longer sustain life and outside colonies would need to be established. Estimates now are that there are only four years left before those who remain will run out of oxygen and, from what I understand, competition to escape the dying planet is intense.

It is generally agreed that the Great American Earthquakes of 2023 marked the beginning of the end. Fourteen million people were killed over six days when the ground opened up from the Six Rivers National Forest in northern California to Tijuana on the Mexican border, and, a week later, with the entire landmass dangerously unsettled, another eight million died on the East Coast when an enormous fissure opened up from Charlotte, North Carolina, to Miami, Florida, devastating that part of the country.

A few days later, speaking from the steps of the Sydney Opera House, President Trump addressed reporters, denying that he had fled the country because he was terrified that the earthquakes would spread north.

"Listen, I don't even know what's going on down there," he said to the assembled journalists as he stood with his family, the Vice President, the Secretary of State, the American ambassador and his entire cabinet, who had also found reasons to be in Australia that week. "They say there are earthquakes, but who knows? The fake-news organizations might have put these images together just to scare us. As you know, I have a property in Florida, Mar-a-Lago, it's a terrific place, very beautiful, probably the greatest resort in America, and they tell me that it's still standing, so who's to know the truth?"

It was at this moment that something strange occurred, a phenomenon that was subsequently watched and rewatched by four billion people over the following months and has been analyzed from every angle. As he spoke and waved his hands in the air, a flame appeared from the tip of the President's right thumb. He glanced at it, frowned, and shook his arm to put it out, staring at the small dark spot that remained in its place.

"What the hell was that?" he asked, looking around, but the flame had been so small that almost no one had seen it.

"Many people are saying that it's the climate change know-it-alls who have instigated some of these things," he continued, his tone a little unsettled by what had just taken place, but returning to his speech, nevertheless. "That it's a plot on the part of the Democrats and the liberal elite, who, let me tell you, are really sick people, some of them. I mean they will just lie and deceive and say whatever it takes to—"

Before he could say another word, another flame sparked, this time running along his right arm, and he yelled out in fright. One of the Secret Service agents rushed forward and extinguished it quickly with his jacket but the President was clearly disconcerted.

"I'm not sure what's happening here," he said, and for once his voice betrayed fear. "But I have some tremendous people on my team, really tremendous people, doing great jobs, and sooner or later the fake-news media—"

And those words, "the fake-news media," were the last that President Trump ever uttered. His entire body suddenly burst into flames in a moment of spontaneous combustion, and as he ran screaming around the steps of the Opera House, his family and colleagues pulled back in fright, watching as he burned to death before the entire world. Ivanka, his daughter, appeared to smile. Soon, he tumbled to the ground, coming to rest at the entrance to the Botanic Gardens, where he continued to cook until all that was left of him was a charred skeleton and a lot of bright yellow hair that seemed completely immune to the flames.

By now, of course, much of the population of the United States of America had attempted to migrate to Mexico, but the government there immediately paid for and erected a wall to keep them out, their own president insisting that they could not take any refugees. "Mexico will not become a dumping ground for everyone else's problems," she declared on national television. "When America sends its people, they're not sending their best. They're sending people that have lots of problems, and they're bringing those problems with them. They're bringing drugs. They're bringing crime. They're rapists." She paused for a moment, considering this. "And some, I assume, are good people."

But, of course, Mexico wasn't safe either, as the earthquakes soon spread there and, within weeks, the entire planet had become plagued by catastrophe. Tsunamis destroyed much of Australia, New Zealand and the Pacific region, Europe was roasted by dormant volcanoes, while the explosion of a dozen or more nuclear reactors in Russia laid waste to most of Asia. Only Africa seemed to withstand the worst phenomena, but soon that continent was overrun by people from around the world, each one desperately trying to cling on to life. But one region could not sustain them all and, as fighting broke out, it was declared a no-go zone.

Within a few years, it became obvious that life on Earth was coming to an end and, as governments tried to build more and more space stations, lotteries began to decide who would be among the first to build a new world in the void. Fortunately for me, my parents were among those who won early places and became part of the group exiled to *Spearthrower Owl,* which has been orbiting the moons of Jupiter for almost fifty years now. At first, they struggled to adapt to their new lives, but when the next generation came along, my generation, we knew nothing of what life had been like before, discovering it solely through the stories we read about in the tablets. As part of that first generation to have been born in space, I have always felt a certain pride that we live differently to our forefathers.

My son, Rick, is one of the chief scientists on board, and it affords me great pride to see the team that answers to his call. Young people divide early into separate fields—scientific, exploratory, cultural—and since I was a child I have belonged to the latter group. There are many other creative beings on board whose work I admire greatly: seamstresses, stele makers, jewelers, sandal makers, dressmakers, stonemasons, wood-carvers, designers of amulets, sword makers, illustrators, crafters of mosaics, glassblowers, arrow makers, playwrights, story writers, novelists, bookbinders and poets.

While I, of course, am a songwriter.

I have a very pleasant studio on Herod Deck. The light here, while artificial, is conducive to creativity and I feel that my work has changed and improved dramatically over the years. As a younger man, my songs were simple tales of life aboard the space station, but in recent years I have been drawn to writing music inspired by the dreams I have of the home planet.

I think, at times, that some of my crewmates consider me a slightly odd fellow, but I don't believe that I'm very different to them. They might specialize in the study of rocks, or flies, or blood, or the nutrients that expand or retract depending on air pressure. I draw songs from my mind. What is so strange about that?

There is no crime on *Spearthrower Owl*. We have everything we need and, if we require something that is not immediately available, we seek out another Being who can provide it. No one behaves in a violent fashion or causes vandalism. We take pride in our station and keep it clean and hygienic. We have no equivalent to what I believe was known as the "police force" on the home planet, nor do we have a military. There are no judges or legal cases, for we are almost never in dispute. On the rare occasions that two Beings find themselves in a moment of disharmony, they invite a third to hear their complaint and it is universally agreed that the decision made by the disinterested party must be the correct one. We nurture no grudges or grievances. We do not compete against each other. We avoid gossip and embrace civility. Social media platforms, as they were called on the home planet, are outlawed.

There is illness, of course, but as a group we live longer and it is unusual for a Being to die before its hundred and thirtieth birthday. Diseases of the mind have been cured, as have most maladies of the body. People tend to pass away in their sleep for no other reason than their organs have finally become exhausted. It is a peaceful way to go and we do not grieve; instead, we celebrate the end of a joyous cycle of existence.

Naturally, we have leaders, but these roles change regularly. An elder is in charge of the station for only a twelve-week period and everyone, at some point, has an opportunity to assume this role. I myself was an elder last year and with the position came the opportunity to suggest new ideas for the station. Qinyang is scheduled to be the elder in three years' time and I am excited to see what she makes of the opportunity. She has a fine mind and I suspect she will surprise us all.

· · ·

The oldest member of our community is the blind woman, Tisa, and, only this morning, I found her in my studio waiting for me when I appeared after breakfast. She has always had an ear for music and likes nothing more than to sit quietly while I work on my compositions, content to be lost in the symphonies I write. Today, however, it seemed that she had something on her mind, and I sat next to her, inquiring whether she was in good health.

"I'm fine," she told me. "Although I won't be if the doctors have their way. They're insisting that I have my operation in a few days' time."

"Ah," I said, for I had heard rumors that Tisa's sight was to be restored now that the solution to blindness had been discovered. On *Spearthrower Owl*, we do not afford Beings the luxury of choosing whether they will be cured of their illnesses or disabilities; each one is obliged to undergo whatever treatment is deemed necessary in order to become a more productive member of the community. "And you don't want to go through with it?"

"I'm one hundred and forty-nine years old," she said, shaking her head. "I have very little time left to me. And I have been blind since childhood."

She had told me before of how, when she was just an infant during a war on the home planet, her house had been destroyed by falling bombs. Her parents and siblings had been killed in the explosion but, somehow, she had survived, although her retinas had become detached and she had experienced only blackness ever since. "What need have I of seeing the world in a different way than I always have? It might shock me into death."

I smiled.

"Will you help me?" she asked. "Will you tell the doctors to leave me in peace?"

I agreed that I would try. Tisa had come to my aid on more than one occasion in my life. It seemed that whenever I suffered moments of grief she had been there, by my side, prepared to tell me that I must continue in this world.

"I will speak to them, I promise," I said, determined to pay her back for her many kindnesses.

"Thank you," she replied, patting a hand on top of my own. "Now, please, play some music for me."

. . .

It is nighttime.

My brother and my son have left my room for their own, having shared an evening meal with me. Before tidying away the detritus of the night and preparing for bed, I make my way to the window and look out toward the sky.

The home planet, on which I will never set foot, is hundreds of millions of miles from here and, as I stare into the darkness, I sense the goodwill of the universe that surrounds me. I think of those people who were left behind when the exile began, and those who will never make it out alive, and those who are now boarding transports and saying goodbye to their friends and family forever.

I have lost many loved ones in my life and rarely been given the opportunity to say farewell. Often, I wake in a state of confusion, uncertain of my identity, unsure if I belong in this time or place at all. I find myself watching as my father cleans a sword, having killed dozens of babies. I am sharing a bed with my cousin, whose twisted legs repulse me. I am buying slaves at a marketplace and being bought as a slave a moment later. I am a murderer. I carve statues into the sides of mountains and watch as an old man floats away on a block of ice. I illustrate letters on an enormous page of calf vellum. I go on a pilgrimage and am seduced by a woman before thrusting my arm into a pot of boiling lead. I climb aboard a ghost ship, watch as a specter appears on the stage of a theatre and hear cries of terror ascend from the base of a well. I listen as a prisoner speaks his final words, witness a man being shot for telling the truth and stare through a window as an army of tanks rolls into the street before me.

I am all these things and more.

I belong to the past, the present and the future.

I am Spearthrower Owl, the greatest ajaw of them all, under whose eternal benevolence the world continues to thrive.

I am at peace.

It is truly good to live among the stars.

ACKNOWLEDGMENTS

For all their advice and suggestions on different drafts of this novel, as well as their friendship, I am indebted to Bill-Scott Kerr, Patsy Irwin, Larry Finlay, Eloisa Clegg, Simon Trewin and Helen Adie.

Thanks, too, to my international publishers for their ongoing support.

ABOUT THE AUTHOR

JOHN BOYNE is the author of twelve novels for adults, six for younger readers, and a collection of short stories. In his native Ireland, he has won three Irish Book Awards and been shortlisted on thirteen separate occasions. He has also won or been shortlisted for a host of international literary awards, including a Stonewall Honor Award and a Lambda Literary Award. A regular participant in international literary festivals, he has also been a member of the jury for the International IMPAC Dublin Literary Award and the Costa Book Award, and in 2015 he chaired the jury for the Scotiabank Giller Prize. His novels have been published in over fifty languages.

johnboyne.com
Twitter: @john_boyne

ABOUT THE TYPE

This book was set in Galliard, a typeface designed in 1978 by Matthew Carter (b. 1937) for the Mergenthaler Linotype Company. Galliard is based on the sixteenth-century typefaces of Robert Granjon (1513–89).